The
UKRAINIAN
in ME

The
UKRAINIAN
in ME

KEVIN ZDRILL

iUniverse®

THE UKRAINIAN IN ME

This is a work of fiction. All of the characters, names, incidents, organizations, and dialogue in this novel are either the products of the author's imagination or are used fictitiously.

iUniverse books may be ordered through booksellers or by contacting:

iUniverse
1663 Liberty Drive
Bloomington, IN 47403
www.iuniverse.com
1-800-Authors (1-800-288-4677)

ISBN: 978-1-4917-6684-2 (sc)
ISBN: 978-1-4917-6738-2 (hc)
ISBN: 978-1-4917-6737-5 (e)

Library of Congress Control Number: 2015907239

Print information available on the last page.

iUniverse rev. date: 05/15/2015

For my wife and boys:
You've opened my eyes and allowed me to
rediscover the world around me.

For Fast Eddie:
You're a true Ukrainian warrior.

For Joyce "J. R." Rust:
It's time to share another laugh.

Also by Kevin Zdrill

Fiction Series (Humor)

No Kiss Good-Night (2012)

Boom Chicka Wah Wah (2013)

Crazy, Mixed-Up World (2014)

Website: kevinzdrill.com

Books available at the following:

www.amazon.com
www.amazon.ca
www.mcnallyrobinson.com
www.goodreads.com

ACKNOWLEDGMENTS

My deep gratitude to these amazing individuals, who have led me on my journey:

Trish Jackson, author, www.trishjax.com
Sue Ducharme, Editor, Owner at TextWorks-EquiText
The Poitras family
Joanne "Hart to Hart"

CHAPTER 1

Hello ... Again

February 2, 5:01 p.m.

Well, here I am, sitting back in my old room in the town of Beausejour, in the province of Manitoba, in the great country of Canada, back at my parents' house. My room in the basement seemed to be waiting, as if it knew I'd be coming back as a soon-to-be divorcée, thirty years old, after being married for nine months, one day, and a morning. My mom is calling me right now; supper is ready. My dad is in front of my basement window, smoking, proud his daughter is home away from "that loser" but not proud his one and only daughter is going to be divorced, his MasterCard still footing the wedding booze. My mom is calling again: "Supper is ready. Come upstairs." My ex is living back at home; he's twenty-eight, and I couldn't be his mother. I can't live on my job as an independent web designer on my own, only getting paid once in a while. My parents are not accepting rent while

I "get back on my feet." I wonder what decade of my life that will be. Looking around at my Ukrainian family, I wonder if it is my destiny to become Auntie Tina, Aunt the Groundhog, First Cousin Garth, Juicey Joycey, Baba Betty, or Best Friend Bernadette. I intend to begin writing this blog to help me discover if this is my destiny, and yes, Mom, I know supper is ready.

*****

I was shivering.

I pushed aside the shower curtain and stepped over the side of the tub onto the linoleum floor. It was just as cold as it had been for the last thirty years. I took a step and a half to my right, as always, to stand in front of the condensation-free mirror.

I knew before I heard it that the fan was running above my head. I glared up at the spinning blades.

I shivered again and hugged myself. Goose bumps covered my legs all the way down to my ankles. I wondered if it was only because of the cold.

I still couldn't believe it. It was too sickening. I felt like throwing up.

It was as if no time had elapsed—as if the last nine months, one day, and a morning had never happened, as if it was only in my imagination.

Dad, as he had during every one of my previous thirty million showers, had come down the stairs with one mission: to turn on that damn overhead fan. There was no way he would allow shower moisture to build up on his painted green walls or on the mirror. He didn't give a rat's ass that the dehumidified cold air would freeze me to the bone.

At least now the paint wouldn't blister.

Yes, it was real. I shuddered at the thought.

I was back living at home with my parents and standing in their basement shower.

It was as real as my wet, long brown hair pressed against my scalp and down between my shoulder blades.

It was as real as the red conditioner bottle I'd left for my father next to his bar of soap nine months, one day, and a morning ago as a joke. It was still where I'd left it, taunting me to return.

I had.

The shower stopped as soon as I twisted the plastic tap to the left, as I had done all my life—minus the last nine months, one day, and a morning.

I opened my eyes and stared at the blue minisquare-tiled walls surrounding me on three sides. I gazed mindlessly into the mirror and focused on my breasts—soon-to-be divorced breasts, as unremarkable as I now was. They held no meaning for anyone. My ex certainly no longer cared about them. He'd never see them again like this—naked, exposed, unremarkable. It was just as well. Sensitive breasts and his callused hands didn't go together.

I reached for the pink towel on the rack behind me. It was the one I always used. I knew it hadn't recently been placed there especially for my return of shame. I knew because it smelled like a mixture of dust, my dad's dandruff shampoo, and the matches he used in the bathroom.

I rubbed the water from my pale skin and then wrapped my hair in the same towel. Out of curiosity, I moved the small glass medicine-cabinet door to the left, exposing the half that had formerly been my side. My toothbrush, toothpaste, floss, brush, and deodorant were still there. Pulsating jabs of paranoia were trying to convince me that my parents had known nine months, one day, and a morning ago that I would return as a permanent occupant of this house, and now there I was, back home, staring at my shit inside the cabinet. I flung open the bathroom door, defiantly naked, to take the walk down the hallway to my bedroom, which was situated at the end, daring anyone—Dad or Mom—to appear and catch their shameless daughter living as though she owned the joint.

No one was there. It was as if they knew their daughter would commit that exact shameless act and did not want to promote an argument on my first day back.

I stopped in the center of my room. For me, it had always been a good size. It was big enough for my double bed, vanity, dresser, television stand with a twenty-one-inch TV, and computer desk without a computer, and it had enough empty space to chill. But now, standing naked in the middle of it, staring at the wall calendar that still displayed the month when I'd left and the flower-patterned duvet, still crooked the way I'd left it, I was struck by the chilling fact that I was back living under my parents' roof.

It really was happening. Time had stood still in my room, waiting for my return.

I opened the closet door and stared at discarded dresses, pants, and tops I'd never thought I would—and never wanted to—set my eyes upon again or slip over my body. I pulled out a pair of well-worn pink sweatpants and a black Roots sweater.

There was one benefit of no longer having a husband to entice: I could now deck my big-boned body in clothing only a serious track athlete dared to wear. I found the size 10 beer-sponsored men's slippers I had won ten years earlier at my cousin's wedding social and slipped my bare feet into them. They were still next to my bed, where I had left them.

They didn't feel as if I had last worn them nine months, one day, and a morning ago.

I flopped down on my bed, not caring one hell what effect the towel was going to have on my hair. *Let it become a rat's nest*, I thought. There was no one to impress anymore. Fingers wouldn't be running through it with passion—not that I'd ever had that kind of passion from my ex, but I always fantasized it could happen at any moment. Did I really believe that was possible?

I took a deep breath and moved my gaze around the room slowly, taking in wallpaper so familiar I knew where every mismatched seam was. Besides the obvious conclusion—this room needed a serious makeover—my observations hammered home the fact that this was the last place in my life I needed to be for any reason.

Heck, I needed a makeover more than this damn room did. Sweet Jesus, I was thirty years old and starting from scratch. I had no job; no money; no higher education; no car, because I didn't have a driver's license; and now no husband. I shivered, although I wasn't cold anymore. I still couldn't believe it. At thirty years old, I didn't have the ability to live anywhere but in the basement of my parents' home, in my former bedroom.

It sucked so bad that it hurt to breathe. The Ukrainian curse had finally caught up with me. My entire family tree suffered from it, and I was the latest victim.

Above my head, I could hear footsteps. My mother stomped. My dad walked with the silence of a cat, but the wooden floor joists still creaked under his weight and gave away his movements. When he wanted to, he could creep through the house with a silence that put me on edge—not that I was ever doing anything that needed to be hidden from sudden discovery, such as drinking, doing drugs, or watching porn. I just hated having someone sneak up on me.

I could hear the plates being placed on the table—one, two, three. Without any doubt in my mind, I knew that third plate would be in exactly the same place I had always eaten. This was my first day back, my first meal. I felt as if it were a prisoner's last meal before execution, except I'd be forced to live in purgatory and not mercifully be beheaded. Any minute now, I would be summoned upstairs to listen to Dad's slurping, chomping, and smacking right next to my left ear, and on my right, Mom would insist I have another pierogi, one more sausage, an extra slice of headcheese, and a second bowl of borscht.

I scrunched my eyes tightly, unsure if I should cry or break out in psychotic wails of nonsense.

When my mother called out moments later, I did neither. I tossed aside the towel from around my head, marched up the stairs to the kitchen, and took a seat—my seat—at the table.

I was officially home.

CHAPTER 2

Life's Influences, Jabs, Digs, Slaps

February 22, 5:30 p.m.

I never intended to get married; it just happened. And what girl doesn't want that to happen? Okay, I confess I wasn't one of those girls. I blame my dad. What the hell? I blame my mom as well. As far as I can figure, they stunted my development of learning about love, being loved, giving love, knowing love, and hurting from love. It took my marriage of nine months, one day, and a morning to learn about love.

It would have helped me had I dated boys when all my friends were dating boys in elementary school. My friend who became my best friend, Bernadette, dated Kenny. Kenny was a sweetheart who held her hand while walking to school, while walking back home, and even during the odd time in the hallway at school when no one was looking. They dated for twenty-one glorious days. Because of Kenny and those twenty-one glorious days, Bernadette earned the ass-kicking status of a girl who could be dated. Kenny shed his shy-guy status, and I watched it all—the girl who was there but not really there.

Were boys not interested in me? I think a few were. Maybe even one for sure. I'd like to believe I had a chance with one boy, my God. I was a girl, and boys liked girls. Maybe if I was into probabilities, I'd say my chances were zero based on the zero valentines I was given by boys each year in elementary school (Bernadette never received fewer than ten after Kenny; my grade-two teacher gave me a blank one that was left over), the zero times I was asked to dance at a dance, and the zero times I was picked to be in any clubs. I'm an optimist. My good old dad told me not to worry. He said I had plenty of time for boys "when I get older," and he never defined *older*, although my impression was over thirty.

*****

Dad began speaking the moment I picked up my fork and knife to cut my first pierogi in half. At the same time, he munched his own mouthful of pierogies, spraying bits out onto the table between us.

I inched my elbow on his side closer to myself.

"Now that you're back home and away from that yollup," Dad said, referring to my ex with a nonendearing term for being an idiot, "you can get your life back on track again."

"It was never off track," I countered in my defense, taking out my frustration on a pierogi with a harsh jab of my fork.

"Marrying that yollup derailed all the plans you had in place for your future."

"I had no plans."

"You had ambitions prior to marrying that loser," he insisted, forking two more pierogies into his mouth while looking my way.

"I lived at home in the basement before I married him. I had no job. Is that the plan you're talking about?" I asked. Dad was obviously confused by the supposed life map that my ex had shaken apart.

He vigorously shook his head, trying to swallow so much dough and potato that I could see it move down his throat in a lump.

"Things were coming together for you. It was just a matter of time." He attacked the ridiculous mountain of coleslaw on his plate.

"I was twenty-nine years old. How much more time did I need before that plan materialized, Dad?" I asked, starting to feel even lower than I had prior to walking up the stairs for supper.

He nodded vigorously, coleslaw juice running down both sides of his mouth. "There was a plan. The loser screwed it all up for you. And ran up my MasterCard for all the booze at your wedding his friends drank."

I defended my ex's friends. "It's a wedding. People are supposed to party. That's why alcohol is served."

"Invited guests drink the alcohol. All of his uninvited friends showed up after the reception, brilliantly timed to avoid having to contribute a gift. Free booze. Yollups. I tuned one of his friends who had a beer in each hand and one in every pocket." My dad was famous for his so-called tuning, which was essentially giving a helpless individual a piece of his mind without mincing words.

I let it go. Dad was right. My ex had invited all of his cheapo friends to our wedding without putting them on the guest list. Avoiding additional meals and giving him bragging rights for showing them a good time on my dad's coin had saved him money. By the end of the night, they had drained every bottle behind the bar. Some of the attending guests had been left with pop to drink.

Mom piped up next to me.

"Nonetheless, everyone had a good time. I know I did."

"Who wouldn't with free booze?" Dad said.

"Enough," cautioned Mom, tossing him her look. She scraped a tab of butter onto her Kub rye bread.

Dad lowered his head farther toward his plate like a wounded animal. It was tough for my fifty-eight-year-old father to reel himself in when he was on a tangent, but he also knew to listen to Mom.

There was a moment of silence that I treasured but suspected was a buildup for a barrage of questions.

I was correct. Dad went first.

"So when are you going to get a job?"

Mom handed him a jar of heavily garlic-infused homemade pickles. He stuck two large fingers deep into it.

"I do freelance web designs," I said.

"I'm talking about a real job where you leave the house and go to another building five days a week with two days off. That kind of job."

"But I like my job," I contested, sipping the glass of milk Mom had set beside me.

"That job does not pay the bills."

"Not yet, but it will."

He shook his head. The pickle crunched as he took a healthy chomp from it. "I want to retire someday. I can't do that with a third mouth to feed."

"Don't be so dramatic," Mom said. "She's young. In time, she will find a good job. For now, she can stay here as long as she likes." She smiled at me as if she had just won the lottery. I was an extra pair of hands to wash, clean, and cook.

Dad grunted. "If you're going to be living back under my roof, then I expect you to help me fix the car."

I glared at him. The car he referred to was the 1994 Chrysler Reliant he had been "saving" for me since 1994. It was supposed to be a hand-me-down that he'd give me once I graduated from high school and got my driver's license. I graduated from high school. I never had the motivation to attempt my driver's test. I took the bus. As a result, the gun-oil-colored Reliant had sat in the backyard for the last twelve years.

"Does it still run?" I asked, incredulous. What car could survive under an orange tarp for more than a decade?

He scowled. "Of course it'll run. I made sure to top off all the fluids before I stored it."

I couldn't help myself. I laughed. "If you call 'storing' letting it sit under that pine tree."

"Don't you worry about it running. But I will need your help, Larissa, with a few minor things to get it back on the road."

"You'll need to get your license," said Mom. I stared at her, feeling betrayed. She knew that meant effort on my part.

"I'm okay with the bus."

Again, my dad's head shook, sending pickle juice flying.

"Ah, no. You need to get your goddamn license and get independent. You're thirty years old and still relying on the bus or other people to drive you around. I'm not doing that for you."

Now the truth was out. Dad was certain he would become my personal chauffeur.

"Just because I'm back here doesn't mean I expect to be catered to. I plan on being fully independent. You won't even know I'm around."

He choked. "Make sure of that by getting your license, and we'll get the car fixed."

I thanked him despite feeling as unmotivated to repair the car as I did to learn how to drive it. At the moment, I could see no purpose to my life. I was a government statistic. I was alone; I was within the zone of becoming another girl riding out the rest of her life in the basement of her parents' house.

My mother reached over and patted my arm reassuringly. "Your father's a great teacher. He'll show you how to drive and pass the test, dear. He taught me, and I passed on my fourth attempt."

"You would have passed on your third had you not ripped the mirror off the parked car," Dad replied.

"There was too much to look out for. I didn't want to hit a little child who might run out into the street."

"You were driving in an industrial area when it happened."

"Well, you never know—a little one *could* have run out from between buildings."

I broke into the conversation. "I'll try to learn how to drive. Thanks. I just don't want to put more weight on by driving instead of walking everywhere." My thighs suddenly felt too large for the sweatpants I wore.

Mom would have none of it.

"You're fine. You have the right amount of weight on you," she said, nodding and passing me the bowl for a second round of mashed potatoes.

"I don't think any girl who's five nine should weigh a hundred and eighty-five pounds, Mom. Thanks." I took the bowl and heaped a large wad of potatoes on my plate. What did it matter if I chunked up some more? Only my doctor would catch a brief naked glimpse of me from there on out.

"These stick-thin girls nowadays look sick," my father said. "I think it's disgusting. I don't need to see ribs." He pointed a butter-laden finger at me. "Don't be stupid." That was as encouraging as Dad ever got with me.

Mom got up from her seat, went to the fridge, and pulled out three chocolate puddings. Apparently, there was no chance in hell I'd ever be stick skinny living under her roof.

I took the spoon she handed me and sank it into the pudding's mushy center. I loved this homemade treat. My sweatpants would just have to stretch a little farther around my hips.

Mom sat down next to me and ate her own pudding. In my right ear, I could hear Dad slurping his from the bowl. Nothing had changed at the dinner table in nine months and a day.

"So?" Mom said, gazing at the ring of chocolate around my lips.

"Very good," I said.

Her brow scrunched. "No. I mean, so maybe it's time to get back in the saddle again and start dating."

I choked on a spoonful of pudding. "I just left my husband a few hours ago."

"I realize that. But the longer you wait, the harder it will be to get yourself out there."

Out of the corner of my eye, I could see Dad nodding in approval.

"I haven't even signed the divorce papers yet." I took another large scoop of pudding, annoyed and amazed.

She waved. "That's all a technicality anyway. The marriage is over, and that's all that matters."

"Well, it matters to me," I said. I could feel the ring of pudding around my lips growing larger.

"Don't get me wrong—I realize you can't remarry until you get divorced."

I cut her off. "The last thing I'm thinking about is getting remarried, Mom. Geesh. I haven't even unpacked my stuff."

"It's just that I don't want to see you go through the remainder of your life alone," she said.

I looked at them both with wide eyes. "I'm not alone! I have you both right here."

Mom nodded, but I could see she was unconvinced. She cleared her throat. "Let me tell you something. The good news is that the neighbor boy—what's his name? Sebastian. You know his mom, Dru—she taught you in junior-high chemistry. You almost failed, but she gave you a second chance with that exam. He's currently not seeing anyone."

I remembered her clearly. That second chance had meant an entire month with a tutor instead of playing with my friends. I couldn't say my memories of Dru were fond ones. And if I remembered her loner son, Sebastian, he had the personality of a cardboard box.

"Is he divorced as well?" I asked, hoping to demonstrate how flawed he was.

"Never married." My mother beamed.

I thought for a moment. "How many girlfriends?"

"None. You'd be his first."

"What am I supposed to do with that?" I barked.

My mother looked at me quizzically. "He's available," she replied.

I put my spoon down and wiped the pudding from around my mouth with the back of my hand. "But is he emotionally available?"

"He's a quiet boy. A good boy. I heard he used to work at the car wash on the weekends."

My eyes narrowed. "If he's to be my future husband, how's he going to support me with a pocketful of coins, Mom?"

She smiled at me. "He won't give you trouble. He's never been involved with the law."

My eyes popped wide open. "Well then, for sure he's a keeper."

"Don't get snarky with your mother," said my dad, running his index finger along the inside of his bowl to ensure he removed every smear of pudding.

"My point is," I began, "good boys don't translate into great husbands. My ex was a good boy who was never in trouble with the law either, remember?"

"He's still a loser," remarked my father, moving his pudding-smeared finger between his lips.

The words fluttered out. "So I don't want to marry another loser."

My mother shook her head. "We're not talking marriage just yet. Only for a date. He's a lonely kid." She looked as if she were about to cry.

"I'm not the neighborhood homeless shelter for lonely boys, Mom. Besides, I've never said two words to him all the time we've lived on the same street. We'd have nothing to talk about."

"Then go to a movie. You won't have to talk much."

I crossed my arms and frowned. I knew there was no getting out of this one.

"Fine. Make the arrangements with his mother. Isn't this great? Mothers arranging their lost-cause adult children for a play date."

My mother ignored my comment and pushed the fruit bowl over in front of me.

"Have an apple. And an orange. They're good for your colon," she said, blinking.

CHAPTER 3

Auntie Tina, Domestic Goddess

February 25, 6:33 p.m.

My auntie Tina never feared getting married. She wanted to get married, lived to get married, and she did it to avoid trouble at age nineteen. She married trouble called Five Star. No, it wasn't a great resort rating or vehicle crash rating or Nolton's movie pick. This was the cheap-ass Five Star rye whiskey her new husband full of trouble drank most days and nights, including weekends. Somewhere in between taking sips of Five Star, removing the cap to throw away, and removing the star from the bottle to stick on their living-room ceiling (because back then you could be proud of how much Five Star you drank, and no one uttered the words *alcoholic, liver damage, stomach cancer, problem drinker, or shitfaced asshole*), they conceived five children, all boys—future troublemakers. In between taking sips of Five Star, sticking the stars on the ceiling, and creating children, her husband also lost his job when the company failed, which meant losing the family home, a living-room ceiling to stick the stars on, and the family car, and soon his full-time job was professional Five Star drinker, which he went at gung ho 24-7, a success in his life.

Auntie Tina was raising five young troublemakers. At a young age, she'd never had to work outside the house, because she was a domestic goddess, and what more could someone expect when you have that status stitched into your apron smeared with baby spit-up? I give Auntie Tina big credit—she lasted eighteen years, nine months, and thirty minutes longer in her marriage than I did in mine, and let me say, that is a tremendous feat not to go unnoticed and unappreciated. She had six troublemakers, which she then reduced to five, and a ceiling void of any Five Star stars, except now she needed to find a job—not just a domestic goddess job but a job-type job that required leaving the house and taking orders and putting up with shit that didn't just come from her five troublemaking asses.

*****

I looked down at the snowmobile boots as I kicked snow away with each footstep. On the walk to the apartment of my best friend, Bernadette, even the brisk, cold February air and snow-covered sidewalk did nothing to stop me from replaying the conversation I'd had with my parents during my first dinner back at their house. I couldn't wait for Bernadette's reaction when I told her this doozy. If she didn't yet understand my desperate plight, listening to what I had to say would erase all confusion.

The snowbanks were piled as high as my chest this year, making me feel as if I were navigating a tunnel. Each house had a marshmallow roof of snow. I could understand my dad's point about owning a car to avoid having to walk. Yet I took pleasure in the pace of walking and the ability to look around, not to mention avoiding traffic accidents on ice.

Bernadette's apartment complex was straight ahead, three streets over from my parents' home. It was a four-story brown brick building with individual apartment balconies and underground parking, much like the other apartments located all over our quaint, small town of Beausejour. In my eyes, because she was not residing under her parents' roof, Bernadette was living in heaven.

She shared this heaven with her ten-year common-law husband, Mike. He was a nice guy as far as guys go. He'd take the time to talk and say hello. His interest waned quickly as soon as the conversation diverged from sports or beer. At twenty-eight, he was the young one in their relationship. I had never seen his clean-shaven face—ever. But Bernadette loved the tightly trimmed beard that covered his bulldog face, his short blond hair, his stocky build, and even the glasses he wore. I think she even loved the remnants of oil on his hands from his job. To each their own.

I entered their building and headed for the elevator that was right across from the lobby. The staircase was next to the elevator, but that meant physical effort, which required more energy than pushing a button. The steel door opened, and I stepped inside. I rode up to the fourth floor alone. In all the years I had been coming to the building, I had rarely seen another tenant, despite there being three hundred apartments.

Once I got off the elevator, I had to walk to the end of the hallway. Some tenants decorated their brown doors with objects, such as bouquets of flowers or inspirational plaques saying to have a great day. Bernadette's had a Coors Lite sticker.

I knocked.

I thought it smelled like popcorn inside. I was right. Mike was stretched out on the sofa in his sweats and a T-shirt, his hand jabbing into a bowl of popcorn, watching basketball on their eighty-inch LED TV. Bernadette was seated at the end of the sofa, pretending to enjoy the plays. She enjoyed sports as much as I did—meaning she liked when the game ended.

Their kitchen was immediately to my left—a slim arm's length from counter to counter. Straight ahead was an open living room, and the single bedroom and bathroom were down a hallway to the right. This had been their home for nearly the last ten years—their home, a home for a couple in love.

I shoved aside my envy and cracked a smile. After pushing off my knee-high winter boots, I walked into the living room.

"Hey, Mike," I called out.

"Hey," he replied, his eyes fixated on the television as if something monumental were on, as if a once-in-a-lifetime eclipse were about to occur, instead of one of the three hundred dunks made during a game. To me, the plays all looked the same—ball up in the air; ball through the same small, round hoop; and not much difference between throws. Mike was Bernadette's sports junkie, not mine. Who knew what my ex was watching right that minute? If I'd had to guess, I would have said his heavy-metal DVD anthology.

I flopped down on a love seat, part of the living-room set they'd bought at the furniture store under a no-pay, no-interest program eight years ago. They were probably still paying for it.

Above the mammoth television was Mike's treasured, flashing Budweiser sign, which was mounted like a deer head on the wall. He had scooped it up when a local sports pub went into receivership. Despite Bernadette's protests that it lit the room in a strange, flashing blue, he never turned it off, and it was there to stay until the day they moved.

My hair was tied back in a ponytail much like Bernadette's. Her gigantic breasts filled out the sports jersey of Mike's that she was wearing. Unlike my own breasts, hers still held a purpose.

"So, babe, what's new?" she asked, sipping Coke from a can with a straw. Mike's legs were draped over hers; she sat upright, her free hand massaging his shins. Bernadette spoiled Mike. I had never given my ex a massage anytime during our dating or marriage. Hairy legs and backs made my stomach turn.

"All hell's breaking loose in Larissa's world back at my parents' home," I said grimly. I pushed my head deep into the leather love seat.

Bernadette looked my way and laughed. "Is the old man already putting together a to-do list around the house? Maybe some roof reshingling for him? Pouring concrete?"

I grinned. "Far worse. He wants me to help him restore that old shit box of a car we planted in the backyard over ten years ago."

The mention of the Chrysler drew Mike out of his game for a momentary comment.

"Good luck getting that Reliant running," he said, keeping his eyes on the play. "By now, every seal will be more dried up than your marriage vows."

I flinched.

Bernadette came to my rescue, slapping him once in the nuts. He got the point and mumbled an apology. But he was probably right about the car; he worked in a garage. Well, he described it as a garage, but it was one of those ten-minute oil-change joints. He worked down in that mysterious hole like some wild animal no one ever saw.

"I'll leave that to my dad to figure out. He's spearheading the project. I'm sure I'll be relegated to handing him tools, not using them."

Bernadette cringed. "Let's hope so. All those metals and oils are murder on your fingernails. It'll kill your manicure in a second."

I shrugged. "I haven't done one of those since my wedding day, and even then it was stick-ons from the drugstore. Remember? I did them on the drive to the church."

Bernadette would have none of that kind of nonsense. She worked in a salon as a hairstylist. Her own hair was always cut ultracool and wildly dyed, and her nails—hell, even her feet—looked damn good. She looked after all of her parts. One of my toenails could have penetrated my Sorel winter boots, and the buildup on my heels could have scratched ceramic tile.

I sighed deeply. "That's just the start, my love. He wants me to get my driver's license. And my mom is supporting him! The betrayal." My right cheek twitched at the thought.

Bernadette stopped sipping her Coke and opened her mouth wide before she spoke.

"Get the hell out! And are you going to do it?" She looked baffled.

"I have to. They're insisting," I replied in a flat voice.

Mike added his two cents. "Don't take the test in the winter. You're sure to screw it up. All the ice and snow makes it ten times more difficult."

I nodded. "I wasn't planning to. I'll need months of training first from my dad."

"Your old man is going to be teaching you?" barked Bernadette. "He's going to eat you alive."

"He's insisting."

"Welcome home, huh?" said Mike with half a grin. He rolled his eyes.

"No shit," replied Bernadette with a sympathetic nod. They both knew my dad and his impatience with imperfection well enough. If a person sank below his expectations, that person took a tuning from him. It didn't matter where you were at the time either. He'd lay a strip on you in front of a priest inside the confessional. Anywhere was fair game.

I dipped my hand into a bowl of stale potato chips. I needed a dose of trans fat to soothe my anxiety. I shook my head and jammed a couple of chips into my mouth. "I just don't get it," I said through the mouthful of food.

"What?" said Bernadette, her brow wrinkled.

"Life."

"What about it?" she said.

"It's too unpredictable for me."

"In what way?" She stared at me as if I were nuts. Maybe I was. I squirmed in my chair.

"I need consistency. I need mundane. Just think—a few days ago, I was you. Sitting on a sofa with my ex, watching TV. All was mundane. My days were consistent—get up, eat, watch TV, eat, go to sleep," I said grimly.

"Sounds boring," quipped Mike.

"Are you saying we're boring?" said Bernadette, glaring at him. He didn't reply.

"And then—boom—one morning, all that consistency is over. I'm living back with my parents, being coerced into to learning how to drive. The simple life I had one day was turned over like morning eggs."

Bernadette looked sympathetic. "I think it was more bad luck than anything, girl. Boring and routine will return for you. You just got blindsided—that's all."

"That's putting it mildly," I huffed. "Men."

"Hey," said Mike. "We're not all like your ex."

Bernadette smiled and stroked his leg tenderly. "My sweetie is the world's best."

Mike's team scored right before the closing buzzer, and he jolted hard into a cheer. Just in time, Bernadette jerked her head away before his legs flew upward.

I shook my head, unconvinced. "To be honest, it's my family curse. I'm destined to grow old alone and destitute, eating cabbage rolls in my parents' basement until I'm so old dementia sets in and I just won't care anymore." I let out a long sigh.

Bernadette looked alarmed. "You really believe this shit, don't you? About this family curse thingy?"

I shuddered. "Shouldn't I? Look at my family, man! Is it normal to move back in with my parents at thirty? Hell, I should have been out of there when I was twenty! Moving back at thirty couldn't say 'loser' loud enough."

"You are so hard on yourself!" Bernadette said, shaking her head. "It's the new economics and not a family curse, girl. Let me tell you straight up—no one stays married for sixty years anymore. No one works at the same job for forty years any longer. This is a disposal society, and since our parents brought us into this shit show, they can support us during the downturns."

I snickered. "Is that your economics 101, Bern? I don't feel much better by it." I crossed my arms in frustration. No one who wasn't in my position could understand the humiliation. Bernadette was in a comfortable, long-term relationship. She had secured her independence. I was still a nomad—a hunter-gatherer with roots showing in my self-dyed hair.

Suddenly, I felt thirsty. I pushed myself up from the chair and headed toward the kitchen.

"Mind if I grab a beer?" I asked, certain Mike's Budweiser sign had flashed enough times in my face to convince me it was fine to drink alcohol alone among friends.

"Go for it," said Bernadette from the living room. "You know where the mugs are."

I opened the fridge and grabbed a beer from a shelf loaded with cans. One thing Mike never let get critically low was his beer supply. I felt like drinking it from the can and wiped the top clean with a rag from the sink.

"*Na zdrowie*," I said, cracking the can and raising it to my mouth. Bernadette raised her Coke can in return.

I flopped back down on the chair.

"You look completely defeated, babe," Bernadette observed.

"That's not the half of it," I replied. "My mom wants me to go on a date with the neighbor boy."

Bernadette snorted pop out of her nose.

"She moves fast!" she said, wiping the pop remnants with the back of Mike's jersey. He was too absorbed in the halftime commentary to notice.

"What's the rush?" she continued. "Doesn't she want to spend some quality time now that she has her daughter back after losing you for the last nine months?"

"Don't forget a day and a morning," I said, giving a smile.

"So who's this mystery man? Not Sebastian?" she said.

I nodded, and she let out a squeal.

"Yuck," she said, laughing.

"I'm going to do it," I mumbled.

She held her free hand to her mouth. "Whoops. Sorry. I didn't think he was your type."

I took a swig of my beer and belched. "Forget it. I don't have a type anymore. I don't know what I want."

"I know a guy at work who'd date you," said Mike, jumping back into the conversation.

I eyed him. "Why do you say that?" I said, hoping this was my way out with Sebastian.

"His last girlfriend had him put in jail for a domestic. So he's looking for someone a little simpler," he said, lifting his head off the pillow for a moment.

I felt hurt. "Thanks for calling me special needs," I said, taking a bigger swallow of beer and fighting back tears.

"Asshole," Bernadette said to him.

Mike realized what he had said and started backtracking. "I didn't mean it like that, ladies. I mean he's looking for a girl who's more the stay-at-home type. Low key, hear me? His last girl was a wildcat. In fact, she was a pretty darn good stripper but too hotheaded."

"Oh great," I replied, remembering I was currently dressed in sweatpants and a sweater. "He'd be really impressed by my pole dancing, the whale-flopping-around-on-the-ground look. Come on, Mike. What the hell kind of matchmaker are you? Would your coworker go from a tight-ass girlfriend to multiple asses?"

Mike shrugged. "Sounds like he would have a lot to choose from."

I made a face at him.

Bernadette seemed interested.

"Perhaps," she began, "we could do a double date. You know, a show of force. That way if this guy is a jerk-off, you wouldn't be alone, Larissa."

Her idea had merit. But I wasn't sure I was at a place where I needed a platoon of chaperones on a date yet. I was pretty certain I could handle Sebastian easily enough on my own.

"Let me think about it," I finally said. "My mom is pretty adamant for me to go out one time with the neighbor kid."

"What's in it for her—some kind of kickback? This should be your choice," Bernadette said.

"I know. I think she's getting pressure from Sebastian's mother to arrange this thing. She's probably getting desperate that her son has become part of the furniture. This could be a simple date for me, a way to break the ice and get back in the scene."

Bernadette shook her head. "All I can say is thank God I am far away from that scene."

"What do you mean?" My eyebrows rose.

"You know, always having to look your best and act your best, constantly focusing on keeping your dates interesting, looking for events to attend, brushing your teeth before bed." We laughed.

"Any idea what you'd do on the date?" she asked. Her question caught me off guard. I hadn't even thought about that. My ex had always come up with plans. I had gone along for the ride.

"Make sure you put out," said Mike. "Knock that ice off." He laughed alone.

"Where'd you find this guy?" I asked, pointing my thumb his way.

Bernadette grinned.

"He's going straight back to the shelter." She pushed Mike's legs off, walked over to where I sat, and stopped. She grabbed my ponytail.

"We need to do some work, honey. If you're jumping back in the saddle, these split ends have the potential to slit your date's throat."

I yanked my hair free.

"Never mind the strands of hair. Look at this body. The first impression any date is going to have of me is that I want to eat at the buffet."

"Funny you should mention that," said Bernadette, glancing over at Mike, who remained stretched out on the sofa. "The other day, I was trying to get my bra on. It was a struggle. Every time I start putting on weight, it goes straight to my chest."

"And the problem is?" asked her boyfriend, smiling her way.

"Ah, like back problems and looking like a circus freak when my chest enters a room two days ahead of me."

I nodded. "I wish some of my fast food went to my chest. It's all ass and thighs for me."

"So here's the solution," replied Bernadette, her eyes bright. "I was talking to Amy the other day. She's battling the same issues. Her kids are eating up all her time, but she's eating up all the desserts and chocolate bars. She wants to start hitting the gym. How about the three of us sign up somewhere and help motivate each other?" She stood in front of me with her hands on her hips.

In theory, the idea sounded great. Beyond that, I knew it meant physical effort. I was starting to wonder where all this energy was going to be squeezed from. Although I was reluctant, I realized I needed every advantage if I were to date because I wasn't currently playing with a full deck.

"I'm in. Just tell me where to go and when to show up," I said, scratching my head.

"Awesome," said Bernadette, obviously pleased she now had three of us on board.

I pointed at her. "I'll tell you right now—I'm in this to lose weight and tone up. I'm not looking to pack on thirty pounds of pure muscle and start to look like those icky female bodybuilders."

Bernadette laughed. "Unless you plan on only eating rice and getting needles full of steroids jammed into your ass, I really don't think you'll ever reach that stage, babe. Sorry. If we're lucky, we might reduce one of our stomach rolls." She leaned over, and I high-fived her.

"If you girls need steroids, let me know. There's a guy at work who deals good shit," said Mike, focusing on his game.

Bernadette looked at me and burst out laughing.

"Obviously, background checks aren't a condition of your employment," I said to him. "It's good to know that when they say full service, it's full service."

"That's how us mechanics roll," he said, looking our way and grinning.

Bernadette shook her head and said, "You mean how you oil-change guys roll. Mechanics take cars apart. You fill them with oil—one hole in, one hole out."

"Now you sound pornographic," I said.

Bernadette snickered. "He thinks just because his name is embroidered on his coveralls, he's a certified something."

"It's guys like me who keep your French manicures clean," he said, finally looking up at her.

I nodded. "He's got a point."

She gave us a sly grin. "Any boyfriend of mine would change my oil for the services I provide for him."

I let out a laugh. "Okay. Let's leave that one for behind closed doors. If there are any moves you can show me at the gym, I need the ones that can give me a waist a guy can wrap his arms around without dislocating his shoulders."

I left Bernadette's place and arrived back at my parents', feeling somewhat elevated, knowing I had the makings of a plan to restore my body to presentable dating quality. In fact, I'd never had a presentable body, so any form of exercise had to produce results. Looking back, I supposed my ex had taken what he could get.

I found my mother in the living room, perched by the front window, where she kept a few dozen assorted plants and flowers. Pruning and developing these plants for the spring outdoor season was her pastime. If I'd owned a yard, I'd have been buying the plants sold at Walmart.

"How was your visit?" she asked sweetly. She was on her knees, holding a pair of scissors in one hand; her other hand was on the carpet, bracing herself. She was wearing her outdoor hat despite the fact that she was indoors. When she did something, she went all out.

"Good." I sat down beside her, hoping I wouldn't be included in the work. I was wrong. She motioned for a pot.

"How's Bernadette doing these days? How's Mike? What was their place like? Did they make you something to eat?"

After Mom asked her barrage of questions, I answered as I always did: "Same. Same. Same. No."

"So you're starving then." She looked at me, concerned, already putting down her utensil to go make me something. I stopped her.

"I'm okay. I'm not hungry."

She didn't look convinced. "Where are common manners toward guests? No matter who shows up here, at any time, they will never leave hungry."

She was right. A fresh jar of pickles was always on standby, plus some ham and pierogi in the freezer, five minutes away from a boil to being served.

I leaned back on my arms, surveying the living room where I had spent my entire life minus the nine months, one day, and a morning. The crushed dark green carpet and the transitional school photographs of me from kindergarten to grade-twelve graduation on the wall were like badges of life. The fuzzy wallpaper behind them still fascinated me; people actually bought it, thinking it fashionable. Way back when I was really young, where the thirty-two-inch flat-screen television now sat in the corner of the room, a mammoth wooden structure with a built-in television and record player had stood. My dad still referred to it as cutting edge. Dad's proudest wall in his house was his so-called feature wall in the living room, which was plastered with multicolored Z-Brick we'd stuck on one weekend when I was a teenager.

I had spent twenty-nine Christmases in that room, ripping apart wrapped gifts while Dad sipped whiskey. Hosting birthday parties, watching Bugs Bunny cartoons, cuddling with my ex prior to getting married—this room owned a lifetime of my memories.

"We decided to join a gym," I said optimistically, trying to seem inspired. The reaction from my mother was positive.

"Good for you girls! A little exercise certainly doesn't hurt. But don't overdo it, okay? I don't want to see you get hurt or start looking like those muscle women," she said lightly.

I promised her I would try my best to continue looking female.

"You know," Mom said with a smile, "I spoke to Sebastian's mom and told her you'd like to date her son."

"Hold on," I said, not trying to hide my horror at the suggestion I was the pursuer. "I'm not the one requesting this date. And, may I add, I am not considering this a date. It's more of let's-go-kill-a-few-hours thing. That's it. That's all, Mom. As far as I know, he may be doing this only because his mom is forcing him. How awkward is that going to be, right?" I looked at her sorrowfully. How pathetic—mothers setting up their adult children on a date.

"She was very excited."

"I'll bet. You're making it sound like I'm interested in her son, when I'm not. He's a geek. I don't date geeks."

"What was your ex?"

"A different kind of geek."

"So is the neighbor boy."

"He's more the freaky kind."

"Give him a chance is all I ask. I don't want to lose a good neighbor."

"Ah, so now the pressure is all on me to go out with this boy and not ruin your relationship with his mom."

"Just treat him nice."

My eyes widened. "What do you think I am, the bogeywoman?"

She looked at me gently. "You know how you can get sometimes."

I reared my head back. "What do you mean 'how I can get'? I'm lovable Larissa all the time."

My mother looked away. "Just be nice. Don't be cutting and negative."

I was hurt.

Mom cleared her throat and changed the subject. "Your dad wants to see you in the garage."

"What for?"

"He's begun work on your car. He wanted you to join him when you got home."

"Fine," I said, pushing myself up from the floor.

The detached garage was in the backyard, meaning I had to put my boots and jacket back on. Then I scurried between the paths in the snow and went inside the garage.

"Hey, Larissa, did your mom send you?" he asked as soon as I entered the double-size garage.

I wanted to be a smartass and reply, "Who else could it have been?" but I didn't. Venting my bruised ego on him was unfair. I walked up to the faded gray Chrysler. Dad was dressed in a pair of green coveralls that I could remember from as far back as four years old. I was certain pure body sweat was holding it together by now.

The car was inside the garage. I was impressed.

"How'd you get this out from under the tree in the backyard to the garage?" I asked with amazement.

My dad, who was not one to hold back on his achievements, launched into his feats of wonder.

Apparently, the car wouldn't start—no surprise there. It couldn't be pushed, because the brakes had seized—surprise there. He'd had Bob from down the back lane bring his pickup truck over. Together, they'd hooked the back of the Chrysler to the back of the pickup and dragged the car through the snow into the back lane. From there, Bob had used the front of his truck to push the Chrysler into the garage, bumper to bumper. Actually, not quite bumper to bumper—Dad proudly displayed the two weeks' worth of newspapers he'd taped together to form a protective cushion, as he described it, to protect the paint. And it had almost worked. The Chrysler's bumper had a smear of last week's news embedded into it. So did Bob's truck, but Dad said he'd buff it out.

He beamed. He stood beside the two-door car as if it were a trophy fish. I fought hard to crank up the same excitement toward an automobile. Having a car meant a money pit—gas, insurance, oil changes at Mike's quick change. And I'd have preferred a shade of pink versus the gray, but there was no way I'd be tossing that request my dad's way. He'd launch into a take-what-you-can-get speech, one I knew by heart.

"Looking good, Dad. Is it ready to go?" I walked up to it and touched the cold metal of the hood.

He shook his head.

"It will be. The damn brakes seized. The battery is shot. And I just noticed something is leaking onto my floor." Mike's words echoed in my head after my dad's last remark.

"It even has a sunroof," he said, pointing at it with an oily hand.

"Does it work?"

"It will."

I was ready to go back inside the house, having seen all I needed to of a car that had stood in our backyard for over a decade and remained exactly the same car, only inside our garage now.

"Just one thing I wanted to say." Dad was not yet prepared to release his hostage.

"What's that?" I asked, rocking from side to side. I was starting to get hungry and planned to hit Mom up for a sandwich.

"Have you gone to visit your baba?"

I shook my head. Baba was my dad's mother. She was ninety-one years old and had outlasted her husband for longer than I had been alive.

"I was planning on it once I got settled in," I said, trying to make it sound as if this visit were a top priority.

"Don't wait. She won't be around forever. At her age, once she's gone, she's gone." I wasn't sure if he was saying this more for his or my sake.

"I realize that," I said, feeling my stomach growl.

"You should be visiting her every week. I know your cousins do." My cousins hadn't just gone through a separation, but I wasn't about to argue.

"I will, Dad. I'm planning on it," I said sheepishly.

"She's old," he said, in case I'd missed it the first time. He nodded and was about to say something else, when the door opened.

It was Auntie Tina, who was sixty-two. My dad's older sister, she had divorced decades earlier and had five adult sons. She also resided with Baba off and on between her own apartments and those of the men she shacked up with. She required a home environment funded on someone else's coin; her ability to work was compromised because of the fibromyalgia she claimed was diagnosed decades ago. She described her pain level as too intense to focus on a job. My dad called her disease bullshit. But if there was one thing she did excel at, it was seeking out men. She made no bones about it, boasting openly that she was after rich men—sugar daddies to provide her with a lifestyle she deserved. Dad also described this lifestyle as bullshit.

"Here you are," she announced, closing the door behind her. She was tall, with dyed-blonde hair and large eyes that looked wolfish under her raccoon hat and fur coat. Her designer boots scraped on the garage's cement floor. She pushed the door closed with black-gloved hands to stop the snow from blowing in.

"Hi, Auntie Tina," I said, waving at her. Her face held a smile that rarely left it.

"Larissa, you poor girl," she said, and she embraced me in a long hug.

I was confused when I pulled away.

"What's wrong?" I asked.

She studied me and said, "Your heart. The pain. The feelings of worthlessness. The ruminative thoughts of taking pills and going to sleep forever."

I took a step back.

"What the hell are you talking about now, Tina?" The annoyance toward his sister was evident in my dad's voice.

She tried to put an arm around me, and I let her. Her voice dropped to a whisper.

"Your poor daughter. Her heart sliced in half by that imbecile. I always knew he was a shitbag."

I looked at her. "Are you referring to my ex?" I said lamely.

Auntie Tina soured. "The bastard that ripped your heart out. Crushed your future. Betrayed your trust. I never liked that douche bag. He seemed slimy to me."

"You only met him once."

"And it left a vile taste in my mouth."

"I did marry him because I loved him."

"A cretin. Stay away from musicians, honey."

My dad called out to his sister. "Your own husband was a juicehead, Tina. Leave my daughter alone. I need her focused on restoring this car with me."

Tina looked horrified.

"That's man's work, Roman. Are you kidding me? Do you have any idea what solvents and grease do to our hands? What man wants to be fondled by sandpaper flesh?" She stared at him stiffly.

My dad's face lit up. "Easy! My daughter is in here with us. What the hell's the matter with your mouth?"

I grinned. Dad still saw me as sweet sixteen. I figured dads didn't ever see their daughters as anything short of virginal. I was convinced they calmed their hearts at night with denial for as long as they could, until the truth was cruelly ripped and shattered by that thing called pregnancy. Since I had yet to spawn a child, my dad's certainty that I was still untouched by any man lived on.

"Come on, Roman. For crying out loud, your daughter was married. She knows plenty—a little about this, a little about that." She smiled broadly at me. All I could do was shrug coyly.

"Honey," she said, taking my hand, "if you want to attract quality men—men with looks, money, a house, and *assets*"—she accented the last word—"you need soft hands, white teeth, hair that smells like an apple orchard, and a sharp eye to spot these catches."

"You're so full of shit," my father told his sister. His arms waved spastically at her from behind the car. "Don't start putting your bullshit into my daughter's head. If your crapola is true, why the hell do you still have to live with our ninety-one-year-old mother when you get dumped? Shouldn't you be chauffeured around right now with your sugar daddy in a Bentley? Shouldn't your two-hundred-dollar haircuts and designer clothes and all that jazz, which our dear mother is paying for, have landed this magic man?" He folded his arms.

She ignored him and looked back at me. "Listen, honey, when you're ready to take it to a whole new level, you call me."

I gazed at her quizzically. "What level?"

She beamed. "I'm talking about bringing out your inner and outer beauty, honey." She read my confusion and mercifully expanded on her cryptic message. "Salons. Professional makeover. The whole shebang. Head to toe. Hair gone from where it shouldn't be. Skin silkened. Teeth like ivory. Layered cosmetics. A piercing near your naughty bits. Body scents to make a man's knees wobbly." She looked pleased with her description.

I smiled casually. "That all sounds wonderful for somebody interested in maintaining it, but I'm more of a one-hit wonder, Auntie Tina. One time, I think I used conditioner after my shampoo, and my ex was smitten by it."

She smiled gently. "Yeah, honey—could that possibly be the reason we're now talking about him in the past tense?"

"Knock it off," warned my father.

I let out a deep breath. She was right. I had gotten lucky with my ex; he'd accepted me as I was, which wasn't saying much. Likely, the new expectations I would face would be higher. That meant more work. Suddenly, the effort to remain married seemed a helluva lot easier than postmarriage.

"Anyway, honey," she said, looking me over and taking in my snowmobile boots, track pants, and navy men's winter parka, "I stopped by to offer my support and network of beauty stores to transform you into a princess. Us Ukrainians have our weaker areas to address. Sometimes our hair is thin, except for the hair creeping out our nose; our skin is blemished; our eyebrows creep together; and our hands are like men's, but rest assured, we can overcome it all!"

"Being a woman sounds so complicated," I confessed, leaning against the car for support. I felt as busted up as it was.

"Just great, Tina," growled my dad. "She was feeling like shit when she got here. I don't need a depressed daughter moping around here like another Groundhog, for Christ's sake." The groundhog my dad was referring to was his second cousin, whom he had nicknamed because of her personal choice to never hold a job, always stay wasted, and reside in the basement of her parents' home.

Auntie Tina brightened. "Relax, Roman. Jesus, you're always so wound up, like a champagne bottle about to burst. I'm surprised your blood pressure hasn't blown your head off yet." She pointed at me. "I'll look after your daughter—don't you worry."

He shook his head. "I worry when my sixty-two-year-old sister, who can't hold a job because of some bullshit pain thing that's never seemed to go away for the last thirty years, wants to motivate my daughter." He grimaced.

"It's okay, Dad," I offered, looking at him with a cocked eyebrow. "I could use some help fixing up some of my rough ends. You're helping me with the car. Auntie Tina is helping me with my body."

His face twisted in agony. "Just don't go slopping all that makeup everywhere, looking like one of those singer freaks on the television."

I smiled, squinting.

I was officially on a beautification mission.

CHAPTER 4

Juiced Love, Shacking Up

March 3, 11:15 p.m.

I confess to never having had the girlie-desire gene to want to get married, need to get married, yearn to get married, yet I did after all—just not happily ever after. I did some things right (waiting until I was thirty) and some things wrong (waiting until I was thirty and marrying a boy who was under thirty and just wouldn't go away). I had no intention of marrying my ex when we met at the bar. I was juiced, and he was juiced—love really does make sense juiced, so it was love at first sight (really, he had cab money to get us home, and I did not). He just sort of stuck around after that night of juicing. If I had been into probabilities, I'd have said after meeting my ex that I'd never see him again, talk to him again, kiss his lips, or sure to Christ marry him. I was wrong. I did all of the above and beyond. Add in divorce.

*****

We strutted away from Amy's minivan like a rock group about to enter the stage for the big show. The reality was that we were in the parking lot of Pump It Up Fitness and about to enroll our unmuscled fat in memberships that would transform our thirty-year-old cellulite-riddled bodies into quarter-bouncing flesh that would make blue-collar men wild.

We held hands and walked in a row toward the blacked-out glass doors of the holy grail, where only the motivated dared to venture into the world of Lululemons, sweat, grunting men, and pounding rock music.

Inside the tiled foyer, we were greeted at the counter by a boy we guessed to be around nineteen, who was experiencing a fresh round of facial acne. He was going to take us through the paperwork and then enlighten us about the world of fitness and the ways of Pump It Up Fitness.

The three of us sat across from Leo, who wore a powder-puff-blue track suit, Pump It Up Fitness's signature color, as he walked us through the documentation for a one-year commitment. I balked. That would last longer than my marriage had. I suddenly got cold feet.

"What's the matter, Larissa?" said Amy, anxious for me to sign by the *X*, waiting with her hand poised to take my pen.

I looked helplessly at her, then at Bernadette, and finally at poor Leo, who simply didn't understand, at his age, what this meant to me.

"I'm just not into commitments anymore," I finally stammered. "I used to believe in them. And then I found out they can be broken."

Bernadette shrugged. "So? If you decide to quit going, no one cares."

I quickly shook my head. "No, I mean, what if the gym pulls this contract from me? Cancels it?"

This time, Leo shook his head. "We don't do that," he assured me. "If anything, we sue those who stop paying on their contractual terms," he declared, smiling.

"See?" Amy replied, pleased. "They won't be canceling on you."

"But I can be sued!" I cried, the pen between my fingers shaking.

"Then just keep paying," said Bernadette, popping the gum she was chewing.

I moaned. Sweat was beading between my shoulder blades.

"I don't know, girls. A year is a long time. I thought my marriage felt like forever, and it lasted three months less than this thing."

"You have forty-eight hours to cancel for a full refund," said Leo. I looked at him hopefully.

Bernadette smiled. "Does that help you?" she said. She'd signed her contract without concern. She had Mike to fall back on—and ten years of assurance. I had nothing but my old bedroom.

I wasn't convinced by Leo's pitch. "What about the other thousands of hours on the contract—can I still cancel? I might find myself getting too much muscle. My dad would hate that."

He looked at me, undeterred. "We guarantee you won't want to cancel."

"Yeah," I said, the pen feeling heavy in my fingers. "I had an even better guarantee in front of God, and that was cancelled."

"Come on, Larissa," begged Amy. "I wanna go see the equipment. And the guys." She was shameless, considering she was a married woman with two kids.

"Okay," I said finally but under duress. "I will sign. But I want to let you know I take offense about having to check off my status. What does my status have to do with me getting fit?" I stared a surprised Leo in the eyes.

"You mean the section that asks if you're single or married?" he asked, licking his lips.

"Yeah, that section."

"So I know who I can date," he said in a deadpan manner. At first, I believed him, until I heard Amy and Bernadette burst out laughing.

Leo joined them. This young boy had a sense of humor. My ex could have used some of it. I signed.

We were now official members of Pump It Up Fitness. It was time to flex our glutes and trim the fat.

Leo grabbed our stack of contracts. He glanced down at mine and then stared at me.

"So how do you pronounce your last name anyway?" he asked, grinning as if I were using it for a punch line.

"Just like it sounds," I replied.

He was still staring at me, looking confused.

"Androshchuk." I finally broke and said it out loud.

"You need more vowels," he joked.

"I'll mention that to my ancestors in the afterlife." I heard Amy snickering behind me. Leo was about to comment, but he closed his mouth and placed the contracts into a drawer instead.

We followed Leo behind the main desk and entered the lair. We collectively gasped. We were probably all thinking the same thing. Within these four walls, with rows of machines, endless stretches of black rubber flooring, and the occasional grunt, we would redefine our futures with toning like that seen on the covers of fitness magazines—bodies we could only fantasize about. We were all now the real deal.

"Leo," said Amy, her eyes as wide as my own, trying to take in seventy-five thousand square feet of hard-body-making machines, "where the hell do we start?"

Leo giggled. "Ladies, there is a machine here for every body part, every muscle, every fiber under your skin." His arm swept out before him.

"I just want the ones that make me look hot," said Bernadette matter-of-factly. "I need something so that when I'm putting the moves on Mikey, I have stamina."

Amy and I groaned at the same time. Leo stared at her.

"Carry on," I said to Leo, gently pushing him forward on his tour. "She comes from a rough background. Her mouth can get a little dirty, like some of these hand grips."

He motioned for us to follow him. He had to raise his voice over the music and noise from the machines. It seemed as if every piece of equipment were being used. I kept surveying the crowd for my fellow fatties, not seeing any. I began to wonder if I needed to start at the more-underground fitness center they all must have gone to before coming to a place like this. Everyone I was looking at already seemed to be in great shape. Why they continued working out was beyond me. I had already decided that once I looked like them, my membership was done.

"So, ladies," began Leo, pointing to his left, "this row contains our indoor cycles. Behind them are our indoor rowers." His hand swung to his right. "These are our ellipticals, and behind them are our recumbent bikes. If you're feeling more adventurous, down here are the cross trainers, and over there are the treadmills."

I was amazed at the diversity. I had no clue what the hell any of them were.

"Hey," inquired Bernadette, "what the heck are those screens attached to the treadmills?"

Good question, I thought, because I was wondering the same thing.

Leo smiled. "All our treadmills, ellipticals, and recumbents have fifteen-inch monitors that pipe in satellite television. As well, they offer Wi-Fi for Internet—"

Bernadette cut him off. "Are you saying we can watch television while we sweat it out?" She was so excited by this prospect that a vein on her forehead started to throb.

He nodded. "Of course."

She screamed. "Daytime soaps while I work my thighs out!"

We high-fived one another. Fitness had suddenly become anything but hard work.

He led us farther down the aisles, coming to a large wall with pegs jammed haphazardly all over it.

"Climbing wall, ladies. Test your endurance and willpower." He pointed to the top, which seemed really high to me.

"Could we fall?" I asked, thinking it a relevant question. I had come there to get fit, not to end up on crutches.

"You could, but it's not likely. Sergio is our certified rock-wall climber, and no one climbs without him present as a spotter." We all nodded. To me, someone named Sergio sounded competent, as if he had grown up on the ledge of a mountain.

Our tour continued past an array of free weights, the area where we'd put on serious muscle. I doubted I'd spend much time in that area. It required a lot more effort than sitting down on a machine and moving my legs to television commercials.

We followed him to another corner of the building. He pointed at a large stage.

"Our facility offers a larger selection of aerobics classes than anywhere else in the city."

"Like what?" said Amy.

Leo was ready. "Like Step, Ride, Core, Kick, Boot Camp, Four-by-Four, Zumba, Power Rack, Stretch, Burnout—"

"That last one sounds like your ex," Amy kidded me. I smirked.

"How do we know what to choose?" said Amy, looking bewildered.

Leo cleared his throat. "We recommend you try each of them over time to find out what suits you best. The classes go from easy to extremely challenging."

"Honestly, Leo," said Bernadette, looking around, "I have no clue in hell what any of those kick-ride-stomps you just mentioned are, but my ass is twitching already."

Leo flushed. Instead of answering, he motioned for us to continue following him. I elbowed Bernadette gently in the ribs to stop her from tormenting the kid. Amy looked as if she were holding back tears of laughter.

He led us to the female changing rooms. Although he wouldn't go inside with us, he described the lockers, showers, steam room, and sauna that were available to all members.

The final part of the tour turned out to be my favorite: the snack bar. There were rows of protein bars, energy drinks, and fresh fruits and a few chairs where we could sit and watch the large overhead LED screens. I was starting to believe I could spend most of my days there, kicking back and only going home for supper.

Leo informed us that his tour was over and that we were free to roam around or have a workout on the machines. None of us was that ambitious, already considering it a victory that we all had shown up and joined. Amy wanted to look around, so I bought a bag of chips, and Bernadette got a large soft drink. It might have been a fitness center, but they still knew how to cater to the weak.

"Girls, what do you think?" I said as we began our own tour among the machines.

Bernadette grinned. "I think this should be fun. How can we go wrong getting fit while watching the cooking channel? Come on."

Amy nudged me. "Look over there," she mumbled, pointing only with her chin.

My eyes popped open when I latched on to what had her juices going. The guy was tall. He was dark. He was buff. And he was sweating. I loved him. So did Amy. And she had no right, since she was married. The guttural sound coming from deep within her made us laugh. She was an oversexed mother of two—even the kids couldn't tire that out of her. The real loser of her sex drive was her husband, who was a long-haul truck driver away three weeks out of every month. Amy was a dangerous woman to let loose inside a gym full of sweating men.

"What would you do with that?" asked Bernadette dreamily to no one in particular.

"What *wouldn't* I do with that?" replied Amy. "But first, I'd eat that skimpy shirt right off his chest. After that, wherever my tongue goes." She exhaled deeply. "I haven't seen my husband's abs in over five years. I forget what abs look like not surrounded by a bulbous ring of fat and hair."

I squealed. "You're awful. I'm shocked your husband lets you out of the house."

"I read the Bible at home," she said, smirking. We all knew the type of books Amy read behind closed doors. She was twenty-nine years old and had two boys under seven. Her flaming red hair matched the energy of her personality. We were always surprised she maintained such a mundane job as a receptionist, sitting behind the counter of a dental office.

Amy pointed at a trio of women working on machines, each taking turns squeezing a set of handles together in front of them.

"See the breasts on those broads? That's what I want. The three of us are the watered-down version of that group."

Bernadette snickered. "Savor your flat chest. My aching back reminds me every day that three Ds equal triple trouble."

"Yeah, but look at them," said Amy, cocking her chin toward the women. "Cleavage. Perky. And how the hell do they also get such tiny waists? Like, come on—that's just not possible," she said sourly.

I nodded. "I'll vouch for that. For every inch I put on my chest, I double down around my waist."

"We will achieve exactly the same as those bitches," Bernadette said, taking on the role of our official cheerleader.

"God, I hope so," I said, stuffing a handful of chips into my mouth.

She grinned. "Our goal is to burn ten thousand calories every workout. Okay?" She looked at us both.

"Let's go for thirty thousand," suggested Amy. "That sounds like more fat to me."

I looked doubtful. "Didn't Leo say it'd take a lot to burn a thousand in a workout?"

Bernadette scowled. "He doesn't realize the focus we have together," she said, slugging back the remainder of her soft drink. "At our age, everything we do to hone our bodies takes three times as much effort as those twenty-year-old tighties."

"I agree," said Amy, nodding. "If those bitches over there do ten of those squeeze things, we'll do a hundred."

We all laughed and looked around us.

"I really should do something today to tone up for my date with the neighbor boy," I said, not feeling motivated.

Bernadette looked surprised. "So you're really going to do it, are you?"

I nodded. "More for my mom than anything else. That'll get her off my back for a while."

"Might be love at first handshake," suggested Amy, grinning.

I laughed. "More like I'll love getting the date over with as fast as possible."

"Do you think you should do a few things here today to, you know, get your pump on?"

I slapped at her. "Listen to you and your terminology. He'll get what he gets. Take this body, or leave it," I boasted, opening my arms wide for the world to see.

"Pretty darn sexy in those capris and baggy sweater, my love," said Bernadette. "But you might want to wash off the ketchup smear," she added, pointing to a remnant from my breakfast eggs on my right shoulder.

My eyes popped open. "You girls let me walk around here all this time in front of Leo and these fit people with ketchup smeared across my chest? I thought you had my back."

Amy laughed. "Your clothes usually contain some remnant of your meal. I didn't think anything of it. Sorry, my dear!"

I groaned. Was this how people viewed me? I was horrified.

Bernadette took my hand. "All that matters is that you look your best for job interviews and dates, 'kay? We don't care what food matter you're fashionably wearing."

My phone started to ring inside my purse. I fumbled for it.

The picture of the caller rolled my heart: my ex. I had forgotten to delete the image of him chewing on his drumsticks.

"Hey," I said, putting the phone on speaker. The girls leaned against machines, listening to the conversation. I kept no secrets from my friends.

"Hey," he replied, sounding as expressionless as always. The only time I ever saw any deviation was when he was playing his drums. Otherwise, it seemed he was wavering on the brink of catatonic.

There was a long silence.

I motioned to the phone, grinning, waiting for him to say something. I often had to be the one to instigate the conversation, but now that we were no longer husband and wife, he was on his own.

The silence dragged on, and I began to wonder if he was even still there.

"Hey," he said again. The girls burst out laughing. "Who's there?" he asked.

I shook my head. "Doesn't matter who I'm with. You're on my time right now, so what's up?" I kept my voice curt.

"Can we talk?" he asked.

I smiled broadly. I loved having him beg me in front of my posse. It showed how much he was hurting. The old adage "You never know what you have until it's gone" was chewing him up inside now. *Good,* I thought. He had wasted nine months, a day, and a morning of my life. He could hurt for all of his reincarnations.

"I have nothing to say," I finally said into the phone. "What's done is done. I've moved on. I told you once I walked out that door, I wouldn't reopen it." The girls cheered me on. Bernadette attempted a victory jump with a split and clutched her inner thighs, grimacing, when she landed.

His voice returned. "I've arranged a meeting for us at the lawyer's. I wanted to give you a call today to let you know the address and date."

I was speechless. My grin faded. "Lawyer?"

"Yeah, I guess we gotta sign off on our shit and stuff like that there." The phone fell silent again.

This time, I was at a loss for words. *More signatures.* Today I was signing my life away everywhere.

"Are you sure?" I caught myself saying, and then I stopped. "Good. Let me know when and where, and I'll be there. No problem."

I could hear explosions in the background.

"What's that?" I asked.

"Just playing the newest release of *Earth Protector* on my PlayStation. It's wild, man. Three-D. Surround sound. You should check it out. I just saved the Earth from a swarm of aliens from the planet Yoman."

Obviously, he wasn't dwelling much on the upcoming legal process to officially end our marriage. He was too busy learning how to deploy his plasma gun.

Amy raised her fingers to the front of her forehead in the shape of a letter *L*. Bernadette laughed despite the fact that she must have been still hurting from attempting that jumping split.

I was too distracted to acknowledge Amy's gesture. "Fine. I can meet you at the lawyer's. What do I need to bring?" There was more silence.

"I dunno. I guess a pen." I could hear more explosions. More aliens had just met their deaths from my ex, the world hero.

Amy raised her knee in a series of quick pumps, simulating shots to the groin area.

"Listen, I'll let you get back to being a superhero. I'll see you at the lawyer's. Thanks for the call." I was about to ask how he was, when the sounds of battle ceased. He was gone.

"Asshole," said Bernadette.

"Total douche," confirmed Amy.

"I want to rip off his nuts." Bernadette's voice rose.

"You're way better off without him." Amy defended me with a slow smile.

I gripped my phone.

I wanted to believe Amy. Inharmonious was the reason we'd separated as a married couple. However, right then, standing inside Pump It Up Fitness, I didn't feel that way.

CHAPTER 5

Bernadette Dates the Yearbook

March 13, 1:05 a.m.

My best friend, Bernadette, made dating in elementary school look easy. She liked a boy, she talked to the boy, she got the boy, and she dumped the boy. I remained a dating virgin until I was nearly thirty years old because my dad told me it would be better that way. Ha-ha—who's laughing now?

Bernadette was a success in school. She was pretty. She had a body. She had big hair. She had hips that shifted hypnotically. She got any and every boy she wanted or didn't want and even had a date lined up for prom six years before prom was on the horizon. The rumor was that she had a waiting list of boys for prom like for an NFL Super Bowl ticket.

Bernadette comes from one of those unconventional families that has multiple mothers and mixed bloodlines and simply scandalous behavior. She wears it like a badge of honor.

Let's backtrack to when her dad was a young man of trouble and married for over three years. He was away on a business trip, doing business and a virgin we'll call Emma (to protect her privacy) he met at a bar one night on business. He gave her his business in his motel room.

Tear out seven months of calendar pages. A knock came one night on his marital door (about eleven o'clock, I am told) from a young lady (who hitchhiked seven hundred miles without having an address, last name, or phone number, though she did have a first name, a town name, and a shit-you-not attitude) he didn't quite remember until she reminded him that while on his business trip, she had given him the business. Now she was bringing his business back home to him. His wife, who was now standing at the door with him, forgot to mind her own business because what this girl had to say made it her business.

The young lady was pregnant with Bernadette (my best friend) and was no longer a virgin, speaking to the man who'd debauched her, making him a father and no less than a husband to her. Being a stand-up guy, Bernadette's dad bade toodaloo to his current wife, who one night was first watching Jay Leno, thinking of the lunch she was going to make for her businessman husband, and then spending the rest of the night throwing lunch meat at him and packing her own suitcase instead. The next day, Emma moved in, in time to give birth a month and three days later to a beautiful girl they named Bernadette, who was destined to become my best friend.

Throw away seven calendars. Bernadette was now my friend in elementary school, living next door to her dad's lifelong best friend, who had two girls seven years older. The parents hung around every day and every night, or so it seemed. Actually, Bernadette's dad and his best friend's wife hung out more often. He gave her his business a few times a week when his best friend was out on business and his wife, Emma, the previous virgin, was out shopping. While she was checking out the bargains, he was checking in with his best friend's wife, whom we'll call Bea (to protect her privacy).

As things go in life, not as planned, Emma forgot her coupons at home and returned early—too early for her husband to finish doing his business with his closer-than-a-brother best friend's wife, Bea. It was a day of destiny and perhaps even a solar eclipse, if anyone had been interested in looking up at the sky and not in the bedroom. Emma found her husband heels to Jesus with Bea on their kitchen table. (Luckily, it was made out of strong hickory wood. Bernadette still has family dinners on that very strong table.) At the same time, Bea's husband, whom we'll call Ron (to protect his privacy), came home, as it was a slow day in the office, with no business to be had, so he figured he'd go home and give his wife some personal business.

However, his best friend, closer than family, was first in line, giving Ron's wife personal business, so he needed to stand in line. Sometimes even best-friend friendships, stronger than blood, break apart for mysterious reasons.

In this case, there was no mystery, with Ron's wife splayed out like a carved turkey on his hickory table and Emma not wanting to use the coupons under Bea's ass. Why, that friendship came to an abrupt end then and there, without Bernadette's dad finishing his business that day. He divorced Emma, he married Bea, Ron married Emma, and in sixty days, Bernadette had a new family. At least she got to keep the same mobile home, because her dad stayed where he lived, and Ron stayed where he lived (next door). Only the cars in the dirt driveways changed, and the business kept on going.

*****

On the day of my date with Sebastian, Mom was clearly more excited than I was. I had decided my predate ritual was to scan through Pinterest on my iPad while stretched out on my bed in a blissful state of calm. I must have entered a pretty intense state, as I fell asleep. This was perfectly fine with me but not my mother. Her predate ritual included an entirely different set of expectations for me to fulfill. My bedroom sanctuary was intruded upon, and I was ruefully awakened by my mom's hand and urgent voice. Unknown to me, prep work was required prior to meeting with Sebastian. My personal expectation for prep work was simply showing up at his house.

She grabbed my hand and pulled me up. I fought as if it were my first day of school.

"You can't look like this," she said, looking me over.

"You mean like myself?" My mind was still foggy, enjoying the remnants of my sleep.

"Well," she said patiently, "we need to untangle your hair and do something with it."

I ran my fingers through it a few times. "How's it looking now?"

Her face slumped. "Don't be silly." She took me by my hand and dragged me upstairs to her bathroom.

"Take a look," she said, pointing at the mirror. "What do you think?"

I stared back at myself. I nodded. "I look ready."

She huffed. "Come on, Larissa. Your hair. There are bags under your eyes. You need makeup. Get out of your robe."

I shrugged. "I dunno, Mom. This is how I look every day. It doesn't bother me."

She released a long breath, signaling her fading patience. "Humor me. These are our neighbors. We still need to live on the street with them. I'd die if Dru spoke badly about us."

I sighed. There was no quit in my mom.

"So do what?" I asked, tossing my arms into the air. "There's only so much that moisturizing is going to do for me at this point. I'm guilty. I went out often in the sun without block and exposed my face. Did I care about future wrinkles back when I was twenty?"

"I warned you. Now the bell is chiming."

I felt hurt. "You used to tell me these were laugh lines," I said, pointing to the creases around my eyes.

Her look softened. "I had to tell you something."

Now I was feeling twinges of desperation. I had a date in forty-five minutes and ten years of reckless living to cover up.

"Okay," she said, taking the lead. She picked up a brush and began brushing her hair in long strokes, displaying the technique. Her brown hair transformed into shiny smoothness. She put the brush down, dug into the cupboard, and pulled out her makeup kit. She took hold of a small brush and began applying foundation to her cheeks and forehead. Another container held what she called bronzer; she swept it on in circles, deepening her color nicely. She opened another container and began applying steady stokes along her lips. They glistened a vibrant red. She used eyeliner to carefully etch around her lids and then plumped up her eyelashes.

She stood back from the mirror, smiling.

She looked beautiful.

I glanced at the watch on her arm. It was time for me to go.

I ran out of the bathroom and down the hallway and headed downstairs. I ducked into my own bathroom, turned the faucet on, wet my hands, and ran my fingers through my hair. I splashed some water on my face and brushed my teeth. I slapped my cheeks a few times, satisfied with the red that gave my pale flesh some color.

I was ready for Sebastian.

*****

If there was a single benefit to the date, it came down to convenience—he lived at the end of my street. Again, I'd dodged the need for a vehicle, reaffirming my belief that I could survive without one. My snowmobile boots pushed aside the snow along the road with each footstep. I had no idea what we'd do that night or what we could talk about. Hell, I wasn't even sure what he looked like up close. Maybe he didn't have his own teeth and had a lazy eye.

A strange feeling overcame me as I was approaching his house. It wasn't eagerness or anticipation. Weirdly, I felt guilty. It was as though my mind didn't register the ring missing from my finger and was still firing me the message *Wives don't date*. But I was no longer a wife. I could date—though I couldn't shake the reprehensible feeling that I was about to betray my husband. I suppose it was only natural, having been separated so briefly. This was like getting back in the saddle when the saddle was still warm from my ass.

For shits and giggles, I tried to remember what I had been doing exactly one week ago. I had been with my ex and his band at the bar before it opened for the evening. He had asked that I record on his iPhone while they rehearsed one of their songs so that he could post it on YouTube. So I'd walked between the band members, holding his phone as steady as I could, taking aim at the expressions of concentration on their faces, fingers moving, and drumsticks being twirled. We had been a couple doing couple things. Afterward, we'd had beers and discussed the history of punk rock. Today, I'd be sitting down with the neighbor boy in a strange house, feeling awkward and misplaced. What a difference a week made.

The house was an unremarkable white bungalow with brown trim that appeared uninhabited until I saw the front window blinds move and Sebastian's mother scurrying away. This was real. It was on.

I gritted my teeth, making my way up the neatly shoveled sidewalk toward the front door. The door opened before I could get close enough to ring the bell. The overeagerness was unsettling. I might have been able to justify it had it been Sebastian's own eagerness that was there to greet me and not his mother's. I had flashbacks of attending birthday parties when I was six years old, the birthday boy's mother welcoming us all in with this same zealousness.

I tried to put a smile on my face to display some level of enthusiasm to Sebastian's mother, whose own face lit up as if we had been best friends all our lives. Her expression gave me a fleeting posttraumatic flashback of the same encouraging look she had worn when she'd explained how wonderful the makeup summer course would be—the best summer of my life, she had promised.

I entered her lair with more than a little trepidation. She wasn't fooling me with that wolfish grin. I was a wise adult now, not a naive preteen.

She closed the two doors behind us, gesturing for me to take off my boots and jacket. Before I could kick the boots aside, she picked them up and placed them inside the closet next to the front door. I handed her my jacket, which she hung up. She reached up into the closet and handed me a pair of blue slippers. I pulled them over my heavy gray wool socks.

She led me into the kitchen and signaled for me to sit down on one of the four chairs around the table. A local talk show played on the small radio on top of her fridge. She sat across from me, continuing to smile. I swiveled in my chair and smiled back. I felt like an idiot, but I didn't know what else to do.

She finally spoke, still beaming.

"This is so wonderful for you to come over, Larissa, and spend some time with my son. He's such a great boy."

I nodded, although I doubted her son's description was entirely accurate.

"I'm sure he is," I said. I didn't really have a choice. I had to be nice.

Her smile grew even brighter in response. I wondered if it was hurting her face to smile so much, and the grin was beginning to freak me out.

"Can I get you some juice? Water?" she asked, bracing against the armrests to push herself off the chair.

I nodded. "Water, please." I would have rather had something stronger. Did she still think I was a kid?

She got up, went to the cupboard, took out a glass, and began to fill it under the tap.

"You know, Larissa," she said at the sink, "to think, all these years we've lived so close together, and you and Sebastian never connected like this before." She giggled. She actually giggled. "Just think—had you developed crushes when you two were little, by now, you'd probably have been married with little ones and I'd be a grandmother."

I reached desperately for the glass. Suddenly, my feet felt hot and uncomfortable inside the guest slippers.

"Well, I don't know about that," I said, swallowing half of the water before putting the glass down on the table.

Sebastian's mother returned to her seat across from me.

"Oh, I'm sure that's how all this would have played out. You two would have likely lived here with us for a few years, banking your money to put a down payment on a house. Maybe you'd even have bought old Davie's house a few doors down, which was sold after his stroke."

I scrunched up my forehead. "Yeah, but he died inside that house after his stroke." I was beginning to wish I hadn't come.

She nodded in agreement. "Sure. But it was in his bed, and they took that away with the sale."

I grimaced. Dead in bed was still dead in the room I'd be sleeping in. *No thanks,* I thought.

"You seem to have it all mapped out," I replied, fiddling with my water glass.

She leaned back in her chair. "I think of these things often, little scenarios in my head."

"Sounds like fun." Actually, she was sounding weirder.

"It is. Keeps me wondering."

"That's nice," I said, looking around the orderly, dated kitchen for something—anything—to talk about that would change the subject.

"Would you like more water?" she offered, pointing at my glass.

I shook my head. My bladder had its limit, and I hated bathroom runs on a date. It was also a sore spot with me that I had never been offered a beer. Whenever I had gone out with a guy in the past, the offer from his family had always been water, juice, or a can of pop, while the guys had been offered the good stuff, such as beer and rye whiskey. I struggled with being treated as if I were pregnant and could not drink alcohol.

I tried not to look at Sebastian's mother and contemplated asking for a double shot of rye just to see her reaction. I couldn't help grinning.

Before I could say anything, she jumped up, grabbed a platter off the dining-room table, and set it in front of me. I stared at an assortment of nuts that I was certain were leftovers from Christmas a couple of months ago. I tried to look interested, hoping it would stop her from talking. It didn't work.

"I've read how beneficial it would be for our bodies if we ate a handful of these walnuts every day and took vitamin D."

I glanced at her. "How so?"

Her face dropped. "I didn't read the entire article, but the headline pointed it out."

I blinked. I recognized that this was her style of prep for teaching her classes. No wonder I'd failed to learn jack shit of anything she taught.

Across from me, the microwave above the stove flashed the time. I realized twenty minutes had gone by since my arrival.

"Hey," I said, "so where's Sebastian?"

His mom's face brightened again. She chuckled, which made me want to puke. "Oh, he's taking his nap."

"Nap? My mom told me he was expecting me at this time."

She nodded, grabbed a couple of nuts, tossed one into her mouth, and chewed. She swallowed hard. "This is not his usual nap time. Normally, he's up by now, except today he seems extra tired. I don't want to wake him. He needs his rest, poor boy."

"Rest? Why? Does he work nights?"

"No. It's good for his digestion. *Reader's Digest* articles say as a society, we undersleep. I make sure he takes a morning nap and another later in the afternoon." She crunched down on another nut. I realized the treat fit the consumer.

This was getting weirder by the minute. "Does he have a sleep disorder? What grown-up takes two naps a day? My friend Amy's two kids used to take two naps a day, but they were infants."

Her eyes softened. "My Sebastian is still a baby at heart."

I stifled a groan. He was sounding more and more like a suck to me. I rolled my eyes. "So what happens now? Should I go home and come back after he's had a chance to wake up? Make sure he's fully rested before his bedtime? Maybe another night is better, when his digestion isn't so exhausted."

She looked at me strangely, and then her face relaxed. "He'll be so disappointed to know you were here and then left without seeing him."

"He can't be that disappointed if he slept through our date," I replied, growing annoyed. He had all night to sleep. I had only so many hours to spare. Dating time was precious.

She waved me off, giggling like the nutcase she was.

I sat back in my chair and blew out air. "Has he been dating a lot?" I said, deciding that if he wasn't present for me to ask, I might as well question his mother, although I would have been a lot happier hitting the pavement and heading home.

"He's saving himself for the special girl to come into his life."

Her remark caught me off guard. Did that mean I was in that category of "special"? *Shit,* I thought.

I hesitated but asked anyway, "What's considered a special girl?"

"We're looking for a girl who will treat him well, respect his needs, and complement who he is as a person." She popped another nut into her mouth.

Did she just say "we"? I began to wonder if Sebastian's mom thought of herself as his dating agent.

"So you're saying he's never been married? Even after all these years? Not even for a little bit?"

Her eyes popped wide open. "Oh, heavens no! He's still as pure as the snow outside."

I wasn't sure if she was referring to his virginity or his mental aptitude, and I sure as hell wasn't about to discuss his sex life with his mother—or with him when he woke up from his Sleeping Beauty slumber.

"How about you, Larissa? Your mom said your marriage didn't last long. She said something like nine months?"

"Plus a day and a morning," I said lamely.

"And I understand no children were procreated," she said.

"No children were procreated," I repeated.

"That's good."

"Why?"

"Well, now you can start a new marriage without any baggage."

"My children wouldn't have been baggage."

"No, of course not. But they just wouldn't have been my son's spawn."

I couldn't help myself. I wanted to throw up or burst out laughing, but I kept a straight face as I said, "I suppose theoretically, we'd have our own children as well to add to the harem."

Her face bunched. "Mixed spawns just don't mix well."

"They can if we give them all equal love." She'd actually thought I was serious. At least my comment had wiped the nutty grin from her face.

She shook her head. "One of the spawn will always get shortchanged with love. I simply couldn't bear to see that happen."

I was about to argue that this was her son's decision, when I heard a loud groan echoing down the hallway. Dru jumped to her feet as if shocked off her ass.

"What?" I asked, preparing myself to leap and run.

She signaled for me to sit back down. *Crap. I should have been quicker. I missed my chance to escape.*

"He's up. My boy's up. Fix yourself another glass of water, Larissa. I always rub his back when he wakes up to settle him in."

"Come again?" I asked, but she was already jetting past me, disappearing down the hall.

I stared at my empty water glass. I was pretty sure my mouth was hanging open. I hoped I wasn't about to be summoned into the room to rub something else in some sort of waking ritual.

I could hear murmuring coming from down the hallway, tempting me to tiptoe over to investigate. However, the potential fear and scarring of what I could witness welded me to my chair. Those were nightmares I could do without.

The first night of discovery after my ex had moved into my parents' house before we were married had been bad enough; while I was brushing my teeth, he'd walked in and sat down to take a dump. My sacred act of maintaining the hygiene of my teeth had been forever tainted by the event taking place behind me, which I had been able to see in the mirror.

I was debating refilling my water glass, when I heard noises coming from the hallway. Sebastian shuffled toward me behind his mother, wearing a burgundy robe, brown slippers, and bed head. Where was my mom to observe his predate preparation? I no longer felt sloppily prepared. We had matching sleep lines on our faces.

He scuffled past me, his slippers making sliding noises on the linoleum, and headed straight to the fridge. Somehow, with his half-open eyes, he managed to locate a little juice box, open it, poke the tiny white straw into the hole, and bring the tiny box to his mouth, closing his eyes entirely while he sucked on it with such force that both his cheeks and the juice box were pulled inward.

I had to look away. I closed my eyes and counted to ten, wishing this were a hallucination. When I heard the final slurp, signaling an empty box, I knew this was as real as the crunch of peanuts beside me.

I opened my eyes to watch his mom turn down the kitchen lights.

"It hurts his eyes right after he wakes up," she said, apparently noticing the quizzical look on my face.

"Mom." It was the first word I'd heard him speak. She was quick to react. She leaped up, removed the juice box from his hand, and tossed it into the garbage can under the counter. She reached for a banana on the countertop by the sink, peeled it, and handed it to him. He swayed with his eyes closed, eating the banana while I watched, fascinated.

"The potassium fires him up," she commented, sitting back down.

"I hope he doesn't get out of control," I replied, wondering if this shot of potassium would at least open his eyes. He ate the sacrificial banana as if it were a Popsicle, sucking it into his mouth and twisting it back and forth until he massaged it enough for it to mulch. When he was finished making love to the banana, his mother took away the peel and wiped around his mouth. If this happened to become the pinnacle moment of the date, the entertainment value was batting one hundred.

He turned and looked at me for the first time. His eyes were finally opening up.

"Hey, Larissa. Thanks for coming over."

I wasn't sure how to respond. His mom hadn't been joking about what that banana would do for his energy. I wondered what would happen if he had a second one.

He leaned back against the countertop, braced by his arms, his robe falling open to reveal a two-piece striped pajama set. Maybe my eyes were misleading me, but the pajamas looked like silk. Only the best for this nerd.

"Well," said his mom, "why don't you two go downstairs and socialize? I'm going to clean up around here. If you need anything, just holler. I'm only one floor away." She smiled at us both.

I got up and followed Sebastian down the hallway that led to a staircase. I treaded carefully on the carpeted staircase so as not to trip in my slippers. I kept my eyes on the belt of his robe, which dangled by his sides as he led me into the rec room.

The room was windowless but a good size, with what looked like authentic wood paneling and a low ceiling. Despite the damp air, the carpet made a crinkling sound under my feet.

Sebastian flopped down onto one of two gray sofas against one wall, the one he apparently often used, since it contoured to his body. I took the opposite sofa. Ahead of us was a projection TV, which was off.

"There's an old relic." I pointed toward the television.

"Sixty-four inches and ahead of its time. In my opinion, these sets are far superior to the LED widescreens. See how the height matches the width? It's the way we view the real world."

Sebastian's world was far different from the one I lived in, and that was an understatement.

I pointed toward it again. "Well, turn it on. Let's watch something."

He shook his head. "Not yet. I use it for an hour a night. That way, I don't wear out the bulbs. They're becoming very hard to find." He took his cell phone out from the pocket of his robe.

"You ever play sudoku?" he asked, staring down at his phone.

"I have no idea what a sudoku is."

He pushed at his screen while I sat in silence without getting a reply from him.

"What are you doing?" I finally asked.

"Playing sudoku."

I was amazed. "When do I join in?" I asked flatly.

"It's a solo game," he said. "Get it up on your phone."

I decided to use his suggestion to text Bernadette.

Freak show!

She was quick to reply with her support: *Told you so.*

"You have big feet," he suddenly said.

He was still focused on his phone, but apparently, he was talking to me, since there was no one else in the room.

"Normal size," I replied, daring him to look up at me.

"Not for a girl."

"Size ten," I said.

"My mom's a ladies' six."

I didn't ask why he would know that.

"Those are my dad's slippers you're wearing," he blurted out.

I looked down at them. "These aren't for houseguests?"

"Nope. My dad wears them when he's home."

"Where is he right now?"

"He's not here."

I felt a surge of awkwardness at the thought of having Sebastian's dad catch me in his slippers. That was like wearing someone's underwear. And it was even worse that I fit comfortably inside a man's slipper.

"Do you have a job?" said Sebastian. He kept his head down, still focused on his game.

I answered while glancing around at the seventies-looking decor of framed photos of dogs playing cards and the fake fireplace across from me, recessed into the wall.

"Actually, I have a great job. A real passion of mine." I wanted to boast more but never liked to give away everything about me.

"Like what? Do you work one of the drive-through windows?"

I thought he was joking, but from what I could see of his face, he looked sincere.

"Drive-through? Why would you say that?"

"You have a drive-through voice. I kind of thought that would naturally be your choice of work," he said evenly.

I thought for a moment about what a drive-through voice sounded like. Static with an echo?

"Not even close. I'm more high tech."

"Like virtual gaming," he said finally.

"Like computers and web designing," I replied flatly.

"Yeah, I guess that was in about ten years ago."

"That's in right now," I said, defending myself, thinking, *What kind of superior job could this banana-slurping boy have that gives him the right to disrespect my gig?*

"I bought a skateboard," he announced, showing some emotion after finishing a level on his game and letting out a long breath.

"But it's winter," I said.

"It's for the summer," he said smugly.

"Do you have your own car?" I asked, believing I had one up on him, even though mine didn't start and the sunroof leaked—but it was still a sunroof.

"I don't drive. My mom drives me everywhere I need to go."

I grinned. "Well, I have a car. I don't rely on my parents."

"Is it a five-liter 'Stang?"

I didn't know what five liters meant, but I knew I didn't have a 'Stang.

"I don't like Fords. I'm a Chrysler gal."

"They went bankrupt in 2009."

I thought quickly. "Yeah, well, the Ford Pinto had gas tanks blow up. I'll stick with a bankruptcy."

He pressed at the iPhone and cleared his throat. "When did you go bankrupt?"

I was startled. "I never did. Why would you think that?"

"'Cause you got divorced. Everyone goes bankrupt when they get divorced."

"Well, I didn't. I'm good with my money," I said sharply. "And I'm not divorced yet; I'm just separated."

"My mom says your marriage didn't last a year. Did you cheat?"

He was getting personal now.

"Not a chance. We grew apart."

"My parents have been married thirty-five years."

"It doesn't mean they're happy," I shot back.

"They renew their vows every year at church."

I snickered. "Yeah, well, that's something I won't be doing this year."

Sebastian pushed himself up from the sofa and held out his phone for me to see.

"Look at my high score. I'm now one win away from entering expert level."

I glanced up at him. "What would that mean for you? Do you win money? Get a badge? A red ribbon?"

He plopped back down in his spot. "It means the top level. And it's going to be hard. I won't have many numbers to work with," he said, and he then looked back down at his phone.

"Sounds dangerous," I said, lowering my voice.

"Do you dye your hair?"

"Why?"

"I noticed gray hairs when I came over there to show you my score."

I flinched. The grays had started shortly after my marriage. I denied the truth to myself; it was always the fault of lighting, not my hair. This weirdo was dismantling my protective shroud.

"Those are lighter-colored hairs."

"They look like gray to me."

"It's the shadows in this room."

"I don't think so. I can see them from here." He glanced my way.

I ran my hand through my hair in an attempt to shuffle the gray hairs around. He continued to look my way.

I changed the subject. "So where do you work?"

He cracked his knuckles. "I do media distribution for a major producer."

"Do you mean like movie trailers for new releases? What media channels do you use? I guess places like YouTube, Yahoo—places like that, huh?"

He looked at me, apparently bewildered. "I deliver the local community newspaper once a week to the homes on our street."

I stifled a laugh.

"I'm also involved with distance education, taking courses over the Internet."

I dared him to elaborate on what those courses might be.

"I'm training to be a stockbroker."

I barked out a laugh.

He seemed unfazed. "I'm starting the first course next week, which is going to be about ethics and compliance. All the good stuff starts after that, when I can get involved with foreign exchanges and penny stocks."

I hoped a penny was all he was paying for the course because there was no chance in hell this bozo could understand foreign exchange rates.

"Well, good luck, Sebastian," I offered, remembering my mom's instructions to be nice. "When you're certified, I'll give you all my millions to invest overseas."

He grinned.

I heard creaking coming from the stairs, followed by the appearance of his mom's feet as she made her way downstairs. She stopped at the bottom, holding her hands together, smiling.

"Sorry to be the party pooper, you young lovers in love, but it's getting close to Sebastian's nasal therapy and then a quick snack before his bedtime."

I looked over at him; he was nodding.

"But he just got up from a nap," I commented, wondering how much sleep he needed.

She beamed. "We've kept this routine ever since he was a young boy. It works well for his body rhythms."

I stood up.

"Thanks for coming over," he said, not standing up in return. I took that as a sign I was hanging up his dad's slippers on my own and seeing myself out.

His mom followed me up the stairs. We reached the front door, and I removed the footwear. She handed me my coat. I put it on, and her arms opened up. I moved in awkwardly for a hug. She squeezed me hard.

"You are amazing," she said. "He had such a wonderful time." She was beaming.

I wanted to tell her his wonderful time came at the expense of picking apart my physical characteristics. Instead, I thanked her in return.

"We'll see you really soon," she called out as I plowed my boots back into the snow on the outdoor walkway. It was a good thing my winter parka was so thick. She couldn't see my body flinch.

CHAPTER 6

Hey

March 14, 7:33 p.m.

The ex called last night. Funny that with only two letters, everyone and anyone knows what *ex* stands for. It never stands for anything good—more like a foul, forbidden, shameful, you-screwed-up-loser title. It's a title for someone who, under God and all of your freaking family and friends and father, who ran up his MasterCard for the booze, became a husband or wife, nicknamed honey bunny or lubber dubber or sweetheart. It's a title stripped to *ex*, as in exited, exonerated, exfoliated, exhausted—out of your life forever.

Almost. Do exes ever go away? It's like they have some lifelong pass now to keep in touch, stay in touch, reach out and touch whenever they wish, which is too often. Why would my ex call me today? Didn't he say everything he had to tell me in our nine months, one day, and a morning, or did he forget one desperately important thing that simply had to be said now, hence the phone call? He called to say hey. He was waiting for his PlayStation to boot up.

Hey.

*****

The treadmill moved quickly under my runners. I reduced the speed from two back to one, a pace more within my control. It was too difficult to keep it up while munching on Kit Kats and chatting to Bernadette, who was on the treadmill beside me. As she spoke, she kept her eyes on the soap opera playing on the TV screen in front of her. We were wearing matching shades of gray, except her outfit was tight-fitting, stink-free fashion workout gear from Lulu, and mine was a baggy sweater and track pants from Costco.

Bernadette kept sipping a mixture of orange juice and, I was certain, a dash of vodka from a bright orange metallic water bottle. I was sure of the vodka because the smell wafted over my way every once in a while.

I kept her entertained with the trials and tribulations of my date with Sebastian.

"What's he looking like these days?" Bernadette asked, glancing over at me. "If I remember correctly, he wasn't much to look at back in school. Kinda that nerdish, shy weirdo you don't want to be left alone with in the same room."

I laughed. "That's pretty much him now."

"And you were alone with him! You broke female safe-dating protocol."

"His mom was close at hand."

Bernadette snickered. "The big question, girl—has he pumped up into a rock-hard man body? That could offset his goofy looks."

I grinned. "Well, he actually put some weight on. His hair is cut shorter. Still greasy, though. He wears out-of-fashion glasses. Oh, he's no longer shorter than me. Now, to answer your question if he has abs for me to run my tongue along, I couldn't see any, because he wore his finest robe and slippers."

"He seems totally weird," Bernadette said.

"He is especially weird," I said. "But it's his mom who's right out to lunch."

"Even weirder then your dad?"

"Hell, I'd take the chunky bits spraying out of his mouth onto my arm at the supper table any day of the week compared to Sebastian and his mother and their wacky rituals."

Bernadette laughed and took a long pull of her so-called fitness drink.

"She rubbed his back, girl! Apparently, it's something she does every time he wakes up." I squealed.

Bernadette choked. "I can't get Mike to rub my back even if I promise him a happy ending afterward."

"I just hope rubbing his back wasn't code for something else."

"Eww," Bernadette screeched. "She filled your water glass with those hands, remember."

"That was prerub."

"Still. There was the morning rub."

I gaped at her, my throat tightening. "I never thought of that."

She grinned back at me before returning to the TV screen.

I broke off another stick of Kit Kat and took a bite.

"I'm not surprised how it went with Sebastian," I said while attempting to keep my feet from tripping on one another. "This is how it is for my family."

"What do you mean by that?" asked Bernadette.

"We don't get normal. We get the strange. The bizarre. The cast-off, riffraff stuff coming our way. It's just the way it is for us Ukrainians. It doesn't come easy. Hell, Sebastian is the perfect example. I get the guy who lives in his robe, gets his back rubbed by his mother, and is going nowhere in life. If that had been your date, he'd have been some corporate executive making a million dollars a year. The only women touching his body would be the ones giving him his weekly manicures and haircuts."

Bernadette laughed crazily. "You certainly live large in your head, my dear! Remember, I have a man who comes home reeking of 10-W30 oil every night. His hands have never been moisturized."

I shrugged. "Still. Sebastian isn't even a step above my ex. He's like a mutant version of him."

"I don't know, my love," said Bernadette. "You might have to reconsider Mike's coworker after all."

"I'm willing to try his buddy as long as I can be assured no disparaging personal remarks are made about any of my body parts. I'm self-conscious about my size ten feet." I took another chomp, my feet moving in a steady, slow rhythm.

She winked. "There isn't anything I can do with your flippers. It is what it is. But I can certainly transform your hair, scrape down those feet, buff them up with polish, and turn bush girl into sexy vixen."

I laughed. "Speaking of bush ..."

Bernadette held up her hand. "You're on your own for that one! I like you. But I don't need to know and see all of you."

We both chuckled.

I popped the remainder of the Kit Kat into my mouth, grabbed both side rails, and continued walking. The level of activity around the gym was unending. We had picked two machines in the middle so that we could observe the flurry of fitness fanatics as a source of inspiration. It helped. I was contemplating moving the speed back up to number two. My long-term goal, that goal being near the end of the contract, would be to begin raising the incline. For now, flat was aggressive enough.

"The thing is," I said, letting out a deep breath, "I have so much to do. I was far less busy while married. Now I have to start looking for a job."

"That's a drag."

"Sure it is—résumés, interviews, questions. Blah, blah, blah. And helping my dad with the car, handing him whatchamacallits. Pretty soon I'll need to start driving with him to practice for the test."

"Don't forget the beautification."

"That too. Auntie Tina wants to take me shopping for my wardrobe. I don't have time to sleep anymore."

"Obviously, that's one problem Sebastian doesn't have."

"For that, I am envious."

"We all should have mothers like his."

"I'll pass, thanks." I groaned. "I love my aunt Tina, but holy shit, I don't want to be in my sixties still stalking the back alleys for a man. I get bed sweats thinking of that scenario. I'll take her fashion advice, but I'm going to be filtering whatever man advice she has for me. I need to do things my way this time," I huffed. "That's why I'm here, busting my ass on this stupid machine."

Bernadette grinned. "This is the cat's ass for exercise, huh? My soaps. Built guys with skimpy shirts. Amy's missing out big-time, having to stay at home cleaning puke from her son's guts."

The beeping from my machine signaled the end of our session, and I was grateful for it. After forty-five minutes, my thighs were screaming. I stepped off. Bernadette followed.

"How about we go for ice cream?" I suggested. She accepted without hesitation.

We climbed into Bernadette's white Volkswagen Golf, still in our workout attire. We decided to try out a new ice-cream place suggested by a local newspaper reviewer. The hype was not only good ice cream; apparently, the owner doubled as a tarot-card reader.

It might have been winter, but ice cream was a year-round treat in our books. We parked in the empty parking lot and ambled through the narrow storefront. No one was inside, so we didn't have to wait in a line.

The aroma of coolness greeted us. A few tables were scattered along the checked tile flooring, and the glass counter revealed dozens of frozen treats. Behind the counter, descriptions of the treat options were handwritten in chalk on a blackboard. A booth with a five-foot-high red cloth wall on a rail stood in the back corner of the room.

No one was behind the counter, which gave us time to study the ice-cream choices. Bernadette said she was going with the Belgian Waffle Delight. I gave in to a dark-chocolate-dipped waffle bowl, supersized. I could afford it after my burn that day at the gym. Dad had warned me not to become emaciated.

"Hello," Bernadette called out. She was not one for patience. She never waited until a red light turned green before she pulled forward when driving. I was always thankful for the passenger-side airbag in her car.

"Anyone? Yoo-hoo."

"We want ice cream. We want ice cream!" I said, joining in.

"And ice cream you shall receive," announced a thick French accent. Our heads swiveled toward the voice coming from behind the red curtain in the corner of the room. He drew back the curtain so that we could see him. He was barely higher than the top of it. His thick dark hair matched the bushy mustache that stretched across his face with an upward curl. Even from a distance, the brilliance of his blue eyes was striking. He segued over to where we stood and stopped beside us.

"Ladies, you have come for an experience."

"We've certainly come for the ice cream, specifically the Belgian Waffle Delight for me," Bernadette said.

He grinned slyly. "The flavors here are far more intense than anywhere else."

"Good," I said. "I'm starving."

I could see him studying me. "In more ways than one," he mumbled, and he nodded before turning his attention to Bernadette.

She rolled her eyes at me.

"Honey," he said, touching her arm gently, "we need to talk after your delicious Belgian Waffle Delight."

She looked confused by his remark.

"You know what I mean," he said gently in his engaging accent.

"I do?"

He ignored her question and walked behind the counter to begin preparing our orders.

"I can see why no one is in here," whispered Bernadette to me. "He's a freak. Maybe a relative of your neighbors?"

I tittered and shrugged.

"Judge me after you've savored the flavor of my shop," he said, startling us both for having heard Bernadette's comment. She grimaced. I knew exactly what she was thinking. He was going to dip his dirty thumb deep into her Belgian Waffle Delight as retribution.

We waited uncomfortably while his back was to us as he mixed and stirred our orders. We'd broken the golden rule of never insulting the chef.

Yet when our treats were presented on the counter, there was no denying they both looked tantalizing. I couldn't wait to sink my spoon into mine.

And then the situation got strange.

When I took out my money to pay for my order, the Frenchman pitched me an offer.

"For you, madam, this treat is on the house. In return, you will allow me to read your cards." The brilliant blue eyes compelled me to say yes. I did.

"Hey, it's a free meal," I reasoned.

Bernadette stood beside me, grinning. "Now I feel left out," she complained, pouting.

The Frenchman handed her ice cream to her.

"Same offer for you, madam. Free if you allow me the pleasure of reading your cards."

She was quick to respond. "Hell yeah!"

We both laughed and took seats at one of the tables.

"You come see me when you're done," he said, and he disappeared back behind the red curtain.

We stared at each other, shrugged, and laughed. *This is the strangest place ever,* I thought to myself.

I stuffed a huge chunk of waffle into my mouth. "Between my fiasco with Sebastian and his mom yesterday and this weirdo," I said in a whisper with my mouth full, "I feel like I'm in a Tim Burton movie. Doesn't this seem surreal to you?"

Bernadette nodded, white ice cream oozing out of the corner of her mouth. She licked it off. "But this stuff is so damn good—it's real for sure," she finally replied.

"I don't believe in that shit anyway," I said.

"What? Cards?"

I nodded.

"I've never had it done." Bernadette stared at me with a serious expression.

"It's all made up. Don't tell him anything about yourself, and watch him scramble. They use what you tell them to make educated guesses."

"I won't," she agreed.

"Besides, anything he tells us is as far-fetched as the *Farmers' Almanac*."

"Sometimes it turns out true."

"Sure. Odds. But mostly, it's wrong."

"Gotcha," she replied, lifting a huge spoonful of chocolate to her mouth.

"Are you ready, mesdames?" asked the voice behind the curtain.

We looked at one another, both trying to contain our laughter.

"I'll come every week if he's going to make me the same offer," replied Bernadette.

"We can make this our ritual after our workouts: a bowl of ice cream and our cards read, confirming we will be millionaires and my breasts will grow to be double Ds with the firmness of an eighteen-year-old's," I said, laughing.

Bernadette grinned. "No joke. Maybe Harry Houdini here can use his magic to transfer over some of my Ds to you."

I wiped off my mouth as well as my smile and tried to look serious. Bernadette did the same. We had already agreed that neither of us believed in things like tarot or horoscopes.

"Let's go do this," Bernadette said, taking my hand and leading me to the booth. I pulled aside a corner of the curtain to find the Frenchman seated across a table from us with his back to the wall. He held an oversized deck of cards in his hand. Two chairs were ready for us in front of the table.

His smile stretched the mustache even farther across his face, signaling for us both to sit down.

"And how was the ice cream?" he asked.

"Even better because it was free," replied Bernadette, grinning.

"I second that," I said, nodding.

His eyes flickered between us while he shuffled the card in his hands.

"All on red," joked Bernadette.

"I'm doubling down," I remarked.

We glanced at one another and both laughed at our silliness.

"What should we call you—Mr. Voodoo Ice-Cream Man?" asked Bernadette, laughing even harder.

The man squinted. "You can call me the Genie."

We both spewed laughter. This guy was a total kook. I was hoping he had enough common sense to keep the place clean of E. coli.

"Are you serious?" said Bernadette, staring at him with a smile.

"That I am, madam." He continued shuffling.

"Is that, like, your stage name here?"

He looked her in the eye, his own eyes twinkling as he shuffled. "You can call me the Genie, and I will call you Bernadette and your friend Larissa." He continued smiling and shuffling.

My eyes popped wide open, and Bernadette's did the same. We stared at each other with our mouths open.

"Holy shit!" she exclaimed. Her mouth still hung open, and her hands went straight to her purse. She took out her ID card.

"I don't need to look at that," he commented, rocking slightly in his chair.

Now I knew our jokes had stopped.

"No, you don't, Mr. Genie," replied Bernadette in a whisper. "I need to make sure you didn't lift our wallets."

"Did Amy give you our names? Come on," I said, still reeling that he knew who we were.

"I know no such person," he replied.

"Then how would you know our names?"

"I am the Genie."

"You're freaking me out," I said, wondering if it would have been better to just pay for the treats.

He took that choice away when he placed a card on the table in front of me.

"What's that?" I said, confused by the colorful picture on it.

"This is called the Three of Cups."

I nodded; it still didn't make sense to me. "So?"

He stared at me. The blue eyes danced. "You have suffered a loss. The loss is a disappointment to you. It has left you feeling despair over what this loss means, and you worry about your future."

I glanced over at Bernadette, certain my eyes were bulging. She didn't look much better.

He laid down another card. "Two of Cups." His blue eyes glittered. "This loss, this breakup, was an imbalance in the relationship. You both had a lack of harmony."

He placed a third card beside the first one. It was a landscape with the sun in the distance.

"Eight of Cups," he remarked, exhaling. "You walked away, creating your loss."

I found myself nodding and breathing hard.

Two people were walking in the picture on the fourth card.

"Five of Pentacles."

"So?" I gripped the table's edge.

"The loss created by walking away isolates you. You are filled with insecurity about your future, worry over what you will become. You have suffered a financial loss from this walking away."

My knuckles were white.

"My God," breathed Bernadette.

Another card was laid down.

"Five of Wands." He hummed a few notes and then said, "You avoided conflict rather than agreeing to disagree with this other person." He placed another card on the table. He giggled. "The Seven of Wands." He tweaked the edges of his mustache with his fingers. "You now live in an environment where you feel overwhelmed. The people in this environment are overly protective of you, controlling what you do and how you do it."

73

I looked over at Bernadette again. Her face was drained of color. I knew she was thinking the same thing: my parents.

He placed another card on the table.

"Three of Swords," he said with a flourish in his accent.

It looked painful. Swords were piercing a red heart. I flinched, awaiting my fate. I was about to die.

"You are embarking on change, initiating change to release your pain; it has provided you feelings of optimism for your future."

He revealed another card.

"Five of Swords." He looked at me, making direct eye contact. "You are open to change. That is why you have now embarked on doing things you have avoided all your life."

He stopped and began shuffling the deck again. His mustache stirred against his face, and his gaze was locked onto my own. Without looking down, he placed another card in front of me and said, "Ten of Swords."

I groaned out loud when I broke eye contact and looked down. A body was lying on the ground with crosses sticking out of it. I clutched at my face. Bernadette put an arm around me.

"I'm dead, Bernadette. I'll never be a mother." Tears built behind my eyes.

"Your crisis has another ending," the Genie sang.

"How will I die?" I cried out. Bernadette squeezed me harder. All this for a lousy bowl of ice cream.

"You will be betrayed, backstabbed by the very person you trust the most."

I flinched. *The dogged family curse! Oh, why the Christ couldn't I have been born Swedish? My destiny is even in the cards!*

I wasn't dying. But my heart was going to be smashed again. "How much can one girl take, for Christ's sake?" I shouted. "This has nothing to do with me! This is because I'm Ukrainian, right?" I tugged at my hair. "Give me a break already!"

"Who?" demanded Bernadette. "Give us a name, goddammit. I want to hang this asshole."

I nodded quickly. I begged. "Even an e-mail address. Please." I had to find this person and stop the heartbreak before it happened.

He shook his head and placed the remainder of the deck in front of me. I looked down at it and then back at him.

"What?"

"Pull a card from anywhere."

My hand shook. It all came down to one last card. What kind of sand in the eye could I expect beyond the betrayal and backstabbing coming my way?

I grasped a card near the bottom and dropped it onto the table as if it were on fire.

The card showed a man riding a horse.

The Genie laughed loudly, tossing his head back. "Knight of Cups. Your knight in shining armor, madam. Romance heads your way."

"Sebastian," squealed Bernadette, shaking my arm.

I reared back.

"For the love of God, no! Please make him ride off into the sunset." I hung my head in my arms on the table. My life was doomed. I could hear his mother's voice asking me to hand her the nasal applicator, a nightly ritual we would share when we lived in her basement.

"Is it Sebastian?" I pleaded with the Genie.

He only smiled at me and shrugged. "The cards do not provide me with names. Just truths about your future."

"So it's true." I exhaled, feeling as if I'd just been sucker punched in the stomach. My next love was the neighbor boy.

Bernadette shook her head wildly. "We have to get ahead of this and change it, honey. I won't let that juice-box-sucking kid take you down, all right?" She looked at me with concern.

The Genie gathered the cards and began shuffling them again.

Bernadette realized she was next and shook her head. "We know enough already."

"This is your dessert payment."

She was reaching for her purse to pay for the ice cream, when he beat her to it.

He placed the first card in front of her. It showed a lone man standing.

"Page of Wands."

He thought for a moment and looked at her with a wide grin. "You're a free spirit, madam. You seek new discoveries. Life is an exploration for you." He resumed shuffling the deck.

I looked at her, and she gave me a wary smile. "Your reputation precedes you," I joked.

"I come from restless seed," she explained.

The Genie revealed another card: a man on a horse.

"Here comes your ride," I teased.

"Knight of Pentacles, madam." His blue eyes studied her. She pushed aside the hair in her face, bracing for his news.

"Your life has become routine. You are bored, and you feel stuck, yet you deny these feelings to yourself."

"Time to dye your hair yellow again," I suggested.

"I guess this is what settling down does to a girl."

The next card showed a cluster of faces.

"King of Pentacles," the Genie said. "You like to be in control. You dominate the people in your life."

"Don't let Mike hear this. He's nobody's bitch," I remarked, laughing.

"This makes *me* sound like the bitch," Bernadette whined. "I got the shit reading. At least you have an ominous future coming up."

"Yeah, goody for me. As if I need more drama."

"Madam," the Genie offered, placing the remaining deck in front of her.

She picked the top card and flipped it over. It showed a person seated, holding his face.

"That can't be good," she said. "I do that when I'm hungover."

"The Nine of Swords," he said, placing his chin on his cupped hands. He stared at her.

"Despair is coming your way, madam. A depression will ensue. Something is not quite right in your life, and you have yet to pinpoint it in order to avoid the consequences. However, you will not successfully identify it in time to stop it."

She slapped the table. "So basically, I'm screwed. I'm going to become a pharmaceutical train wreck." She looked at me and then back at the Genie. "Thanks for the bowl of ice cream, buster. That went right to my ass, and your reading went straight to my head." She stood up. "Come on, honey—enough of this freak show." She grabbed my hand and pulled me up.

"Next time we go for ice cream, we're using the damn drive-through."

CHAPTER 7

Tunings and Rants = My Dad

March 18, 2:22 a.m.

My dad never wanted me to marry my ex. Not that I got that impression from my dad from a feeling or a hint or some magical, dreamlike inspirational thought. He told me so.

My dad was never a person to mince words, hold back, cut back, or restrain himself from vocalizing his opinion whenever, wherever, and however the urge exploded within, which was often—almost always.

I learned as a small child to mentally prepare myself for him to give a tuning (a rant, a reaming, a piece of his mind) to anyone, anywhere. It could happen in a Canadian Tire store (if the staff avoided him in the aisle or didn't offer the appropriate knowledge, answer, or question or if the part he wanted wasn't there).

A trying-to-please waiter could get a tuning anyway because my dad got wacky on the Wiser's

Whiskey and decided to be Jay Leno without the chin or humor and ended up insulting the waiter into quitting. There didn't have to be a reason—if some kid was walking down the street and a swear word (!) came out of his mouth, that gave my dad justification for a tuning to watch his mouth or else (or else what?). (This was before kids carried guns, knives, bats, and grenades.)

Do you know how to get rid of neighbors? Move my dad in, and watch them clear out—tunings to the neighbors; their kids; their relatives; their dog, cat, bird, and car; the snow and leaves; paper; music; voices; very existence. My dad tunes all day every day. It is important to note we (a blue-collar Ukrainian family from "that area of the city") moved into "their" area of the city, among the white, crisp, starched white collars of professors, doctors, lawyers, CEOs, CFOs, COOs, and every other three-letter title my dad doesn't know. The only three-letter title he knows is SOB, and those people don't like to get tuned. But they do anyway.

My dad possesses no genetic code called shame. It didn't take more than a year—actually, two months, really—for our Ukrainian blight to show itself. First, we painted our house bright green with yellow trim. My dad tuned everyone else for their blah-blah browns and whites. We walked around our yard wearing sombreros (don't ask); lit bonfires in the backyard and front yard (in the middle of day, when it was thirty-eight degrees Celsius, burning plastics and anything else that could burn); and changed our car oil in the driveway, putting the car up on blocks of different-sized wood and plastics we hadn't yet burned to save the eighteen dollars and ten minutes we'd have spent at the shop down the street, to keep "those assholes from getting rich" (on eighteen dollars), because we had all day Saturday to do the oil change. I got to watch and hand him rags every time the oil missed the bucket (which was often) and the oil-plug thing wouldn't go back in properly. ("Yollup Japanese assholes!" he'd say. It was a GM-built car.) Oh shit, let's not even get into when metric started taking over imperial and all my dad's tools began to become obsolete. We got to hear a tuning rant about our dear government every minute of every day for ten years. Thank you, government, for our tuning.

It was okay to park our car on the lawn; we didn't have a double concrete driveway, as the heavily starched white collars around us did, and grass was grass—easy on the rubber. At first, I'm sure our neighbor who spoke seven languages better than I did English on my best day, taught advanced university courses all his life, won awards, and had tenure coming out of his ass was fascinated by what he watched from his kitchen window. As with a car accident you just have to watch, over time, fascination becomes annoyance and then morphs into outright indignation—"How can you do that in my neighborhood?"

My dad was good with his hands, a little off with his abilities, and crazy with his imagination and execution, missing the mark most times. My dad didn't believe in trading in his car every few years, as the others (yollups) around us did, because they were built to go three hundred thousand miles, unlike that "Jap crap" that fell apart, rusted out, blew blue exhaust smoke, and cost our countries jobs. My dad spent nights, weeks, months, and years with a torch, a belt sander, a hammer, and sheet metal, cutting off rust on his GM car and replacing head gaskets in the driveway, using Asian-made parts (they were cheaper—"If these domestic yollups don't learn, they'll see").

Why buy a new car when we can paint ours a new color every spring? That's why we have a Canadian Tire store—for their vast array of car spray paints and the chance for my dad to give a tuning to a sales clerk who doesn't know the answer to the question of whether the paint needs a primer first (this really happened, and the clerk was fifteen and still had dinosaur wallpaper in his bedroom).

Our neighbor would get to witness a massive poly tent built out of shaky wood frame (which would be burned along with the poly later in the heat of the summer) go up in front of his kitchen window every spring like spring flowers, flapping in the wind, surrounding the family GM car, which now freshly soldered, the sheet metal free of rust until next spring. With a case of Canadian Tire spray cans and one roller to even it out, my dad would transform his car into a cheery new color—green, blue, orange, yellow. In theory and execution, my dad's poly tent idea would get the thumbs down from any professional spray-booth guy, since yes, the tent mimicked the concept sans being hermetically sealed, dust-free, or lint-free. Fumes, fibers, and free spray mist were sucked out under my dad's flapping poly. The wind swirled all this shit around inside, resembling a green fly strip. Every year, we had a custom car displaying a seasonal archive of what was blowing around our street that year.

*****

The transit bus stopped directly in front of the strip mall that was home to the lawyer's office where my ex had arranged a meeting. When I'd informed my dad of my ex arranging a mutual lawyer for our divorce, he had gone ballistic. He was sure I would be taken advantage of because the lawyer would work harder for my ex than for me, since he had been hired by him. My dad was adamant I should hire a lawyer who could swing a hammer for my rights. Frankly, I didn't see the point since we were in agreement about ending our marriage. Why would I want to repeat myself to my own lawyer, who was going to say it all again to my ex's lawyer? To me, using the same lawyer was all about economies of time.

I stepped off the bus and walked toward the strip mall. The blue sign for the lawyer, Mr. Singh, was situated in the middle of the mall, sandwiched between a Subway restaurant and Frame Your Own Prints store. It stated that he specialized in family law, specifically divorce.

There was money to be made in heartbreak.

The office didn't look anything like the glamour I was used to seeing on TV, where law offices larger than my parents' entire house were on the sixtieth floor, overlooking downtown through wall-to-wall glass windows. Mr. Singh's establishment looked more like a tattoo joint.

Still, I had to give my ex credit. He had taken the initiative and found us a lawyer to handle our affairs.

I pulled the door open and stepped inside. The place was small, and there was a strong odor of cigars. Three steel-and-black-vinyl chairs were lined up against the front window. A wood-panel divider separated the seating area from the receptionist, who sat quietly behind a desk, wearing a headset. Behind her was a wall of paper files in various colors. A hallway beside the files revealed a series of offices with glass windows. Somewhere in one of those offices was a man who would be altering my life on paper. I was in awe of his power.

The door to a unisex bathroom opened, and out walked my ex, wearing his standard attire: acid-washed jeans, black sneakers, a black concert T-shirt one size too small, and a baseball cap. His bushy hair ballooned out under the sides of the cap.

His expression remained passive when he saw me walking toward him.

"Hey," he said, taking a seat next to where I stood. He smelled of hand sanitizer.

"You just get here?" I asked. I dropped into the seat next to him. Today was the first time I had seen him since we'd walked out of our apartment door together, handed our landlord our two keys, and taken separate buses in opposite directions.

I had gone to my parents' home, and he had gone to his parents'. They were empty nesters no more.

Physically, he hadn't changed. The cheesy mustache and wispy beard remained. I'd sort of figured those would have gone, to signify a new beginning. His round belly bulged out from his shirt when he sat down. For nine months, I'd often rested my head against that belly while watching movies. In those happy days, that white mound of flesh had been my happy zone. Today when I glanced at it, I felt a remoteness.

He crossed one leg over the other, holding it in place with his hands. Despite the winter snow, he wore his sneakers without socks, as he did year-round. His feet vacillated between foot rot in the wet summer months and frostbite in the winter.

"I caught the wrong bus and got here an hour ago," he said, staring at an uncut fingernail. "I've registered us with the secretary. We're good to go."

"Thanks for taking care of this," I said, meaning it. "Where did you find this guy? Is he any good?" I spoke quietly, although no one else was in the room with us.

"On Kijiji. The first twenty minutes is free. So talk fast." I nodded, impressed. My ex was still a tight ass.

"How're Mom and Dad?" I asked, unbuttoning my jacket. His parents had always treated me well. I knew our marriage breakdown had hit them hard. In fact, they were the only two who'd cried when we announced it. Even I hadn't shed a tear.

"They miss you," he said, turning to look my way briefly, and then he looked back at his nail. "They asked for you to come out to the hootenanny."

I looked at him, surprised. The hootenanny was a yearly event his family hosted every fall out at his parents' farm. It was a traditional day of outdoor baseball in the backyard. It had been going on for four generations. I had taken part our first year together as a married couple, thinking I had a lifetime of hootenannies. I was wrong. My one homerun would become my only home run. And now I was being asked back like an alumnus.

"That would be nice," I said, surprising myself with the answer.

He smiled. "I'll let my mom know. She'll be happy."

It felt odd making plans with my ex on the same afternoon we were about to officially kiss off our marriage. But I felt comfortable being around his family, especially compared to the strangeness of Sebastian and his mother.

I felt compelled to update him on my adventures.

"My dad is making me get my driver's license. He's even fixing up the old Reliant in the backyard."

My ex looked surprised as hell. "What about your bus pass?"

"It's going to be on waivers. Soon I'll be swearing at the gas stations every time they raise prices before a long weekend, like every other motorist."

He was about to reply, when the secretary announced we could proceed to the office.

I followed my ex down the hallway and turned left into a windowless office that must have faced the adjoining Subway store. I could smell freshly baked Subway bread mixed with the sickly sweet scent of cigars.

A man who introduced himself in a clipped accent as Mr. Singh, our lawyer, rose from his desk to greet us. His suit jacket was dark purple, and he wore a pressed white shirt and red tie. His dark skin contrasted with the shirt, and short, curly black hair covered his head. Every finger sported a thick gold ring cluttered with what looked like diamonds, but they could have been cubic zirconia.

He smiled and signaled for us to sit down across from him. Dozens of thank-you cards were scattered across his desk and on shelves behind him—a testimony to his great work in making people single again, apparently.

"Welcome," he said, and he sat down again. "Is this the first time for both of you?"

I looked at him with an eyebrow raised. "I guess so. I've never been here before."

He smiled warmly. "I meant first divorce. Fifty percent of my business is repeat—second, third, fourth divorces. Even fifth-time divorces have become popular in the past year."

Who could survive five broken hearts? I thought, wanting to meet such a person to see how hardened and embittered he or she had become. By that point, a person would have become so stone cold, his or her wedding vows would end with presigned divorce documents.

"First for me," I said, looking at my ex, who was also nodding in agreement.

"Okay, no problem. It's a little easier and faster the second time because I have a template already filled in with your particulars. Keep that in mind," he said.

I shifted in my chair.

He twirled the pen in his hand. "One thing I'll suggest for future marriages is to register with me at the same time you do with your marriage certificate. That way, I'll have a file started should things go sideways."

"Not much of a vote of confidence for marriage," I said.

He shrugged. "Stats are stats, Larissa. Marriages don't work. If you want my advice, procreate and get the hell out. At least the kid will know who the father is, and your chance of being a victim of domestic violence decreases by eighty-eight percent."

"Fascinating," I replied.

My ex grinned. "See? I told you he's good."

"That's why you pay me the big bucks." He shuffled some papers on his desk and began writing. His gold cufflinks scraped against the desk. He kept his head down as he asked us questions and wrote notes.

"How long was the marriage?"

My ex answered. "Nine months and one day."

"Plus a morning," I added.

"Did you engage in sex with one another during that period of marriage at least once?"

"More than once," my ex replied, smiling and nodding.

"Was it consensual?" he said.

"I think so." He looked at me, startled.

"Yeah, it was," I agreed, nodding at him reassuringly.

"Are either of you contesting the termination of this marriage?" He cocked his head slightly.

We looked at one another and shook our heads.

"We're both good with it," he said.

"Good with ending the marriage," I added.

"Is there a need for restrictions, such as restraining orders?"

"Nope," stated my ex.

Mr. Singh glanced my way. "You can be candid, Larissa. Do you require a restraining order?"

I reared back. "No, I'm safe."

He cocked his head once more at us both. "So no for both of you?"

We nodded in unison.

"Now," Mr. Singh continued, "in terms of income splitting and pensions, we can look at the industry norm of fifty-fifty. What would you place the household income at during the period of the marriage?"

86

I looked to my ex. "I'd say it was about eight thousand dollars." He confirmed by nodding.

Mr. Singh looked at me. "I'm talking about the combined household income."

"Eight thousand."

"What about pension plans?"

"None," said my ex. "I'm self-employed as a drummer. Larissa was picking up odd jobs here and there. Hey, man, we lived on love."

Mr. Singh wrote something down and crossed something out.

"Okay. What about pets, favorite mutual prized possessions, inheritances, assets?"

I took a deep breath. "I bought a cat shortly after we moved to our apartment. He ran away the next day. Other assets ..." I searched my memory.

My ex jumped in. "I guess my drum throne that was once sat on by Keith Moon of the Who—yeah, I'd say that's definitely a prized possession."

Mr. Singh looked up, nodding. "Value?"

"Oh, at least twenty bucks, man. No way I'd settle for anything less. I paid ten."

Mr. Singh flinched and struck something else out.

I rubbed my face. "There is the half set of CorningWare we bought at that garage sale. Do you want it?"

My ex waved me off. "We bought that with our empties anyway."

I agreed with a nod.

"And all the furniture, we rented. All that shit went back to the rental company," he said, stroking the wisps of his chin hair.

"We didn't own a car," I added.

"Nah," my ex agreed. "A cash hog."

"Hey," I said suddenly, "what about our wedding money? That term deposit we set up with it?"

My ex slapped his leg. "No kidding. How the hell did we forget about that? Good memory." We high-fived.

"I knew there was something missing," I said. I pointed at Mr. Singh's paper while he waited, poised with his pen. "Write down three hundred dollars. It comes due in ten years."

He put a line through something else.

"I suppose that wraps it all up," said my ex, beaming. "I'd say we're pretty darn amicable about the whole thing."

I looked at him and smiled. "Having gone through the experience myself now, I really don't understand why so many couples make this a difficult thing."

Mr. Singh raised his head. "They have assets."

I tossed my hand into the air. "Perfect example of why you shouldn't. Divorce and assets will make you an embittered couple."

"Hell yeah," stated my ex, slouching back down.

Mr. Singh reached into a filing cabinet, pulled out a sheet of paper, quickly scribbled our names on the top, crossed out a few paragraphs, and pushed the paper in front of us, along with a pen.

"This is a standardized separation agreement since you both have no assets to speak of, along with both parties not contesting anything. Sign this by the *X*, please." He grinned. "You actually qualify for my no-fee divorce filing. Congratulations."

We signed.

Mr. Singh placed his pen on his desk and sat back in his chair.

"I'm going to provide you with a few of my cards. Please pass them around to all your married friends."

My ex and I stood, shook hands, and made our way back to the front of the office and out the front door. We stood on the shoveled front walk, breathing in the crisp air.

"That went well," I said. "You done good, cowboy, picking him." I punched him lightly on his shoulder.

He shrugged. "It helps we're both on the same wavelength about ending our marriage. Nothing personal at this point, just business."

"Yes sirree. Just business. We're basically walking away with the shirts on our backs."

"Just the way we came into the marriage."

"Well, it's good to make it official. I was having a hard time saying for certain I was divorced until it was on paper, just in case, you know, we got back together and had to explain it."

He stuck his hands in his pants pockets, nodding. "Me too. I always prefer things in writing. Otherwise, it's just your word against mine that we're divorced. Now there's no going back."

He was right. There was no going back.

I looked over at him. "Well, thanks for a whirlwind nine months of romance. At least I wet my feet with what marriage was all about."

"No problem. If we never get remarried, at least we won't go to our graves wondering what we missed out on."

"Been there; done that," I said, slapping my hands together.

"Hey," he said, looking around, his breath billowing in the cold. "I've got a gig coming up with a new set of cover tunes—you should come by and check it out. I've finally learned those new beats that I was working on just before we decided to divorce. They sound pretty wild in a new track we perform."

I knew what all the *Cosmo*-type magazines said—"Stop doing things with your ex when it's over. How can the wounds heal when he's still involved in your life?" Blah, blah, blah. But hell, if it got me out of the basement for an evening, why not? I'd bring the girls with me for support.

"I'm in," I said. "I can't wait to hear those beats. I know you were working hard on them."

He smiled. "Awesome. I'll text you the details." He had to cross the street to catch his bus. For mine, I needed to stay on the side we were on. I watched him go. His distinguishable, shuffling gait of boredom still seemed familiar. What wasn't familiar was that I wasn't walking next to him as part of a married couple.

His bus arrived first, and I watched him get on and wave at me through the window. I waved back.

I was divorced.

CHAPTER 8

Unearthing the Groundhog

March 20, 3:05 a.m.

My father's second cousin's nickname, Groundhog, might need some explanation. Her name isn't actually Groundhog, but after this blog, nothing more will need to be explained. She is a classic spoon-fed Ukrainian utilizing tradition via textbook, old-country folklore on how to be a Ukrainian kid and maximize those attributes. Groundhog has perfectly mastered a Ph-freaking-D in the art of her craft.

At fifty-five, she lives in the basement of her parents' home; her parents, who are in their mid-eighties, have failing health, but steadfast and true they remain to their only daughter. Their a-hole son, in their eyes, abandoned them to live halfway across the country decades ago to, God forbid, start his own life with a woman, raise kids, and have a career and independence.

Sure, Groundhog remained loyal to her parents by sacrificing her own independence to reside in their basement. But her attitude was inexcusable toward her parents—living rent-free, cost-free, and maintenance-free; doing no shopping, cleaning, or cooking; and always demanding, complaining, shouting, and bitching. The basement had always been her turf, and it remained her turf. She protected her turf in the semidark. Her parents tossed food down the stairs as her gruff voice called out, "Get me smokes and Wiser's Whiskey."

*****

I lay down on my bed next to my laptop to check out Facebook before heading outside to help my dad work on my car. He'd said he was making progress but could use me there to hand him stuff. I was the stuff hander.

My twenty-two-year-old cousin, Garth, with his shaved head, was online with Facebook, and we got to chatting.

"Just finalized my divorce," I wrote to him.

"The city's most-eligible bachelorette is back on the market," he typed.

"Don't forget desirable," I added.

"LOL. Of course. Now the manhunt is on."

"Any suggestions?" I asked, thinking that as a guy, he should know how a man needed to be hunted.

His reply came back quickly: "Online dating, Cuz."

"What do you mean?"

"Get set up with an account, profile. Input what kind of man you are seeking."

"That simple?" I wondered what kind of man I was seeking.

"Hell ya. Got myself a profile. Instantly got myself a handful of honeys."

"I'm not looking for the hive. Just one bee."

"You can weed out the riffraff without stepping out your door," he typed.

"Doesn't get better than that," I typed, agreeing. Riffraff was what I dreaded the most about getting back in the market—the endless cycle of shit dates, bad dinners, and awkward hours.

His return message advised, "If you want a night of sex, set your profile for it."

I reared back from my laptop. I hadn't even considered sex. I was unprepared for being single again. Sex was a whole other awkward area. What if those guys wanted me to perform like the girls Amy had shown me on the Internet one drunken night? Gone were the days of lying on your back for a few minutes. These broads were all about stamina, stunt work, and bent-out-of-shape sex positions. My hips could not possibly move like those I'd witnessed, unless they were fractured. Amy and I had eaten an entire bowl of popcorn while watching one of those girls take a thirty-minute pounding; she probably had gone for a burger and fries afterward, as if nothing had happened.

I was simply looking for conversation at this point. I could hold off on spreading my thighs for a few years, perhaps even into my forties.

"What site should I use?" I typed. "I'm looking for normal dudes." I didn't want guys with fetishes or character flaws. It was bad enough my ex was into drums.

"Singlenomore," he replied. "I've met lots of great gals. Got a hottie right now I've been getting with. Looking deadly serious, Cuz."

I remembered Dad was waiting for me in the garage. I panicked. "Congrats," I typed. "You inspire me. Gotta run. Keep me posted on your love life."

My dad was devoid of patience. When he said to meet him in five minutes, he really meant twenty-five minutes before he'd asked me.

I walked to the back door, thinking I'd set up a profile once I'd finished handing stuff to my dad.

I slipped on my snowmobile boots, parka, and gloves. The weather guys said an early spring was heading our way. I couldn't wait to get out of the winter gear and into flip-flops. There was nothing sexy about a girl wearing a fur-lined, hooded parka.

Inside the garage, my dad had rigged up lights on extensions cords all around the car. The scene resembled an archeological dig.

I hadn't closed the door before Dad was barking out a question.

"Did you go visit Baba yet?" He raised a hand. "You know she's not getting any younger. She's not going to be around forever." He glared at me and then stuck his head back under the hood, where the car's engine was located.

I walked up to him.

"I'm going. It's on my to-do list. I've been busy job hunting," I lied.

His voice was muffled. "Don't be looking for those executive-type jobs. Make sure it's a job you're qualified for. You have to work yourself up the ladder. Start at the bottom, shoveling shit like all the rest of us."

"Where's the bottom for me?"

"Don't get smart," he barked. "And can you hand me that thingamajig? We need to remove the entire kit and caboodle." His left arm was flailing out, trying to reach what he wanted. I guessed it was the tool on the car's fender. I grabbed it and placed it in his hand.

I heard a clunk.

He swore. "Put that light over here."

I wasn't sure where "here" was, with half his body embedded in the car. I grabbed one of several lights swinging around us and tried to point it where I thought he might want it. It must have been close enough. He continued working without saying more about it.

"How'd it go at the lawyer's?" he said. "Did you nail that yollup to the wall?"

I leaned against the car. "It went very well. We settled everything we had to."

"I hope you got half his pension."

"He doesn't have a pension."

"He's got to pay you alimony, you know. He's going to pay through the nose, too."

"We agreed not to."

Dad dropped his tool. "Beans!" He weaseled his way back up to Earth and looked at me as if I were nuts. He looked pained. "No alimony? What the hell's the matter with you, Larissa? He has to pay you. The yollup should also pay me back for the booze at your goddamn wedding."

"We worked it out not to."

"Then sue his ass off. Don't let him get away with this. I don't give a shit if he cried in front of you. Don't fall for that bullshit," he said sharply.

"He's not getting away with anything. We didn't have anything."

"That's a load of bull crap. No wonder he wanted you to use the same lawyer. They're all in cahoots."

"No one is in cahoots, Dad. This was all aboveboard."

He shook his head vigorously and pointed a greasy finger at me. "You got screwed." He bent down and dug through a toolbox. "I'll give him what for if I ever see him again."

"No violence," I cautioned. "We both agreed to end the marriage."

My dad looked wounded when he stood up. "Don't become like my sister, Tina—all fake, crippled up with no job, and looking to sink her fangs into any man with a debit card." He sighed. "Please, no more shaming our family."

"Don't take it personally, Dad," I pleaded as I spoke to his headless body buried deep in the car. "This is the family curse, plain and simple. We're Ukrainian. Shame is as genetic as the hair sprouting from my earlobes."

My dad grunted. "Do you have a screw loose? There's no family curse, for Christ's sake, Larissa. When you marry a goddamn yollup, that's just plain stupidity. No different than the piss head my sister dug her claws into either."

Once I'd finished handing Dad stuff and holding things, I ducked back into my bedroom and closed the door. I had official dating business to attend to. It was time to register as a woman in need of a man. I was not yet desperate, not quite ready to settle, but ready to show my head, like the spring groundhog.

Singlenomore displayed color photos of smiling, blatantly happy people of all ages, hair colors, and skin colors wrapped in the arms of the opposite sex, obviously connected with their soul mate by the service. I just wanted a guy who had a soul and no ambition to procreate.

Frustration quickly set in over the work required to set up an account. I was a little taken aback by all of the check boxes I needed to fill in order to allegedly find my perfect match. With so much technology, I'd expected that listing I was interested in a guy would have been more than enough.

Apparently not.

I had to list my hobbies. I discovered I did not have any hobbies.

I had to list activities I enjoyed doing. I discovered I did little.

I had to list music I enjoyed, movies I'd watched, books I'd read, and pets I'd loved. The NA button was getting used too often.

I was starting to resent all of this private stuff I needed to give up for the world of men. What would be left to tantalize and razzle-dazzle them if they knew everything about me before they looked me in the eyes over a candlelight dinner on their coin? Where was the mystique? Would I have anything left in my bag of tricks to pull out during the awkward silence?

I suddenly became uncomfortable. These strange men would know more about me than my parents did.

How should I answer how much alcohol I drank? Did three ounces a day make me sound like cheap drunk who spread 'em after the fourth shooter? Or if I answered that I never drank, was I going to lure every churchgoer trying to take me to Sunday Mass? I wanted to avoid the extremists. I checked off that I drank sometimes, a nice vague statement that drew no definitive conclusions.

I was relieved when it came time for the meat and potatoes: What was I looking for in a man?

I had my thoughts. Since the time we'd ended our marriage and I'd moved back home, I had been thinking about this often.

What did I want in a guy? Did I want someone totally different from what my ex was all about?

That'd mean someone who held a professional job, probably wore a suit, had a paycheck direct-deposited every two weeks, and owned a car or maybe two—one for winter and one for summer. Perhaps he had three dogs, a house, a small mortgage, and grown kids from a previous marriage that had ended only because she'd died after being struck by a meteorite. Maybe he ate no meat, was tall, had abs, carried three unused credit cards, and could cook without using the microwave.

Who was this man?

Was he out there somewhere, waiting for me?

Was that what I wanted? Could that person make me so happy that I'd enjoy spending the rest of my life with him? I needed a person who could endure my family and not leave the supper table midway to go have a quiet cry in the bathroom. I checked off my fantasy-guy list: someone who was over six feet tall; was into fitness; had no pets; was career oriented; enjoyed music, television reruns, and restaurants; and loved to cuddle. I was living outside my comfort box.

The final request was to upload a photo. I rarely took selfies. I figured, *Let the cyber world see me as I am.* I used the laptop's camera to snap a few photos. The pictures would have qualified for a passport—grim, devoid of personality. The effort to get off my bed to apply makeup and style my hair made my choice to submit the passport photo look good. *Good enough for a customs agent, good enough for a dating prospect.* I took one liberty. With a slight edit, I moved my eyes a little farther apart for a more-exotic appearance.

I hit the save button. Confirmation came back instantly that I was now live. The bait was cast.

A twinge of hope crept into me. Maybe life wasn't so bad after all. I might not stay single and reside in my parents' basement forever.

I rested on my bed until curiosity aroused the need to check out some of the guys online. Cousin Garth had left me with the impression of a utopia of desirable men swarming like piranha around a floundering carcass.

I logged into the site and opened the quick summary that listed rows of random guys looking for love and laughter.

Each photograph had a quick bio attached.

Something was wrong.

Todd, twenty-seven, recently paroled, was looking for a short commitment until his upcoming resentencing hearing.

Carl, forty-two, wanted his third wife to be his last.

Chaz was twenty-five, but his face was difficult to discern under his tattoos.

Mick, thirty-three, might not have had any arms, but he still could dance up a storm.

Joey, twenty-nine, had a photo of Pinocchio as his profile picture. I had no idea in hell what that meant.

Corbett, thirty-six, was just getting out of a homosexual relationship and wanted to "try the other side" for a while, he said.

I logged out and put the laptop beside me on the bed. I rolled over the opposite way, cradling my head.

Was Garth serious about this site and his success, or was I being played? So far, all I'd found were misfits, creeps, losers, and fakers. In comparison, my ex and his shortcomings looked a hell of a lot more manageable than some guy doing time in the prison system. I watched *Lockup* on weekends. I saw what went on inside the cages.

I panicked.

Could my divorce be reversed? Had Mr. Singh filed the papers yet, or could I get him to retract the whole damn thing? I was an idiot for signing off on my marriage before investigating my alternatives.

Fear ate at my guts. What creature was going to respond to my profile?

I closed my eyes.

I cried.

CHAPTER 9

Hard Act to Follow

Desperation pushed people in different ways. For me, it was motivation to hit the shopping malls in the hopes of trading my extensive inventory of ten-year-old sweaters and track pants for clothing that had buttons, color, and no logos.

The task was daunting, so I was bringing all of the troops. Bernadette, my mom, and Auntie Tina surrounded me; with that many years of collective female fashion sense, I had to have some degree of success.

"Honey," Auntie Tina said, rubbing my shoulder and smiling as we walked into the city's only fashion mall, "I will transform you into a Cinderella. I've been tweezing, shaving, moisturizing, defrizzing, flat-ironing, bikini-waxing, exfoliating, and manicuring since eighth grade, all while sleeping on a silk pillowcase to reduce wrinkles. I raised boys who never changed their underwear until it stuck to their skin. I'm ready to pass along forty years of self-help to a female in need."

I looked at her hopefully. "If you can simply make me recognizable as a woman from a distance and smell like one close up, your job will have been successful."

"Cut yourself some slack," said Bernadette. "With our toning program at the gym, you'll soon have a pair of hips."

"And I'll need to learn how to walk with them," I said. "Anyone know how to teach my ass to shuffle from one side to the other?"

"Don't you worry, honey," said Auntie Tina. "I'll show you the hypnotic sway that captures men's attention."

"No pole dancing, Tina," warned my mom, glancing her way.

Tina laughed wistfully. "My age has its limitations."

Bernadette glowed at my aunt.

We kept walking through the mall.

"Listen, girl, after five kids, you could say I know how to work the pole, and it wasn't the one for dancing, honey."

We all burst out in laughter.

Tina pointed to a store, and we turned in that direction.

"Shoes, girl." She grinned. "A woman's best friend. We are starting at the bottom and working our way up."

I had never been in a store that sold only shoes. Every piece of footwear I'd ever owned had come off the shelves in Walmart. I chose seasonal clearance over style.

We gathered around a salesgirl as my aunt explained her strategy.

"Ideally, every woman should own a dozen pairs of shoes. That's minimum—daytime, nighttime, formal, ultraformal, friend's house, job interview, daily employment, special event, in the bedroom."

We all looked at her in awe. Even the salesgirl was impressed, nodding in agreement, believing she was about to rack up the mother of all sales.

"I own two pairs of shoes," stated my mom, needling. "Boots and runners, and I've managed to survive a lifetime."

My aunt looked skeptical. "You're also married to my brother. He wouldn't notice if you were without feet."

"He's practical."

"He wore rubber boots to my wedding," Tina spat, still apparently smarting decades later.

There was no defense for Mom on that one. The event was a legend within my dad's family. Considering he was part of the wedding party, the family portraits had become priceless. Among my friends, he had become a celebrity.

"So where do we start?" I asked, breaking into the conversation before purses began to fly.

My aunt refocused, surveying the sections of shoes.

"First," she began, looking down at my snowmobile boots, "we've got to get you out of those shit kickers. The type of guy those turn on are not the type you want breathing beer breath over your face, honey. Let's look into a pair of knee-highs." She led me by my hand to the wall where several pairs were set up. She motioned to the sales associate to bring out a pair of the black knee-high boots with five-inch spike heels.

"Size?" she asked, looking down at my feet, trying to take an educated guess.

I hesitated. "Let's try a ten."

The sales associate appeared troubled. "I doubt these boots come in that large a size."

"What do you mean?" asked my aunt, stepping between us.

"Well, typically, we have very few requests for these types of boots in the larger sizes."

"Just go look," snapped my aunt.

"I'm not even sure I could walk in those," I said, glancing at the five-inch heel.

She waved off my concern. "These will accentuate your calves."

"Tina," said my mother, "you can't even see a calf with the boot going up to the knee."

The sales associate came back cradling a large box.

"This isn't the exact floor model, but it comes in a ten. We only have the more-popular sizes of eight and smaller in the boot on display. Sorry." She pulled out the black boots. There was no spike heel, making this boot seem far more manageable. I sat down to slip it on.

My mom, Tina, and Bernadette stood in a half circle around me while I unbuckled my snowmobile boots and slipped them off.

"Don't you sweat in those because of the felt liner?" said my aunt, leaning forward to squeeze the felt's thickness.

"Always," I replied, "but it doesn't bother me."

"It should if you're slipping them off to get down with a man," Auntie Tina replied.

I grabbed the new boot, looking for a zipper.

"It's a slip-on," said the sales associate.

"All this length, and it's a slip-on?" I said, amazed.

I started to try to push my foot in, when the sale associate stopped me.

"You'll need to remove your sock."

I looked down at the thermal wool sock I had on.

"That's a boot by itself, Larissa," said Bernadette, grinning.

"I hate cold feet."

I slipped it off. Horrified, I stared at my discolored toenails, which had been growing all winter.

"Those feet need some loving," stated my aunt.

I jammed my foot into the boot.

The first six inches went well, but then it became tighter and tighter. I gripped the leather as hard as I could. The sales associate also took hold; we yanked and pulled in short bursts.

"You have a set of powerful calves," said Bernadette. "Must be all the treadmill work we've been doing."

My mother looked pained. "You girls—I warned you to not be bulking up to look like a man."

We tugged some more.

My calf was too large. We stopped, defeated. I couldn't get my foot halfway down the boot's length. It took Bernadette and the sales associate working together to pull it free from my leg.

"Too bad," said Auntie Tina, making a face. "They are beautiful."

The sales associate smiled. "And this week, they are half price. Four hundred twenty dollars.

I choked. "That doesn't fit my budget either." I grimaced. "Next, give me something with a helluva lot less leather and price. My whole wardrobe has to be under four hundred."

"You really want to challenge me," replied my aunt grimly.

"I can't help it. I just got divorced. Money is tight."

She nodded. "My point why you must zero in on money exactly. If they don't have a net worth, they don't have any reason to be knocking on your door."

The disgust on my mother's face was apparent. "Money doesn't buy love, Tina."

"Who needs love?" she replied. "As far as I last remembered, it's a big house that keeps you warm in the winter and a fancy car that keeps you off a bus. Love has nothing to do with either of those."

Bernadette's eyebrows rose. "She has a point."

"Don't egg her on," cautioned my mom.

"I just need some cheap footwear," I said.

My aunt signaled to me. "We'll find something that works under those sizable calves, honey. We'll leave those powerful gams to clench around a man's neck. Let's refocus now on a dress shoe. If you're going to be dating, believe it or not, the man will be focusing on your feet."

I groaned. The cutting of my toenails was just upped a notch in importance.

"Take a look at these," said Bernadette, pulling a pair of shoes off the shelf. My aunt gagged.

"Are you nuts?" my aunt said, pushing them away. "Platform shoes like that are suited for the strip show. Guys who sit ringside at those events have no money. And if they do, they blow it on skanks. Besides, you're a tall girl. With these clodhoppers, you're going to tower over the men, and they don't like that. Unless"—she grinned— "they have a fetish for Amazon women."

"I hope," my mom said, turning to Tina, "your mother's asleep when you're Googling all this garbage in her apartment."

"All factual," she said.

"So what do you suggest?" I asked, looking around and feeling overwhelmed.

My aunt snatched a pair of leopard-print shoes.

"These are statement makers," she said, holding them like a prized trophy catch.

"Hey, they match the underwear I have on right now," said Bernadette, smiling. "They're Mike's favorites."

I scowled. "How the hell am I supposed to wear those now, knowing I'm wearing your underwear?"

Bernadette perked up. "It gets Mike's juices flowing. I guarantee those shoes will do the same to your men."

"Sure. Except every time I look down at these, I'll be thinking of you prancing around in the same pattern of underwear in front of Mike."

"Try them on," urged my aunt, ignoring the conversation.

"These are best sellers," said the sales associate. "Size ten?" she asked again.

I nodded. "Ten." I couldn't blame my size on my feet swelling as the day went on.

I sat down on the bench. I wanted desperately to put the snowmobile boots back on.

The associate brought a box over to me. She opened it and handed me one shoe to fit on my naked foot.

"Please tell me these are under fifty bucks."

"Forty-nine dollars."

I smiled and thanked her. At least the price fit.

I wiggled my foot inside the shoe. The flesh on the top of my foot oozed over the top.

"Let's try on both," suggested the associate.

With both shoes on my feet, I held out my arms with Bernadette taking one side and the associate the other. On three, I was raised to a standing position. There was a moment of silence while I caught my balance and got control of the swaying.

"Thirty years old, girls," I said. "First time in heels." There was applause.

I took a tentative step forward. "Walking in these babies is far less supportive than my steel-toed, rubber-soled snow boots."

"Don't look down. Look straight ahead," advised my aunt.

"Focus on an object in the distance," suggested my mom. I locked my eyes on the cash register.

"You got it, girl," cheered Bernadette. I felt like a rehab patient taking my first walk after a hip replacement.

I stopped and turned around.

"What do you think?" asked the sales associate.

"I like the way they feel," I said. "I suppose with a little practice, I could wear them on a date and not walk like I have blisters."

Auntie Tina beamed. "Just wait until I get those sweatpants off you and get you into a slinky dress. That is our next mission, right after you pay for those shoes, honey."

"Okay," I said, feeling empowered. "I'll take these." I wobbled back to my bench. I gave each shoe a quick tug, releasing my feet. I covered up the red marks left behind by slipping on my wool socks.

"Great choice," said Bernadette, leaning over and smiling. "Seriously, those are hot. The guys will love them."

I looked up at her. "I didn't realize dating was all about the shoes."

"And what goes on after you take them off," said my aunt.

Bernadette grinned, jabbing her thumb back at my aunt. "She's hilarious."

"I think she missed menopause."

I walked up to the cashier to pay for the shoes.

Mom came up beside me. "You be careful in those."

"I'll try my best." I laughed. "It's hard being a woman."

She shrugged. "Most men don't care about that stuff," she said, pointing at the shoe box. "They want a meal on the table when they get home from work. You do that, and they're happy enough."

Bernadette caught the conversation. "I don't cook shit for Mike. I work too. It's everyone for herself after a day of working."

Mom grimaced. "That's why we have so many broken marriages. The woman doesn't want to be a wife anymore."

Bernadette wasn't buying it. "Ten years for me and Mike, and no complaints from him. He's happy with the arrangement. When I dish him up a hot meal, it's in the sack."

My aunt shrieked. "I like this gal," she said, embracing Bernadette in a one-arm squeeze.

"We should hang," she replied, grinning.

"I'd love to."

"Hey," I said, coming between them, "remember that today is about me, girls."

"And our mission continues," replied my aunt. She led us out of the store, and we continued through the mall.

My aunt said devilishly, "See that gentleman sitting over there by the water fountain?" She pointed to a hunched-up guy wearing a ski jacket and drinking a coffee by himself. We all nodded, uncertain what she was getting at.

"Vulnerable," she said, grinning hawkishly. "Everything about him screams, 'I need a woman'—the slumped posture, unkempt hair, his desperation, the puppy-dog face. Exhausted by lonely nights, he hasn't laughed at anything other than himself in months. I could hook this guy in ten seconds." She snapped her fingers crisply.

"All this from a simple glance his way?" asked Bernadette, enthralled by her new friend. "I see a guy sipping coffee. Probably waiting for his wife, who's shopping for bath salts."

Auntie Tina glanced at us with a tiger smile. "To the young and naive, like you and Larissa, that's the assumption you'd make. But you missed the ringless finger, mismatched socks, and stained pants. No wife lets a husband be seen in public wearing soiled clothing. And the coup de grâce—his glance our way. Took us all in, ladies. Long before you even noticed him, he noticed us. He picked out in our group those of us looking for a piece of action. He formulated a plan long before we saw him holding a coffee and making our own judgments. He's leaving the ball in our court as to how we use this information."

Bernadette barked out a laugh. "You got all that from that guy sitting and drinking coffee?"

"Are you back on your medications?" asked my mother, frowning.

"Ladies," said my aunt, continuing her strut between us, "this is from years—decades—of man hunting. I've been able to evolve it highly to a keen degree."

"Then why are you still single?" asked my mom. "With this advanced human-sensory thing you have going, I'd figure you'd have corralled the most-eligible moneybags by now."

We continued walking while my aunt justified her singleness.

"Despite this amazing ability to sniff out the men," she said, taking long strides, "I'm still vulnerable to the guy being a dud."

"All that female posturing, and flaws remain in your system," said my mom, shaking her head.

My aunt was undeterred. "All part of the pursuit and capture, my dear." She put an arm around me. "Next up is that sexy dress, leaving your man salivating to see what's underneath it."

I felt queasy. "I think they'll be horrified by the discovery. Some things are best left to the imagination, and my body is one of those."

Bernadette walked up to my other side, putting her arm around me.

"Our physical training will change all that, girl. Think rock-hard abs, sexy calves, and tight arms with no underskin hanging."

I groaned. "I wish. But I'm finding I'm hungrier after the workouts. I keep stuffing my face. There's no way that increased appetite is going to make anything look sexy on me."

"Color and cut," said my aunt, determined. "It does amazing things for our bodies."

"God, I hope so," I replied, not sure how much a girl could fake before the truth came out.

My aunt led us into a store with pounding music, mannequins, and rows of clothing. She knew what she wanted and headed straight to the back of the building.

We stood in a circle around her.

She pointed at me. "You have hips. You have a powerful set of calves. We need to give you a waist and prop up your boobs."

"Gee. You're talking a full rebuild," I replied.

"Nothing I can't handle." She yanked a dress off the rack. "Try this one on. I love the pattern."

I took hold of it, doubtful.

"Are you sure? This might work as a hairnet."

"Go on," she urged.

"Seriously, this is the size of a facecloth."

"It stretches."

I walked over to the changing rooms and was let inside. Once I took off my jacket, sweater, and sweatpants, I glanced at myself in the full-size mirror. The mismatched panties and bra glared at me. Now the details started to count.

The dress was a one-piece. I stepped into the top of the dress with one wool-socked foot and then followed it with the second foot. I started pulling the dress up toward my hips. It was stuck against my thighs. I pulled a little harder. I heard a stitch give out. I stopped. There was a gentle knock at the door.

"You need a hand?" It was Bernadette.

"Get your ass in here," I said urgently. She slipped in the door. With the two of us in the room, the confined space was tighter than the dress.

"Nice torn underwear," she said.

"Shut up. I never thought about this when I was getting dressed this morning."

"Do you own a pair of matching undies?"

"I'm not even sure. These panties are my mom's."

She looked stricken. "That I didn't need to know."

I flinched. "They fit."

"They're your mom's!"

"Never mind. My immediate problem is getting this napkin over my hips." I looked down in desperation.

Bernadette's brow furrowed. "This could be a challenge."

"It already is. I heard something ripping," I said in my softest voice.

"If we get this one on, make sure we take a different one off the shelf."

I cleared my throat. "You pull from the back, and I'll work the front."

She got behind me and dug in her fingers.

"Who the hell do they make this shit for?" she said.

"Not for women like us."

"Healthy and powerful," she muttered.

We yanked.

The dress reached my hips.

"Almost there, girl," she puffed.

"Is it normal not to feel my toes?"

"This might be one of those new-style dresses you wear once and cut off at the end of the night."

I snorted. "It will be if I keep tearing this thing."

"Just don't sneeze."

"I'm afraid to swallow my gum."

Bernadette heaved. "Pull your stomach in a bit so that I can hike up the back a bit more."

"I am."

"Okay. Pull your ass in."

"How's it looking?" my aunt said from behind the door. "An attention-getter, isn't it?"

"It's certainly got mine," I shouted through the door.

"Let's see how hot you are in it," urged my aunt.

"Are you sure there isn't a size bigger out there?" I called out.

"I'm sure. Keep in mind," her voice said, "this style is supposed to be a little snug."

"Snug?" I grunted. "My belly button is poking through."

Bernadette helped place the straps over my shoulders. I looked in the mirror. I stared at a bulging sausage.

Bernadette shrugged.

I opened the door. My aunt's and mom's smiles faded.

"Yeah," my aunt said, "that's not gonna cut it, honey. Sorry. How starved was the model when the designer stitched this thing together? Come on. No real woman carries flesh that would fit into it."

I reddened. "That's what I've been trying to tell you."

She turned. "I'll go see what I can find in a two-piece."

"And make sure it comes in double digits, will ya?" I demanded.

Bernadette got behind me again. "Let's see if we can peel this thing off you."

"God, I hope so. I think I've lost a bra size."

"It'll all spring back," she said.

"Good. I can't afford to lose any," I said while we rolled the material down my back.

More ripping sounds came when we reached my hips.

"This thing is ready for the discount bin," Bernadette joked.

I took a deep breath. "Perhaps I need to stick to designer sweaters. At least I won't get lightheaded from my rib cage being squeezed."

"Now you know what I go through carrying around these monster jugs."

"I feel for you," I said, nodding.

I pulled on my own clothes, instantly appreciating the comfort. I grabbed the dress and walked out to find my aunt and mom.

They were milling about, looking frustrated.

"Nothing here, honey," said my aunt. "This shit is made for schoolgirls."

"What now?"

"We are regrouping. Designer stores are out. Off the rack is in. One way or another, honey," proclaimed my aunt, "we will transform you into a trophy wife."

CHAPTER 10

Job-Type Job

I realize people in my generation don't want to work—work hard, work at getting ahead. We try hard to do it our way or no way at all. I embarked on the pursuit of doing it my way or no way at all.

I left high school and drifted into work as a video-store-rental clerk (for one summer), weekend gas-station cashier (for five weekends), flower-shop pruner (for six weeks), salon floor sweeper (for a Friday, Saturday, and Sunday), bank call-center operator (for four months), road-repair flag girl (for seven weeks), Lazer Clinic employee (for four weeks and one treatment of Botox around my eyes), weekly community newspaper deliverer (for eighteen months), and restaurant hostess (for one shift).

Now that I am living back with my folks, I decided I am going to become a home-based web

designer. I enjoy being freelance. I hate having
no income.

*****

It was time to buckle down and appease my dad.

I arrived at my baba's apartment at noon for my first visit since
my divorce. Actually, I hadn't made a visit during my marriage either.
I recognized that was disrespectful, but marriage had made me lazy.
It was far easier to continue lounging on a sofa in my apartment
than to make the effort to travel across the city to say hi. I had made
several phone calls to prove I still existed.

I pushed the buzzer. My baba lived on the third floor. At one time
or another, she had resided on the second floor and twice on the first
floor, and she was now back for a second time on the third floor, all in
this same three-story building. Her reasons for transfers ranged from
the south-side view being too warm, the wind on the north side being
too cold, the parking lot noise on the west side, the laundry-room
rattles on the east side, a bachelor suite that was too small, and a one
bedroom that was too big. She kept the caretaker in a perpetual state
of painting each time she left a suite. The building's owner would
have stopped any other tenant from transferring so many times but
took a soft stance for a Ukrainian baba in her nineties.

A voice crackled on the intercom inside the vestibule where I
stood.

"*Tak.*"

"Baba, it's Bernadette."

"Tak."

"I'm here to visit you."

"Who's there? *Ya ne rozumiyu? Yak vas zvaty?*"

"Baba, it's Bernadette."

"Baba?"

"No, it's Bernadette."

"Do I know you, tak?"

"You should. I'm Roman's daughter."

"Bernadette! Why didn't you say, *luba*? Come in. I upstairs." The door buzzed. I silently thanked my mother for providing me with the apartment number. It avoided more intercom confusion.

I took the elevator to the third floor, trying to think of something—anything—for us to talk about. Conversations on mutual points of interest were severely challenged when separated by three generations.

Baba was waiting by her door when I exited the elevator. Her suite was halfway down the hallway. She stood in her patterned apron, fluffy slippers, large-rimmed glasses, and autumn-red babushka, wearing her always-present cockeyed grin. I was tall, and I towered over her under-five-foot frame, which did not speak to the powerful personality she possessed.

"Hello, Baba," I said, reaching down to embrace her.

"*Dobrogo ranku, lubov moya*," she said, her hands giving my triceps a light squeeze. "It's been so long. Your *tato* is saying you going to stop by. I never see you."

I silently cursed my dad.

"I know," I conceded. "So much has been happening. But here I am." She led me into her apartment, gently closing the wooden door. There was a strong smell of garlic.

"Is Auntie Tina around today?" I said, looking around. I wanted to thank her for scrambling to salvage my shopping spree and for finding me a few reasonable fits. I wouldn't be the dancing queen in any of them, but it was a step up from my sweaters.

Baba shook her head, looking up at me. "She out at mall, doing shopping."

"Man shopping," I wanted to say, but I didn't. It wasn't my place to inform Baba of her senior-citizen daughter's man-scanning abilities.

I grinned and sat down at the kitchen table. "She was a great help to me the other day, picking out new clothes now that I'll be dating again."

Baba joined me at the two-person table.

Her face darkened. "Idiot husband ruined your life. The son of bitch."

I smiled despite her profanity. "I can't blame my marriage's failure all on him."

"Tak. Why not? Son of bitch broke 'till death do you part.' Now you to die alone like me." Her eyes were troubled.

I stiffened. "Oh no. I plan to date again. Maybe even one day remarry."

Her eyebrows lifted. "I have perfect boy for you." She tapped her gnarled finger on the wooden table.

I looked at her, not hiding my shock. What crowd was she hanging with that would match someone with me?

"Really. Where did you meet him?"

She braced her back, smiling proudly. "He very, very good boy, luba. Perfect for you. He delivers meals here every week."

I sank in my chair. "Is that so?" I said, forcing myself to sound cheerful. "At least he has a job."

She nodded once, determined. "He very hard worker. You see him carrying meals all day. No complaints from him. A good boy."

"Good to hear." I smiled weakly.

She pressed on. "I like this *cholovik*. I talk to him this week, tell him you interested."

I held up my hand. "Well, let's not rush into anything just yet, Baba. I've only just signed my divorce papers."

She cursed silently. "The good ones get away if you wait. I tell you—someone snatch him fast."

"Has he just become single?" I ventured.

She spat. "No, he single years. We talk."

"So there's a good chance he'll be single for a while yet."

Baba muttered to herself. "He be taken any minute. He hard worker. They go first."

"As you have said." I stifled a moan.

"You not getting younger," she said, leaning over the table to try to pinch my arm. "Babies no come easy, luba."

"I know."

Her eyes clouded. "I don't be around forever," she announced. "I need see babies before I die. I no wait and wait. You have many babies."

"Yeah, well, I prefer to be married and have a daddy I know is the daddy to the children."

She got up from the table, went to the fridge, and pulled off a piece of paper.

"Here card," she said, handing me the paper. It was a business card for meal deliveries.

I glanced at the name. "Willie. Interesting." *What was his mother thinking?*

"He nice boy," she said sharply.

"Sometimes the nice boys are the weird boys, Baba."

"Everybody weird these days. He good boy. You two make me baby."

"I haven't even met him yet. Hell, our fluids might be incompatible."

She cackled. "He not like that son of bitch you married. This boy treat you right, *lubov moya*."

"My ex treated me good, too," I said defensively. "It just didn't work out."

My baba shook her head and shuffled to the fridge, where she began pulling out food.

"That's okay," I said. "I'm not hungry."

Baba told me to be quiet.

Hungry or not, when I sat down at Baba's place, she was going to feed me, so I went along with it.

She placed a casserole of headcheese in front of me, tossed a handful of pierogi into water she had boiling, opened a container of sour cream, and took out a few slices of rye bread and a jar of pickles, and it was time to eat.

"Put meat on your bones," she said, shaking her head disapprovingly. She added, "You looking sick."

I grabbed a slice of rye bread and a pickle. "I've joined a gym. I'm trying to tone up."

"Gym?" She scowled. "What you need gym for? I grew up on farm. Carrying milk. Shoveling manure. Do housework—no gym. Put on muscle? Look like man? Nonsense." She slapped a jiggling slab of headcheese onto my plate.

"The gym is to get into shape."

She scowled. "Problem you kids. Girl look like boy. Boy look like girl. Disgusting." She got up and scooped out the pierogi from the pot. She took one for herself; the remaining eight went on my plate. She tossed a huge gob of sour cream next to them.

"Eat." She smiled. "You need strength. Make baby."

I shoved a large forkful of headcheese into my mouth.

"This is fantastic," I said.

"You learn cook. Learn our heritage—headcheese, pierogi, cabbage rolls, the pickles."

I agreed with her. I knew nothing about cooking our favorites. What kind of Ukrainian wife would I be? The kind of wife who would be buying microwaved hamburgers and poutine.

Baba pointed at me. "We make pierogi at church. You come. Learn." My baba wasn't asking.

I grinned. "I would love to. It's time I learned the secrets of the craft."

She looked pleased. Then she squinted at me. "Easter eggs? You know how? Easter coming up."

I shook my head. I didn't want to admit my only experience had been once in elementary school, when we'd spent an hour dyeing Easter eggs.

She smacked her lips. "Here," she said, standing again. She walked over to the kitchen counter and brought over a tray of supplies, tools, and an egg.

"Is this for making eggs?" I surveyed the tray of bowls with colored liquids, a pen-like thing that looked like a dental applicator for cleaning teeth, wax, and a candle.

She sat down across from me. "I give Roman shit not teaching make Easter egg. Tradition important for you to carry on for us." Baba was right. But I still blamed my ex for influencing me to play video games for the past nine months. I realized I didn't have a valid excuse for the previous fifteen years.

"Easter coming up. I always make eggs."

I was impressed. At her age, she was still motivated to paint Easter eggs.

She lit a candle and began heating the wax, her hands shaking so visibly that I considered moving my chair back a bit to avoid being splashed. I held firm, ready to accept it as my punishment because someone in her nineties had to start teaching me the art of Ukrainian Easter-egg making.

"Luba, these pencil lines—I drawn over egg for design," she pointed out proudly.

She grabbed the dental tool and held it under the candle flame.

"What is that thing?" I asked, pointing.

"The *kistka*."

"The what?"

"Kistka. How we apply wax."

"I get it. You can apply the candle wax with the tip of it."

She glared at me. "Beeswax."

She traced the kistka along her pencil line, leaving behind drying beeswax.

"Now," she said, placing an egg into a steel spoon, "dip egg in first color. I choose blue. Blue happy color for me."

"That's actually red," I said just as she dipped the egg inside the cup.

"Tak? Oh shit. Damn eyes." She adjusted the glasses on her nose. She then pulled the newly dyed egg out. "Small hole in egg to drain."

I saw the hole; it was far from small. I agreed with her. She had covered it with wax.

"Beautiful colors." She smiled. She traced more lines, leaving behind a wobbly line. She dipped the egg again into another bowl of dye.

"Hold egg under heat from candle; melt wax." I watched as she held the egg under the flame, rotating it. A little burned-flesh scent wafted over to me. She took a paper towel and wiped away the remaining wax. Before us was a multicolored Easter egg. It might not have been a work of art, but it was beautiful to me.

"Done." She smiled, pushing her dentures out for a moment with her tongue. She looked at me. "Teach your children, tak. Pass on generations." She stared at me with a heated expression. "I won't be around forever. You learn now. Damn your tato."

CHAPTER 11

The A List

Job hunting had changed with the explosion of the Internet. I enjoyed not having to touch stinky newspaper, read tiny job ads, carefully cut them out with scissors, print off a hard copy of my cover letter and résumé, write out an envelope, lick a stamp, and mail it. Job hunting was not a leisure activity for me. I preferred lounging on my bed and scanning websites full of job ads on my laptop while flipping between my Facebook, Pinterest, TeamBuy, and Twitter accounts. Whenever I found a job that interested me, might match my qualifications, or met my criteria, I simply attached my résumé and hit a button to send it. Today, nothing in my screening process qualified. I was determined to become somebody—a Larissa success story. Employed full-time would be a remarkable achievement. No one in my family tree had amounted to anything considered white collar. Our collars were either stained dark colors or striped. I felt as if the upcoming generations of Androshchucks were stacked hopefully on my shoulders, cheering me to break free of the black mold.

I had no idea what type of job to look for that would make me happy and, more importantly, make my dad happy. We had conflicting views on happiness. I wanted flexibility in a job. Ideally, I would be calling the shots on the hours, preferably five-hour shifts, with an adjustable lunch hour consisting of an hour or more; full medical benefits; paid parking, because I would be a car owner; and mobility within the company for when I became bored. For my dad, happiness was a job that required me to attend five days a week or more, forty hours a week or more, running me ragged for thirty-five years or more. His happiness translated to misery for me.

Admittedly, I was distracted from that morning's job seeking. Earlier, I had been propositioned by my first Internet date reply, and I had accepted.

My date with "rugged, outdoor-type-of-guy" Daryl was arranged for later that week. His reply message to me was to be prepared to spend the day outside. He would pick me up in the early afternoon. Already, he was two up on my ex. He had a driver's license and a vehicle. Even more impressive, he'd planned an activity agenda without asking me. This guy looked promising. He was five years older than I. I figured that age, thirty-five counted for more maturity right off the bat. He listed his job as sales. Another plus, he had an income. The dots were aligning for Daryl; he could become my future husband. His was the only reply I had gotten.

Not wanting to blow this opportunity, I tried on a few of the clothes I had bought with my aunt. On part of the shopping spree, we had acquired what she called "tricks of the trade" for me. I now owned supportive undergarments that sucked in my stomach, smoothed out my thighs, bulged out my ass, and pushed up my breasts. From the outside, I actually looked proportional and borderline sexy. Undressed, I was sure to scare the living shit out of my dates.

I returned to my computer screen and scrolled through the job ads. Hundreds listed fit my C list: restaurants, retail outlets, gas stations, car dealerships, telemarketing firms. All required interacting with hordes of limitless strangers and fake smiles. I was all about keeping it real. Dozens of jobs made my B list: receptionist, hairdresser, wedding planner. All required some level of specialized training, none of which I had. My A list was harder to flesh out among the swath of Cs and Bs—specifically, corporate trainer, human-resources manager, plant manager, research assistant, resource teacher, chemical engineer. These positions met all of my requirements in a job: respect, money, paid time off, and my own office. Unfortunately, there were a number of challenges for any of these positions, namely professional designations and experience. I had neither. However, I remembered once watching a daytime talk show about a woman who got her dream gig and broke the shackles of a man's world simply by applying. She charmed her way inside and rode the corporate ladder to the top desk. That was all the womanly inspiration I required to reach out and be someone.

I submitted applications to my entire A list.

CHAPTER 12

Stubble Equals Trouble

Daryl sent me a text, advising about the need to dress warm and expect to spend the day outside. I enjoyed his ability to plan a date himself, but for me, winter and outside didn't dance together. Bernadette advised me to go along with his plans. She assured me the time for resistance and pushback began after the relationship had been established. Until that time arrived, we shut our mouths and went along with the man's antics, sporting a smile and fake enthusiasm. It sounded devious yet enticing. I had obviously played by the book for too long.

I was relieved that I could wear my winter boots that day, providing me a reprieve from attempting the leopard-print shoes just yet.

Daryl said he'd be at my parents' house at one o'clock. I waited inside by the front door.

My mom tried to be crafty about her curiosity to set eyes on Daryl. She came around with tidbits and updates about the neighborhood I didn't care about.

"Just so you know, the McKenzies are having their dog neutered," she said. "In case you were wondering about the Froebes, they've been down south for the last month."

Later, she added, "I overheard we might be having community mailboxes installed this summer."

My dad was far less stealthy. He simply stood directly in the middle of the living-room window, staring outside. It was his house, and he could stand there if he wanted to.

"I hope he's nice," Mom said, her face pinched with worry.

"I hope so too."

"Make sure he buys you dinner," Dad ordered from the window. "At a sit-down place with a menu in your hand," he added.

"Remember," my mom whispered, "it's okay to say no on the first date."

I planned on saying no for all of my dates.

"I guess," my dad said, annoyed, "I'll be working on your car alone today." He wheeled and stared.

"I hope you can get by for one day without me there handing you tools. This could be the man to sweep me off my feet and out of your downstairs bedroom forever."

He grumbled something I couldn't make out. He then remarked loudly, "Is this him, driving the pickup with a camper and snowmobile on the back?"

I jumped toward the door and stared at the vehicle. I wasn't sure.

Mom, trying to peer around my shoulders, looked frightened.

"I hope to God he doesn't expect to take you out in that thing," she said, clutching her hands.

"I don't think so," I replied weakly, fearing this was Daryl's source of outdoor activity. I glanced down at the snowmobile boots I was wearing.

A horn blared in staccato.

"Atta boy," my dad said. "A pure gentlemen. Too lazy to get his ass out of the truck. I'll bet he'd make you drive if you had your license."

"Please be careful," stressed my mother. The horn went off again.

"Sounds like a hothead," Dad said, trying to stare down Daryl from the window.

"I'll be all right," I assured my parents, not believing my own words.

"Do you want to bring my whistle?" Mom offered as I was stepping out the door.

"Don't pay for his gas!" Dad's voice rang out as I made a quick run toward the truck. The horn went off twice more. I approached the passenger side and opened the door.

"Are you Daryl?" I asked before jumping in with the horn-honking potential psycho killer prowling the neighborhood.

"Yup, hop on in," he said, smiling. "I was revving up your old man with the horn. Each time I hit it, he'd do a little jump in the window."

I climbed into his truck, using the step.

"Well, it worked," I said. "He was wanting you to come inside like a gentleman."

Daryl laughed, putting the truck into drive and hitting the horn one last time. "That's off the table now that I've fired him up."

I looked over at him. "Your profile photo doesn't have the beard." His beard was long and full. The photo of him on the dating site was clean-shaven. The beard gave him a rugged, unkissable look.

"Yeah, I've been growing this bad boy for a while. I like to surprise the honeys with it."

"You've surprised me."

"Wanna touch it?" he asked, glancing my way.

"Not at all."

He laughed some more. "Just joking. I thought I'd ask in case you have a fetish for running your fingers through facial hair."

"For the record, I don't."

He looked down at my boot-covered feet.

"You've dressed accordingly for our day," he said, steering down the street. "We're going sledding."

"What's that?"

"It's done on that thing at the back of my truck. A Two-Up by Ski-Doo. Notice my jacket," he said, nodding to the decal on his arm that said Ski-Doo. "My favorite brand. I've been riding all my life."

I corrected him. "Not all your life, since you'd have been too small to grab the handlebars as a baby."

He looked at me strangely.

"Well," I said, "just to let you know, I've not been sledding"—I used my fingers as air quotation marks around the word *sledding*—"since I was a young girl, and that didn't go very well, so I'm not sure what to expect getting back on again."

"Expect the thrill of a lifetime."

"I thought the same thing before my marriage," I said dryly.

Daryl gunned his engine. "No man can compete with a Rotax four-stroke engine and Rev-X platform while hanging on for your life."

"This is a date and not a sales pitch, right?"

"I'm passionate about my ride," he explained.

"How about your women?" I ventured.

"That too, which is why I have a twin seat."

"So romantic," I breathed.

He scoffed. "This beats a horse-drawn sleigh ride."

"At least on the sleigh ride, I could look you in the eyes when we spoke, not at the back of a helmet."

"Staring at my helmet might be more attractive than staring at this," he said, popping all of his teeth out of his mouth into his hand.

"What the hell?" I said.

He held up a full set of dentures.

"Lost all my Chiclets two years ago when I drove my face into the windshield of the sled."

"My God." I held my hands to my mouth. "All your teeth gone."

He slipped the teeth back in so that he no longer sounded shitfaced drunk when he spoke.

"What the heck happened?" I asked, still trying to absorb what I had just witnessed in Daryl's show-and-tell.

He laughed. "I was following the boys down a path at night. Yeah, hell, we were going a little too fast. But hey, that's what livin' is all about—being on the edge."

"Sounds like you crossed that edge."

"Missed the turn. I couldn't see through the snow fog my buddies kicked up. Slammed into a few trees. Wrote off my sled and my teeth."

"And you still find this fun why?" I shrugged.

"I could have just as easily been hit by a drunk driver while standing at the side of the road."

"Except you weren't. You were driving your snowmobile and hit a tree."

"The worst thing about it, insurance wrote off my machine."

"What about your teeth?"

"Hundred percent replacement coverage for my Chiclets. For my machine, the bastards gave me sixty percent."

I was puzzled. "Weren't you wearing your helmet? I thought that was the law for things like that."

He shook his head. "The strap broke while I was putting it on, and it kept shifting on my head, so I was free-balling it."

"Do you have a helmet for me that works? I don't want to free-ball it. I like my teeth and have no dental coverage."

He nodded toward the rear seating area. "I have all the gear we'll need today."

"Great. I know you said we'd be outside, but I didn't realize we'd be plowing through snow drifts."

He winked. "This will be a date you won't forget."

"Bring me back home with everything I left with, and I'll be impressed."

"We're not doing trails today. We're sticking with open terrain and ditches. It's a good way to kill a few hours."

"And not us," I added.

"I haven't done that yet."

He steered his truck off the main highway, and we entered a snow-covered road that weaved between trees and a frozen lake.

"Say," he said, grinning, glancing my way for a reaction, "how the hell d'you pronounce your last name anyway? I've never seen one like that before."

"Like what?"

He laughed. "Well, you know, like it's misspelled."

"I can assure you it's not."

"You should double-check just to be on the safe side."

"Thanks for your concern, but I can assure you Androshchuk is spelled the way it was meant to be over a hundred years ago."

We reached the edge of the city limits, and Daryl pulled the truck to a stop.

"Showtime," he said, grinning as if he had just been handed a huge tax return. "Grab a pair of mitts from under your seat. I'll get the helmet for you."

I opened my door and jumped down to the ground. There had been nothing on Daryl's profile about owning snowmobiles. I made a mental note that the expression "rugged outdoor guy" likely referred to someone who had multiple recreational vehicles, such as boats, snowmobiles, ATVs, and dirt bikes. I feared that group of guys might turn out to be too adventurous for me. Where was the balance between laid-back musician and hell-bent outdoorsman?

I reached inside and pulled out a pair of massive mitts that reached my elbows. Daryl came around to my side and plopped the helmet over my head.

"How did you know pink is my color?" I said of the helmet.

"When I bought it, I figured it was a universal chick color."

"Your mother taught you well."

"It's all about being sensitive to that female crap," he said, beaming.

"Sounds like you have it down pat."

I surveyed the area, which was a vast nothing. It was devoid of trees, just pure openness covered in snow. I tried to visualize what provoked the pleasure of driving around in this barren plain of nothing. To me, it would be like shopping in a store without any products—boring. One would steer the snowmobile one way, turn it that way, and go another way. At least driving a car was fraught with challenges, such as racing stoplights and running stop signs. Out here, there were no laws to break or crosswalks for old ladies to chance. That apparently wasn't on Daryl's mind as he hopped up on the attached trailer and turned a key that started his Rotex Ski-Doo. The roar and the plume of stinky exhaust made me gag. I took a step away. Conversation time was apparently over.

The trailer tilted backward as Daryl navigated his machine to the frozen turf. In an attempt to showcase his skills and the power of his Rotex four-stroke, he gunned the engine and was gone, leaving me alone in a waft of snow dust. This must have been his way of exuding male courtship.

I watched him make a large arc while I breathed into my helmet, which was beginning to fog up. Maybe he gave all of his dates the helmet to bang their heads in frustration.

Daryl decided to make his return by driving up toward me at a rapid speed and then coming to a stop right where I stood. There was no door for him to open in a gentlemanly gesture, so he simply nodded for me to mount behind him in the second chair. Thus began our intimacy; I bumped it up a notch as I gripped my date from behind.

I jockeyed into position on the raised second seat.

The voice that boomed around both my ears nearly caused me to fall back into the snow.

"Hey, I forgot to warn you," he said. "I've activated the helmet headsets so that we can converse."

"I'd much rather you concentrate on steering. We can converse once we're sitting across from each other in a restaurant, nice and safe."

"You're going to love this."

"How do you know that?"

"Why wouldn't you?"

"Oh," I said, "things like the cold, speed, personal injury, and death. Those are just off the top of my head."

"Listen." His voice came eerily around me while I stared at the back of his helmet. "You can hang on to the straps down by your knees, or you can grip around my waist."

"Which do you suggest?"

"If you grip around my waist, don't squeeze too hard. I have a colostomy bag that's getting kinda full."

"Say what?"

"Yeah. In that sledding mishap, I also lost a section of my lower bowels from the handlebars."

"Are you sure this is safe?" I asked. Then I said, "I enjoy using toilet paper."

His voice boomed in my helmet. "Trust me."

"I really don't know you well enough for that to happen."

In response, he gunned the throttle, and the Ski-Doo leaped forward. I screamed. He laughed. My arms dug around his waist. If he was going to scare the shit out of me, I was going to squeeze it out of him.

We shot across the open field. There was nothing smooth about the ride. It was a paint mixer of jostles and jolts. I was certain I'd bite my tongue off. What chance would remain for someone to desire marrying a tongueless girl? Daryl didn't understand that.

My grip on his waist remained firm. I buried my body against his, unable to see anything ahead of us. I preferred not to see my upcoming death. Even if I'd wanted to look around, I couldn't have. My heavy breathing had completely iced up the inside of my visor. He'd steer the Ski-Doo into dips filled with snow, and we'd roar out the other end in a shower of white spray. His laughter did nothing to spur my own. If my mom could have seen her daughter now, she'd have fainted.

For me, the ride seemed to go on for hours. In fact, when Daryl pulled up next to his truck, he said we'd been gone for forty-five minutes—forty-five minutes of my life I would never get back.

Daryl leaped off the machine, leaving me to disembark on my own. My legs shook from squeezing the seat so hard.

"What'd you think?" he asked, taking the helmet from my hand.

"Besides the fact I couldn't see through this stupid thing," I answered, pointing to the frozen visor, "and we went around in circles, I'm not sure I really see the point. Everything hurts. God knows how much Absorbine rub I'm going to need tonight." I rubbed the ice chunks from my eyebrows. "You actually find this fun?"

"Hell yeah," he boasted. "It's freedom. No boundaries. Go wherever you want to go." His grin was huge. All I could envision was that mouthful of teeth hanging from his lips earlier in the date.

"How about we go get something to eat, Daryl? I'm starving. I need something to settle my stomach and arrange my kidneys back in the right place."

This time, the climb back into his truck was daunting. My arms shook weakly. I flopped onto the front seat.

"You really need to do something with the height," I said. "I feel like I'm climbing up into a school bus without steps."

He started the truck. "This is a dually raised diesel." We started moving. "I need the power for pulling and transporting my camper and snowmobile on the back."

"You do a lot of traveling with it?"

"I live in it."

We turned back onto the highway, heading toward the city.

"I get it. Saves you money on hotels," I said.

He shook his head. "I mean that's my home back there."

"You live in this truck?" I said, stunned. That detail wasn't on his profile. There were key pieces of information to consider in choosing a new spouse—such as "Are you homeless?"

"You can't be living back there," I said, laughing. "Are you kidding me? It's only the size of your flatbed."

He winked. "Everything I need is back there."

"Except space."

"Don't be fooled," Daryl replied. "There is a sit-down kitchen table, a bed, and a microwave."

I looked at him in disbelief. "Why?" I raised my arms in question. "I've heard about affordable housing, but shacking up in the back of your truck seems insane. It's wintertime, man! It's got to be freezing back there."

"Built-in heater," he said cheerfully. "It's surprisingly comfortable. My common law didn't think so."

I laughed out loud. "You were living there with your girlfriend?" My body buckled with giggles.

He grinned. "Seven months. You don't realize how much time you can save commuting to work when you park outside the office the night before. She loved it."

"And what happened?" I looked at him, amazed.

"Someone tried to steal the truck one night. She was in the back, sleeping. The bandits got as far the Manitoba-Ontario border before she awoke, realized the truck was moving, and jumped out the back when the truck stopped for gas in Richot."

My eyes lit up. "That's crazy! Where were you when this happened?"

He shrugged. "I had gone around the corner to buy a two-liter of Pepsi at the store. When I came back, she was gone. I figured she'd needed something and drove off to get it. So I waited for a couple of hours. By then, it was around one in the morning."

"And you still think it's safe?"

"Hey, I've been living in this truck for three years. Shit's going to happen no matter where you live."

I was flabbergasted.

"What're those garbage bags behind us in the backseat?" I asked. "Your food?"

"My dirty laundry. That reminds me. I need to stop by the cleaners tonight to get it done. I'm down to my last pair of socks and underwear."

I shook my head, grinning a sick grin.

"Listen," he said, pulling into the parking lot of McDonald's. "Dinner's on me for putting up with an afternoon of sledding." He steered into the drive-through and stopped at the meal board. "Anything you want. It's on me. Even the Happy Meal."

I looked at his face. "Are you serious?"

"Absolutely. Fast food is the only meal I eat every day."

"You keep surprising me," I said, crossing my arms and looking past his body to the menu board.

"I only eat what's deep fried or between a bun."

Another missing profile statement. I began to question what the screening criteria were for this dating service.

I looked at my options. "Okay. I'll have a Big Mac and fries then."

He nodded. "Good choice."

He crept up to the speaker to order.

"Hello. Welcome to McDonald's. What can I get for you today?"

"Two Big Macs. Two fries."

"What size fries?" the female voice asked.

"Large for me," he said. He looked my way.

"Small."

"Small fries for the second order."

"Drinks?" asked the voice.

Daryl looked at the speaker.

"Make it a large Coke." He turned my way. "We can split it."

"Get two straws then," I replied, thinking he was joking.

We pulled up to the window to pay. He took out his wallet.

"Eighteen dollars and twenty cents," the employee said. Daryl handed her his debit card.

"Good thing it's payday today."

He punched in his numbers and handed back the debit machine.

"Next window, please," said the employee at the window.

We pulled up just as the bag was being handed to him. I was forever amazed at how food could be pulled out of storage, cooked, put together, packaged, and placed in a bag after someone ordered it and moved his or her vehicle twenty feet. I assumed anything was possible, now knowing that people could reside in the back of their pickup trucks for three years.

Daryl handed me the bag and steered his truck back into traffic.

"Aren't we going to pull over and have a romantic dinner in the McDonald's parking lot?" I asked. "I enjoy watching the rats near the waste container while I eat."

He laughed. "We're eating on the run. I need to drop you off. I still have a few more deliveries to make today." He took out his meal and handed me mine.

I looked at him, confused. "For what?"

"I deliver meat," he said, taking a large bite out of his Big Mac. White sauce spread across his lips.

"To who?" I asked, opening the bag, removing my burger and fries, and putting them on my lap. I tore open a packet of salt and sprinkled it over my fries.

"I work for a company that sells frozen meats to homeowners. I'm the guy who drives around dropping the stuff off. I took a break for us to go sledding."

"Won't the buyers be waiting for their deliveries?"

He shrugged, taking a huge bite out of the burger. Juice oozed over his beard. He left it.

"A couple of hours won't kill them. Besides, I have it in the back of my trailer."

I laughed. "We've been carting around your customers' meat all afternoon?"

He waved me off. "I do that all the time. No one complains."

I pushed a batch of fries into my mouth with my finger. "Is that your full-time job?" I asked.

He nodded. "Been doing it five years. I like it. I'm not shackled behind a desk, you know what I mean?" He shoved a finger load of limp fries into his mouth.

I agreed. "I'm basically a freelance web designer. I make my own hours. I'm also looking for something else to help pay the bills." I slipped two french fries into my mouth.

"I never understood that computer crap. Too much frustration, punching things on those little keyboards."

"You get used to it." I took a bite from my hamburger.

He motioned to the drink in the cup holder. "It's for both of us."

"I'll pass. Been trying to cut down on my sugar," I lied, not wanting to taste Daryl's spit. It was difficult enough watching the Mac sauce hardening into his beard.

"Say, listen," he said as the truck pulled up to a stop in front of my parents' house. "Let's do this again. I really didn't get a chance to know you," he said, licking the remnants of the burger from his fingers.

I looked away. "Leave it with me," I said, opening the door and taking the plunge to the ground, missing the step.

I watched him pull away and tried to avoid breathing in the diesel fumes. As I made my way to the front door, I thought about the need to examine the profiles of prospects on the website more closely. The need to read between the lines of bullshit was apparent. There was obviously a code book out there that explained all of the shit that could pop up once a person was being held hostage on a date. I knew one thing for sure: I was through being blindsided by a so-called romance taking place on the back of a snowmobile with a man who shit inside a plastic bag and fine-dined me in a fast-food drive-through, not to mention the fact that he had no teeth.

CHAPTER 13

Shark Tank

Auntie Tina prowls the mall every weekend. She is eyeballing canes, walkers, crutches, and wet coughs. She has her hair professionally styled every Friday and her nails every second week. She tans in a salon weekly. She takes her work seriously. Her sales pitch is precise, direct, compassionate, heartfelt, and sexy. She is a mature woman looking for a mature gentleman who wants a mature relationship. Auntie Tina bagged three previously widowed men (one of them divorced five times) on her Saturday-morning stakeouts with great success.

The trouble is that relationships with people in their eighties become day by day. I'm not talking about a blowout fight, a brawl, boredom, or another man or woman; I mean a "See ya—I've died" relationship ender.

She is three for three. Her longest just about beat mine at eight months. He died in the shower as she was getting soaped up, we're told. The other just died in his sleep. The third died during the third hour of *Titanic*. The coroner waited until the ship sank before hiking the body away.

Now Auntie Tina stalks the Starbucks in Safeway, going for a healthier male who can afford high-priced groceries and higher-priced gourmet coffee. As it turns out, she struck a bold-flavored man this time. He is seventy-nine, Ukrainian, and a long-retired city worker; has been divorced once; has two grown daughters; and is now living in the country. He stopped at Starbucks to get a free biscuit.

Auntie Tina caught him at the right time. She offered a free coffee at McDonald's. He accepted.

*****

I jumped out of the Prius cab, followed by Amy, Bernadette, and Mike. In the darkness, we staggered over a snowbank in our shoes, hanging on to each other for support and balance.

Last Call Bar and Grill was set back off the street, a windowless one-story brick building with one steel door in front. It was a hotspot for Beausejour headbangers on weekends. Tonight, behind the steel door, my ex's band was to perform their best cover tunes to the last-call patrons. My posse would be among the rabid crowd to support his group.

I nodded at Amy and the eye-grabbing miniskirt she was wearing. Her legs were built to be exposed. She owned it.

"Any trouble getting a babysitter for tonight?"

She grinned. "My girl came through again. I let her have her boyfriend over, so she never says no."

I smirked. "Do you think she might be too preoccupied with him to babysit?"

She shrugged. "Hey, with my hubby driving around the country for his work, leaving me alone to parent, I need a break too."

I laughed. "The things that go on when the man is away, huh?" She high-fived me.

"So are we ex-groupies watching your ex perform now that you're divorced?" asked Amy, struggling to navigate toward the door in her high heels.

"Hanging around with my ex postmarriage makes us pathetic," I said, grinning, clutching Amy's arm for support.

"Any reason for a night out works for me," said Bernadette, following me.

"I think this is weird," said Mike, walking up to hold the steel door open. "Instead of cheering on your ex, shouldn't you be throwing things at him?"

"We divorced on good terms," I said. "Besides, he did all the legwork to arrange a good divorce lawyer. The least I can do for him is support his band."

"The last time we saw him perform, it was all psychedelic sixties crap," complained Amy.

"Hey," Mike said with a smile, "I respect any group that can play the entire seventeen minutes of 'In-A-Gadda-Da-Vida' and then make an extended version with another twenty minutes of their own jam. Pure brilliance."

"I finished three martinis before your ex finished his drum solo during that song," said Bernadette, looking at me wistfully.

"You know musicians—they play what they like, not always what the crowd wants to hear," I replied as the door closed behind us.

A large man with no hair and a black T-shirt stood by a table, collecting the five-dollar entrance fee. Mike handed over a twenty-dollar bill.

"On me," he said to us.

I was impressed. "You just spent more than my date did the other day."

"Where'd you find the guy?" Mike asked, frowning at me.

"The Internet."

He looked disappointed. "I told you I know a stand-up guy who works with me. Charlie won't let you down."

The bouncer stamped our wrists with a red ink dot. The Cult blasted "She Sells Sanctuary" from inside the bar's dance area, the same area where my ex would be performing.

We checked our coats with the attendant behind a counter.

"You're looking hot, girl." Amy complimented my new wardrobe from my aunt.

Bernadette agreed. "I never in my life thought I'd see you wearing a dress to a nonfuneral event."

"You're going to fire up your ex's ole lust," warned Mike. "Did he ever see your legs in a dress, not shrouded in sweatpants?"

"Hell no," I replied, laughing.

"This you don't need to be displaying." Bernadette grabbed the sales tag dangling from between my shoulder blades and snapped it off. "Good price!" She winked.

"Don't you spot-check yourself before leaving the house for tags, tears, and stains?" said Amy, now scanning my body for wayward items.

"I haven't bought anything new to wear in years."

Amy nodded. "No problem with that, Lars—just don't let the world know."

"How're the new shoes?" Bernadette nodded, pointing at the leopard prints.

"I keep my eyes focused on an object ahead," I said, laughing, "and they hurt like hell."

We started walking down the hallway toward the roar of music. I felt a twinge of excitement burning in my gut.

Amy came up from behind, putting her hand on my shoulder.

"Maybe he'll sing you a love song. Serenade you to come back to him."

"I sense a Kiss tune coming up," said Bernadette, smirking.

"Larissa, I hear you calling, and I can't come home right now. Me and the boys are playing," mimicked Mike.

"You guys are cruel to a newly divorced woman," I said, smiling. "I'm hunting for fresh meat now."

"First round of beer is on me," said Mike as we entered the main area.

"Where'd you find this prince?" I asked, glancing over at Bernadette. "I need one like him. He'd take me to a restaurant where I can hold the menu in my hand."

"Yeah, big spender," Bernadette said to him, "did you get a raise you aren't telling me about?"

"It's two-for-one tonight, so don't get so excited," he confessed.

"Where's the crowd?" asked Amy in the nearly empty room. "Why's it always dead whenever your ex plays with his band?" A few staff members were walking around. Three people leaned against one table.

"It's Thursday night, right?" I asked. We stopped in a circle. I sensed our common feeling of discomfort.

"Sure is," Bernadette replied. "You said be here at nine. It's nine."

"What the hell? Another empty bar for him to perform in," I said, nodding. "Apparently, some things never change."

"That's his drum kit up there," said Mike, pointing to the main stage. "The bass drum skin reads 'HeeBeeGeeBees.'"

"He's supposed to start at nine thirty," I said, feeling awkward that once again, we would be the only ones in the bar when he performed.

"I'm going for our beers," said Mike, stalking off toward the empty bar. I looked around the room, which would easily have held three hundred people.

"Hey," I heard a familiar voice call out. My ex walked across the room toward us, smiling and holding a pair of drumsticks. His gut bounced under his black T-shirt, and his baseball cap covered most of his fluffy hair. I recognized the jeans he wore by the torn and flapping cargo pocket—they had been given to him by his grandmother six years earlier.

"Is this the wrong day?" I said. "There's no one here. I see from the lack of bar crowds that nothing has changed for your band."

"Yup. Right day." He looked around, smiling for no apparent reason. "This is pretty typical for this place. Most of the regulars show up after the show."

"After?"

He tapped his sticks together. "This is a hard-core metal bar. We're doing Gordon Lightfoot cover tracks with a seventies fusion of acid rock." His gaze moved across my body. "You're looking nice."

I was taken aback. He hadn't complimented how I looked the entire nine months we were married.

"Thanks," I replied. "The girls and my aunt took me out to spruce up my wardrobe for my dates."

He stopped tapping his sticks. "You're dating?" He looked hurt. The wispy hairs above his lip twitched.

"Sure. Don't want that saddle to get cold. In fact, I was on a pretty wild one the other day. I went sledding. You know, one of those big four-stroke Rotex types. A two-up," I explained confidently. "Boy, did we ever put on the miles."

"You did something outdoors? In the winter?" he said. He cocked his head to the side, searching my face and waiting for the punch line.

"Snowmobile mitts and helmet, too. The whole shebang. Followed by a romantic dinner." I heard Amy snicker behind us. "How's your dating been?" I asked, trying to deflect his questions before she ratted me out.

He twirled his sticks. "I haven't thought about it. All my shit hasn't been unpacked. The boxes are stacked in my parents' shed."

He nodded at my feet. "Fancy shoes," he commented. "No socks. You always wear socks."

I took an awkward swirl. "Tossed away the wool socks. Even shave my legs every day." I hiked up my dress a bit to flex a beefy calf.

"Humph," I heard my ex exhale.

"Hey, buddy," Mike said to my ex as he walked up carrying our beers. "Can I buy you a round? Don't want you to feel left out."

He grinned. "After the show, Mikey. Gotta keep my focus on the gig."

"So you going to blow the roof off this place tonight or what?" asked Mike. He took a long pull on his beer bottle.

"Got a whole new set we're rolling out tonight. A tribute to Gordon Lightfoot," my ex boasted, glancing back at my shoes before heading off toward the stage. I felt Bernadette poke me in the back.

"Let's grab a table," I suggested, pointing to one off to the side of the band. Mike motioned to the waitress to bring a round of shooters.

It was going to be one of those nights.

I was feeling good about myself. Auntie Tina was right. If you dressed like you meant it, people around would take you seriously. That night, I was feeling all woman.

We lifted ourselves onto barstools around the high-top wooden table. Mike and Bernadette sat across from Amy and me. I traced a finger through the condensation on the outside of my beer mug.

"I think your ex was displaying a wee bit of jealousy," said a grinning Amy. "There's actually a woman under the track suit and work boots."

"Poor bastard is probably thinking he got screwed," Mike said, laughing over the top of his beer mug.

I shook my head and took a long swig of beer. "There was never any reason to get dressed up. You get lazy after a while."

"You were lazy before you had a chance to get lazy," said Bernadette with a laugh. "Going out to the bars with you was like taking along someone lost in the bush for a month who I'd just found."

"Now it's different," I said. "Losing my marriage was a wake-up call. I refuse to be my aunt Tina at her age—single and living with my parents. I need to be proactive."

"Your aunt is hilarious and cool," replied Bernadette.

"Don't be fooled by her charm," I said. "You're seeing pure desperation to not die alone."

Our shooters arrived, and we each grabbed one. We held them above our heads.

"On that note," said Mike, "let's drink to tormenting our exes."

"You don't have an ex," reminded Bernadette, "and it had better stay that way, buster." She downed her shooter with the rest of us.

Mike reached over and squeezed her in a hug. "You're mine forever, sweet chili."

"You'd better put a ring on it," she said, flipping up her hand and wiggling her fingers, "before I'm swept away by Mr. Five Karats."

"You're an expensive piece of ass," said Amy, grinning.

"I'll say," I remarked. "I gave mine away for a quarter karat—I'm still convinced it was a cubic zirconia."

"You girls are all about the hardware," said Mike, signaling for another round of shooters. "What about relationships for love?" We all looked at him and then at each other. We burst out laughing.

"Hardware, my love," said Bernadette. "Hardware."

I pointed at him. "How much longer are you going to torture this fine gal?"

"Ten years," said Amy. "Murderers do less time."

"I don't see her running off because of it. She must be enjoying the relationship without an outlandishly expensive ring on her finger," said Mike. Our shooters arrived, and he distributed them among the group.

"But, honey," said Bernadette, hugging him around the waist, "see these beautifully manicured nails? Think how a beautiful, glittering diamond would complement them."

"Shut up and drink, girls," said Mike, ducking the questions.

I admired his backbone for sticking to what he believed in—or didn't believe in, holding off on putting a ring on his girl's finger in this case. On the other hand, he was damn lucky she hadn't bolted by this point.

We held up our glasses once again just as the lights dimmed, and feedback echoed in the room.

"Showtime," announced Mike. We all knocked back out shooters. I was already feeling lightheaded and giddy.

"Good thing we're here, or else your ex would be playing to the staff," commented Amy, noting the addition of one other group of two.

With a drumroll and an explosion of bass and electric guitars, the band kicked in. The lead singer belted out an acid-rock version of

"If You Could Read My Mind." My ex played as he always did—as if he were having a seizure and being electrocuted at the same time. His rack of drums kept his head and shoulders visible, along with his flailing arms. Actually, the band didn't sound bad. A round of beers arrived, and I took one from the waitress.

The set went for eight songs. One thing was certain: my ex put a new spin on Lightfoot's crooning.

The lights came back on for an announcement of a drawing. The winner was the individual with an entrance stamp of the letter *A*. Amy let out a drunken howl. She wobbled up to the bar to collect her prize. I was beginning to wonder how I was going to navigate my way out of the bar, being three sheets to the wind and in heels.

Amy returned, flopping against the table and holding an envelope in her hand.

"What'd you win?" slurred Bernadette. Mike's endless rounds had taken a toll on us.

She fought to make her fine motor skills work, opened the envelope, and extracted the two pieces of paper. She held them close to her eyes.

"Two free passes for one session of naked yoga," her drunken voice said.

We squealed.

"My muff would shut that program down," I breathed.

"Then let's go, girl," she said, leaning toward me, her eyes rolling in her head.

"What do you mean—go do the class?" I tried to focus on her two heads.

"Yessum. Let's see if we can make the instructor gag with your seventies muff."

"I told you to shear that thing down," said Bernadette, beginning to laugh hysterically.

"I may need to be drunk to do it," I said.

"Then let's go right now," she said, grinning wildly.

"One word for that," said Mike, pointing at the passes in Amy's hand. "Gross."

"Why not?" challenged Bernadette. "Is seeing strippers any different?"

Amy grinned. "She got you there, smart boy."

He shook his head. "Strippers are professionals. That's their job. So they make sure they're clean and cut," he said, for some reason looking my way with his last remark.

"I'm just saying," he continued, "for a lot of people, keeping things under wraps is far better for everyone."

"I'm in," I said to Amy. "Me and my muff."

She cheered. "Downward dog, baby!" We drunkenly hugged.

"I feel like a hot dog," I said, suddenly pushing my barstool back. My body moved, but my feet were wedged onto the stool's crossrails by the high heels.

I fell backward to the floor.

Mike stared down at me sprawled out on the floor. He laughed. "Nothing beats low-end meat after a night of drinking at the bar. Sop up all that beer and shooters." He pointed down at me. "Larissa, I've paid for your drinks, but sure as hell, I ain't carrying you if you can't walk in those stripper shoes."

"Shut up, and help me up," I cried out, raising my hands for Bernadette and Mike to lift me to my feet. Being drunk mercifully stifled the embarrassment I should have felt.

Amy grinned. "Maybe practice a bit more at home before strapping those bitches on your feet. They aren't your slippers."

"Stupid chairs," I said, trying to take a swift kick at one and missing. I wobbled.

"Should we say good-bye to your ex?" asked Bernadette, grabbing my arm to steady me.

I shrugged. "I don't know where he went. But I'm starving."

We got our coats and left the building. Outside in front, a hot-dog cart was set up and selling to arriving patrons.

"Doesn't matter how shit-ass cold it is, the dogs must go on," said Mike with a laugh as we staggered up to the vendor.

A line was forming at the door to enter Last Call.

"Your ex was right—the place is filling up now for the heavy metal," pointed out Amy, shivering. Her short jacket and matching-length skirt were inadequate for the weather.

"He always was a guy to buck the trends."

Mike nodded. "Evidenced by your nine-month marriage."

"Don't forget the day and a morning," I added.

"Four dogs with the works," Mike said to the vendor. The smell of the smoldering onions made my mouth water. I was sure my stomach would be saying something different when the grease hit the beer.

"How're your feet?" Bernadette gestured downward before wrapping her arms around herself and shivering.

"Killing me," I said, laughing. "Good thing I'm half in the bag, or else I'd be crying."

"I should have told you to always break new shoes in at home a little bit at a time. It's foot suicide to wear them for a night right out of the box."

I winced. "My size ten feet have swollen to twelves for sure."

Bernadette was about to reply, when Mike handed us our hot dogs. My ex came walking out the front door.

"Hey," Mike said to him as he walked up to our group. "I was planning on buying you a round after the set. Where the hell did you go?" He took a chomp on his hot dog, his breath coming out his nose.

"Forget about it," he replied, turning toward me. "So what'd you think of the set?"

I sloppily wiped a smear of mustard along my cheek with the back of my hand.

"It was the first time I never cried listening to the Edmund Fitzgerald song. I like the heaviness you brought to it, especially that double bass drum during the amped-up bass guitar solo." I belched.

Amy laughed. "That's the kind of thing you want to hold off doing on your dates, honey. You can only get away with that when you're married."

My ex looked at me quickly. "Are you going on more dates?"

I took another bite of my hot dog, replying with my mouth full. "I hope so. If someone wants to go out with me. I'm a member of this dating website. A lot of the guys are losers."

Amy pointed at my face. "Another no-no. Mouth closed when chewing, and no talking and chewing at the same time. So many bad habits from being a married woman."

Mike scoffed. "Ah, Bernadette does that all the time. Even spits out her mouthful of toothpaste in the kitchen sink. And we're not even married."

"Close enough," Bernadette remarked. "Besides, that's not nearly as bad as that spit cup you keep next to the bed."

"Hey, I have to clear my sinuses in the middle of the night." He looked wounded.

"Yeah, except you have six months of sinus juice in it."

Amy gagged. "Do you two want me barfing up this hot dog after listening to your stories of bodily fluids?"

My ex stared at me. "Well, if they're losers, then just delete your profile from that website."

"I mean," I said after swallowing the hot-dog remnants first this time, "some are pretty good."

"They can't be worse than Sebastian and his mom," said Bernadette.

My ex looked at me quickly. "The guy down the street? You dated him, too?"

"I did. But it's not going anywhere."

His eyes narrowed. "New clothes. New boyfriends."

I shrugged. "What's a girl to do? Times have changed. Us gals can take the initiative and go after what we want. We don't need to be wallflowers. I'm shaking free this Ukrainian curse, baby! Look out—because you'll all be reading about Larissa one day on Yahoo news. I'm no longer going to be the neighborhood gossip."

"I see," he said.

"And tomorrow Lars and I are going for a session of hot naked yoga," said Amy, laughing and banging her shoulder into mine. "She's going to show the instructor her man muff." She roared harder.

His eyes lifted. "Public exposure, too?" He tweaked his beard with one hand.

"Hey, Amy won these tickets from your place here tonight. There're free. Ukrainians don't let freebies go to waste. I know my dad would use them before seeing them go into the trash."

"Don't need that visual," said Bernadette, gagging.

"Are you sure I can't get you a hot dog?" asked Mike, taking his final bite. "They're freaking good after a few beers, my man."

My ex shook his head. "Nah, I've got to go back inside and start packing up my gear." He waved and moved toward the club doors. His shoulders hung low.

A couple of taxis came to a stop in front of the club, looking for patrons in need of a ride. We needed one.

"Let's get going," stated Amy. "I need to get home before I start puking all this through my nose. Everything is spinning. I feel brutal."

We opened the doors to a cab.

I laughed. "I'm undecided which will be safer for me: you puking on me now or tomorrow during our naked yoga."

CHAPTER 14

Romance: Gobble, Gobble

April 8, 3:10 a.m.

How I got engaged—well, you know what? It was so romantic.

My ex has romance in his genes like Man o' War was bred to run. Knowing the vast bloodline in my future hubby-to-be, I was enthralled, fantasizing about what his approach to woo me would be. I was not let down. His baba and gigi were still farmers, and once a month, we trekked up north, a three-hour drive, to visit. They raised turkeys and had a barn with three hundred gobbling birds. Twice a year, our visit would coincide with insemination. I got to chase turkeys into a corral. My ex and Gigi would grab a bird, flip it upside down, and insert a steel hose into it. The bird would stiffen with the intrusion, squawk, flutter its eyelids, and strut off when released. Much to my chagrin, I was promoted to bird holder one blustery weekend.

How could I say no to an eighty-eight-year-old Ukrainian with a heavy, husky accent?

The bird was strong, feisty, and full of fury. For the second bird, I dug in my heels and leveraged my 160-pound body. The third bird was surprisingly passive. I held it firmly and steadily for the insemination tube. The boys just stood still—for what? "Come on—do her. Do her now," they said. The chickypoo didn't squawk, squeal, or move a feather. I was about to let the forty-pound bitch drop, when I saw the bling. The ring was around its neck. *Hello.* My soon-to-be ex was down on his knee in turkey shit, with Gigi grinning, nodding, and spraying insemination into the air like confetti. In Gigi's other hand was a metal jug of his home-brewed smodka, ready for celebratory shots.

This was romance.

I replied without hesitation, "I do."

*****

Flared Star Yoga Studio was in the basement of the city library. The instructor rented a small, windowless room. The smell of musty books filled the air.

I squeezed my eyes, still feeling the banging behind them from the hangover.

"The only reason I'm doing this is because I'm either still drunk or too hungover to know any better," I said, looking and feeling like a beaten dog. It was two o'clock, and Amy didn't look much better. In fact, I could smell vomit on her.

She clutched a half-empty water bottle in her hand. "I really didn't care if we did this or not. I'm here more out of curiosity about what kind of people actually do this naked."

"And those people could be doing the same thing to us," I said.

She sighed, lifting her arm and smelling underneath it. "I suppose I should have showered. But the thought of water hitting the tub floor made my head hurt, so I didn't."

"I can't tell you how good it is to be wearing my winter boots again," I said as we made our way down the narrow cement staircase. "My feet are torn up with blisters from those shoes last night."

Amy made a gargling sound. "My mouth tastes like shit." She moaned. "I just hope we're not the only two people here for this," she said. "I'm struggling to keep my eyes open."

"Are my eyes as red as yours?" I said, looking her way. She stared at me and nodded.

"I was hoping it was the lighting."

We stopped at a steel-gray door. A piece of computer-printed paper on the solid door indicated the yoga studio was inside. We pushed the door open and entered.

Amy whispered next to my ear, "This is going to get up close and personal." She surveyed the twelve mats pushed together between the walls.

"Is it supposed to be so warm in here?" I said, feeling sweat beading on my forehead.

"A tropical blend of heat and steaming flesh," Amy mumbled.

Of the twelve mats, only two were empty.

"We'd better claim those while we can," I said, not liking that they were in the middle.

Amy exhaled. "I think those would be the same as the front-row seats no one wants to use at movie theaters."

"I'm going to have my nose stuck in the ass of the person in front of me," I whispered, horrified.

"What about the poor bastards behind us?" Amy said.

A man, noticing our growing distress, got up from a center front mat and walked over to us. He was tall, wore his long hair in a ponytail, and was thinly muscled. A sheer piece of fabric was wrapped around his waist. It didn't hide any of his assets.

He held out his hand. "Welcome to my yoga class. I'm Devon. First time here?" His blue eyes were warm.

Amy held up our passes. "Won these last night."

He smiled widely. "A fantastic way to experience this type of yoga."

"You mean naked," said Amy.

"Self-exploration," he said.

"You mean the person behind me exploring my ass."

He grimaced. "The experience is for deepening your own sense of love."

"I'll be showing my love with downward dog, my friend," Amy quipped.

"You'll get past the lack of clothing once we tap into your psychospiritual soul." His hands clasped together; the blue of his eyes sparkled.

"As long as that's all that's being tapped around here," Amy said skeptically. "I don't want no funny business—you hear me? And no cameras. My husband thinks this is an aboveboard, regular yoga class. If he knew his wife's ass was going up in the air on display, I'd be in the shit book."

I held up my hand with a question before he could address any more of Amy's concerns.

"Because we'll be undressed, do I need to be groomed? I haven't been attending downstairs in months, so things have grown in— you know what I mean?" I said, lowering my voice. "Is a certain grooming standard required?"

His eyes fluttered. "Again, we are focused on what is happening for us on the inside. Our physical bodies are present in whatever form they arrive here."

Amy pointed at him. "I'm holding you to that."

"All participants are respectful of space. Part of the reason for close proximity is to help us remove the feelings of discomfort and awkwardness we learn from wearing clothing."

"Well, just to let you know, we're not lesbians," stated Amy defiantly.

"I'm divorced from a man," I added. "She's married with children."

"We accept all within our studio," Devon remarked.

"I don't want to be seen as fresh meat—hear me?" Amy said, nodding and pointing her finger at the instructor. "This had better not be a pickup joint for your sexual pleasures."

"Trust me," Devon said, clasping his hands. "This will be a spiritual awakening for you both."

"I'll be happy for it to take away my hangover," I replied, feeling dehydrated. My mouth was dry.

He pointed to a door that led to a changing room and said that inside the room were white robes to wear initially.

We entered the tiny changing room and saw gym bags from the current participants. There were no lockers, just a single wooden bench seat. *How many naked asses have sat on that piece of oak?* I wondered.

"I'm glad to get this parka off," I said, sweating from the heat.

"He's a little weird," replied Amy, slipping off her boots. I noticed she was wearing mismatched socks.

I rubbed an eye with my hand. "This whole thing seems a little weird. It made sense last night when we were shitfaced."

Amy laughed. "Everything made sense last night, even your ex's cover version of Gordon Lightfoot. Now even that spooks me."

"Well, we're here now. Can you not look at me while I get naked?" I said to Amy when I was about to remove my sweatpants.

She stared at me. "You do realize what we're about to do for the next hour, right?"

"I know," I said, "but at least I will be in a spiritual place. Right now, I'll simply feel naked."

Amy laughed. "Wait until I get to show off my stretch marks. That'll be a wake-up call for any guy who hasn't seen the real deal of a mother."

I snickered. "Instant fantasy killer. At least you have a legitimate reason for your stretch marks. How do I explain mine on every surface of my flesh?"

"Turning thirty. Simple as that."

I slipped on the robe. "I wish my body would hurry up and get in shape from our workouts. I'm not seeing results versus the energy output."

Amy chuckled. "My husband is certainly seeing energy versus results, girlfriend."

I laughed, impressed. "Glad to know that. Thank you."

"You're sounding like you're losing your motivation. Maybe my exploits will inspire you."

"Yeah, well, thanks. Actually, it highlights more of what I've lost from my life and what I'm still missing."

Amy tied her robe. "You're doing all the right things. Your divorce was a minor setback in your life."

"When do I start moving forward?" I tied back my hair. "I no longer have a husband. I really don't have a job. For sure I have no income. I'm living with my parents. And in moments, I'm about to get naked with a group of strangers with the very real possibility it will be broadcast on YouTube."

"Then show the world your best side," said Amy, laughing and pushing me toward the door.

We reentered the silent room. No one spoke. Everyone was on his or her knees, staring at his or her mat. The instructor signaled us to take the mats in the middle.

While I was trying to decide between the two mats remaining, a thought occurred to me: *Who will be in front of me?* One was a female. The other was an older guy. I wanted the chick. Amy must have come to the same conclusion. We jockeyed toward the mat behind her. She was nimbler, and my swollen feet betrayed me. With a slight shove from her hip, I was propelled to the mat behind the old dude. I glared at Amy, who was grinning wildly.

She mouthed the word *Enjoy.*

I sneered back at her.

Devon instructed us all to move to our knees, place our foreheads on the mats, and breathe deeply. I pressed myself forward, my nose inhaling whatever had last been smeared on the mat. My stomach hitched. Beer rose up the back of my throat. I coughed.

We were instructed to lean back so that our heads touched the mats behind our feet. I had not been gifted with womanly flexibility; my thigh muscles burned, threatening to rip from my hips. When we were instructed to move back to a seated position, I realized my robe had moved up from my thighs, offering the old man an upside-down front view of my sanctuary. When we moved back to a kneeling position, I scanned Amy's pinched face.

"I'm gonna hurl if I have to lean back like that again," she whispered desperately.

"Everyone," the steady voice of Devon directed, "close your eyes and lean forward—deep breaths. Visualize your place of tranquility. Allow your robe to fall from your body. Focus on the peacefulness in your personal place of tranquility. We become one with our origins of birth. As we are born naked to this physical world, our minds remain in our spiritual world."

My mind was racing. This was the real deal now. The let's-do-this-for-shits-and-giggles attitude didn't seem funny now that I was sober. I was naked in a roomful of strangers with an old man in front of me and my naked friend beside me, whom I'd watched birth her last child. I dared not look behind and into the eyes of the person riding up my ass. We remained strangers.

"Tabletop," Devon called out. We followed his lead, lifting our torsos with our legs and arms. My thighs and shoulders burned.

"Cat," he said, giving the next direction. I rolled my back into a hump as he said, "Deep breath. Deep breath."

Next, he said, "Cow."

I moved to my hands and knees, arching my back. So did the old man ahead of me. I broke spiritual code and looked. Two saggy balls hung low. I moaned. My face flushed with shame at the horror I was providing the person behind me. My gynecologist had a more-impeded view.

"Downward dog," he said, and we moved into a standing triangle. It was all out there now. I kept my head down. The image ahead of me was burned into my mind for a lifetime.

"Twist," Devon said. I looked to my left.

Amy was facing me, laughing. "Worth the price of admission, hey?"

Before I could reply, Devon said, "Forward fold," and we repositioned. Saggy Balls was pinching his goods out between his compressed legs. My ex had performed this look for me one night shortly after we were married, and I'd found it funny. I wasn't laughing now.

"Modified crescent lunge," Devon said, giving the final command, followed by a chant. I grabbed my robe and put it back on. I nodded to Amy, signaling an exit to the changing room.

"Did you see what I had in front of me?" I whispered to Amy as we began to dress.

"I couldn't help but look," she said, giggling. "I never knew ball hair turns gray."

My stomach rolled.

"Next time we're at the bar and I win anything," she said, "buy me a shooter and tell me to forget about it, okay?"

I slipped my boots on. "Deal."

I zipped up my jacket and faced Amy while she pulled on her toque. "Do me a favor—let's forget this spiritual awakening ever happened."

CHAPTER 15

Straight Talk

Today brought two changes in my life. From the wet smell, there was no denying that spring had overtaken winter. The second change? I was seated in the reception area of a chiropractic office, awaiting my scheduled appointment for a job interview. I was about to become a professional. My dad could finally begin to brag to his friends that his daughter not only earned an income but also had a direct-deposit-type-job that didn't require a uniform or an embroidered name tag.

The season of change was upon me.

My dad was ecstatic. The job interview signified hope that I was soon to become employed. This, in turn, meant income and rent money paid to him.

I tried to dampen his enthusiasm by reminding him that this was my first interview for a semiprofessional class-B job. In the past, these types of job interviews had simply amounted to showing up. The interviewer, usually the boss or a severely underpaid assistant manager, would be amazed and delighted if one out of ten applicants arrived, and he or she would hire the person on the spot out of desperation. I couldn't remember being asked a single question other than the spelling of my name and size of a uniform.

That was my style of job acquirement.

That day, all bets were off. Similar to the quickly melting snow outside, my soul was about to be exposed and dissected.

My advanced preparation, which meant a few minutes spent Googling job-interview questions, was quickly derailed when ads for hair coloring appeared, and off I went on a tangent. Ten minutes later, I ordered a Revlon lipstick package; interview questions were ignored. I'd wing it.

I looked around the office. It was decorated with pastel wall paint, dozens of color photographs of smiling kids treated successfully by the doctor, an overhead flat-screen TV promoting the health benefits of chiropractic, and a sign warning that missed appointments would be charged to the patient. These guys meant business.

The receptionist answered a phone call while taking payment from a patient. That was impressive multitasking and far beyond my skill sets. I wondered if it was her job I would be assuming. Did she realize I was her nemesis?

Another employee walked around the corner and then sat down at the desk. Judging by her waddle, I guessed two things: she was pregnant; and it could be her job I would take over. I made a mental note that being employed did have its advantages. I would be entitled to maternity pay following my pregnancy. Being paid to sit at home raising a kid seemed like a dream gig. I was now further irritated at my ex for having foiled the potential we'd had for a stay-at-home paid leave. Being paid to watch soaps was a fantasy come true, and I had blown it.

I wore one of the new outfits selected by Auntie Tina, a casual business suit that came with striped pants, a white top, and a matching striped jacket. It made me appear far more intelligent than I was. Her advice was that first impressions counted more than actual competence once you were on the payroll. I wasn't going to challenge her wisdom. My dad called her a master bullshitter.

Another woman came quickly around the corner, carrying a file folder. She wore a black blazer and dark pants, and her hair was styled smartly. She wore the knee-high boots I could not.

"Larissa?" She signaled for me to follow her. I hopped up and tried to keep pace down the long hallway to a room on our left. I hoped this wasn't the speed she expected all of her staff to walk at while on duty. *Somewhere there must be labor laws prohibiting such outlandish expectations,* I thought.

We entered a small room with a round table in the center and two chairs. She directed me to take the chair farthest from the door.

She smiled and held out her hand. I took it and gave it a weak squeeze. "Hi. I'm Jodi. Welcome to my clinic. I'm one of the two chiropractors. My husband is the other one." She slid into the chair across from me. She opened the file folder; I could see my résumé in it. I had a sudden thought—I had forgotten to run spell check before sending it off.

Jodi adjusted the designer-frame glasses on her face while scanning my résumé. She crossed her legs and sat back in her chair.

"So, Larissa, tell me a little bit about yourself. Who is Larissa?" She looked up at me, peering over her Guess glasses.

I cleared my throat and pulled on my jacket to straighten it, thinking about who I was.

I took a deep breath. "I'm just a simple girl. Well, not simple, but you know what I mean, right? A girl who likes the simple things in life."

She smiled quickly. "Describe what 'simple things' mean for Larissa."

I sat back in my chair. "Ah, like things that don't stress me out. You know, I like easy mornings without an alarm clock. Things like avoiding conflicts or confrontations that bring me down." I brightened, now on a roll. "Give me a day without an agenda, and I'm in my comfort element. I thrive on going with the flow. And for me, that's huge because I've always been criticized for being too high-strung." I beamed.

"When you say 'high-strung,' what would be an example?" Her pen poised over my résumé.

I pointed at her. "That's an easy one. Look out if you wake me from my afternoon nap. I can get to be, like, a real bitch. Twelve hours at night and two hours in the afternoon. That's something I'd want to talk to you about once I got started here."

She looked at me and then back at the résumé.

She held her mouth open for a moment and then asked, "What else can you tell me about who Larissa is?"

I sat back with my hands behind my head. This was going well.

"I wear a size ten shoe. Unless it's a dress shoe—then my feet swell a size. My marriage lasted less than a year. I live back at home with my parents in my old room in the basement. My dad is going to be teaching me how to drive. My ex and I never had our driver's licenses. We strove to protect the environmental future of the children we never had. Oh, I recently learned how to make Ukrainian Easter eggs. Oh wait—I guess I grew up in a loving household. Both my parents were there for me. I have no siblings, so I had to fend for myself. I did pretty darn good in school, mostly Cs and a few Ds, but they said that was okay. And besides all that"—I shot Jodi a large smile—"here I am." Who needed Google?

"Interesting," replied Jodi, slowly nodding at me.

"I thought so too."

She rested a hand against her face. "What can you tell me about Cervical Holistic and Wellness for Life Chiropractic Center? What brought us together here today?"

I snickered while thinking about it. "I'm here more by default, really. My A list of jobs all declined me. I was hoping for an executive job with a nice office and windows. A secretary would be a bonus. To be honest, I don't know anything about your clinic. I sent out a bunch of résumés in a shotgun approach, hoping something would stick."

She stared at me. "Do you know what we do here?"

"Sure. You adjust bones and stuff like that." I shook my head. "I've never had it done myself." I lowered my voice, leaning forward. "Truthfully, I really don't believe in this voodoo thing. But I see commercials on television saying it works."

Jodi lowered her notepad. "Well, I can assure you what we do here is certainly not voodoo. We strive to achieve optimum health and wellness for our patients here. For many, we are their primary health-care provider." She pushed up her glasses.

"Impressive." I nodded. "I might even start coming here myself. I've not been too impressed with the way my doctor does my physicals."

"We strictly offer manipulation of the neuromusculoskeletal system," she replied flatly.

A question occurred to me. "What are the benefits here as an employee?" I asked, deciding we'd had enough of the small talk about me. I wanted to know the meat and potatoes. "Is my gym membership paid? That's certainly health and wellness, in my opinion."

"We strongly encourage our employees to remain physically active outside of work. It reduces stress as well as absenteeism."

Another thought occurred to me. "So do coffee breaks. My last job, when I was pumping gas, didn't allow for structured breaks, and I hated it. If you can actually believe it, my manager wanted me to go out and serve a customer just as I had heated my soup. Let's just say that didn't end well."

Jodi cleared her throat. "Customers have to come first, so I understand what your manager's expectations were about."

I thought for a moment. "What would be nice is a subsidized transit pass, Jodi. It took me three buses to get here. I know that at some point, I will have my own car, but my dad isn't exactly getting that thing repaired fast."

"We leave transportation to and from work to the employee's volition." She wrote a note on the résumé. She looked up at me before I could ask another question. "Tell me a little bit about your strengths."

I stiffened. We were back to more about me. "I'm a dedicated employee. When I work, I work. Now, I'm not saying I dedicate my life to one company. You can see that based on my résumé. But if things are going well, I'll stick around at least for a few months to a year."

She scribbled some more notes. "Okay, what do you think is a personal weakness?"

"No doubt chocolate."

"In a job?"

I thought for a moment. "I get distracted easily. I'm just being honest. If I get a text or a friend wants to FaceTime, I'm likely going to answer it. It's like checking Facebook constantly. I seem compelled to do it."

"Even at a workplace?"

"I'd be lying if I said I wouldn't."

"I appreciate your candor." She wrote another note.

"Thank you," I said proudly. The interview was going well.

"Larissa," she said, leaning forward, "let's talk about workplace conflict. How do you handle it? What if you became involved in a confrontation with another employee? What is your approach to dealing with it?"

I ran my hands through my hair. This was a tough one. I didn't want to seem violent.

"I tend to just walk away. If she wants to be a bitch about something, I want nothing to do with it."

"Would you let management know?"

I hesitated, contemplating if this was a trick question to snag me. "I'm not out to get her into trouble. I don't rat out my coworkers. So my answer is no."

"But what if it affected the patients' care?" she said.

"I would apologize to the patient and simply tell them, 'She's a bitch. Sorry. I hope it doesn't happen again.'"

"That's how you'd handle the conflict?"

"Absolutely. Everyone's a winner." I crossed my arms.

She cleared her throat. "Larissa, where do you see yourself five years from now?"

My face stretched into a grin. This was an easy one. "Hopefully as an executive somewhere in an office tower. Maybe even knocked up. I hope to God to be remarried. But I could be traveling. I always wanted to backpack Europe."

"Very ambitious." Jodi tapped her pen against the folder.

"I think so."

"So, Larissa," she said, shuffling in her seat, "our office hours run from 7:00 a.m. until 7:00 p.m. We stagger our shifts so that our staff experience all of them. On Saturdays, we're open from 8:00 a.m. until 4:00 p.m."

I held up my hand.

"Yes?"

"I'd prefer weekends off. I work out on the weekend with my friends. But I'm still a team player. I'd be willing to work during the week—ideally between 11:00 a.m. and 3:00 p.m. I've heard these types of swing hours are better for employee mental health."

Jodi was shaking her head. "It doesn't quite work like that here. I need you to acclimate to our office hours. It's only fair to the other staff."

"I get that, but then it's not fair to me. They have more seniority, so how can I compete with that if I've just started? We either need to draw straws or flip coins."

Jodi sat back in her chair. "Are you sure you're motivated to work? I'm sensing some resistance to being a team player."

I pointed at her and then around the room. "I need to work, Jodi. Absolutely. My dad is kicking my ass to get out of the house. I think I can do well here. With a little tweaking of the hours, we're definitely on the same page."

"We are?"

I nodded. "I can shoot the shit with anyone who comes in. Make them feel comfortable. I'm good on the phone. No one can talk as much on one as I can. On top of all that stuff, I'm good with people."

Jodi closed my file. She stood and looked directly at me before speaking. "Considering everything you've said, I don't believe you'd be a good fit within our organization."

I stood too, staring back. "Say what? You don't even know me, and after a few questions, you've decided I wouldn't be a fit?"

Jodi grimaced. "You bet. I've been doing this for a long time. I can flesh out the ones who would simply be considered a bad hire."

I stood my ground. "We haven't talked salary. I might not have even accepted an offer had there been one. I don't come cheap, you know. You pay for good help."

She began to lead me out the door, back toward the reception area. She coolly stated, "I'm certain somewhere out there is a company ready to pay what you're worth."

I snorted. "At least I'm honest with you. Go ahead—pick the one who lied the best. Two weeks into this gig, you'll discover your new hire smoking dope on her bathroom breaks and stealing from the payroll. She might even sell your client list for a case of beer."

I walked past the receptionist, glaring at her.

"Now I know why you look so miserable working here," I snapped. With a jump to my step, I closed the door behind me.

*****

I kicked off my boots and threw my jacket onto the railing when I arrived back home. My dad was out, and my mom was in the front room, watering her plants. I grabbed a handful of cookies from the kitchen and joined my mom in the living room.

"How'd it go?" she asked.

I shrugged. "A waste of my time. After a few questions, she'd decided I'm not a good fit. Whatever the hell that means."

"And it's a job you wanted?" My mom looked at me skeptically.

I shrugged once more, sticking a piece of cookie in my mouth. "I did. But not anymore. The hours suck. And there's a lot of time sitting and answering the phones."

"I think every job has its own downsides," my mom said, laughing.

I forced a smile. "Everything is going in slow motion. Spring is here, and I still don't have a job or a boyfriend." I looked around the room, chewing wistfully. "Even your plants have grown since I've been home."

"Listen," Mom said. "I realize I'm not a matchmaker, nor is Baba. But is there anything to lose in trying a date with her Meals on Wheels boy? Honestly, if it doesn't work out, don't go on a second." She looked up at me while I crunched on the cookie.

I opened my eyes wide. "Do you know how pathetic it sounds that I need to be set up on dates by my baba?"

She shook her head. "No one's judging you on the context, Larissa."

"I am."

"You're being too hard on yourself. Relax. Enjoy your life."

I flinched. "I feel defeated."

"You feel sorry for yourself."

"Mom," I breathed. "Let's talk about the elephant in this room: the family curse. We're screwed no matter what we do, what choices we make. We're all given a ship with a hole welded into the bottom of it."

I pointed at my mom with a cookie. "I look at you guys and all the years you've been married. At this point in my life, I could never live long enough to be married as long."

My mom laughed harshly. "Stop being dramatic. Marriage isn't about how long you can hold it together. It's work, plain and simple. Your dad and I haven't lasted this long just because we were meant to be together in a marriage."

"I realize that."

My mom replied flatly, "Really, it seems like you don't. Maybe if you had worked harder with your ex, put in some effort, things might be different right now."

"I figured I had time," I sputtered, cookie bits spraying from my mouth.

My mom pointed the water jug at me. "There you go. If you're counting on doing tomorrow what needs to be done today, you're a day late."

"Impressive. Did you just make that up?" I grinned.

"I sure did. Except it's the truth."

I nodded, staring at the ceiling. "I hear you."

"So that's what I mean when I say spend a day with this Meals on Wheels guy. Have fun with him. Even if it amounts to nothing, it's an experience."

I nodded. "All right. All right. I'll do it. Especially if it means I reduce the risk of becoming Auntie Tina at her age, stalking the malls and grocery-store aisles to man hunt."

Mom burst out with a laugh. "You're damn straight you don't want to be her. Do you have any idea how many malls she's been banned from already? A few more, and she'll have to relocate to another city."

"Who would have thought she was bad for business?"

"Can you image the poor men? They wouldn't know what the hell was happening to them. I think at one time, there was talk of making a formal warning for all the city's nursing homes, too."

"She's a character."

"Your aunt hired a good lawyer who put a stop to that one. He contested that if the men were lucid enough to dress and travel to and walk the malls unassisted, they weren't vulnerable."

"That's a stretch."

"It worked."

"Money well spent, I'd say."

My mom turned to me. "Look. Now that you're back at home, I'm planning a small birthday party for you."

I started to protest, but she cut me off.

"Listen—just us, Amy, and Bernadette, okay? We haven't had a gathering in years." There was no saying no to my mom when she had a plan. "Is there anything you want as a gift?"

"A man in my life," I moaned.

She smiled. "Maybe Baba's meal-delivery guy will deliver his heart to you on a platter."

CHAPTER 16

www.juanita.milf

May 22, 9:13 a.m.

Had an update from Cousin Garth this morning. I e-mailed him last night, asking how the cyber love affair was going. Apparently, it's hot, hot, hot.

Cousin Garth had never dated, held hands with, kissed, or touched a woman; felt a woman's hand run through his hair; or had Valentine's Day cards or a girl. This Internet cyber vixen was his first.

Ah, to be twenty-two again.

He spent three glorious days with Juanita. He forwarded pictures from his Facebook of her nice mobile home in a park in Texarkana.

I noticed in the pictures lots of neighbors hanging around with Juanita at her mobile home. A social lady, our Juanita was. Cousin Garth proudly corrected me. Those were Juanita's family members. Immediate family. All-of-her-children family. All-six-of-her-children family.

The youngest was three years older than Cousin
Garth's twenty-two. This remarkable cyber woman
of free love, Juanita, had sown the seeds
from six men. Cousin Garth attested she was a
passionate, fiery woman of sixty-two, belying
her inner age of thirty. My head swam. She was
moving from the heat of Texarkana to the wheat
fields of his parents' home in Beausejour.

*****

Today was the day to learn how to navigate the dreaded parallel-parking drill. My dad finished arranging some makeshift poles on the street in front of our house to create a parking spot.

I watched him roll two winter tires on their rims from the garage to the front yard, grunting. I heard his typical muttering and swearing under his breath, complaining about the effort.

He measured the distance required for the poles, based on the driver's handbook stuffed in his back pocket. He'd placed a mop upside down in the middle of one tire. In the other one was my mom's Swiffer. It wasn't pretty, but it would do the job.

Now it was up to me to perform. The pressure was intense. I'd heard a rumor that most people failed parallel parking, even those who succeeded on the road test. The parallel-parking challenge had become a formidable barrier to getting the magic piece of paper that proved I'd passed my driving test. If I was to relinquish my bus pass, my fate could come down to the space between those two poles.

Dad was determined that twenty feet of concrete was not going to prevent his daughter from a lifetime of adding to the traffic and smog.

"Larissa," my dad said, signaling for me to join him beside the Reliant, which was already parked in front of his makeshift testing arena. "You've read the handbook, right?"

I nodded.

"Does it make sense?"

I nodded again.

"Good. Because I'm going to teach you how to do this in a way that is completely different from that stupid book."

"Will I still pass?"

His face grew dark. "This is how I've done it for the past forty years."

"And it'll conform to the standards I need to pass?" I asked, still doubtful.

"If it doesn't, I'll be going over there and giving the instructor what for."

"Okay, just remember," I warned, "threats may not go over well with a government agent, Dad. Think back to what happened to you when you did that at the Worker's Compensation Building. Handcuffs don't suit you."

"Those yollups do everything by the book, even if it doesn't make sense."

"It's called law."

"I call it bull crap."

"Show me what you got," I said, pointing to the car.

"Get in the driver's seat," he directed as he walked around to the passenger-side door.

It was sweltering inside the car. "Is there any way to fix the air-conditioning?"

"Roll down the window," he said. "Then it's fixed."

I rolled it down. "But the car has air-conditioning."

"Fixing it will cost more than the car is worth. Besides, this is ninety horsepower. You'll get shitty gas mileage with the air-conditioning running."

"At least my makeup won't run."

"Put less of it on," he grunted.

I pressed further. "I find it distracting trying to focus on driving while I'm sweating so profusely."

"Listen," he said, fastening his seat belt as if we were going farther than the twenty feet ahead of us. "Your mom and I traveled across North America in the middle of summer while she was pregnant with you. We had no air-conditioning. We sweated like horses. I drove without pants on, and my underwear stuck to my ass."

"Dad!"

He nodded. "This is a true story. There were times your mom's eyeballs were rolling in the back of her head from the heat. But we did it."

"And that was fun?"

"You do what you got to do, Larissa. That's my point."

"So you're not going to fix my air?"

"Be thankful you even have a car. My parents never gave me a car—I can tell you that for certain."

"That was forty years ago. Things have changed."

"Not while I'm alive."

I gripped the steering wheel in frustration. "I'll talk to Mom about this."

"Do that, and you'll be changing your own winter tires."

"Okay. Forget the air conditioner."

"Atta girl. Now park this car between those two doohickeys."

I put the car into drive, crept slowly forward, and turned into the space. The pole rocked in front of us.

"Fail!" my dad shouted. "You hit the car in front of you."

"You mean the tire."

He pointed at the front window. "Think of it as a car. Now you have an insurance claim. Increased premiums with the yollups. A blemish on your abstract. Do that again within the same year, and your license is gonzo, kiddo."

I punched the steering wheel.

"Watch your road rage, bucko; that isn't ladylike. Now back up, and try it again." He gestured for me to move back onto the main road.

I shifted into reverse. A horn blared behind me. A car moved around us; I looked in time to see the driver show me a raised middle finger.

"No manners anymore in this world," Dad grumbled.

I backed up behind the tire. I moved the shift into drive and decided to try a different approach. I drove past the front pole, stopped, and reversed, rotating my wheel gently so that my bumper entered the parking space. The pole waved in my rearview mirror.

"Fail," my dad said flatly. "Again."

"Shit, Dad."

"Language."

"I'm thirty years old!"

"You're still my daughter. Keep your mouth clean."

I took a deep breath and stared at him. "So what am I doing wrong? This is driving me crazy."

He looked over at me. "You don't have any idea?"

"If I did, I wouldn't be hitting those stupid poles."

"Take this seriously, or you won't pass your test."

I tossed up my hands. "I am taking it seriously. You don't realize how stressed I am over this."

He cleared his throat. "Try it again. This time, when you pull past the front pole, stop, go backward, and wait until you see the pole in the side rear window. Then crank the steering wheel and continue backing in until you see the rear pole in the other rear passenger window. Straighten the car at that point."

"Can you write all this down?"

He grumbled. "Just do it, and don't get smart with me."

I pulled forward, watched for the poles, and swung the car into the space. No poles were shaking when I put it into park.

"Amazing," I said, not believing my eyes. This attempt had been accident-free. My dad opened his door and looked down.

"Fail."

"I didn't hit anything!"

"Too far from the curb. We're halfway in the street."

"Shit!"

"Mouth!"

I clutched the steering wheel.

"This is hopeless," I protested, exhausted, leaning my forehead against the steering wheel. "No matter how many times I try this, I won't get it right. Our family is cursed, plain and simple."

"Do you have a screw loose?" he bellowed. "Drop this curse shit already."

"We're Ukrainian."

He cut me off before I could say more. "Deal with it. We're also tough and stubborn."

I let out a long breath and straightened in the driver's seat so that I no longer resembled a crash-test dummy.

"Relax," he said gently. "You're getting better every attempt. We'll keep trying until you get it right."

"I just want to pass." I groaned.

He looked at me earnestly. "Your mother and I want you to pass too. You have to pass."

CHAPTER 17

Cradle Robber

May 29, 4:20 a.m.

I shit you not, Auntie Tina is getting married. Yes, love does come down the Safeway aisles in front of Starbucks. Her retired Ukrainian city worker, seventy-seven, now living in the country, said "I do" to her proposal. Forget old-fashioned manners. Time is of the essence when on government pension.

They are in love. They are compatible. They have the same interests. They are both alone. He has a full pension. He has a house. He owns his car free and clear. This was meant to be.

Already, my father is ranting: "What the hell is my loony-tunes sister thinking? Who is this clown? She's after his money. Her marriage won't be half as long as Larissa's." Thanks, Dad.

*****

If there was one thing I was getting better at with dating, it was learning how to avoid my parents sticking their noses into it.

Much to the dismay of my mom and dad, I chose to meet Baba's Meals on Wheels guy down the street from the house. The pressure of the date was enough without the inquisition from my mom or my dad's infamous stare-down.

Willie must have thought my instructions to pick me up at the street corner were funny because his first response when he pulled up in his red Subaru Outback was to ask me how much it was for a date. At least he had a sense of humor.

"Nice car," I commented, climbing into the passenger's seat.

He glanced over at me. "A gift from my baba on her deathbed. It was her thanks for all the meals I brought to her over the years."

"Was she your client?"

"Nah. But I made sure to take an extra meal to her every day, writing it up as a fictional client."

"Does that mean you weren't afraid to lose your job? I think that's considered fraud."

He laughed. "Wowie, I lose my thirteen-dollar-an-hour job. Starbucks, here I come."

I grinned. I liked his attitude. He seemed like a no-bullshit type of guy who wasn't afraid of his own shadow.

"Family looks after family," he said defiantly. "I made sure my baba had a warm meal every day. Since I took this gig, I realize how many older folks sit alone, rotting and starving in their rooms, forgotten by their families. Not my baba. Every day, I visited her with a meal."

"I have to say your actions are so cool. It sounds like you cared for her right to the end." Tears welled in my eyes.

"And guess what?" he asked, a determined look on his face.

"What?"

"She had twelve children and twenty-seven grandchildren. No one but me came to see her."

My eyes shot wide open. "That's disgusting."

"It is. Actually, I prefer the word *pathetic*."

"And you got this car for all your kindness?"

"Not that her death was a good thing, but I have to say the timing couldn't have been better. The day after she died, some assholes stole my car from the parking lot of my building during the night. The cops found it two days later, completely burned to shit. I need wheels to deliver my meals. Her car keeps the seniors of this city fed."

"Including my own baba," I said, in awe of this great man.

"She's a great woman," he said, nodding. "Even though I'm bringing her a meal, she treats me to her homemade pierogi and cabbage rolls. We'll sit and watch a little television and chitchat."

"No wonder she pushed me to get together with you. Obviously, she knows you very well."

He winked. "Absolutely."

"She's been pretty disappointed with me lately. She was giving me shit the last time I visited her because I hadn't learned some of the Ukrainian traditions."

He looked over at me. "Such as?"

I grinned. "Easter eggs. I guess I fell through the cracks. This is something we're all supposed to have learned growing up. Although I think my dad takes most of the heat from her for this misstep."

"All in good time," Willie replied smoothly.

I nodded. "She hated my ex. Never liked him even after we got married."

He smirked. "I know. She told me everything during my deliveries to her place. It's kind of surreal meeting you because I feel I've known you a long time!" We both laughed.

I cleared my throat. "Did she describe to you our family curse? That all Androshchuks are destined to fail at whatever we do? I'm convinced it's the reason my marriage sank."

He squinted at me and then smiled. "Curse? No. She left that piece out."

I squinted. "Are you willing to risk becoming tainted by me? Your future—hell, your own life—could be at grave risk." I braced myself for his rejection.

He laughed. "I like a woman of mystery. I'm all in."

I slapped my hands down on my lap, relieved. "So what's the agenda for us tonight, Willie? Where are we going?"

He turned down a street. "Thanks for agreeing to a late-night date. I have meals to deliver morning, noon, and early evening."

"Ten o'clock is fine. Hell, I have no job, so I get to sleep in tomorrow. You're the one who's going to feel tired in the morning."

"I actually sleep very little. If I get four hours a night, I function well."

I laughed. "Knowing that, we'll need separate rooms if we marry, since I like my twelve hours a day."

"Girl!" he shouted. "There's beauty sleep, and then there's sleeping your life away."

"Right now, I don't have much of a life to sleep away."

"Tonight we will change that attitude," he replied with a grin.

"Good. I need my life rebalanced."

"I'm your Mr. Fix It."

"I like the sound of that," I said, smiling. I found Willie easygoing. Even though this was our first conversation, it felt as though I had known him for years. The night was off to a good start.

He cleared his throat. "Since this is a blind date, I thought why not keep it simple?"

"I like simple."

He scrunched up his face. "People go all out on the dating scene, thinking that if they can blow the other person away with a night they can't forget, they'll win over their heart. Trouble with that is they don't keep it up."

"I hear ya." I nodded, agreeing. "It's impossible."

"I've always wondered why, when two people are dating, it's all about activities. Every friggin' date has to be an activity. And they have to be mind-blowing yet—the best themed restaurants, fancy nightclubs, the theater, concerts, houseboat rentals, exotic getaways, eight-course home-cooked meals."

"All of which sound amazing."

"Of course they are. And that's my point. All that time is spent looking and behaving our best, laughing at stupid jokes, forcing conversations, and pretending we're loving to learn how to play pool. The thing is—all of it is unsustainable and exhausting. By month seven, you're just wishing to dear God that instead of yet another late night out, why can't it be popcorn on the bed in your underwear, watching infomercials?"

"Willie, you're a realist, my friend."

"Think about it, Larissa. Do you see married couples going on like that?"

"Hell no!" I shouted.

"They can't possibly. So when all that shit is gone, what do you have left?"

"Tell me."

"Sitting around drinking from your own can of Pepsi in silence, probably pissed off at your spouse over some stupid little thing, but the only way to even strike up a conversation is with a fight."

"And what's the moral to all this foolishness?"

"Just be yourself, my friend."

"That simple," I whispered.

"That simple. Which is why our date tonight is at Willie's house, with Willie just being Willie. And I can guarantee you, years from now, I'll be the same guy you hung out with tonight. I may not be glamorous, but I flash in my own ways."

"I'm digging it, Willie. You just described my previous marriage. I'm tired of the mating dance. I want to get straight to the morning after."

He grinned at me in the darkness, the dashboard lights casting a soft glow on his face. "Your baba told me you're a good girl. I like that."

I laughed loudly. "True enough. In fact, I'm thinking of joining her at the Legion to learn how to make pierogi with all the other babas."

"She'd like that," he agreed softly.

We drove in silence for a few blocks before Willie looked over at me.

"There's chemistry here, Larissa. Notice how the lack of conversation wasn't awkward. That's chemistry."

"Heck yeah. I was just thinking the same thing. I wasn't racking my brain, thinking desperately of something to say just to fill the space."

"All needless filler. Really all it is."

"Speaking of filler," I said, "do you have any family in the city?"

"Family," he said quietly, "are my clients. I haven't spoken to my parents in years. I was never the person they wanted me to be. Not that they had alternatives. I'm an only child. Spent a lot of time alone in my bedroom, trying to kill time. My parents thought that was weird, but I was bored."

"Are your parents here in the city?"

"Born and raised here. In fact, they live close by me. It's one of those mutual 'Let's not see each other' agreements." He looked at me with a cocked eyebrow.

I stared at him, horrified. "That's pretty sad."

"What's sad is Baba fending for herself while her lawyer son ignores her right until her death," Willie said fiercely.

"I'm sorry for bringing up a sore topic."

"Forget it about it," he said, navigating down the street. "On paper, you'd think parents are always there for you. Go against the grain even a little, and you're in their shit book forever. No forgiveness there, man."

"I can see that," I agreed. "My dad was set in his way of seeing the world. Either you were part of it, or you were the problem."

He glanced over at me. "What's your dream in this world, Larissa? Do you ever fantasize at night about what the world could look like when you awake the next morning?"

I thought about what he'd said for a moment. "Freedom," I replied. "To be who I am without judgment. I'm scared to let it all hang out because I know damn well I'm being judged on it. Why the hell do I have to justify everything I do?"

"That's my point."

I surveyed him. "Females have it tough, Willie. There are invisible barriers around us everywhere. I've lived all my life riddled with self-doubt. My inner critic relentlessly torments me so that I barely feel adequate. I'll bet you can't say the same thing, right? Men never question their confidence."

"Like what?"

I shrugged. "You might go out and say, 'I'm going to get my driver's license today.' Meanwhile, I'll have practiced as much as you, but I'll be saying to myself, 'I'm going to blow it and fail.'"

"That doesn't make any sense," he said. "Why would you think that?"

"It's how we're hardwired as females. Hey, we may look confident. We'll act confident. And we'll have our successes. But, Willie, despite all this, for every one of those instances, I can tell you that deep inside, we're shitting an internal brick of self-doubt."

"That sucks."

"Sure it does. Toss in people questioning our decisions and pushing back with resistance, and it's no wonder we're riddled with feelings of inadequacy."

"Which means if Larissa was to wake up tomorrow, she'd be ripe with inner confidence and kick-ass attitude."

"I'd settle simply for waking up not scared to look at the face staring back at me in the bathroom mirror."

He tapped my hand. "Don't worry, girl. That will come."

Willie pulled in behind a three-story house. "Tonight our theme is to free our minds from labels and persecution."

"Anything goes," I said, feeling relaxed. Sebastian could have used a few lessons on being a man from Willie—a world without sudoku, napping, and motherly back rubs.

"Home sweet home," said Willie, putting the car into park and hopping out. I followed his lead.

"Nice place," I said as we walked up to the back door. The home was huge. There were windows all over the wooden exterior, which would provide plenty of sunlight inside during the day.

He stood in front of me, key in hand, and glanced back, smiling before he unlocked the door. We walked on wooden floors to the end of the narrow hallway, turned right, and climbed up a scuffed wooden staircase. We bypassed the second level, continued to the third floor, and stopped at the fourth and final door at the end of a long hallway.

"This place must be a bitch to clean," I said, thinking about the rooms and staircases. "Why'd you get a place so large? Do you have ten kids you're about to introduce me to? I promise not to scream too loud," I said, laughing.

He chuckled and popped the door to the room open.

"This is my room," he said, flipping on a light switch. He closed the door behind us.

"Corner room. Away from the ruckus, hey? I think I'd be too exhausted going up this many stairs. Why didn't you take something on the main floor?"

He looked at me and then around the room. "This is all they had."

I was confused. "Who's 'they'?"

He walked across the room and turned on a stereo. "The landlord. This is a rooming house. I rent this room."

"You live in this room?" I laughed, looking around at the setup. "Where's your bathroom? Kitchen?"

He took off his jacket and tossed it onto the floor. "Kitchen is on the main floor. Laundry in the basement. Bathroom down the hall to the left. I share it with only three other tenants. They're pretty good about giving me time to shower."

"Giving you time?" The words fluttered out of my mouth.

"Sure. If one of them needs the toilet, they'll wait until I'm done with my shower rather than come inside. One guy who used to live on the second floor would come in even if we were inside. Pissed us off. He breeched his probation and was sent back to finish his time in jail, which solved our problem."

My head was still swimming over the concept of Willie's living accommodations. I swung my arms around. "So you're saying that in this entire massive house, only this room is your personal space? No other room on this floor?"

He nodded. "I'm a minimalist."

"No shit," I replied, observing the artifacts in his room. "Quite an interesting collection of … stuff, Willie," I replied, trying to figure out what the hell a miniature model city was doing set up in the corner of the room, fighting for the limited space.

He pointed to his surroundings. "Computer and desk. A few chairs. Sofa that I crash on. This is living large in a small space. And the beauty is that it's all for a hundred fifty bucks a month."

I was impressed. "What's with the model city?" I asked, pointing toward it on the floor. "Is it the child in you still emerging?"

He laughed and opened the door of a bar fridge. "You'll know soon enough. Beer?" he asked, holding two in his hand.

I accepted. He handed me a bottle. We each took a swig, and he signaled for me to sit with him on the sofa.

"You had me fooled," I said. "When we pulled up, I thought this was your house. I was thinking health care is the field to get into for the bucks."

He snickered. "We're not unionized. The pay sucks. With a roommate, I could afford an apartment, except it's a pain in the ass having another person invading my personal space. This works perfectly for me."

"At least you won't get out-of-town relatives dropping in unannounced for a place to crash."

"Even the Jehovahs leave this place alone since the time one of the tenants placed a photo of a sabbatical goat on the front door. I think it represented some kind of occult sexual worship or something bizarre like that."

"Spooky," I said, leaning back on the sofa and feeling relaxed.

"The photo of that creepy goat I could live with. But the guy was whacked. I mean, this dude used to burn his own flesh for hours. The other tenants could smell it in their rooms."

"What for?" I squealed, enjoying the campfire ghost story.

Willie laughed. "Are you nuts? Who the hell was going to ask him that question?"

"Did anyone hear chain-saw sounds coming from his suite at night?" I joked.

"No. But one time, the dude hiked out a rolled-up rug from his room and tossed it into the trash bin out back. Everyone wanted to unroll it to see who was inside."

I burst out in laughter. "Lovely. Did you do a head count to see which tenant was missing?"

"The freaks living in this building take the spotlight off me," replied Willie, taking another long draw on his beer. He stared at me from behind the bottle.

I was confused by his comment. "What do you mean?"

He pointed to his nose, his lip, and then his ears. "The studs and rings. People's first impression is that I'm about to strong-arm their wallets."

The circle of rings on his lower lip and in both ears had caught my attention when he'd pulled up in his car. The device that opened a sizable hole along one nostril had certainly made me look twice.

"To be honest," I said with a laugh, "not much surprises me. I think of what you've done as body art." He seemed to relax at my comment, which probably indicated to him that I wasn't about to bolt.

"Great," he said, pulling at his shirt. "I've also split my nipple in half to symbolize my good side and bad side." I flinched when he lifted his shirt and exposed the handiwork.

"Which half is your good side?" I asked. "I could think of ways to get that point across without the use of a scalpel, like maybe a badge on my jacket. Did you ever think of that one before you had someone saw your nip in half?"

He laughed, pulling his T-shirt back down. "It's how I roll outside the box of most people's reality."

"What do you mean?"

Willie hopped up to replace our beers and returned to his seat next to me.

"Are you about to tell me you're from another planet? I'll be up front—if there's any space travel required for an abduction, I suggest we get on the mother ship and start the tour. If I'm home late, my mom is going to freak out."

Willie let out a barking laugh. "Your baba was right about your sense of humor. It's wicked, Larissa."

I grinned, falling back on the sofa with my beer in my hand. "Growing up, I learned to defend myself with humor."

He stared at me. "Probably the best way to explain my world is to show you. Are you up for it?"

I hesitated and then chuckled nervously. "Beam me up, Scotty."

He saluted me, and we clinked bottles. I was enjoying the evening with this meal boy.

"Here's the thing," he began. He stood up and stared down at me. "It's an interactive expression of myself." He pointed at me, smiling. "Are you game to participate?" He took a swig of his beer, awaiting my response with a sly grin. I wanted to be cautious—to get to know him better and maybe even find out his last name.

"I'm in!" I roared with laughter to hide my uncertainty.

He held up his hands. "Are you sure? I don't want you feeling pressured."

"Don't worry; you won't do jail time. I'll even sign a personal waiver."

His eyes glittered. "I heard your dad's a ballbuster."

I zipped my lips. "This stays within this room. I promise."

Willie seemed content. He walked over to a green tote and pulled out a plastic bag. He returned to the couch and sat down.

"What's in the Safeway bag? All your Club Card savings?"

He looked amused. "My world's inside this bag."

"I hate to say it, but you're sounding like someone homeless."

He reached his hand inside and hesitated. "Are you sure?"

I shifted in my seat. "Dammit, man, you'd better not be a serial killer. I'd hate to go to my grave because I got suckered by a dude who delivers meals to the aged."

"They always say the quiet, nice ones are the least suspected." He reached into the bag and pulled something out.

I flinched. "Are those balloons?" I stared at the red and yellow items. Killers usually carried rope, not rubber balloons from Dollarama.

He squirmed. "I have a thing for balloons."

"I did as a kid. How fun was that when the helium came out and we'd do that crazy stuff with our voices?"

He cleared his throat. "It's a little different for me. Balloons serve as a personal release when I watch a woman inflate them." I waited for the punch line to come, but it never did. Willie looked serious.

I fluttered my eyelids. "You're losing me. Watching a woman inflate a balloon is a turn-on for you?" I was not sure if I should laugh or not. "It's a piece of rubber enlarging."

He handed me a bunch of sagging rubber balloons. "Try it?"

"That's it? Just inflate them?" I asked.

He nodded, almost dreamily.

I separated the balloons and selected the yellow one.

"Do the red," urged Willie.

I started blowing on the red balloon and watched it grow with every breath.

"Keep going," he whispered, his eyes fixated.

The balloon burst.

Willie's eyes glazed over. "Again," he breathed, handing me another red one.

I started puffing. "This is going straight to my head."

"You're a sport."

"Thanks for the endorsement," I replied, stopping to catch my breath. I glanced at him with a crooked smile. "But I feel like throwing up." I started huffing and puffing again until the balloon was the impressive size of a basketball.

He gestured for me to stop. "Okay, tie the end, please."

I laughed. "This one took a lot out of me, Willie."

He rubbed his hands and stared at the balloon on the floor between us. "I need you to sit on it," he stated.

"Say what?" I couldn't help laughing.

He appeared anxious. "I know. It sounds crazy."

I got a grip on my laughter. "More like ridiculous." I grasped the balloon on the floor and hovered over it. "No one can say I'm not a team player." My ass made contact, and I wobbled for balance. I clutched at the coffee table for support.

Willie's face was distorted with concentration. "Torture it, girl. Bear down."

I squeezed my thighs. The rubber shrieked against my blue jeans. The balloon burst.

I fell to the floor on my hands and knees.

I pushed myself up off the floor and grabbed for my beer before sitting back down next to him. Willie looked as if he had just experienced a crop circle being etched into a field.

"Are you okay?" I said, noticing the perspiration on his face.

"Brilliant," he replied with a grin.

"Sorry my fat ass burst your balloon," I stated, staring at the remains of the abused balloon.

He swiped the back of his hand against his forehead.

"Say," he said, looking down at my socks. "What size are your feet?"

I pulled them closer to the couch.

"'Kay, let me be clear: I'm a size ten, but that's at the end of the day, with some swelling." I reached down and pulled my socks tighter. "I got my dad's feet, not my mom's."

"I think they're perfect."

"Well, thank you. No one's ever complimented my feet, but I'll take it, I guess." After hundreds of dollars in makeovers and clothing, my feet took all the credit.

"Hey, they're sexy as hell." He got up and grabbed another round of beers from the fridge. "You seem like an open-minded gal." Willie hovered in front of me.

I took the beer he offered. "When you start having me blow up balloons and then call my feet sexy, I start wondering if there's a live YouTube feed somewhere in your room." I laughed.

His face brightened. "I don't confess this to many people," he said, lowering his voice. "You seem like someone I can trust."

"Hold it right there," I said. "If you're about to give up murders, I'm weak, Willie; I'll squeal like a piggy under police interrogation. I'm weak." I pushed a finger into one ear.

He smiled crookedly. "It ain't like that." He playfully slapped my finger from my ear.

"Good. I can't handle heavy shit like that. I'm still guilt-ridden about when my mom coached me to lie to my grade-three homeroom teacher that I had been sick on Friday, when really, we had all gone to the beach."

He grinned. "My confession doesn't involve misleading the school system, but I like your mom's style. No one gets hurt by a little self-gratification."

"Easy for you to say. But I was looking at the greatest teacher in the world, telling her my throat hurt so bad I thought I had polio."

He released a belly laugh. "You've been too hard on yourself for the last twenty years."

"I'll carry that guilt to my grave," I said, grinning and swigging my beer.

He fidgeted. "Would you mind carrying one more secret to your grave?"

"There's only so much room in those graves, Willie."

He chuckled. "This won't take up too much space. I have a little thing I like to have done to me. I'd like you to help me with it."

"Done to you?" I was mystified. "If you're thinking I can stretch out your nostril any bigger, you've got the wrong gal. I throw up at the sight of orifices being abused."

He laughed, tipping his bottle at me. "Actually, it's pretty tame compared to that, but it requires you putting on something for me."

I barked out in surprise. "Like what?"

He grinned, saying nothing as he walked back to the tote and retrieved an article of clothing.

"This," he said, holding it up.

I laughed. "Is that Wonder Woman?"

"It should fit."

I stared at the gold trim against the red and blue material. "It even has the stars across the crotch," I commented, smiling.

"How 'bout it?" He dangled the costume in front of me.

"What the hell? How often does a person get to be a superhero for a night?"

"Tonight is your night." He grinned, tossing it to me.

I snatched it in the air.

"I'll stand outside the door. Holler when you're ready." He sounded excited.

The door closed, and I slipped off my pants and top, slid both of my feet through the one-piece outfit, and wiggled my body into it. The halter top stopped at the top of my boobs. I commended myself for purchasing new underwear; my bra straps were exposed. I karate-chopped the air and sent a snap kick toward the door. I was ready for action.

"Willie, I'm ready to tackle crime."

He jumped back into the room.

"Ta-da!" I said, striking a pose.

His eyes lit up. "Wonderful! Here." He scurried over to the tote again. "You've gotta wear the crown!"

"You have your very own tickly trunk, huh?" I laughed, took the gold crown with the red star in the middle, and slipped it over my hair, across my forehead.

"Oh baby, you are ready!"

I laughed some more. "I'm ready, but for what remains a mystery."

Willie frowned. "Just one more thing, please."

"Like what?"

"Ditch the socks."

I looked down at my purple woolies. "Really?"

"I need them bare. You'll see."

"But the underwear is staying on, buster."

He grinned and nodded.

I slipped off the socks.

He motioned me to the corner of the room, where the toy city displayed miniature high-rise buildings, simulated paved streets with cars, a park, and a train station.

"Here's the catch," he said, lying down on his stomach outside of the city. "I'd like for you to walk along the streets. But do it slowly." His face lit up. "And kinda grind your feet into the road as you walk."

I barked out a laugh. "Are you serious?"

"Absolutely. It's a little thing of mine."

"Listen up, meals boy. You're a little freaky—hear me?"

"Like I said, I don't groove to the regular beat."

"For Christ's sake, promise me, Willie—don't ever bring this up to my baba. She's nearly a hundred years old. Your world doesn't exist for her."

He laughed. "I ask the same of you! How'll I ever sit across the table and eat pierogi while knowing she wants to beat my head in with the wooden spoon?"

"Deal," we said in unison.

I took a tentative step in the city. The ball of my left foot ground into the fake asphalt roadway. I wobbled. "Can I be arrested for drunken walking?" I asked, laughing.

Willie was too busy concentrating to reply.

"Step on that car," Willie urged suddenly. His fingers gripped the flooring.

I planted my right foot on top of the taxi.

"More pressure!" he whooped.

I bore down. The car burst under my foot. Plastic scattered. Willie moaned.

"Again. Do that next car, Larissa." It was a minivan. I took another step, placing my foot on the roof.

"Grind it," he breathed, his chest rising and falling rapidly.

I let out a war cry, thrusting downward and shattering the van. He grunted.

"You okay?" I asked. He ignored me, focusing on my feet.

I navigated the street, heading toward the park.

"Crush that picnicking family," he breathed.

"I can't, Willie." Instead, I redirected my foot, blasting apart their picnic table with my big toe. Willie nodded, satisfied.

I sought further destruction. I headed toward the train station.

"Oh yeah, do it." He squirmed. I took another step and lifted my right foot against the boxcar. I heaved, hearing a satisfying crack.

"The caboose. Do the caboose," he directed, his face flushed.

I had an idea.

I took a step, squatted down, and planted my ass on the toy train. I let my weight go, and the train shattered.

"You like that?" I commented, half laughing. "That's a Larissa kiss-my-ass special."

I had reached the end of the city.

"Sit on my head. Crush me," he urged from his prone position.

I stood up, wobbled over, and stood above him.

"Wonder Woman is here to rub out crime, slimeball," I bellowed, bending down until I hovered above the top of his head.

"You got me," he replied, bracing himself.

I thrust down in a series of dips, banging the top of his head.

"Take that from Wonder Woman, you criminal scumbag."

I stood back up, laughing hysterically. My ex would never believe I had just jammed my ass onto a stranger's head while wearing a Wonder Woman costume. I refused to get dressed up even for Halloween.

Willie pushed himself up. "Sweet Jesus, you rocked it, girl. You'd make your baba proud, being such a fine crime fighter." He shook his T-shirt. "I'm drenched."

I pointed to my swath of destruction in his toy city.

"I hope you're okay with smashing your models."

He cut me off. "You did exactly what I needed you to," he breathed. "Those beautiful size tens were made for crushing—let me tell you that." He grinned broadly.

"If you say so. They've been a pain in the ass to find footwear to fit."

"Listen," he said, reaching for the crown I'd removed from my head to hand him. "You've been a sport, but it's getting late. I have an early set of meal runs tomorrow. Would you be okay if we called it a night?"

I beamed. "I've had a wonderful woman time, Willie. Thank you for the strangest night of my life."

He laughed, still flushed. "Hey," he said, handing the crown back to me. "Keep it as a memento. Someday your kids will ask for the story about how you got it, and you'll have to tell them the truth." We both laughed and hugged.

"I'll leave out the part about trying to crush your head with my ass. Sorry. I don't need expensive psychotherapy bills. And," I said, "I'm not sure a relationship is in our tickle trunk of tricks. But I'd love to continue to hang with you as friends. What'd you think of that?"

He grinned and nodded. "I'd be friends with Wonder Woman any day of the week, girl."

CHAPTER 18

The Writing is on the Wall

I could hear my phone vibrating on the nightstand. I turned the ringer off every night to keep from being awakened until I felt like it. Rousing myself from slumber always had to be on my own terms. Right now, some inconsiderate person was challenging my independence. Despite the window blind, my room was bright with sunshine. I flipped open one eyelid. The LED clock displayed the time as 9:45 a.m. That was insane. My face went puffy if I awoke before eleven. The vibrating wouldn't stop. My agitation surged, compelling me to find out what jackass was tormenting my rest. If it was Dad trying to be funny, I was prepared to give him a tuning.

I wriggled toward the phone, staying under the blanket, and stretched my arm until I could grasp it. It was still vibrating. Whoever the chickenshit calling me was had his identity blocked.

"Yeah?" I said flatly.

"Good morning. I'm trying to reach Larissa."

"Yeah," I replied flatly again. I rolled onto my side, smothering the phone against my ear and pillow. I went into a fetal position.

"So is this Larissa?"

It wasn't my father's voice. He'd have been bitching me out by now.

"Yeah, why?" I answered, not tempering my annoyance.

"Really? Larissa of Think It, Do It Web Design?"

"Yeah, yeah, yeah," I whispered, just wanting to slip back into dreamland.

"Are you okay? Your voice is really muffled."

I shifted my head an inch. "What's up?"

"My name is Dalton King."

"Okay, good," I mumbled, cutting him off.

"I'm the owner of a company called Company in a Box. Without getting into details at this point, I'd like to entertain discussions on how your company can assist mine."

"What do you mean?" I mumbled.

"We need to move on this quickly. I sent you an e-mail this morning at six and haven't heard back, so I'm calling you instead."

I choked. Was he joking? Why would this dude think I'd be looking at e-mails any time before noon?

"Meet me at my office at eleven forty-five."

"Today?"

"Absolutely," his voice boomed. "I'll provide you a synopsis of what I need, and you can run what your company can accomplish past me."

I rolled onto my back, grabbing the phone.

"Are you saying you're looking to hire me to build you a website?" I had been speaking to a potential customer, one who could actually pay me, unlike my friends, who traded concert tickets for my web-design service fee, and I had been talking to him as if I were sleeping off a bender in the drunk tank. I cleared my throat. "Mr. Dalton, ah, Mr. King, sorry if I seemed a little abrupt; you caught me in a bad moment. I was just concluding a tremendous business meeting that required, unfortunately, someone being let go. Human misery puts me off my game—but only momentarily."

"Nature of the business. I get that. Nothing personal," he said with a grunt.

"Sure, sure. Exactly my thoughts."

"Can I count on you being in for today's briefing?"

I sat up in bed, pushed aside my hair, and tossed back the cover.

"Mr. King, for sure I will be there. Normally, I'd have my secretary take down your address and details, but I'm out—out in transit. Let me grab something to write on. I'm in my car right now. I'm pulling over."

"Good. Don't get yourself in an accident."

"No sirree," I said, flopping out of bed and landing on the carpet. The phone skidded along the floor. I scrambled on my hands and knees, grabbed it, and looked around for a pen and something to write on. I had nothing. I grabbed my purse and took out a lipstick.

I calmed my voice. "Okay, Mr. King, I have my Day-Timer ready. Where am I to meet you, sir?" I took down his instructions, writing the address in bold red letters on my wallpaper.

The call ended. I looked at my clock. I had two hours to get rid of my bed head, dress, Google the bus route, and get on the bus.

But it was a gig—with potential income!

I took a deep breath. If I could land this baby, I would forgive Mr. King for ruining my morning sleep-in.

*****

I walked off the bus with an impressive ten minutes to spare. Considering it had taken three bus passes and sheer luck with timing to catch the connecting routes, I thought I even looked presentable, with my hair in a ponytail and makeup fixed. Dalton King would never know that two hours earlier, I had been in a scissor lock with my blanket.

I stood in front of a towering, windowless, expressionless warehouse building that held within its corrugated-steel walls the potential for a future paid gig. I carried my laptop under my arm in a show of competence. Its hard drive held no past work to display, because this was my first legitimate design job. I didn't count the site I'd set up for Bernadette's boyfriend, Mike, so that he could boast each Monday about how many beers he had drunk that weekend while watching sports on his television.

I took a deep breath, staring up at the mammoth building. Was I a big-enough woman to rub shoulders with big business?

To hell with it. I had nothing to lose. It was time to stifle my inner critic and grow man balls. This was the big leagues, and I wanted a piece of it.

My high-heeled shoes clicked on the cement with my long strides. First impressions were all about the entrance, and I wanted mine to be epic.

I slung my purse over my shoulder and gripped my laptop, and with my free hand, I pushed the glass door forcefully open. I barreled inside, ready to bark out that Larissa had arrived.

There was no one to greet me. The echo of my footsteps stopped when I did. The entrance from outside led to an empty room lined by walls that pushed up two stories to the rooftop. A second set of doors faced me. I resumed my strut and rushed the door. For added dazzle, I leaned my foot against it, as well as my body. The door didn't move. I plastered my face against the pane of glass.

I staggered back, dazed. My lipstick was smeared in a squiggle along the pane. What the hell kind of business was this if a customer couldn't get inside? I walked back to the door and pushed. Again, it wouldn't budge. A cold sweat swept across me. What if I was in the wrong building? I would miss the appointment and lose the gig for certain. I started second-guessing myself. Had I transcribed the wrong address from the one I had written on my bedroom wall? I pushed again. Nothing moved. Now it made sense why there was no staff or office. This building wasn't where I was supposed to be. I screamed. Pissed off, I kicked at the door.

"Goddammit!" I yelled. I lifted my laptop above my head, tempted to smash it against the tiled floor. What was its use if I couldn't land a job with it? I calmed myself and lowered the laptop, realizing my mom was still paying for it.

I stared at the tiled floor, breathing hard, angered. My family curse was smacking the shit out of me at every turn. I couldn't do anything right to get ahead of it. This was my first big job break, and I'd screwed up with the incorrect address. I shuddered. I was doomed to become another Groundhog, hibernating in the basement.

As I turned to go, I spotted an object next to the doorframe: a black button.

I pushed it. A buzzer sounded, and the door lock disengaged. Sheepishly, I pushed at the handle. It opened effortlessly. My heels clicked on the polished marble flooring that led into a reception area lined with darkly stained wood and hosting a glass water feature mimicking a waterfall.

A woman greeted me with a concerned smile. "Is your nose okay? I saw you take that header into the pane of glass."

I touched it gingerly. "Actually, it was more my lips that smeared your door. Apologize to the cleaners on my behalf. And sorry for hoofing your door with my foot."

The receptionist grinned. "Great war cry you let out! Sorry for the experience. We've needed to keep it locked ever since one of our competitors became so upset over an account we snatched from him that he stormed in here with a group of his friends and busted up our lobby with baseball bats."

My eyes opened wider. "Must be big money at stake for someone to react in that manner." I glanced around, impressed. "Well, I'm here to speak with Mr. King about assisting with website development. And I hope I'm not stepping on someone else's toes. The last thing I need is my dad's front door being booted in. He just got it from Home Depot this year and installed it himself."

She laughed. "Dalton's only considered *you* for the job. We desperately need this to work. Our sales have been hurt by not having a functional website, and I don't want to start looking for another job. Dalton's an amazing guy to work for."

"I don't usually get breaks like this for a working gig." I smiled at her. "How long have you been here?"

"Five years. The best five years I've ever had working anywhere. How many people can say work is fun?"

I nodded. "I work for myself so that I can dance to my own tune. I create my own happiness, although it can be lonely being the only one at the top." I laughed at my own joke.

The receptionist said, "Larissa, how about a latte, dark-roast coffee, Fiji water?"

"Sounds great," I said, feeling more relaxed. I figured I'd might as well get a few freebies in case I didn't land the gig.

"I'm Dana," said the girl, standing up and walking to a counter behind her desk.

"Let's make it a latte," I said, thinking it was the most-expensive drink.

"Coming up," replied Dana.

"Fancy digs," I said, looking around while Dana prepared my drink.

"To think Dalton started this company working out of his father's garage."

"You're shitting me."

"No, I'm not," she said, walking up to me with my drink in a mug with the company logo. I made a mental note: the mug was coming home with me—another pregig perk.

I was just going to inquire when I could meet with Mr. King, when another door opened to my left. A man with a mane of black hair rushed up to me. He wore gray dress pants, a black sports jacket, and a red sweater.

"Larissa!" His voice boomed and echoed around the room. "Bang on time. I appreciate that. I've got about thirty minutes to give you a quick tour and explain what I need. An incident came up at a factory, and I need to head out of town."

"Going out to bust some kneecaps?" I joked, quickly realizing he didn't get it. "Ignore that comment." Dana giggled from behind her desk.

"Let's get under way," he said, signaling for me to follow. I wasn't sure how long his legs were, but my heels clanked like a racehorse on the street as I attempted to keep up. Walking in heels was still new to me. I was far too inexperienced to be moving at a fast trot.

He held a door open for me.

"Thank you," I breathed, moving into a room that appeared to me to be the size of a community center.

"Welcome to my world," he said with a smile, signaling for me to continue on with him. He spoke as we walked. "This is a two-hundred-thousand-square-foot warehouse. Notice the shelving reaches thirty feet up. I've maximized the volume of space to make it cost effective."

"Mr. King, I'm overwhelmed by the amount of stuff you have everywhere. How the heck do you find anything?" The rows seemed to go on forever.

"Believe or not, we know exactly what we have and exactly where it is on these shelves. The system in place is highly efficient and accurate. When an order comes in, my staff can have it boxed and ready for shipping within hours. Where you come in is getting everything on our shelves in front of our potential buyers. They need to know as precisely as we do what we have for sale, what it does, what it costs, and how many we have in stock."

I looked around, stumbling while looking up. "Are you serious? You want all these things on a website? There's gotta be thousands!"

He looked over at me. "Ten thousand, to be precise."

I swore under my breath.

"What's that?"

I turned quickly to face him. "Impressive," I replied, trying to hide my embarrassment.

"Over here"—he pointed—"is my fleet of forklifts. I have ten, and each of them is automated—driverless. I think back to the day when a stepladder was my tool to get product on and off the shelves."

"These things drive themselves?"

"Yup. And lift the product on or off the shelves without error. I paid one hundred thousand per machine—worth every cent."

I gasped. Was this guy a moneybags? In my mental calculations, the math added up to a million dollars. I felt my palms sweat as I wondered what kind of magical, automated website he expected from me. I had played around with the sample websites provided in the developmental package I would use to design a website. I had yet to fully put a site together using all of the tools and applications.

"Right now, I have a basic website. The site was set up by a summer student intern a few years back. It has our company name, our address, and a general description of what we do and what we sell. It's Mickey Mouse. I need my customers to be able to see the products, get details on them, and, ultimately, purchase them. I'm losing business to my competitors because I'm in the Stone Age as far as web purchasing goes. I'm desperate to turn this around—and fast. That's my mission in a nutshell." He frowned. His large frame towered above me, which didn't happen often, because I was tall.

I glanced around the rows of product. "So what exactly do you sell?" I asked.

He handed me a thick catalog.

"Flip through this archaic thing. It would take someone an hour to find something they need in it—if they didn't fall asleep first."

It felt heavy in my hands.

He stopped and turned toward me. "What do you say, Larissa? Are you up for the task? Can you transport my company into the age of smartphone shopping? Something so interactive, so cutting edge that my competitors will beg you to work on their sites, too? Of course, I'd be disappointed if you helped them."

I gawked at everything and tried to think. "I'm intrigued," I said, playing coy.

He nodded. "I understand. You'd be basically committing all your developmental time to my project. I need this to roll out by winter, if not sooner. I can't expect you to put all your other accounts on hold just to work on this. What's that worth to you?" He zeroed his eyes in on mine. I tried not to let them waver. I had no clue what to charge. I had no other accounts to work on either, but I wasn't about to blab those facts to him. I blurted out a number.

"Twenty—" I began, intending to finish with "Twenty-six hundred," but Dalton cut me off.

"Twenty thousand it is. You come way too cheap. But I'll ensure a bonus if this damn project comes in on time and sings to the masses."

My knees buckled. Everything in me screamed to come clean, to tell him he was $18,000 off from what I was going to charge. The devil in me stifled my self-doubt and made me say, "Good. I'm going to take a hit with all my other customers to dedicate myself to your project. But even though I know I'm low-balling my competition with this bid, you seem like a hardworking guy who deserves a break." I flinched. My mother would have been horrified at the bullshit sliding so easily out of my mouth.

He asked how many hours I'd need to gather information and to get to know his products. I replied, "Lots."

He replied, "Okay." He asked where he should sign.

"Nowhere. I trust you." There was no need to explain I had no contracts to offer.

His smile broadened. "You have a unique negotiation style," he said. "I've come to expect a series of tug-of-wars that quickly turn into a shouting match. But you're a straight shooter, and I like that in business." He grinned. "You know what you want and go right for it."

This was Big Business, with a capital *B*—an honest-to-goodness, no-phony-baloney corporation. I did something I had never attempted.

I held out my hand, and we shook.

I pumped once and then twice, firmly.

I was now in on the action of Big Business.

*****

Stretched out on my back on my bed, I flipped through the Company in a Box catalog. This shit was boring. This guy sold *stuff*—tape, plastic wrap, staples, cardboard, ass wipes. I was in awe trying to visualize who the hell bought this stuff from him. The website needed a bold red disclaimer right up front: "Enter with extreme boredom." Mr. King sold packaging materials. Who cared how many millimeters of square, circular, or ribbed foam balls he had? He sold FRAGILE stickers in fifteen sizes, colors, and fonts. I tossed the catalog across the room and rolled onto my stomach. *Shit job. Dammit.* I had shaken on it, and now I was obligated. I needed to listen better at these business meetings. I thought of the poor son of a bitch in the warehouse all day, packing and unpacking packing materials and unloading pallets of tape by the truckload. The poor dude must have screamed when walking through the doors of a Staples store on his days off.

How did Mr. King hire people to work at his business? Did he disclose up front what they were signing up for? If they knew, they'd remain working at Starbucks, grinding French roast with a smile. Who the hell would possibly want to see his website? Who was I designing for? I flipped onto my back again, staring at the ceiling and trying to envision that person. Did this individual utilize this website as a front in case his wife walked into the room the moment he switched from a porn site?

Why wasn't this gig for something I cared about, such as a flower shop, lingerie, shoes, purses, sunglasses, or wine—things I actually needed to buy? I had never in my life bought tape, staplers, and cardboard boxes. These items always just seemed to be in the drawer when they were needed. No one actually went out and bought them. They were always just there.

I understood now how Mr. King had discovered my website. Everyone else had told him to get lost. I was the last girl standing. I didn't need this headache. But I did need money. I stared at the stippled ceiling, as I had for the last two decades. I groaned, got up, and retrieved the catalog from the floor. *One more time. Corrugated cardboard—two millimeters, five millimeters, fifteen millimeters ...*

CHAPTER 19

Extra! Extra! Read All About It!

June 17, 8:30 p.m.

When I think of my marriage—or, rather, when I was married and living as a wife, a kept woman, someone loved and sanctioned under the eyes of God—I can't help but wonder what people thought of me when it ended. Was there backyard family whispering? "He was no good for her. She married a loser."

"She's the loser—the poor guy. It lasted as long as I thought it would. Thank God I gave a little wedding gift."

"Kids these days don't try or give a damn. Her poor parents—supporting her again."

"What a waste of booze at the wedding. Let's hope we don't get invited to her *next* wedding."

"Who gets to watch the wedding video on the first-year anniversary?"

Yeah, yeah. The whisperers all smugly develop and share their hypotheses; tear down the marriage; and analyze whatever they know, suspect, guess, or make up. "Oh, they had money troubles. He was a drummer, and you know what they make. She's never held a job for longer than three months."

"They've never lived on their own; they're both so young."

"Her parents spoiled her."

"He made eyes at her maid of honor. I saw it."

"No one knew how to cook."

"They both wanted the same side of the bed."

That is, until the first family gathering, and God forbid it's a wedding, when you face everyone as a divorcée for the first time. For many, the last time they saw you, you were wearing white, crying, saying I do, kissing over spoons, wearing your hair firmly in place after two cans of salon spray, dancing with all your heart with your heartthrob, having a garter ripped from your thigh, and puking wine over your dress later in the hotel room. You have to deal with the looks—some sad, some disdainful, some righteous, some perplexed ("What happened? You were so perfect together"), some philosophical ("It happens for the best"), and some mean-spirited, usually from those who are drunk ("Maybe next time you'll do better").

"Rest assured," the bride will tell you. "You'll find Mr. Right soon enough, Larissa. I know because I did." That's when I wanna puke wine over her dress.

*****

Dalton King asked me to wait outside. He was five minutes away from my house. A business meeting in my area had just concluded, and he wanted to pick me up to show me his latest product.

A raised white pickup that looked something like a tank rounded the corner just as I walked outside.

I stepped back from the curb when the horn beeped and the front headlights flashed. It pulled up, black exhaust puffing from the pipes.

"Hop in," Dalton King called out, leaning over and pushing open the passenger door. "Thanks for being flexible on short notice."

"No problem," I said, hoisting myself up into the cab and pulling the seat belt across my body. The truck started moving forward. "I was working on your website when you called me."

He beamed. "I cannot wait to see the magic you've created for my company."

"So far, I'm not pulling any rabbit out of a hat. I'm just one girl working on a major project."

"As far as I'm concerned, you're my company's Wonder Woman."

I looked at him strangely. "Why would you describe me as that?"

"Wonder Woman?"

I nodded, biting my lower lip.

"She overcomes adversity."

"Is that all?"

His eyes widened. "Are you offended by the comparison? If you are, I apologize. That wasn't my intention." He looked horrified.

I studied him through my sunglasses. The comment wasn't offensive; I was scared as hell he had seen pictures of me dressed up at Willie's and was now convinced I was into fetishes.

"Nothing like that at all," I said. "No one's ever held me in such high esteem, putting me alongside an international superhero. By the way, you don't happen to know a guy named Willie, do you?"

"I think you deserve the crown," he said. "And no, I don't know any Willie."

I wished I had the crown Willie had given to me to slip on my head right that minute. Dalton King's reaction would have been priceless.

"If I can pull off this gig and develop the website, I'd be honored to wear the crown. Although, at this point, I'm really far from that."

"Deal," he replied, grinning. "I have total faith in you and your abilities."

"I really don't know what you're basing that on. It's not like I can take the credit for Apple's successful resurgence. Although I did buy an Apple, adding to their bottom line."

"You are your own worst enemy, Larissa. Stop beating yourself down. Believe in yourself," he said. "My first impression of you was someone who will get the job done. I can sniff out a fake in a second. In this business, it's not what someone says but their actions. I get a good vibe from you. Take that to heart."

I didn't know what to say. My expectation had always been to brace myself for being shit on. Having someone gush over me was not normal. But it did feel good.

"Okay. No more Ms. Negativity. I'll let my can-do attitude flow all over your truck like a shaken pop can."

"Everything inside is Scotchgarded. Let it all out."

"This truck interior is too nice to do that. Look at that screen on the dash. It's bigger than my laptop. This truck shouts la-di-da big shot."

He laughed. "I enjoy nice things because I can afford them. Let me tell you—a few years ago, I drove a two-door car that burned oil, kept running when I took the key out, and was finally yanked off the road by a highway patrol officer for not being roadworthy. I know what's it's like to live check to check—or less."

"I wish I had a check to live off," I said, laughing.

He looked at me seriously. "Stupid me. Where the hell has my head been?"

"What do you mean?"

"I'm so focused on launching this project, I've been irresponsible, forgetting you've taken this project on without up-front seed money. You've committed all your time to it. Here you are, indirectly telling me, 'Hey, man, I'm starving.'"

I was horrified. "It's not like that at all."

He shook his head. "I'm writing you an advance for ten thousand dollars. The work will get done—I have no doubt."

My head swam. *Ten grand.* That was like $10 million in my books. I could afford those knee-high boots without them being on sale.

I gushed. "Way too much, Mr. King. My up-front costs are okay."

He waved me off. "No way. Even if it's just to cover coffee for all those long, late hours. And please, for the love of God, call me Dalton."

"If you insist," I said, grinning.

"I do. And take the advance, okay?"

"Thank you." I was keeping my mouth shut. My dad would shit if he saw a check for ten grand. "I'll use it to buy a one-way ticket to Bali. That's been my unattainable dream escape vacation."

Dalton grinned and winked.

I shrugged. "Not that I ever expect that to happen. A dream is all Bali will ever be for me. I'm up against a multigenerational curse. If I'm lucky, I might get a day drive to Steinbach."

Dalton barked out a laugh. "Steinbach! That's your substitute dream vacation because of this curse? If you want my opinion, and you're getting it regardless, a curse translates to low self-esteem."

I shook my head vigorously. "You don't understand. This is the real deal, buddy. I can describe dozens of family members brought down by this thing."

He laughed harder. "I don't understand how your dream trip to Bali is decided by a curse. If you want something, you go out and get it with hard work, plain and simple." He glanced over at me, as if expecting me to nod my approval.

"I'm trying," I conceded. "I'm just up against centuries of extreme odds."

He chortled. "Consider your curse a piñata and this gig your stick to smash it to be free! You're going to beat the hell out of it and release all future Androshchuks to live unafraid of their shadows."

I nodded, fascinated at how a person could be so full of confidence and positive energy. I wondered how many boxes of Fruit Loops Dalton loaded up on every morning before he left his house.

We pulled up at a large manufacturing building on the far edge of the city.

"Let's go," he said, jumping out. "You've got to see this machine I've just bought."

I hurried after him, chuckling about men and their toys.

We walked through a large overhead door into a warehouse loud with noise. Dalton signaled to a man in a white hardhat, who nodded. He drove over in a golf cart. Dalton and I climbed into the front seat next to him. We motored past rows of equipment.

At the end of the room, a machine sat alone. We stopped, and Dalton jumped out, wearing a large grin.

"Sam, fire this bad boy up. Show Larissa what it can do."

"What is it?" I asked.

He pointed. "It practically gift wraps pallets of goods."

"You mean with that plastic stuff?" I asked, noticing the Saran-wrap-like spool attached to it.

"You bet," he said, rubbing his hands together. "Gone are the days a guy has to walk around the pallet in circles with a hand wand of wrap, sealing the goods. This baby does it in seconds—and far more efficiently."

The machine started and began circling the pallet of boxes, stretching the wrap around until no gaps were left.

Dalton crossed his arms, wearing a large grin. "Laser eyes read the pallet and guide the arm around the goods. The tension of the wrap is adjusted by the machine, which also maximizes use of the wrap. Look at that," Dalton said, raising his voice in a cheer. "In ten seconds, it's done. I'm selling these machines now. I want this to be the focal point of my website. The automation has to be demonstrated because that alone sells it."

My heart sped up. I couldn't screw this project up. This guy was expecting serious results. As if he'd read my mind, he turned to me.

"How's the deadline? Still within reach?" His gaze bored into my eyes.

I lied. "Bang on."

"Good. I have millions of dollars behind this project to drive my sales. If this were to misfire, I'd have to fire half my staff."

My guts knotted up. Now I was responsible for ruining lives. Why had I answered my phone during my nap? I silently cursed.

"Don't start swinging the ax yet," I joked, trying to bring levity to the chat. "At least give me a chance to screw it all up."

He looked at me for a moment before bursting out in a laugh.

"I like your humor. It's dry, but you get me every time."

"Thanks. Most people refer to it as being a smart-ass."

"I find it funny. But I've been labeled as eccentric, which, to me, means weirdo."

"In your defense, I don't find you either weird or eccentric, but the word *intense* fits."

"My staff would define intense as 'ball-breaker'." He grinned.

"Something you won't be able to break on me, being a girl. So being a ballbuster is okay."

"I'll count on you to keep me in check. My staff would appreciate it if I develop a softer side."

"If you get too soft, you'll become a slacker like me. That isn't any better than being a ballbuster. Then you start to hear murmurs of 'Deadbeat' when you enter a room."

"I'll just drive over them with my truck. That stops murmuring really quick."

"I like your style. I bet you sleep well at night."

"Like a newborn."

"And your dad's not revving the lawn mower outside your bedroom window on Sundays, attempting to wake you up, I bet."

He shook his head. "That's why I own my own home. No one gets into my locked backyard."

"So I can't sneak in there late one night to toss stones at your window to wake you up to share an earth-shattering idea for your website? Too bad."

"I never thought of that," he said, looking troubled. He reached into his wallet, pulled out a key, and handed it to me.

"This works the lock and gets you into my backyard. I'm going to leave a pile of stones beneath the window for you to throw. I hate good ideas going to waste."

We laughed.

"Let me get you back home. You've been a sport coming out here on short notice. We should do a more-informal meeting over dinner one night to keep the project on track."

"Don't run up more costs over a dinner."

"It's a business write-off. Not to say that's the reason to do it. I take all my suppliers and contractors like you out at least once a year as a token of appreciation."

"Well," I said, smiling, "just let me know when, and I'll be there. I might even be able to drive if I pass my driver's-license test later this summer."

He looked at me quizzically. "Did you lose it?"

I laughed. "No, why? I haven't gotten one yet to lose."

"Odd. When I first contacted you, I'm sure you mentioned you were driving at the time and had to pull over to write down my contact information."

I flushed.

"You sure I said that? I was riding my bike, if that's the case."

My ears were on fire.

"No, I'm certain you said you were driving your car and needed to pull over to talk. Listen—be honest. If you've lost your license for drunk driving or some other conviction, I should know about it. I can arrange transportation for you for our project. Not that I condone reckless behaviors, just so you know."

I was cornered. "Okay, you got me."

"What do you mean? You do have a criminal conviction?" He let out a long breath. He visibly braced himself for the bad news.

"Nothing like that." I hesitated, reddening. "When you called me the first time, I'll confess I was napping in my bed. I thought it wouldn't sound professional to inform a new client of that, so I made it sound like I was driving my car. Fact of the matter is, I don't have a driver's license or a car. However, my dad is just finishing restoring his Chrysler Reliant for me and has been teaching me to drive. Should I pass my test at some point, I will possess both a license and a car."

Dalton laughed. He kept laughing until his eyes watered.

"I've got to hand it to you, good job on sounding convincing that morning. If your skill with my project matches your ability to think on the fly, I'm in for one helluva website."

"I'm happy you can laugh at me, not fire me for lying."

"Fire you? By going for your driver's license, you're showing drive, ambition. People like you make others successful as well."

"Thank you for your accolades, but I'm wondering—do you have me mixed up with someone else? Ah, because I've never made anyone else successful. If anything, I've been known to be a burden on people."

"That's stupid talk, Larissa." He turned and faced me. "Believe in yourself, and others will believe in you. Don't sell your abilities and skills short. I believe in you, and I have yet to see anything you've accomplished."

"This is going to be a major letdown—let me prepare you."

"See? There you go again, self-deprecating. Stop it already!"

"I hear you. Sorry. I simply don't have evidence to prove success. There are no trophies, plaques, ribbons, certificates, or letters from the pope saying Larissa is a success."

Dalton jabbed at his own chest. "Success is in here. Everything else you just described is artificial."

He wiped the corner of his eye with the back of his hand and glanced over at me with a raised eyebrow.

"So does your secretary really exist, or was that part of your theater acting?"

He had me.

"Part of my fib. Yes." I crunched my eyebrows. The lies kept piling up like cigarette butts in an ashtray.

"Damn, woman, you're good. You fed me that line like it was gospel. I should put you on my sales team!" He laughed. "You'd be top performer."

I tried to share in his laughter, feeling like a complete nob. At the time, shooting my mouth off with bullshit had seemed like the right thing to do. I changed directions to redeem myself.

"If I pass my test and get my license, I'll have something material."

"You *will* get it. Not *if.*"

"I'm thinking of holding off for a while to keep practicing."

"Does your father think you're ready?"

"He thinks I will be. So far, we've attempted parallel parking, and that hasn't gone so well."

"Then just go for it. You'll be ready. When your old man says you are, trust me—he will know."

"You don't even know my dad."

"From the attributes I see in his daughter, I can deduce he is a good man."

"You might want to tell my mother that."

He laughed. "I expect you to take the test," he said. "If you don't, I'm firing you from my project." He looked serious.

"What!"

"You bet. Consider passing your license test as part of completing our contract."

"Excuse my nongirl language, but that's bullshit."

"That's business. Take it or leave it." He studied me while we climbed back into the golf cart to return to his truck.

I needed the cash.

"Okay, I accept. I have no choice."

"You always have choices. In this case, you made a fabulous one."

I looked at him doubtfully. "Oh, sure. As if deciding under duress is a good choice."

"Trust me. Years from now, you will look back at this decision and understand what I mean."

"Great. The thought will comfort me while I'm still living in my parents' basement, waiting for supper to be called."

"That," he said, laughing some more, "remains to be seen."

*****

Mom finished pouring me a hot chocolate. I sat curled up in the fuzzy one-piece Spice Girl pajamas I had bought a decade earlier as a joke. The feet had additional padding to mimic platform shoes.

Dad had been in the bathroom for the last half hour, doing business. I was describing to my mom the complexities of the website I had been hired to design. Her eyes were glazing over, when the doorbell rang. We both looked up at the clock on the microwave at the same time: 10:35.

No one ever came to our place after eight o'clock. We looked at one another.

"Not for me," I said, knowing I had not arranged for a visit from a friend.

"Couldn't be the police with bad news," Mom said. "All of us are here at home."

"Unless Dad called from the crapper because he's stuck."

Mom pointed at me and laughed. "Could be. He's been in there longer than normal."

She put the kettle down on the stove and left the kitchen to answer the front door. I sipped from my mug. I had a few more minutes left before I removed the mud mask I had put on to clean my pores. Mom had had a good laugh when she saw my green face. She'd declined to join me, saying she looked young enough.

I heard the door open and voices murmuring. I chuckled to myself. Whoever was at the door this late had better get the hell out of here before my dad finished his business and found out someone was violating his stay-away-after-hours clause. This was his time to read the newspaper, drink his rye, and have a smoke.

I heard the toilet flush. Time was running out for the poor victim talking with my mom. I sipped at my hot chocolate some more. It was good. My face was starting to itch, a sign the mask was hardening.

The door to the bathroom opened. Dad would have to walk past the front door to get to the kitchen and then the living room. The slaughter was about to begin.

I decided to hold off for a few minutes before going to the bathroom to get rid of the mask. Listening to the tuning would be worth the wait.

My dad's voice rose.

I couldn't make out what the uninvited guest was saying in defense of the late-night intrusion. I heard shuffling on the front landing. Dad had probably threatened to throw his rye glass at the person, and now the yollup was scrambling to get out the front door.

I heard footsteps coming up from the landing toward the kitchen. I couldn't wait to get the scoop on what idiot had shown up this late.

Dad entered the kitchen, followed by my mother. She was followed by Dalton.

Oh crap. I knocked over my hot chocolate.

"Larissa," boomed my dad, "look who's here. This fellow says he hired you to design his company's website. Now, here's a man who believes in hard work—still at it this late at night. Come on in," he told Dalton, gesturing for him to sit beside me.

"This is a different look for you." Dalton grinned as he sat down beside me at the kitchen table. I could smell the leather of his dark-colored jacket.

I wanted to crawl into a hole. I felt like a stuffed-rabbit carnival prize inside my pink onesie.

"Ah" was all I could say. My mom reached over and wiped up my spilled hot chocolate.

"Drink?" my dad said loudly, slapping Dalton on his shoulder.

"Of course," Dalton replied, his usual confident self.

"Larissa," Dad said, looking at me, "one for you to replace your cocoa?"

"Hot chocolate, actually."

"Oh, she doesn't drink," said my mom.

"Bullshit," said my dad, banging the bottle of rye down on the table between us, along with three glasses. "Employees drink with their bosses." He filled each glass halfway. "Marina, get the ice rack."

My mom brought it from the freezer and placed it on the table. She whispered to me, "Pace yourself."

My dad dropped two cubes in each glass, leaving behind a spray on the table.

We all picked up our glasses.

"*Za zdorovie*," proclaimed my dad.

"*Salude*," added Dalton, nodding.

"A toast," I said, clinking my glass and seeing everyone look at me.

"To what?" asked my dad.

"What?" I said, confused.

"What are we toasting?" asked my dad, annoyed at having to wait before he could drink. I realized my mistake.

"To the success of my website because of Larissa's talents," stated Dalton, intervening. We clinked glasses and took a drink.

I coughed and swallowed hard. It felt as if the Five Star were on fire and going up my nose.

Dad pounded his drink back without a hitch. Dalton finished his glass.

I looked down into my glass, frowning at chunks of something— dirt?—on top of my ice.

"You gave me a dirty glass," I said to my dad, glaring at him.

"It's that shit falling off your face," he said, pointing at me with his empty glass.

"Huh?"

Mom was also pointing at me.

"Oh Jesus!" I shouted. "Oh shit." I jumped off my chair, slipped on the linoleum in my platform Spice Girl onesie, and fell. Green chunks showered the floor. I felt myself being lifted to my feet. I looked up and saw Dalton.

"You okay?"

"No, I'm not. Why didn't anyone remind me I had this stuff on my face?"

"Why bother?" said my dad, refilling our glasses. "I can't figure you out anymore."

"She's trying to look younger," my mom said, defending me.

"Mom!"

"Beauty is beauty," said Dalton. "Don't mess with it."

"I'll drink to that," said my dad, lifting the bottle to refill the glasses. "That's why I married my wife." He squeezed her side, and she jumped.

"Excuse me," I said, rushing for the bathroom. I was horrified. How professional could I look dressed in a one-piece with my green face flaking off onto the table? Dalton was sure to fire me tomorrow. He was the type who required a woman who looked polished no matter what time of day or night it was. Well, now he knew for sure I wasn't one of those women. I was a train wreck around every freaking corner. I couldn't see Dalton's receptionist, Dana, ever being caught in this kind of dumb, compromising situation. She exuded put-togetherness.

I scrubbed my cheeks with warm water and looked at my red face in the mirror. *What a loser.*

"Larissa," Dalton called. "Hurry up. We have business to discuss. Your dad's going to get me drunk."

I dried my face roughly. I thought about applying makeup. *I should apply makeup, but holy shit, what difference would it make now?* I crept back into the kitchen to laughter and jovial conversation.

"I bet you do your best creative thinking in your pj's," Dalton stated. "Nothing beats individuals who can be themselves without fear of judgment. I can see why you're a success."

My dad beamed. "She's a chip off the ole block," he declared.

"I can see that," agreed Dalton. He grinned at me again.

"Our daughter is practicing to pass her driver's license," said my mom.

Dalton beamed. "Yes. She mentioned that to me today. She has a very creative mind, so I don't believe she'll have any trouble passing." He grinned and nodded across the table. "Obviously, your dad's instructions will also see that you succeed." He raised his glass.

"So what brings you by our humble home?" Dad asked, pouring another stiff shot into each glass. My mother intervened, removing mine just as the bottle came around. I silently thanked her; my head was already spinning enough.

Dalton grinned. "Business." He nodded toward me. "Larissa and I are in the crucial stages of launching my website. I have several million dollars of potential business at stake."

My dad coughed, slapping the table. "*Cahki*! *Cahki*! Several million!" My dad was used to working with numbers for our family budget in the hundreds.

Dalton nodded aggressively. "Absolutely. In fact, once Larissa's website hits the cyber world, I expect thirty-five percent jumps in my revenues each year."

"Sounds like it should put thousands in your pocket," replied my dad.

"Thousands? Mr. Androshchuk, thirty-five percent equates to fifteen million per year."

My dad gurgled. "Holy shitsky. That's a lot of zeroes."

Dalton beamed. "Amazing, isn't it, what one enhancement can do for a company? The future of my company and eighty employees rests on your daughter's shoulders. It's out of my control now."

"Mr. King," breathed my mother, her gaze wildly flicking from Dalton to me and back, "are you sure you want to risk all that with my daughter? All she has is a small computer."

"I say my daughter deserves a son-of-a-bitch bonus if she pulls this off," said my dad.

"I couldn't agree more," said Dalton, nodding. He saluted my dad with his glass.

I took a sip of the juice my mom had given me to replace the rye.

"Speaking of the website," said Dalton, "how are we for timing? After the addition of the machinery we viewed today, are we still on track for a late-fall launch?"

"I'd say we're going to avoid our drop-dead time frame easily," I said, repeating a term I had read about on the Internet, which I thought sounded official.

"Good. Just be open with me if anything starts to go sideways. I'll throw whatever resources you need your way. Speaking of which"— he reached into his jacket pocket—"I owe you this advance, as per our agreement. Sorry for my oversight. I've added in a little compensation for my carelessness."

My dad slurped at his glass. "Couple bucks for gas money?"

Dalton placed the check on the table. My dad's eyes bulged. "Are you shitting me?"

"Sir, she deserves this and more."

"Hell!" My dad pointed to me. "You might as well sign it over for room and board and every twenty bucks you've promised to pay me back over the last twenty years."

I snatched the check away. "This is business revenue. Talk to my accountant."

"I am," he said, staring at me.

"I'll need to consult my banker first. Make sure my receivables are paid up."

"Good thing I love her," said my dad, "or she'd be living in a shelter right now."

"All bark," I replied, laughing. "You won't let me sleep without a night-light."

"You're in safe hands with your father," confirmed Dalton, tipping the glass to finish the last remnants. He looked at my dad. "Mr. Androshchuk, thank you for your wonderful hospitality." He vigorously shook his hand. He turned to my mom and kissed the top of her hand. "Mrs. Androshchuk, you are very gracious to accept me at this late hour."

Dad spoke up. "Nonsense. We love guests like you at any hour. Feel free to bang on our door at three in the morning if you're driving by."

I looked at Dad strangely. Who was this man?

Dalton shook everyone's hand. He took mine last and pumped it quickly. "Thank you for your dedication to my project." I nodded my drunken head.

My mom scurried over from the fridge with a package for Dalton.

"Mr. King, please take these with you. We never let anyone leave without a plate of food."

He accepted with a smile. "What is it?"

"Homemade pierogi and headcheese. Larissa is going to learn to make pierogi with her baba for the local church. She's learning to be a good cook." My mother winked.

He smiled and glanced my way. "I appreciate it. Single guys take whatever meal handouts we can get."

My mom's eyes widened. "Oh. You're not married?"

He shook his head. "Tonight would have been microwaved Mr. Noodles. Now I can eat gourmet, thanks to you."

My mom rubbed her hands together. "Why wouldn't your girlfriend make you something to eat?"

"Don't have one."

"You don't have a girlfriend?" my mom said. "Well now."

"Marina!" shouted my dad from the kitchen. "Not every man needs a woman in the kitchen. I'm sure with his cashola, he's got a maid, cook, and cleaner at his house every day."

"Listen, Mr. King," said my mom, ignoring my dad's remarks. "Tomorrow is Larissa's birthday. Did you know that?"

His eyes lit up, and he looked up, catching my own. "Well, actually, I did not. Today has been full of I-did-not-know-that surprises from your daughter." I blushed.

My mom carried on. "I've put together a little party—family and a few close friends. You're probably very busy with meetings and business to come. But consider yourself invited."

"Mom!" I yelled, intervening. "He's a really busy guy. Don't be asking him at the last minute like this. Now you'll make him feel obligated." I grew even redder.

"I'm in," he replied matter-of-factly. "What time?" He grinned at me. I shook my head.

My mom squealed. "Six. There will be food and cake, so don't eat."

"Wow. Now I feel like I was just paid a bonus! Two days of home-cooked meals. Mrs. Androshchuk, you might never get rid of me now!"

My mom's face lit up. I covered mine with my hands.

The door closed behind him.

My dad stood at the top of the stairs, arms crossed, his eyes penetrating my own.

"Okay, little girl," he barked. "You're sitting on a shitload of money. I'm letting you live here rent-free, thinking you're so broke you couldn't fit a dime between your cheeks."

I grinned. I leaped up the stairs past him.

"It's in a safe place," I called out, heading back into the kitchen. "I'm—oh, whatchamacallit—being responsible, investing in my future."

I glared at my mom.

She smiled back slyly.

CHAPTER 20

On The Count of Three

My mom made me wait downstairs while she prepped the kitchen for my surprise birthday party. It wasn't a surprise, because she'd told me about it. The fact that I let the guests into the house as they arrived decreased the surprise even more. But my mom still wanted to make it a surprise, so I waited in my room for her call. Meanwhile, I could hear everyone walking around above my head, laughing. Someone asked for a lighter. No one smoked, so I heard my dad leave the house, the aluminum door banging behind him, to get the barbecue starter from outside.

From my bedroom window, I watched my dad walk to the barbecue, grab the lighter, and rush back toward the house. Once again, the door slammed, followed by a scurry of footsteps. Quiet ensued. Standing by the edge of the stairs, I waited for my mother's voice.

"Come on up, Larissa!"

When I walked into the kitchen, the lights went on, and everyone shouted, "Surprise! Happy birthday!"

I lit my face with the corresponding look of happiness.

In the middle of the kitchen table was a cake. Thirty-one burning candles sent up plumes of black smoke.

"Hurry up and blow this damn thing out before the smoke alarm goes off," urged my dad. His concerned eyes kept gazing toward the plastic detector on the ceiling, directly above the rising smoke.

I ran up, took a deep breath, and felt my face glow in the heat from so many candles. Nothing says "You're too old for candles" like eyelashes curling from the heat.

I blew. Nearly a dozen went out.

I blew again. Two remained.

My group of supporters cheered me on.

One more blow put out the hangers-on.

A victory cry went out from my supporters.

"Thanks, everyone," I said, looking at Dad, Mom, Bernadette, Amy, and, strangely enough, Sebastian. I was convinced my mom truly believed if he was around often enough, something would stick.

"Speech!" Amy shouted, grinning. She held a jumbo glass of red wine.

I held out my hand. "Firstly, where's my wine glass? Second, growing old sucks. The top of the birthday cake gets destroyed by candle wax."

"I'll still eat it," replied my dad. "Don't throw that out," he cautioned my mom. "We paid good money for it."

Bernadette came up and hugged me. "Happy birthday, girl."

"Thanks, hon."

"Your wine," said Amy, handing me my own glass. I took a large sip.

My mom beamed. She held a glass of red wine. "A birthday party like I used to throw for you."

I smiled. "When I was six," I said. "Long before my innocence was stolen by being careerless, manless, divorced, and homeless and living with my folks."

"We're doing everything in our power, dear, to get you back on your feet," commented my mother.

"Yeah," said Bernadette, "don't take it personally that they're setting you up on dates, fixing your car, and pushing you to get your license and a job. Worry only when you come home one night and find all your shit inside the garage. Until such time, consider yourself a lifer here." She cheered. We tapped glasses.

I grinned. "I just hope to God we're not all here in the same circumstances when I'm turning forty. If that happens, I beg someone to set me on fire, not the candles, okay?"

My dad held up his hand and shook his head. "Hold on. The only lifer in this house is the property tax. Adult children are supposed to leave the flock and procreate in their own nest."

"All in good time," my mom assured me, nodding. She sipped her wine.

Amy defended my single status. "Don't rush into bearing children. Look at my hips," she said. "These babies are bent out of shape forever." She slapped her thighs. "Thank God my husband doesn't mind looking at a wide load from behind." She winked.

Sebastian stared at her as if he were trying to figure out what she meant. Bernadette picked up on it and laughed. "I've always wondered what effects childbearing will have on my body," she said. She squeezed her bosom between her arms. "Can you image how much bigger the girls are going to get filled with mother's milk?" she said. "It'll become a safety issue for Mike." She laughed.

Stealing a quick glance at her, Sebastian flushed red.

"Enough of this sex talk," my dad interrupted. "Let's get these gifts opened so I can have cake. My guts are rumbling."

"For a guy who's constantly eating," I said to my dad, "you're skinny as a rake. Why couldn't I have gotten your genes?"

"You wouldn't want his knobby knees and bull-legged walk," my mother said. "I gave you the best parts—womanly hips and a little chub to help fill in the gaps."

"That chub is why I'm spending all my time now in the gym, trying to work it off, Mom," I whined.

"A waste of time," my dad said. "Wasting your money so that you can go to a place and walk." He took a huge gulp of rye from his glass. "You can do that shit outside for free."

"But inside the gym, we can stare at the guys," Amy said.

"Don't let your husband hear that," warned my mom.

She grinned devilishly. "It's okay as long as I look but don't touch."

Bernadette burst out laughing. "Mike doesn't even like the looking part. I've got to make sure when I'm with him I'm wearing my darkest sunglasses."

"Can we please open the gifts?" asked my dad again.

"Okay," I said, sensing he was getting himself wound up, "let's get this over with." I walked over to the kitchen table and took a seat. My mom was about to hand me the first gift, when the doorbell rang. Everyone stopped talking except my dad.

"It had better not be that idiot neighbor calling the police again because we're too loud. I've had enough of his shit."

I shook my head. "That happened because you were snow-blowing at three o'clock in the morning."

"I wanted it done before I left for work," he said, defending himself.

My mom left the kitchen and disappeared toward the front door.

"Well now!" she said, and I heard her voice rising. "I thought you had forgotten about my invite."

I groaned.

I had been hoping Dalton would forget and miss the family mayhem. Parties never reflected my family and friends at their best. I braced myself in my chair for his arrival.

"There's the party girl!" his voice boomed. His wide grin sparked up the room. He reached over and shook my hand. "Happy birthday."

"And who is this?" Bernadette elbowed me.

I announced, "Everyone, this is my boss, Dalton. Dalton, this is everyone."

"So are you *the* Dalton? The tape guy?" Bernadette asked, sliding up beside him.

He nodded. "Tape is one thing I warehouse. I'm more like the supply guy."

"What's the company name? Maybe I've shopped there."

"Company in a Box. And likely, you haven't. I mostly sell to wholesale buyers, not at the consumer level."

"Interesting name," said Mom to Dalton.

"Give my mother the credit. She came up with it one night when we were brainstorming."

"Oh," said Mom, her eyes lighting up. "You're a family guy."

"Family means a lot to me, yes," he replied.

"I hope we don't spoil that idyllic image of family you cherish," I stated sarcastically.

He laughed. "I don't scare that easily. And sorry for being late," he said, placing his gift on the table next to me. "I wasn't sure what gift to buy, so I was scrambling through the warehouse in a panic."

"You didn't need to buy anything," I said.

"Don't be ridiculous. It would be terribly inappropriate to attend a birthday party without a gift."

"Never mind the gift," my dad said, waving Dalton to the counter next to him. "Get over here for a shot of whiskey, my man." He poured into the glass and filled it halfway.

"Mix?" he asked, eyeballing Dalton to see his reaction.

"Hell no, Mr. Androshchuk. And ruin a glass of fine whiskey?"

"Atta boy," my dad replied, raising his glass in a salute. They both took a swig.

Dalton's eyes watered, but he smiled at me. "Sorry," he said. "Carry on like before I intruded."

My mom handed me the first wrapped gift. It was from Bernadette.

I pulled apart the haphazard wrapping. Inside was a pair of black Lululemon tights. I held them up, studying the size.

I looked at her, laughing. "These won't fit, will they?"

Bernadette nodded. "They are guaranteed to make you look three sizes smaller."

"Sure they will," I said, "because all the fat and blood will be squeezed upward, expanding my head."

She laughed, along with everyone else. "We've got to use every angle we can to look our best. It's all about illusions. Just keep the lights dim when you take them off. It does take about a half hour for the marks on your legs to disappear."

"Interesting womanly secret," said Dalton, nodding and grinning.

I blushed. "Cover your ears. I don't need you knowing how fake everything about me really is." He laughed, raising his glass in acknowledgment.

Sebastian reached over, handing me his gift inside a decorated bag.

"Thank you," I said, taking it from him. "You shouldn't have."

He smiled at me. "My mother said never to attend a party without a gift. She picked this herself."

I reached inside the bag and pulled out a set containing three small bottles.

Sebastian cleared his throat. "There is coconut scent, vanilla, and India spice."

"What is it?" I asked, studying them.

"They're for your back rubs."

"Back rubs?" I looked perplexed.

"Sure. The same kind that I get from my mother when I wake up. I figured since you're at home, your mom can do the same thing."

The room went quiet. Amy snickered. Dalton's eyes widened.

"It's a long story," I said, feeling I had to clarify Sebastian's remark to Dalton.

"No worries," he said, cutting me off with a laugh. "What happens in the family stays in the family."

I looked at Sebastian gently. "I'm not sure this is something I want my mom to do, Sebastian."

"I could, honey, if it makes you feel better," Mom said.

This time, Bernadette barked out a laugh.

"It puts me in a good mood," Sebastian assured me.

"Perhaps," I said, placing the bottles back inside the bag, "I'll use them to moisturize my legs after I shave."

He looked crestfallen.

Amy shoved her gift in front of me. "It's in the card," she said, smiling. I opened it up and snapped it shut. It was a hundred-dollar voucher to a sex shop.

"Hey"—she shrugged deviously—"you gotta fill your downtime on your own."

"What is it?" asked my dad, trying to peer my way.

"Yes," insisted Dalton, smiling and leaning forward. "Show us."

"Never mind," I said, putting it under my butt. "Amy's being silly."

"What the hell kind of gift is that?" Dad asked, shaking his head.

My mom asked if I wanted her gift now, and I quickly nodded. The box looked professionally wrapped.

"Thank you," I said, taking it from her and pulling at the ribbons. I lifted the box lid. "Something sensible, I hope."

"Enjoy," she said, taking a sip from her wine glass. I heard the ice cubes in my dad's Five Star whiskey clink harshly when he saw what I lifted from the box.

"Sexy bra, Larissa!" shouted Bernadette. "Wahoo!" She took a spoon and tinkled her wine glass.

"We're seeing a new side to your mother," said Amy, making a growling sound.

"I'd say your mother is dressing you for success," joked Dalton. "You'll be prepared for your presentation at my office."

"The salesgirl," said my mom, looking around at everyone, "told me this lifts everything up and makes you two sizes bigger."

My dad cut in. "Three sizes smaller down below. Two sizes larger above. What the hell kind of clothes are people wearing anymore? Does everything you wear have to squeeze the shit out of you?" He stared at us in disbelief.

The flowery pink bra felt solid in my hands.

I saw Sebastian's hand start to reach out as if to touch it and then retract quickly.

My dad must have seen the same thing. He stepped between us.

"Marina, grab my thing for Larissa, will ya?" His package was on the countertop.

"Nice wrapping, Dad," I said, admiring his use of newspaper and duct tape.

"It works. It goes in the garbage anyway."

"Good job," Bernadette said, patting his back.

"Hey," Dalton said approvingly, "good taste in tape, Mr. Androshchuk; you've used a brand I sell."

He smiled at Dalton and raised his glass. "See? I have good taste in whiskey and tape." They tapped glasses. "Now open the goddamn thing so we can have cake. This rye will start burning at my ulcer if I don't get some food in me."

I tore at the newspaper, which I noticed had that day's date on it. I stared at a long yellow cable in my hands.

"Is this some kind of extension cord?" I asked, clueless as to what I was holding.

My dad beamed. "These will save your life one winter day."

"How? Where are the instructions telling what they do?"

He pointed. "Booster cables. When the battery on the car won't start, these babies will get it going."

"Can't I just use the car key?"

"Not if the battery is dead." He grabbed a cable, squeezing the gold prongs at the end. "You attach these to your battery and the other end to another car's battery. Sends the juice through to your battery so it will start. But you need to be careful because the batteries can blow up in your face."

"Roman!" shouted my mom. "Why are you giving our daughter something that can maim her? You know she's not good with car stuff."

He smiled. "Open the card."

Inside was a roadside-assistance membership.

"You now have twenty-four-hour roadside assistance. Give the tow-truck driver those cables, and let him do it. All you have to do is make the phone call."

"Now that is my style," I said, grinning.

"A damsel in distress," replied Bernadette. "Not only will he boost your battery, but if you're wearing the Lulus and power bra, I can assure you he'll tow you home and treat you to dinner."

I turned to my dad and smiled. "Thanks, Dad. These gifts are everything a girl could want."

"A man of practical nature," agreed Dalton, chuckling. "I can see where you get your common sense."

"I'm okay with being practical," I replied, "but these would have been nice in pink."

Dad grimaced. "The cords are yellow to stand out at night."

Dalton pointed and grinned. "See? Practical."

"Okay, smarty-pants," I said, snatching his wrapped package from the table in front of me. "Let's see your creative side." He blushed and slurped at his drink.

I tore at the plain red wrapping paper.

"Nice tape job," I commented, glancing up at him with a wink. The corners were folded perfectly.

"Thank Dana. I'm all thumbs."

"Don't worry about stuff like that," said my dad, pouring whiskey into Dalton's glass. "Guys are not about finesse. We're built to stampede."

I started pulling out items from the box: a twelve-pack of pink markers, a ream of pink paper, pink work gloves, a pink stapler, and a twenty-pack of pink gel pens.

He shrugged at me sheepishly and grinned. "I had to scour the warehouse to find all those pink items. I can attest they are not in great demand."

"A-plus for effort," I said. "And I'm still putting them on the website."

CHAPTER 21

Speech, Anyone?

Auntie Tina's reception, you'd think, would have upstaged mine, considering this was her second shot to work out the kinks. I should have suspected the brevity of the wedding announcement, planning, and execution were an indication of the shenanigans to come.

I guess when your groom is staring down eighty candles, time is of the essence. Maybe it was the green farmer's coveralls he wore. Maybe that's not a big deal—everyone has his or her own style—but perhaps wearing a clean pair not worn in fields would have been a better choice. I am uncertain how a professional photographer could balance out Auntie Tina in her flowing, billowing white dress and John Deere in his green scrubs.

Our family has a tradition that any major family event, gathering, or reunion, such as notable birthdays, deaths, and anniversaries, be held in the Bok Choy Chinese Restaurant basement.

Auntie Tina had a ghetto blaster set up beside the guest register, playing Nestor Pistor's greatest hits. The head table was set for two—no bridesmaid or best man.

Auntie Tina looked so happy holding her new husband's hand, leaning over and whispering to him—or maybe yelling because his hearing was a little soft. He seemed a little stunned. Or maybe it was past his nappy time.

Auntie Tina's son, my cousin Pete, took the microphone, making my dad's speech sound like Christ's last supper. You always hear of speeches that are showstoppers or astoundingly embarrassing like Bush's, historic like Obama's, or the kind my cousin Pete gave, when no one wants to look anyone in the eye afterward. Cousin Pete is a big boy—and apparently pretty darn protective of his mother.

Cousin Pete, never one to be eloquent, stood in front of his family like a sergeant before his troops in *Full Metal Jacket*. I almost wanna paraphrase, quote, mimic what was said. Because she'd been previously married to a yollup, his mother's life had been tough. He said she is a strong woman who deserves the best, expects the best, and will get the best. And (for this part, I must quote him) pointing his finger at Farm Guy and glaring, he said, "If you ever let my mother down—if you ever make her sad, if you ever hurt her in any way—I'll fucking kill you."

Auntie Tina wiped tears from her eyes.

*****

As soon as I pulled open the door, the rush of voices from inside the Legion hit Sebastian and me. The abandoned appearance of the windowless white-stucco exterior of the building belied the buzzing excitement on the inside. We stopped at a wooden table, where two female seniors sat looking up at us. Beyond them were rows of similar tables lined with bundles of gray hair bent over, furiously working.

"*Dobrogo rankoo,*" stated one of the females behind the desk. "Are you here for pierogi making?"

"Unless it's shuffleboard night, we're here to help her baba make pierogi," stated Sebastian.

They turned their eyes toward me and asked, "*Yak vas zvaty?*"

I wasn't certain, but I decided they had just asked me my name.

"Larissa. My baba asked us to come along and learn the art of pierogi making." Their eyes lit up.

"So you the *don'ka!*" They glanced at one another and nodded and then looked back to me.

"We heard about you," said the woman to my right, whose hair was hidden by a red kerchief.

"And I hope it was all good," I replied, smiling and studying them both.

"*Ni,*" said the one to my left, whose hair was covered under a wreath of fresh flowers.

"Shameful," replied Kerchief.

"What you doing growing up?" said Wreath. "Not making pierogi with your baba."

"How do you pass to your children make pierogi if you don't know?"

"I don't have children," I said, taking a step back.

Eyes opened wide on both babas. One said, "*Vybachteh,* your age—no children and no make pierogi?"

I held up both hands in front of me. "Hey, I'm still young."

Kerchief snickered. "I birth ten kids your age, not includes three still died."

Wreath added, "My kids make pierogi at two years old." She scowled.

Kerchief nodded. "Before my don'ka walked, she push roller on kitchen table, smoothing out dough."

Wreath stared her steel gaze into me. "My don'ka—she look your age. She seven kids, all make the pierogi."

"I—"

"My mom buys the pierogi from Safeway's freezer section," said Sebastian, grinning.

Kerchief's face compressed. "That not pierogi. That frozen turd."

Wreath agreed, souring. "No way pierogi finger-pinched. Pierogi made by machine hard like puck."

"I like them," confessed Sebastian.

"Taste like poop."

"My mom's are handmade," I said, feeling the heat rising.

"Your mom make the pierogi, and you don't?" Wreath said.

Kerchief shook her head. "Shameful. You get married without make the pierogi?"

"I'm divorced," I said. "My ex didn't know how to make pierogi either."

"He man. He make money."

"He didn't do well at that either. He's also living back at home with his parents."

Kerchief soured. "Generation you kids not learning what we learn by our *maty*. Shameful."

"Blame it on the parents," said Sebastian, nodding. "My mom made sure to teach me everything." I glanced over at him, startled by his remark.

"Look," I said, "today my baba will instill in me the knowledge I should have gotten as a young girl, okay? I already learned Easter-egg making from her," I boasted.

"But no pierogi at home by your maty."

"Lord strike me down," I replied, frustrated. The babas flinched and crossed themselves.

"Table one twenty-nine," said Wreath, shooing us away.

"Tough crowd," commented Sebastian, looking back at the two babas. He glanced around as we walked into the main area. "Wow.

Look at the mounds of dough," he breathed, glancing around in wonderment at the tables as we began navigating between them.

"Soon our hands will be kneading in those mounds," I said, feeling good about finally doing something productive with my baba.

"My mom gave me gloves to wear so that I don't catch something," confessed Sebastian.

"Isn't it the other way around—so you don't contaminant the food?"

"She said bacteria can enter a wound on my hand. I could lose it to an infection."

I grimaced. "We're making pierogi, not working with rusty shards of metal. My baba will shit if you put those gloves on."

"My mom said there's no guarantee my tetanus shot will save my limbs."

"When did you get the shot?"

"I went with my mom this morning to the clinic. Look at the red mark on my buttocks," he said, pulling down the waist on his blue jeans to show me the injection site.

"Sometimes you freak me out with the things you do," I said, shaking my head. "And keep your pants up here. These babas will boil you in hot water if they see you stripping like that."

He shrugged.

We pushed past more tables. "I can't believe there're more than two hundred tables in here. I'll bet half of the city's seniors are here making pierogi."

"I hope we get to eat." He was rubbing his belly.

"Just what I need—more dough, straight to my hips."

"My mom says curves define a woman."

I winked at him. "I'm actually starting to like your mom. Not."

I spotted Baba near the middle of the room. She was lifting a bowling-ball-size chunk of dough from a bag and slamming it on the table. I could just make out her head above the table of dough.

"Baba! We made it." I grinned. "Here is my friend Sebastian. We're here to learn everything you know."

She looked up and didn't smile.

"*Pryvit.* You late. Look at dough I carry to table myself. Shame on you, making someone nearly one hundred years old lug around heavy dough."

I glanced over at Sebastian, who looked every bit as horrified as I was.

A woman from the table behind us spoke up. "My son came here with me to help carry the dough," the baba said. "He even helped your baba carry her potatoes. Where were you?"

I sensed a growing uprising around us. I realized I needed to respond quickly before Sebastian and I became the victims of a geriatric mob beating.

"Everyone!" I shouted among the roar of voices and activity, grabbing the attention of the immediate tables around us. "I apologize on behalf of myself and my friend for arriving late. In no way did we wish to offend anyone or make my baba lift and carry all this dough and potatoes. We ask for forgiveness and to work in peace, please." There was a scattering of nodding heads.

"Enough yakking. Roll up sleeves. Start," barked my baba, signaling for us to gather around her table. Sebastian and I went on one side of her.

"*Ty*"—she pointed to Sebastian, already forgetting his name— "roll out dough." She handed him the wooden rolling pin. "Christ's sake," she said, "make dough not too thin, or pierogi fall apart in water."

"Where's the measuring tape?" he asked, looking around the table.

"*Vybachteh?*" Baba looked up at him weirdly. "Use eyes," she said, poking him several times in the forehead with her stubby finger.

"Ouch," he said, rubbing his head with the back of his hand.

"Larissa," she said, "I cut pierogi shell with glass cup. You take potato; put healthy dollop in middle. Pinch, pinch, pinch for good seal." We heard a snap of latex. Baba looked over at Sebastian, who was slipping on his gloves.

"What hell those for?" she asked, slapping at his hands.

"Protection against infection."

She lifted herself on the tiptoes of her slippers and poked him once in the chest with her finger. "Toughen up," she said, shaking her head. "You generation soft. I dug bare hands through cow shit on farm. After that, fed babies, chop vegetables, made stew before wash hands. Look," she said, holding up her arms. "Ninety-one years old. Not dead. All babies grow up. Tough like bull."

"Gross," he replied, scrunching his face.

"Not like your mom, huh?" I said to him, laughing.

"Roll! Roll!" Baba commanded. "We behind. We make six hundred pierogi. Not one less."

"With everyone here, that'll take no more than an hour," said Sebastian, swinging his rolling pin. "That's about twenty pierogi per table, based on my math," he added smartly.

"Watch mouth," snapped Baba. "We," she hissed, pointing at us, "make six hundred pierogi. I make most pierogi every year," she added, sweeping her arm around. "Roll. No slow me down."

Sebastian took the hint that Baba meant business and began working his rolling pin over the dough until he had a large sheet of it in front of him. Baba snatched it away and began plunking down her glass, cutting out circles. I peeled them off as fast as she moved along the dough. Sebastian had already spread flour and was rolling out his second slab of dough.

Baba's eyes widened at me. "Stuff, luba! Stuff pierogi, Christ's sake. Iris one stack of completed pierogi," urged Baba. I started scooping a double finger of orange-colored potato filling into the center of the dough and pressed my fingers gingerly along the outer rim, ensuring the edges were lined up. I admired the finished product. I had made the perfect pierogi.

"Luba," snapped Baba, "faster pinch. People eat, not put on mantel."

I pinched faster.

Beside me, the flab under Baba's arms wiggled as she moved her cup in a continuous line. Sebastian had two rows of sweat running down each side of his face.

Baba looked at me and then at Sebastian, her white dentures grinning back at us. "You kids do okay."

"My arms feel huge," boasted Sebastian, smiling while he rolled. "Feel how thick they are, Larissa," he said. I glanced over at his spindly arms sticking out of his T-shirt.

"Pass!" I shouted over the increasing roar of voices as the pierogi frenzy was reaching a fever pitch. "And never mind your arms—my fingers are killing me from pinching all this dough."

"You kids soft," said Baba. "I not feel bottoms of feet twenty years, and I stand, no complain. Luba, keep pinching. Ty, keep rolling."

Sebastian looked grief-stricken. "How will we know when we've made six hundred? Should I start counting?"

Baba banged the glass cup against his table several times. "Keep rolling. We stop when pierogi at top of garbage pail," she said, pointing to a full-size green trash container.

His eyes shot open. "That thing is huge, Baba. We can never fill that with pierogi."

"Six hundred pierogi fill pail. Every year, I do myself."

"What are you made of?" he asked, startled by her revelation.

She cackled. "Stuff you never be."

"Half hour!" a voice rang out over an intercom.

"Dirty bananas!" Baba shouted, hip-checking me so that we stood side by side. She grabbed the circles of dough and began filling and pinching in a frenzy.

"Quick, kids," she urged.

"I'm almost out of dough!" exclaimed Sebastian. "This is my final ball."

I grimaced. "It's the curse, Baba! We're screwed!"

"Blah," growled Baba. "I be damned—no curse stop us today!" She pointed her finger at Sebastian. "Grab dough in pail next to you."

"It's for the other table."

"Grab," she snapped.

Sebastian didn't hesitate, reaching down and pulling up another large ball of dough.

"Betty," said the woman at the table next to us, "you just lifted my dough."

"You owe, Abigail. You idiot son smashed tomato plants in my garden."

She scoffed. "Betty, good Lord, that was twenty-nine years ago! He was ten years old."

"I never forget. Today you come good."

"That's ridiculous."

"If no, I press charges. Take pick, Abigail. Milton gets criminal record? You live with guilt." She kept stuffing and pinching without missing a beat.

"Charges!"

"Kiss job at gas station bye-bye. He never move out your house."

Abigail sneered. "You're ruthless. Take my dough, and leave my son alone."

"Good. He enough problem upstairs," she said, pointing to her own head.

I looked at Baba with admiration. "You play for keeps."

She grinned at me. "Tak. It dog-eat-dog world. Let no one get in way when make pierogi. Stand up for yourself as *zhinka*," she said proudly, pushing back her tiny shoulders.

"Zhinka? What's that?"

"Woman," she stated, strengthening her stance in her slippers. Beads of sweat ran down from underneath her patterned babushka.

Coming from an independent four-foot-nine ninety-one-year-old, her advice held true after nine decades of battling self-doubt and consuming it for lunch. For me, it was obvious Baba had no shred of self-doubt anywhere within her skin.

When the buzzer went off and time was called, our garbage pail was stacked, with pierogi sliding off the top. Afterward, I got to shake the hand of the priest at my baba's church, where all our pierogi were going to be sold for fund-raising. Today I felt good about myself. I'd fulfilled a piece of my heritage and given something back to the community.

I high-fived Sebastian and Baba. I might not have been selected for any sports teams when I was a young girl, but that afternoon, I was part of a team that was something more special.

Dyakuyu.

CHAPTER 22

Backseat Drivers

My dad was pacing by the garage door when I walked up. I wore my rubber boots and a light coat. I wished I owned a pair of driving gloves with the knuckles cut out.

Wearing his green mechanic's jumpsuit, he wheeled toward me. "Jesus, Larissa, about time. I want to get this done before it gets dark."

"It's only noon. Are we going to be driving for eight hours?"

"I don't like leaving things to the last minute."

My shoulders slumped. "Next time, we should start at the crack of dawn."

He glared at me. "Come over here so that I can show you something." I followed him inside the garage to the back of the car.

He pointed. "These are brake lights. One on each side, plus this one in the middle of the rear window. These white sections light up when you reverse."

"Okay," I responded, uncertain what relevance this information had for me. I would be inside the car while I was driving.

"You need to make sure before you go anywhere to test all the lights every time, and make sure they're working."

"Why?"

His face flushed. "Because you'll get a goddamn ticket—that's why. It's a punishable offense to drive with a burned-out light. Do you want to be pulled over? It also goes against your license. You know what that means?" He gestured. "More money to pay for your license and insurance."

I was confused. "If I'm driving, I have to be inside the car to make these lights work, right? How do I get behind the car to check?"

He looked at me as if I had two heads. "You get someone to watch for you. Or you back up in front of a wall and watch the reflection against it. Same rule of thumb for the headlights."

"All right," I said, not convinced it was practical.

He leaned down and rubbed the license plate with his finger. "Keep this doohickey clean. If the police can't read it, they're going to get you."

"You make them sound like they're waiting for me."

"They are. Even if you can't see them, they're around, waiting."

"Now you're starting to sound really paranoid, Dad."

"Believe you me. Don't think you can get away with anything." He signaled for me to follow him to the other side of the car.

"This is where the gas goes," he said, flipping open the small gray door. "Unscrew this, and stick the nozzle inside. Don't overfill it. Make sure you screw this thingamajig back on until you hear one click."

"Can you write all this down?" I was becoming overwhelmed.

He scowled. "Never let your gas get below half a tank, especially in the winter. Check your tire pressure every morning. In the winter, make sure to untie your block heater cord from the wall socket, or you'll rip the entire kit and caboodle out."

We both turned when we heard shuffling feet approaching the open garage door.

Dalton stood there, his hands tucked in his jacket. He wore a shit-eating grin.

"What's up?" I asked, unsure why he was outside my garage and how he knew where I was. My question must have been obvious in my expression.

"I was walking up to your front door, when your mom flew out to say you were in the garage with your dad. She told me if I was fast enough, I'd catch you before you left to practice driving. I told her I wouldn't miss this for anything!" He looked pleased with himself.

My brow furrowed. "I know you didn't come to my house for this. Is there something we need to discuss about our project?"

"Actually, yes. However, this takes precedent." He pointed to my car. "Remember, part of your contract with me is gaining your license." He grinned.

"If that's the case," said my dad as he opened the driver's door, "you'd better get inside too." He motioned Dalton toward the backseat. My dad then motioned for me to join him on the passenger's side.

"Thanks for the offer, Mr. Androshchuk," replied Dalton. "I most certainly will." Dalton squeezed his large frame behind my seat to access the backseat.

"Are you sure we shouldn't be doing this alone?" I asked my dad. I was thinking of the liability if I crashed and maimed Dalton.

"This will be a good lesson for both of you." He started the car. The tiny four-cylinder engine rattled and shook, but it ran. He glanced back at Dalton. "Even after years of driving, bad habits develop."

"Everybody, put on your seat belt," my dad commanded. "Larissa, watch me. Put your foot on the brake to shift into drive. Look both ways before letting your foot off the brake."

We slowly pulled out of the driveway and crept down the back lane toward the street. This was my dad's normal driving speed. As a passenger over the years, I'd developed a tremendous sense of patience.

When we stopped at the end of the back lane, he shifted into park, unlatched his seat belt, and hopped out of the car. He scurried around and opened my door.

"Your turn."

I froze. "What do you mean 'my turn'?"

"I don't need to drive. I know how. Get out."

"You can do it, Larissa," said Dalton from the backseat.

"You don't know that," I fired back, annoyed.

"Skedaddle," my dad urged. "My hemorrhoids are aching from standing. Bending over this car all winter has taken a nasty toll on them." When I still didn't make a move to get out of the car, Dad tugged at my jacket sleeve. "There's only one way to learn, and that's by doing. Out."

"Do it, Larissa," agreed Dalton.

"You're such a backseat driver," I shot back at him as I pulled myself from the car. "Shouldn't you be signing off on some multimillion-dollar deal right now?"

"Those can wait. Right now, my biggest investment is in you."

I strode around to the driver's side and got behind the wheel. The dashboard suddenly looked like an airliner cockpit—buttons, levers, dials, and steering wheel, all under my care and control. The car slumped to the right when my dad sank inside.

"Buckle up. Let's hit it." His belt snapped into place. I felt Dalton leaning in between us.

"Around the block, James."

"Would you shut up?" I said nervously, scanning the dash.

"Let's stay in the area for now," my dad mercifully suggested.

I pulled my seat belt across my chest. Suddenly, my boobs felt too big, too protruding. I stepped on the gas pedal, and the engine revved. A red needle surged in front of me.

"What's that?"

Dad snorted. "Nothing to be concerned about. You need to focus on the dial next to it. The speed limit around here is thirty kilometers in the back lanes and fifty on the streets. Don't go a kilometer over."

"Come on," urged Dalton from over my shoulder. "My warehouse forklift crew drives better than you."

"That's not saying much," I said roughly.

I grabbed the shifter on the steering column and clunked the transmission into drive. As I released my foot from the brake, the car started rolling forward.

"Turn signal! Turn signal!" barked my dad.

"Which way?" I screamed back, thrusting the turn signal left to right.

"Yee-ha!" shouted Dalton in my ear.

"You're stressing me out, idiot!" I shouted over my shoulder.

"Turn, turn, *turn!*" my dad shouted. "You're going to hit the curb." His arms flailed.

I yanked the wheel to the left. The car straightened.

"Slow down!" he yelled. "You're speeding."

I glanced down at the speedometer. I was way over the limit. I jammed my foot on the brake. The car lurched to a near stop. My dad braced his hands against the dash. Dalton's body smacked into the back of my seat.

"Jesus, Larissa," Dad said, "go easy. You're driving like a yollup."

"I'm sorry!" I screamed. "There's too much going on."

"Yield sign!"

"Shit!" I braked hard.

"Don't swear like that!"

I merged onto another street.

Dad's voice screeched. "Watch out for that imbecile! He's all over the road!"

"So are we," said Dalton. I felt his hand dig into my headrest.

"Stop riding the brake! You're going to wear out the shoes," cautioned my dad.

"I can't help it," I moaned. All four limbs felt detached from my body.

Dad poked at my thigh. "Use one leg. Why do you have one leg on the brake and the other on the pedal?"

"There are two pedals. I have two feet," I said.

I came to a stop at a four-way intersection.

"Count to five," my dad advised.

"What for? There's no one here."

My dad snapped. "That's the law. Complete stop."

I started to move forward.

"That was only four," said Dalton.

"Will you quiet down back there?" I said, staring at him in the mirror.

"Your dad says it's the law. You just broke the law."

My dad grunted. "That's a fine and two points on your license for running the stop sign," my dad said.

"But I stopped."

"Not good enough." I could see my dad shaking his head.

"How about some radio?" suggested Dalton. "I could use some Human League from the eighties."

"No distractions," my dad warned. "Focus on your driving."

He pointed at the car ahead of us. "You're following too close. You won't be able to stop in time if he slams on his brakes."

I braked in frustration. "Is this far enough?" I said, glancing quickly his way.

"Good," he replied gruffly. "Count to seven, using a landmark to gauge your distance."

"Why's there so much counting?" I whined.

We stopped at a red light.

My dad stared at me. "Do you know what's wrong with the distance to the car in front of us?"

I glanced at the car and back at my dad. I was at a loss.

"Too close," he said.

I made a face. "I need to count here as well?"

"Think about this, Larissa—you're right behind his car, where the exhaust is coming out. We're inhaling his toxic fumes. We could die."

"I don't want to die," Dalton groaned.

I rolled down my window. "No one is dying." I beeped my horn to get the guy ahead of me moving before we died.

"Are you crazy?" said my dad, clenching his teeth. "That guy could be a psycho. You hitting your horn could set him off."

"What good is the horn then?"

"And never make eye contact," he added.

I wailed, "Dad, I can't do this! I'm destined to take the bus forever! The bloody family curse has it out for me," I said.

My dad barked, "For Christ's sake, Larissa, would you stop this shit about a curse? You sound like a maniac. There ain't no family curse, so stifle your yap about it. It's the yollups we bring into our family that curse us. Enough of this phony baloney, already. So shut up and drive."

I winced at his tuning.

Dalton spoke up. "You really do believe in that curse, don't you, Larissa? You know, Mr. Androshchuk, your daughter truly believes it."

"Well, she's full of shit. There ain't no curse. Maybe just a touch of family stupidity."

We started moving. I changed lanes.

"You didn't shoulder-check."

"I looked in the mirror!"

"Not good enough. Stop being lazy. You can't see past your blind spot without shoulder-checking."

A horn went off behind me.

"He's waving at us," said Dalton, looking out the rear window.

"Ignore him," my dad said. "Don't let him intimidate you."

"I could be a psycho, so why's he honking?"

"Just keep your speed five kilometers under the posted limit. Remember, it's only a suggested speed for optimum road conditions. Today there's a lot of water from the melting."

"He's right on my ass, Dad!"

"He's giving us the finger," stated Dalton matter-of-factly.

"I'll give him what for in another minute," growled my dad, getting into road-rage mode.

"Dammit, he's not letting up. I can't even see his front bumper."

"Jam your brakes," urged my dad.

"He'll hit me!"

"It'll show him what for."

"Do it!" shouted Dalton.

"There's too much testosterone inside this car!" I yelled, and I made a sudden right turn off of the street, losing the tailgater.

"That was a way-too-dangerous turn," said my dad. "And you didn't use your turn signal."

"You wanted me to have the nut job ram us, but my evasive turn to get away was too dangerous?"

"Where are the police when you need them?" complained my dad, shaking his head. "I get so cheesed off by this."

"Can we call it a day?" I pleaded. "My nerves are shot."

"This is the best day of my life," said Dalton, grinning, bending forward against the back of the front seat.

"The bus is starting to look pretty darn good, Dad," I said, heading back toward my parents' home. "I'll take campy smell, poor connections, and waiting in the cold over the stress of driving. This is insane! I nearly killed us; other drivers wanted to kill us. Plus, the possibility of death by carbon-monoxide poisoning—this did nothing to boost my confidence."

"Every time will be easier," said my dad, nodding.

"Count me in," said Dalton, popping his head between my dad and me. "This was a blast." He beamed. "Larissa, I've even forgotten what I was here to talk to you about!" He laughed again. "It isn't often someone is able to make me lose my train of thought when it comes to business. I congratulate you on being the first!"

My dad grunted. "Buddy, I hope my daughter's driving isn't anything like the effort she's putting into your project, because let me be clear right now: if she runs your business into the ground, there's no way in hell I can afford to feed another mouth in my house. Got it? You're on your own."

CHAPTER 23

Double Trouble

It was a first—going on a double date with my best friend, who was in a secure long-term relationship and was more of a chaperone than a date. But there was safety in numbers, and I was leery of the quality of Mike's referral for his boy at the Quick Lube. Changing oil as a career at age twenty-six didn't exactly scream "motivated" to me. Perhaps I was being overly critical, but the following day, with a killer hangover, my awareness of what made a good man a good husband and, ultimately, a father was expanding beyond functional. I didn't think I was asking too much. In my opinion, now that I was divorced, I'd earned the right to become more selective, more demanding about whom I allowed into my life as a partner.

Moving into my thirties, I had less to sacrifice, and time management became more important now. The twenties were meant to be sacrificial years—blissfully uncaring, unfocused, experiential times that shook off having been a handheld teenager. That unbridled living had ground to a halt now that I was divorced and one year into my thirties, when several clocks began their ticks. Biologically, my baby-making years were now in the direct spotlight. My egg counts were plummeting daily; genetic failings increased each month. If I wanted five children, I'd be hard-pressed to squeeze them all out in the same decade without being in a state of continuous pregnancy. I'd have no boobs left after that ramped-up childbearing agenda. And the closer I got to forty, what man could I land, when I'd have wrinkles so deep that even foundation couldn't fill them in without a ladle? I'd be viewed by any man as having a huge expiry date plastered on my forehead. Men would see my shelf life in years, not decades, knowing full well my best years for him were well behind me.

Guys didn't struggle with issues of time. Most aged well, like a good portion of beef. They were like wines that only got tastier the longer they sat before they spoiled. It usually took a guy a few decades of life to grow out of his boyhood looks into a rugged man with ground-in razor burn. Procreation was still doable at age seventy. Men's bodies didn't burn up with menopause. They even had pills to keep their sex parts working. We women had bodies that left parts behind each year as we got older.

Bernadette sent me a text telling me to dress for the outdoors. She suggested runners and long pants but refused to indulge me with the activities planned for our megadate. I wasn't about to challenge a date that I could go on without wearing high heels. This was all about getting back to my comfort level.

I agreed to walk over to Bernadette and Mike's apartment to meet Charlie there. He was going to be a few minutes late. He was stuck at work, fixing a vehicle after an oil change stripped the oil plug. I had no idea what *stripped* meant or where an oil plug was; I only hoped he'd wash his hands before leaving work.

I walked up to Bernadette's door and knocked. I could hear their voices through the door. It sounded as if they were having an argument. I debated whether I should wait a few minutes and come back. The shouting stopped. I felt uncomfortable.

I heard footsteps quickly approaching the door, and the lock was flipped open. Bernadette opened the door. She was wearing a robe.

"Going casual tonight?" I tried humor, seeing the redness of her eyes.

"Come on in," she said softly, signaling for me to pass her as she closed the door.

"Is this the right night?" I asked, seeing Mike drinking a beer and staring out the patio door.

Bernadette walked past me into the kitchen.

"Hotshot over there," she said, pouring a glass of water, "told me to find a pair of jeans that fit my large ass. How's that for support?"

I looked his way. He was taking another sip of his beer.

"I meant it," he said in reply. "Wear something that will be comfortable. Those did not look comfortable."

"It wasn't your ass in them."

"I just don't get why you take everything I say so personally. What I said wasn't an insult; it was a goddamn suggestion."

Bernadette stood her ground in the kitchen. "After all the working out, I don't expect to have my ass called large."

"Get over it," Mike replied. I could see Bernadette stiffen and grip her water glass harder.

"You know how to bring a girl's self-esteem down without even trying," she said tearfully.

"Yeah, really, and it's not about your own body-image issues? Why the hell do you want to wear tight jeans if you know your ass is too big in them? That doesn't make any sense to me."

"No, you think my ass is too big. I guess you're embarrassed in public about its freakish size."

"See what I mean?" he said, pointing to her and looking at me. "Her misplaced perception keeps growing until I puke at the sight of her."

She came out of the kitchen, livid. "Should I wear your coveralls from work so that my entire body is hidden? Maybe I'll put a veil around my face so you don't have to look at that either."

"Now you're being ridiculous."

"You're being a jerk."

I wasn't sure what to say. This was the first time I'd witnessed Bernadette and Mike scrapping. They were one of the most-passive couples I knew.

I tried to lessen the tension. "Look, guys, you're not setting a good example for how I should behave on my date with Charlie."

"Maybe I should date Charlie. You can have Mike and get criticized all night," said Bernadette.

"Go for it," he said. "See how long he puts up with your whining and lack of confidence."

"I get it. Now I'm weak." She slammed a cupboard door, scurried past me down the hall to her bedroom, and slammed that door.

"Why do women need to be so ultrasensitive?" Mike asked, glaring at me. He finished his beer and walked to the kitchen.

"Mike, I think it's more a question of just thinking about what you're going to say. We do take comments more personally."

"No guy would give a shit if someone called his ass fat."

"Sure. But mention something about his car in a negative way, and watch the reaction."

"The difference is we don't have a hissy fit. We might have a few words, shake it off, and go have a beer afterward. You won't find us running off to sulk in the bedroom."

"You should know after all these years that she's sensitive to comments about her body."

"It gets tiring. There's got to come a point when it doesn't matter like that to her. Ten years, and she reacts the same stupid way."

"It's called being respectful."

"Is it really?" he asked, taking a new beer from the fridge. "I walk on glass around here, too afraid to say shit about anything, because it might set her off. What the hell kind of communication is that?"

I shrugged. "You've done it for ten years. It can't be that bad."

"Did you and your ex fight over stupid stuff like this?"

I laughed. "We didn't fight at all. We weren't together long enough to piss each other off."

He snickered. "You spared yourself all this crap. Charlie's going to be here soon. I'll be embarrassed if he sees Bernadette having a fit. Do you have any idea how much the boys at work are going to lay into me?"

"What does it matter what they think?"

"It matters a lot," he replied. "We spend eight hours a day together. They're my posse."

"Posse," I scoffed. "You guys change oil."

"My point is," he said, "when we are together, it's about laughs and not taking things seriously. When you girls get together, it's about bitching about your men and your boss and the girl down the street who looked at you the wrong way. All I know is that you girls cannibalize one another."

"We express our feelings."

He pointed down the hallway. "Great way to express your feelings."

The buzzer from the downstairs vestibule rang. Mike pushed a button.

"Come in, Charlie," he said. "Bernadette, get dressed and get out here. Charlie's coming up."

"Why don't you go see her in the bedroom? She'd probably want you to do that," I suggested, knowing that was what I would want.

He shook his head. "And reinforce her behavior? I don't think so."

There was a knock at the door. "Yo, Mike," a voice boomed.

I looked at him. "'Yo, Mike'? Really?"

He grinned. "That's my boy."

"He is over fifteen, right?" I asked, knowing that dating a minor wasn't cool.

Mike raced past me and flung open the door. Charlie was a short, wiry guy wearing a baseball cap. He yelled and jumped up, banging his chest against Mike's. I wanted a replay to make sure I had seen two grown men act that way.

"Brother, how are you hanging?" said Charlie, strutting inside the apartment, still wearing his blue work coveralls with his name stenciled on the front pocket.

"All good. All good." Mike went into the fridge and grabbed a beer for his coworker.

Charlie took it and lifted it to his mouth, tilting his head back until half the bottle was drained. It was followed by a belch.

"I've been craving this all morning. Freakin' plug got stripped, and I had to dink around for an hour regrooving it. Freddie made me charge the customer nothing."

"He better not take it out of your check."

"Who knows with that goof?" Charlie said, shaking his head. "He's a company man."

Mike turned toward me as I stood watching the two of them banter.

"This is Bernadette's friend Larissa. This is Charlie."

Charlie held out his hand to shake; I noticed it was stained black. I reluctantly held mine out and felt the roughness of his skin. I checked "body massage" off my future list of things to do with Charlie. I hated exfoliations.

"Hey, Larissa. Cool." Charlie grinned, taking a slug of his beer with his free hand. I saw his gaze work its way down my body and back up. I shivered, having just been visually judged.

Charlie was a few inches shorter than me and had acne scars scattered across his cheeks.

"So you work with Mike," I said, already knowing the answer but unsure what to say.

"If you want to call it work," he replied, laughing with Mike. "Most of the time, we're pranking one another."

"And your boss is okay with that?" I asked.

Charlie waved me off. "Most of the time, we're down in the pit. He never comes down there."

"The pit?" I asked, but I received no answer.

Mike suddenly laughed. "Remember that time you changed the oil buck-ass naked?" He high-fived his buddy.

"The guys up top were pissing themselves, trying to hold it together, seeing me down below wearing just my boots."

"Sounds like a blast, I suppose," I said doubtfully, wondering if Bernadette knew what the hell was going on at Mike's work.

"The guys got a kick out of it."

Mike laughed. "If we're ever looking for a laugh, Charlie will do something at work to make it happen."

Charlie barked, "Like the time I chugged half a can of ten-thirty oil and then vomited all over the back of John." Mike and Charlie howled.

This is a stand-up guy? I hoped Bernadette was going to make an appearance before I found out Charlie also cross-dressed on weekends, making it impossible to move forward with our pending date.

I heard the bedroom door open and watched Bernadette make her way toward me, as if reading my mind. She had changed into baggy jeans; her makeup hid all signs of crying. Her hair was tied back into a ponytail.

"Hey, Charlie." She nodded at him. He waved back.

"Are we ready to get silly on the town?" Charlie replied, looking at each of us.

I nodded. "As long as no one drinks motor oil, okay?" They laughed, not realizing I was serious.

I caught a glimpse of Mike, who looked away when Bernadette stared at him. I figured an apology for his comments was not coming anytime soon. I sighed. *Nothing like starting a double date with tension in the air.* I wondered if it was a full moon.

I sat in the front seat of Charlie's red Mustang. Mike and Bernadette squeezed into the backseat. Because of the argument, there was no hand holding between them. There was no hand holding between Charlie and me because his hands were disgusting. I feared scuffing my fingernail polish against his skin.

"Are you into thrills?" Charlie asked me as he shifted into fourth gear. We passed slower traffic.

"I'm not sure how to answer that one," I said. "If you're talking about putting me inside a room with three dozen pails of ice cream, yes, I'm into thrills. If your thoughts include me jumping from a plane, forget it—you can do the death dive yourself."

He laughed. "I know nothing about you. Tonight's all about experimenting and learning about one another."

"As long as it involves keeping our clothes on. My ex patiently waited six months before he saw me once run from the bedroom to the bathroom in my underwear."

He beamed. "So you have an ex-boyfriend."

"Ex-husband."

"Second divorce?"

"First. Give me more credit than that."

"Just asking. You never know these days." He grinned and slapped the dashboard with his hand.

I looked at him. "Does it matter?"

He nodded. "Better having a second ex. You'd be collecting good juice from two ex-husbands."

"Well, I'm not. We're both broke, so I hope you're paying for whatever thrills we have tonight."

"He can afford it!" shouted Mike from the backseat. "He bonuses every month for changing the most cars."

"Now she knows how much I make," scolded Charlie. "That's how they get you for alimony."

I crossed my arms. "First, I have no idea what you make. Second, you're getting ahead of yourself, as if we're going to get married and divorced and I'm going to live off your alimony."

"Isn't that why women get married?" he said in all seriousness.

Bernadette finally spoke. "How about for love, Charlie?"

He snorted and wiped his nose with the back of his hand. "Dream on. I don't buy that shit for a minute. If it was true, every divorced woman should walk away from the marriage with the same change in her pocket she brought into it."

"With that attitude, you'll never be married," she said sternly.

"Good. I'll die rich and in the same house I bought."

"I'll be there to support you, buddy. Dudes don't give up on one another." Mike slapped the back of Charlie's seat.

Charlie grinned and pointed toward the backseat. "With bros like that, who needs women?"

"In that case, why am I riding with you in your car?" I said.

"A dude's still got to have fun."

"Let's see how much laughing you're doing before this night is over," I said, shaking my head.

"Sorry, Larissa," said Bernadette. "I should have known a-holes hang with a-holes."

"Ouch," said Charlie. "What's with your bedmate, Mikey boy?"

"You tell me," he replied. He took a shot at Bernadette. "Must be that time of the month."

"I sense rising aggression in the car," said Charlie, twirling his hand. "I believe our activity will help eliminate some of this, ladies."

Bernadette snickered. "Only if it involves us kneeing you two guys in the balls."

"I can tell you that won't be happening," replied Charlie. "But feel free to go nuts behind the wheel." We pulled into a roadside amusement park that featured bumper cars, go-carts, and paintball.

"This is the date?" I asked, looking at Charlie.

"There's a slight hint of man date involved." He laughed.

"I thought wearing your work coveralls covered that aspect of man date," I quipped.

He shrugged. "Why change from something I'm comfortable wearing?"

"How about," said Bernadette, climbing from the backseat, "because you smell like oil?"

He turned to his work companion. "Mike, does my smell bother you?"

Mike shook his head. "Like a fine cologne, my friend."

"The smell of Bengay would turn you on," said Bernadette, walking up beside me as we headed toward the entrance gate.

"Is this what double dating is about?" I whispered to Bernadette.

"Sorry," she replied. "I'm feeling like a real bitch tonight after the comments from Mike."

I put my arm around her. "Don't worry about it. Let's try to make the best of this night and salvage it."

"More like shelve it. I'm still so pissed."

"If it means anything coming from me, your ass is looking mighty hot," I said, slapping it with my hand.

"Watch it," she warned, "or you'll be coming home with me."

"At least I know your hands are clean."

"That's something I've always insisted on—that Mike never come home with dirty, oil-stained hands. He scrubs them raw at the shop."

"I'm keeping my fingers crossed no opportunity arises where Charlie has to hand-toss a salad for us."

She laughed. "I'll intentionally vomit in mine to keep from eating it."

"Hey," I said, "you missed the two of them body-slamming each other in the chest when Charlie arrived."

"Believe me, I've seen that stupid move dozens of times whenever any of those guys get together. I warned Mike—no guy in his late twenties should have any desire to rub chests like chimpanzees."

"Come on, ladies," beckoned Charlie. "I've just paid your admission. Come choose what color bumper car you want to drive."

"I sure hope they have my hot pink here," I called out sarcastically.

"Interesting choice of dating activities, Charlie," replied Bernadette, shaking her head. "Do you think giving your date whiplash leads to romance?"

"I've got to know that my woman is tough."

"That's what dogs are for," she replied.

He ignored Bernadette's comment. "Everyone, choose your battleships!" he cried out, fist-pumping Mike as they climbed into bumper cars.

Bernadette and I took cars that were side by side.

"I didn't need to shave my legs for this," I commented to her. She grinned back at me.

"I have on my granny panties," she replied.

"Have you ever done this before?" I asked, waiting for the cars to move.

She shook her head. "I think we just steer this thing around the floor."

"Where's a mall to stop at?"

She laughed. "These would be perfect on Black Friday. We could mow aside the people who are in our way for the bargains!"

"That's why I order online—with a bowl of potato chips next to me on my bed."

A buzzer went off, and I felt my car power up.

Bernadette shot off past me. I pressed a pedal, moving my car slowly ahead. There were two other cars on the floor besides those of our group. They were kids, and I steered carefully around them. I was smiling at the little girl driving one, when my car leaped forward, struck from behind. I let out a squawk. It was my date, Charlie. He was laughing hysterically.

"Gotcha!"

I was about to tell him that wasn't nice, when Bernadette's car came out of nowhere, broadsiding his vehicle. He slid to the side.

"Street justice!" she cried out to him.

"Way to go, girl!" I shouted. She gave me a thumbs-up just as Mike plowed head-on into her. She let out a wail. "Asshole!"

Enraged, I planted down my pedal and steered straight at Mike. He saw me coming and moved his car out of the way. Where he once was, now the little girl I had smiled at moments earlier appeared. I took her out. Her look told me I was no longer her friend.

It was now on between Mike and Bernadette. Bernadette's car weaved among the other drivers, stalking Mike. Mike swung his car around, facing hers. Both headed straight at one another, unwavering. The frontal impact sent both cars shuddering to a stop. Charlie's car steered out of the crowd, striking Bernadette on the side.

"I got your back, bro," he called out to Mike.

I saw my moment and seized it. Charlie was busy giving Mike a thumbs-up. He failed to see me heading right at him, broadside. I heard a satisfying grunt of surprise when I connected.

"Payback!" I shouted, and I pulled away.

He signaled to Mike for a joint attack against me.

I steered my car frantically, trying to prevent the two quick-change oilmen from cornering me. Bernadette joined my defense by running block. She launched her car between me and the two boys, taking a double hit. She was flung around inside her car like a doll.

I steered my car around and headed right for Charlie. The weight of my car forced Charlie's to rebound into Mike's. Before Mike could stop spinning, Bernadette walloped him. He was thrown the opposite way.

"What the hell?" he shouted, staring angrily at her. The attendant must have noticed the growing hostility; he shut us all down. The two little girls let out cries of disappointment. We all climbed out of our vehicles, breathing heavily and rubbing our necks.

The attendant glared at us when we walked past, heading toward the bumper-car entrance.

"Nice moves," Bernadette said, complimenting me.

"You too. We held our own." We joined hands while we walked.

"These girls think they owned the track, huh?" said Charlie. "How about we take it to the range?"

"Paintball," agreed Mike, nodding. "You two up for it?" He gave a questioning, beckoning look.

I had never shot a paint gun or any gun. *How hard could it be? Point and shoot?* "Yeah, we're up for it," I replied for both Bernadette and me.

She leaned over to me. "Go for crotch shots."

My eyes lit up. "You're nasty." I laughed.

"We can blame it on bad aim since it's our first time."

"Mike might not be able to use his parts for a while. You'd only be hurting yourself," I cautioned.

"After today's comments, he ain't getting a piece of my fat ass for a long time."

We entered a small wooden building that had a desk and counter; guns were displayed on the wall. A teenager was eager to help us.

Each of us was given a white bodysuit with a hoodie. We were handed miniature rifles and two hundred rounds of ammo. I was bracing myself for the cost, when Charlie pulled out his wallet and paid for everyone. It was my turn to be impressed—until the two-for-one coupons came out. His bonus remained intact.

"Girls," said Mike, rolling his hood over his head, "prepare to be annihilated."

"This is for fun, right?" I asked, pouring the pellets into the gun as the attendant had demonstrated.

"I can truthfully say no one has ever hit Mr. Stealth," replied Charlie, attaching his extra ammo onto his belt.

"Who's that?" I asked, confused.

He pointed at himself. "Me."

"You have a nickname for this?"

"You betcha. Be prepared to not see me coming. Your ass is grass."

"At least it's not fat," said Bernadette from behind me.

"Drop it already," said Mike, shaking his head.

Her face darkened. "The only thing I'll be dropping is you with this rifle."

Charlie whistled. "Sounds like you're a wanted man, hombre. Don't worry—Mr. Stealth has your back."

Bernadette laughed. "In that white getup, looking like an overgrown doughboy, how can I not miss you, Mr. Stealth?"

He scowled.

The attendant read the rules of fair play. The intention was simply to stalk and shoot. The competition was point-based, so every time someone was hit, he or she added points to his or her tally. Each player had a different color of paint to determine ownership of hits. My paintballs were red.

"Are you ready?" asked Bernadette, walking up to me, holding her rifle. Her white hoodie was cinched tightly around her face.

"Hell yeah." I smiled. We out a war cries and jumped toward one another, banging our chests together. It was time to battle.

We ducked into the playing field one at a time, spaced a minute apart to give each of us a chance to move into position. I was first, and I scrambled along the maze of walls, rooms, stacks of plastic logs, and boulders with strobe lights going off. I began to sweat in my white jumpsuit as I ran like a felon, holding my rifle aimlessly. It suddenly occurred to me that I was going to be shot at and hit. This was going to hurt. My mind was already preparing excuses for my dad about how I'd lost $10,000 of dental work. Unless the television news recorded my plane crash-landing into a field and me walking away minus my teeth, I would never hear the end of it.

I was quickly disoriented by the flashing lights and occasional clouds of dry ice being pumped from somewhere. I stopped running when I noticed a set of wooden stairs that led to a wall about ten feet tall. Images of men on rooftops flashed in my mind. "Shoot from a vantage point" was the one thing I'd taken away from sniper movies. I climbed the narrow stairs and slithered on top of the narrow rooftop. I was a sitting duck if anyone saw me first. There was no other way to get down but the stairs in front of me. I lay prone and placed the rifle in front of me, trying to hold it steady despite my gasping breaths. Despite all of the cardio training at the gym, I was still breathing as if I were giving birth.

I waited.

I prayed it wouldn't be Bernadette I'd shoot. We all looked alike in the white jumpers.

It wasn't long before I saw a shadowy figure below me, creeping out of the fog, about ten feet away from my wall. My stalker was walking cautiously in a half crouch, rifle at the ready. I couldn't tell who the hell it was, but I had to take my shot.

I pulled the trigger.

The rifle started barking out a stream of paintballs. I arced it along the floor and across the figure twenty feet from me. I cut a line of red splashes across his head, back, and shoulders. He went down. I'd earned six points.

The figure let out a wail. I scrambled down from my perch.

"Charlie!" I yelled when he stood up and I saw his face. "I shot Mr. Stealth!" I held up my rifle and fired off a few victory rounds into the air.

He looked at me, stunned, and I pointed my finger at him. "Gotcha, hotshot. You ain't so stealthy after all, oil boy." I dashed off in the opposite direction before he could respond. I heard repeated rounds coming far from my left.

I rounded a corner, surprised to see someone hightailing it toward me. Without even thinking, I raised my rifle and fired off a round. Red opened up on his forehead. It was Mike. Before I could say anything, Bernadette ran up behind him, squatted, raised her rifle, and screamed, her finger jerking repeatedly, pumping out a stream of balls. Mike caught the majority in his backside. Two went astray and hit me on the shoulder; I screamed.

"Goddammit, that hurts, Bernadette! Ow!" I rubbed my shoulder. She ran over to me and gave me a hug.

"I'm so sorry!" she said. "I only meant to hit that bastard."

I grinned. "Guess what? I tuned Mr. Stealth back there. He didn't see me coming!"

"You're kidding me!" she squealed. I looked over at Mike, who was groaning.

"Is that your green across his groin?"

She laughed, grinning. "Told you I would."

I was about to reply, when sprays of blue began showering me and Bernadette. Charlie had run up behind us, firing.

"Not my teeth! Not my teeth!" I shouted, dropping my rifle and holding my hands over my face. I felt tiny punches littering my body. Bernadette was screaming too.

The gunfire stopped.

Charlie ran up and stopped in front of us. "See? I told you I'd get you. Didn't see me coming, did you?"

Bernadette growled. "You were hardly stealthy, running up to us in the middle of the path. Only because I was talking to Larissa did you get the drop on us, you dick. Never mind. I can see Larissa dirtied your virgin jumpsuit. So much for never being shot, loser. And just so you know, your buddy here with the red dot on his forehead and splattered backside was our handiwork. He took one to his junk because you weren't there. You let your boy get slaughtered."

I grinned. "It was especially awesome screwing those guys like that."

"Mike!" Charlie yelled, running over to his friend. "You're a fucking mess. Can I help you, man?"

"I got all this shit under my mask."

"Perhaps my ass won't look so big with one eye closed," called out Bernadette.

"My nut sack is on fire too." He heaved. Charlie bent over him, trying to help him to his feet.

"Come on, guys," I beckoned. "Game's still on. I still have a shitload of ammunition to hit you with."

Mike shook his head. "I can't see straight."

"I can see the welt on your forehead from here," Bernadette said.

"Yeah, it's huge, Mikey," confirmed Charlie.

"Sorry," I said. "You must have a really big forehead. I didn't even really aim."

"I'm calling it quits," Mike said. "The guys at work are going to have a field day making fun of me for looking like this."

"Quit?" shouted Bernadette. "You guys are the ones who wanted to come here. It was all your idea. You take one headshot and you're out?"

"You also shot me in the balls. I can't feel anything to my knees. Thanks."

"A woman scorned," she replied.

"Let's call it off," said Charlie. "I can't let my boy get hurt any more. Besides, I've been shot now. It sucks. Why play when I can't be Mr. Stealth?"

"Are you kidding me?" I said. "You lose your title, and you now want out?"

He nodded, removing his helmet.

Bernadette shook her head. "See, Larissa? Under all that chest hair and strut, guys are soft. Never be intimidated by them." I nodded, agreeing with my friend.

"Let's go change," she said, taking my arm. "We'll meet you losers outside by the car." We walked off.

CHAPTER 24

Give Me Your Best Surprise

July 17, 11:39 p.m.

Did I tell you I like surprises? Bernadette gave me a good surprise last night at 3:22 a.m., banging on my parents' front door. She was crying. Her eyes puffed. My mother was at the door, doing up her housecoat. My dad went ranting back up the stairs and down the hall, took a piss, and headed back to the bedroom.

Bernadette had gotten a surprise she didn't want, need, expect, or understand at 2:00 a.m.: a get-the-hell-out-of-my-apartment surprise. Her boyfriend/common-law husband—whatever you wanna call him—had now become a leech/douche bag/ asshole and booted my friend from their place after all these years. He had had enough moods and demands and not enough sex.

For Mike, the novelty of shacking up with an older woman had lost its allure after ten years. All his friends were notching scores with twentysomethings who slept with their makeup

on, left the bras at home, shaved everything
every day, preferred going to bed at 7:00 a.m.
rather than waking up at 7:00 a.m., grocery
shopped at Shoppers Drug Mart, and thought it
was cool to have a flashing neon Budweiser sign
over the big screen.

We sat around the table, me blurry-eyed from
waking up unexpectedly, my mom the same, and
Bernadette from crying—three women consoling
each other with matcha green tea. I couldn't
remember the last time I had been up and sober
at 3:30 a.m.

It was decided Bernadette would stay across
the hall from me in the spare room. My mother
was appalled at how young men treated women
these days. It was the least we could do for
her until she could get back on her feet.

*****

Sitting inside Bernadette's favorite dessert café, I stared across the
table at her. Her eyes were still red from crying. Really, she hadn't
stopped crying. She was just out of tears. She was dry-crying by
that point. I'd thought getting her out of the house into a public place
and stuffing her face with the fattiest treats she enjoyed most would
help her get a grip on her pain and tears. My plan wasn't working.
Bernadette had been staring at her death-by-chocolate cake with
double fudge for the last fifteen minutes, since it had been served.
I had eaten my vanilla-and-raspberry pudding within five minutes
of receiving it. Every so often, Bernadette would let out a large,
startling gasp; wipe at her tearless but red eyes with the napkin; and
moan. Her birthing sounds were starting to annoy several tables
around us.

I sipped at my water, waiting for her to say something. So far,
there had been no adult conversation, just her gasps and moans.

I was unaccustomed to seeing Bernadette without makeup, and today her face looked ashen; her hair was matted and unwashed. The end of her nose was swollen and red from her blowing it. She resembled a woman who had just had the floor of her life ripped up from under her. The reality was that she had, now that Mike had thrown her out. His move was the biggest blindside we'd ever witnessed.

"Are you going to eat that?" I finally asked, teased by the cake long enough.

She waved it at me.

I pulled it across the table toward me.

"Why, Larissa?"

"I'm hungry, I guess."

"Why'd he do this to me?"

I felt like an idiot. We weren't here for the fudge. I stuck a chunk into my mouth anyway.

"I wish I knew," I replied, talking with my mouth full. I wanted to know as badly as she did. No one had heard anything from him.

"Has he responded to your texts?"

She shook her head, letting out a moan. She held out her phone, showing me all of her texts. There must have been hundreds.

"I thought you guys were solid," I said, meaning it. "Ten years. It doesn't get more secure than that."

She let out a wail. More heads turned toward us, this time from behind the counter.

"I gave him the best years of my life." Her lower lip quivered.

"You still have your thirties."

"I gave him my ovaries."

"Physically, they're still inside you."

"They're old now. I waited because of him. And now they're rotten."

"Your eggs are the same age as mine. We can share if it comes down to it."

Bernadette muttered, "I feel like the biggest loser, justifying that for all these years, it was okay he did not propose to me."

"The ring doesn't mean security. I had one. Look where it got me." I flashed her my ringless hand.

Her brow furrowed. "At least you had a formal commitment to plan your future. Obviously, I was a fool for accepting his word."

"You had love."

"Really?" she protested. "How real was his love if he could do this to me?"

I shuddered. "He is a guy after all. Would we really expect anything more?"

Bernadette snapped, "With my guy, I did. He promised me a lifetime. We shared an apartment lease agreement together!"

"As good as the paper it's written on," I said, pointing my spoon at her.

She pressed her face into her hands. "What am I going to do? How do I go on?"

"Like me—depressed, hopeless, suicidal."

"You've got your family," she moaned.

"So do you. You're now living with them."

"Mike! Oh Mike! Come back!" she wailed through her fingers.

I lowered my head to avoid the icy looks from everyone inside the café.

"You might want to keep it down. I don't think Mike is listening," I suggested, not wanting to be booted out before I finished her dessert.

"I just want to smash his neon Budweiser sign over his head."

"Is that just a thought or an upcoming action? Action equals an assault charge, and he's not worth going to jail for."

"I want him to hurt like I do."

"That'll just hurt his head, not his heart."

"He's ripped mine from my chest, squeezed it in his oil-stained hands, taken a bite from it with his crooked teeth, and tossed it away."

I glanced at her. "That image is going to haunt my dreams, girl."

She moaned. "Cursed? You think you're cursed? He booted me out of our home," she said, turning angry. "Who does that to the person they love?"

"Were you guys still fighting after our double date?"

She nodded slowly. "I was still pissy at him for the fat-ass comment he made."

"And?"

Bernadette looked uncomfortable. "We had it out after we got home. Royally."

"Please don't tell me my double date was the reason for the demise of your relationship. I can't live with guilt of that magnitude."

"He said he was fed up with my moodiness."

"That's PMS."

"He said younger women don't let their moods dictate how they treat their men."

"What the hell is that supposed to mean?" I said, shoveling a large spoonful of fudge into my mouth.

"They want their men happy, so they keep their moods in check," Bernadette said.

"It's called having no self-respect."

"He said I'm too sensitive. It was like walking around broken glass, never knowing if I was going to blow up."

"So he doesn't like you being a girl," I protested.

She wailed, "He's trading me in for a younger model."

"How much younger can he go before jail time? You're only thirty!"

"One guy at his shop is dating a twenty-year-old. He says she's all over him from the time he gets home from work until he goes back to work the next day."

"Okay, so he's got himself a horny twenty-year-old who probably can't spell her own name. How long do you think that relationship is going to last before she gets bored with smelling the same odor of grease and runs off with a guy her own age? Besides, trying to have supper with her hopping up and down in his lap gets too awkward. Sure, it makes for a great work story, but eventually, the guy's stomach wins out. He'd rather stuff his face with a steak than see two breasts bouncing up and down between him and the plate of food."

"We never had dinner-table sex," she whispered. "I let his needs go unmet." She wailed some more.

"Neither did I," I said, trying to put it in perspective. "There's nothing romantic about washing spaghetti sauce off your ass."

"Oh Mike. I'll do you on the table," she moaned.

"Listen, you've got to move past this."

Her eyes flew open. "How? Ten years! What confidence will I have to feel secure again, Larissa? Fifteen years into a relationship? Thirty years?"

"I think by thirty years, you'll both want out desperately, and it'll be a welcomed mutual run for the door."

Bernadette balled her fists. "I'm just used goods. What man will want me now after I had sex with the same guy for ten years?"

"Well, last I checked, most men will still take you even after birthing six kids. Besides, with your jugs, you have a guaranteed concert pass. You let those babies swing free and bounce, and mass traffic accidents will follow you down the street. Me? I couldn't get a honk or an obscene call."

Her eyebrows arched. "I need a man. I need Mike."

I shook my head knowingly. "I hear ya, girl. Except Mike doesn't want you. He wants girls who are too young to have corns on their feet."

"I feel so alone," she whispered.

"It's been less than twenty-four hours."

"I had the names of our two children picked out: Billy and Baily."

"They won't expire," I said. "You're that much more prepared for your next man. One less thing you two will have to worry about."

"Oh Christ, the pain, Larissa. It's deep inside my chest," she said, jabbing her finger so harshly into her breastbone that I could hear it. "I feel like I am about to die."

I tried to redirect her. "You should try your cake. It's simply to die for."

"I'm not hungry," she croaked. "I'll never eat again in my life."

"You know, that's a good approach if you're going to stay with my folks for a while. My dad starts to bitch about the food bills."

She looked at me. "I'm not moody, right?"

I paused. It was a defining friend moment. I responded, "Not at all. He's nuts for thinking that."

"Exactly what I think." She stared at the tabletop. I was about to suggest again that she try the fudge, when she rubbed her hands in her hair angrily; the end result was a mash of frizz.

"That goddamn genie," she growled. "His stupid ice cream and his stupid cards cursed my relationship."

"I had forgotten about him." I laughed. "Could he possibly be right about our lives?"

Her face darkened. "Ten years of sweet romance. And then one bowl of Belgian Waffle Delight and that stupid Nine of Swords, and—*swoosh*—my entire life turns to shit."

I thought about her statement for a moment, realizing the potential. "Hey, now that we're both single women, we can tear this town apart in search of fresh kill—you know, tag-team the guys. Be like the fearsome twosome. Maybe even get some kind of street cred that makes us irresistible."

She wept. "I want my Mike."

I looked at her with raised eyebrows and wiped the last of the cake from my lips.

"He booted your ass out. Why would you want him after all that? He kicked you out in the middle of the night. You left with all your belongings in garbage bags. You want him back?"

She raised her head, eyes red, lips quivering.

"Yes."

CHAPTER 25

Strike Three

I asked Bernadette to join me for my ex's family baseball game outside the city for three reasons. One, she had a car to drive us. Two, she was crying at the kitchen table during breakfast, and Mom glared at me as if to say, *Get her the hell out of here.* Three, she needed to burn off some of her Mike pain by swinging a baseball bat and yelling from the outfield.

I wore my yellow track pants, a T-shirt, and a baseball cap. I studied Bernadette as she drove. She was wearing oversized sunglasses, black sweatpants that ended at her knees, and a black T-shirt with her hair pulled back. I was certain she had not showered since Mike had given her the boot. "What's with the all-black attire?" I said, nodding toward her outfit.

"I'm a widow in mourning."

"Mike's not dead."

"My heart is."

I grabbed a pack of gum from my purse and popped a piece into my mouth. Bernadette took one and chewed slowly.

"Be prepared," I warned Bernadette. "My ex's family is a little weird."

She stared out the front window. "I'm not too worried."

"Just don't agree to go into the barn, no matter what they tell you."

She glanced at me. "Why not?"

"Like I said, they're a little weird. They have this first-timer initiation for people who come to their farm. When I got suckered into going inside, I was doused in pails of melted butter and rolled in chicken feathers."

"What the hell for?" she asked, alarmed.

"Apparently, it's a century-old tradition brought over from Ukraine."

"Sounds weird."

"I told you."

She let out a long sigh.

"Have you heard from Mike?" I asked, bracing myself for the answer.

She sniffled. "Yeah, one text: 'How you doin', babe?'"

"That's sweet."

"And then he asked if I had consulted a lawyer."

"Endearing. I could give you mine."

"Nope." Her head shook. "I don't want to do that in case he comes to his senses and wants me back."

I was shocked. "You'd actually do that?"

"In a heartbeat. I love him, Larissa. He's my heartbeat."

"He's more like an arrhythmia. I'll warn you now that if you try going back, I'll kick your ass."

"It's tough," she breathed. "I have no one."

"Neither do I. I'm so hard up I'm playing baseball with my ex's family today. How sick is that?"

"You're no different, keeping that door open."

I shook my head over what she said. "This is different. I'm not looking for a way back in. We're done. Now it's a friendship. And don't forget we ended on good terms. I wasn't shooed out of my place in the middle of the night, scrambling to fill garbage bags with my belongings along with a frozen turkey."

"No, but you hosted a huge wedding and stiffed your dad for all that booze. He was telling me all about it last night."

"It's a bit of a sore spot for him."

"I'll say. He downed two whiskeys and said at least forty 'yollups.' All I could do was nod my head, afraid to say the wrong thing."

"And that's another reason I could never rekindle with my ex. My dad wants his head. Actually, he also wants his testicles. He said he was kicked in his nuts by my ex for running up that booze tab."

"Your dad has an edge."

"He's a vocal person. His doctor would never accuse him of holding in his feelings."

Bernadette let out a moan, squeezing and shaking the steering wheel.

"Are you having a stroke?" I gripped the seat. *Should I be reaching over to grab the wheel from her?*

"It's the only way for me to release the buildup of toxins around my heart."

I tried to settle my own pumping heart after her unexpected fit. "Try to give me some warning before you do that, all right? I nearly shat myself."

We drove in silence for another twenty minutes before the trees began to thin out to open land. The large red barn was my marker that confirmed we had arrived at my ex's parents' house. He called it the farm, but no farming had ever taken place there. His father had dreamed of a retreat outside the city with a red barn. He'd bought the land, built the barn, and kept nothing inside it. The only animals that grazed his land were deer, and those he shot with a rifle from the second-floor window in the barn.

Bernadette steered the car off the highway onto a gravel road, where we moved slowly on small rocks that crunched under the car's wheels.

"Why would anyone want to be out here?" asked Bernadette, puzzled. "There's no Walmart."

"I know. There's a whole lot of nothing out here."

Bernadette wrinkled her nose and rolled up her window. "And it smells."

"That's called a septic field."

"Gross."

We pulled in behind a series of cars and pickup trucks. We could see bases being set up in the field beside the house. My ex's cousins were milling around, tossing balls and running short sprints.

We opened our doors.

"I have zero energy," complained Bernadette, shuffling next to me.

"Suck in this beautiful air."

"I should have stayed home and listened to your dad."

"Believe me, you'd rather be hit in the forehead with an errant pitch than hear him rant."

A woman ran toward me. I recognized my ex's mother's beefy frame. I had not seen Charlene since we'd announced our divorce. I wasn't sure what to expect, but I checked her hands to see if she was carrying any sort of potential weapon.

Her empty hands were outstretched to either hug me or choke me.

She wrapped her arms around my waist, burying her face in the nape of my neck and rocking me.

"Bernadette, we've missed you so much. Nothing feels the same anymore."

I was shocked by her remark. This attitude was far different from that of my dad, who wanted to murder her son.

"I've missed you guys," I replied, meaning it. The family had its quirks, but they treated me well, like family.

She kept me in the clinch. "I pray every day for a miracle," she said, her voice muffled against my shoulder.

I wasn't sure how to respond.

"Pray with me, Larissa," she said, and she began to recite a biblical passage I didn't recognize, since I was off religion altogether.

I mumbled something in response. She squeezed me and pulled away, smiling.

"Such a beautiful girl," she said, still clutching my shoulders.

"I wear makeup now," I replied, blinking.

She placed her rough hands against my face, pressing in both cheeks.

"Such a beautiful, beautiful girl."

I could see Bernadette staring from behind her sunglasses.

Charlene stepped back.

"Thanks," I replied, not sure what else to say after the hug, something I rarely had gotten from her son. "You were always so kind," I said to her, meaning it.

"My husband is so excited you decided to come today. He's got your catcher's mitt ready."

I didn't own sporting equipment and refused to buy any, especially for a one-time occasion. Charlene's husband had bequeathed me his own glove, which he had used for decades. This had become known as my glove.

"How is Aleksander?" I asked, knowing his son's divorce was a major disappointment. We were the first in their family's two-hundred-year family tree to break the sanctity of marriage. I considered it a good sign that he still thought of the glove as my glove. To me, it was a symbol I wouldn't be banished to the barn for another feathering.

Her face darkened. "My poor Aleksander has another hernia. This time, he was carrying our old toilet down the staircase and felt something let go inside his waist. The toilet crashed down the staircase and through the wall. Turns out half his guts were pushing out."

Hernias were a family trademark for all of the men in my ex's family. The doctors could never say for certain if the issue was due to a weak hereditary muscle structure or just plain stupidity for carrying and lifting objects way too heavy for a human man. My ex had two mesh implants, the first one by age fourteen. At that time, he had been proving to his aunt how strong he was; he had started an isometrics fitness regimen a week earlier. He'd gotten down and picked her up off the ground, grabbing her by her thighs. His aunt weighed four hundred pounds. The soles of her nylon-covered feet had just left the ground, when they'd all heard something let go from inside my ex. The next month, he'd had surgery to insert a mesh to keep his insides inside. The year before we married, he had been helping his lead guitarist carry his Marshall stack amplifier out to the van after a gig. There was a reason the eighty-pound speaker had built-in carrying handles on each side—it required two people to carry it without injury. My ex, besides his love of drumming, also loved eating pizza. He had been in a rush to catch the pizza joint before it closed for the night and had taken it upon himself to carry the Marshall alone. He had torn open next to his original mesh implant. He'd felt too ill afterward to go get the pizza.

Aleksander had so much scar tissue from nine hernia operations that it was almost inconceivable there was anywhere left to tear. Apparently, there was. One old-fashioned five-gallon toilet had proven everyone wrong.

"Well, I hope he's able to participate today," I said, trying to sound enthusiastic, knowing he was one of the better guys at batting.

Charlene smiled. "He and I thought it through, and I've wrapped a roll of duct tape around his waist. He said it'll hold everything in so he can play."

Knowing Aleksander, he'd play even if he had to drag his guts behind him.

I turned and pointed. "Charlene, I'd like to introduce my best friend, Bernadette. I think you met at the wedding."

Charlene gave Bernadette a hug. "Of course I remember. Your boyfriend gave me ten percent off my oil change on Wednesdays. Did he come too?" She started looking around.

Bernadette stiffened.

"He left me," she said before I could head off the flow of wound juice from her emotional hernia.

"He left you?" replied Charlene. "He's such a nice guy. I said to Aleksander afterward what a wonderful couple the two of you made. And he gave me ten percent off my oil change to boot."

Bernadette heaved and then burst into tears. I reached over and hugged her and said to Charlene, "This is all pretty fresh. It just happened the other day. He kicked her out of their apartment in the middle of the night. All she had time to do was pack her stuff into garbage bags."

Charlene was outraged. "He's just lost me for a customer, the heathen."

"I thought it'd help if she came out and played today. Fresh air and family fun is the world's best medicine," I said.

"The absolute best, dear. You're part of our family. Welcome," she said, hugging Bernadette again. Bernadette wiped away tears with the back of her hand.

"Listen, girls," Charlene said encouragingly, "we're just about ready to start. Why don't you saunter over to the field? My son should be out there somewhere too," she said, looking directly at me and winking.

She walked away, and I signaled for Bernadette to follow me.

Bernadette walked beside me with her head down.

"Who would have thought?" I said. "When we were in elementary school, could we ever in our lives have envisioned this exact moment in time?"

"What do you mean?" she asked glumly.

"Both single again. Girls on the prowl."

"And about to play baseball with your ex-husband's family on their farm," she added.

"Yeah, that too. We have brand-new futures about to be written for us."

"Perhaps today I'll meet a farmer, hook up, move out here, and smell shit all day long."

"See what I mean?" I beamed. "A new future."

"Can't wait," she said without enthusiasm.

We stopped and chatted with a group of people. I recognized some who were part of my ex's family. Others must have been locals.

"Hey, you guys made it." I recognized my ex's voice. I turned to see him sauntering toward us from the barn.

"Hey," he said, nodding toward Bernadette. She waved.

He grinned at her from under his baseball cap. Heedlessly, he stroked his fingers through his wispy beard. "Thanks for supporting my gig at the club." He faced Bernadette. "Larissa texted me about what happened with Mike. Pretty crappy stuff, man. What surprised me was that he seemed so happy at the club. Did you guys have a blowout or something?"

Bernadette's tears were hardly dry after speaking with his mother, and I wasn't about to let the water flow again. I redirected him.

"How's your dad doing?" I asked. "I heard he's in need of another surgery."

He slapped his hands together. "Stupid toilet. I swear they need to put caution labels on them for one person not to carry them alone."

"Do you think that was the problem?" I asked.

"My dad wouldn't have tried if he'd been warned how heavy it was going to be."

"Okay, but shouldn't he have stopped when he picked it up and realized it was far heavier than he'd thought rather than trying to continue down the stairs?"

"You know my dad—once he starts something, he has to see it through."

"I heard it fell through the wall."

"Now it's sitting inside the dining room, against the china cabinet. After all that, the darn thing didn't break."

He nodded toward Bernadette. "Do you need gear?"

"What do you mean?"

"Glove?" he said, pointing to his hand.

"Sure, I guess. I've never caught a ball, so I'm not sure how useful I'll be."

"This is for fun. No one expects to be struck out at bat or get picked off at the bases."

"Then I'll need a glove."

"Right- or left-handed?"

Bernadette looked blank. "I really don't know."

My ex took out his wallet and tossed it at Bernadette. She caught it.

"Right-handed," he said, pointing at his wallet in her right hand.

"Cool," she replied. Even I was impressed. Creative thinking was a rarity.

She handed back his wallet, actually smiling a little.

"If you need help with the bat, I'll show you."

"Just be careful she has proper form," I warned. "We're workout partners, and I can't have her on the injured list, or my motivation to attend will quickly flatline."

"You betcha," he said.

"Hey, did I mention I landed a gig designing a website?" I said gleefully.

"You did?"

He smiled. "That should prove to your dad there is money to be made."

"Once I actually get paid, I'll be flaunting it in his face. He won't be able to say his daughter is a deadbeat."

"Live your life the way you want it. That's my motto," he said.

"Perhaps that's not a healthy approach—may be the reason we're both living back at home with our parents."

"Three hots and a cot. Where's the problem with that?"

"Lack of independence?"

"I happily forgo independence every time my mom dumps my laundered clothes back in my room and puts them away."

"The least you can do is fold and file them," I said, shaking my head. His old habits hadn't changed from when we were married.

He shook his head. "I'd feel wrong taking away something she enjoys doing."

"She enjoys doing that as much as I did when we lived together. Not."

"Obviously, I didn't marry my mother."

"No, you certainly did not." I laughed, throwing a punch at his shoulder.

A whistle went off, signaling the beginning of play.

There were twenty of us in a circle. Gloves were handed out, and two teams were assigned. I was included on the team with Bernadette, my ex, and his mother. His father was on the opposite team.

My team was at bat first, and my ex was first to have a go at it. His dad was pitching. My ex nailed his first swing, sending the ball soaring past the outfield. He trotted in for a home run.

I was third to bat.

Aleksander winked at me and tossed me a pitch someone swinging a toothpick could have hit.

I missed.

"Head up, Lars," said my ex. "You can rock it out."

I connected with another mercy pitch from his dad. I ran.

I rounded three bases and was heading toward home plate, when the ball was thrown to the catcher. My head must have been blocking his view because when I dipped to slide, the ball bounced off his forehead; I made the run. By the time I stood up, my ex's cousin already had what looked like a horn protruding above his eyes.

"I'm so sorry," I said, meaning it.

He laughed it off. "I've been hit there so many times I get a contusion by sneezing too hard."

"Do you want some ice?" I offered.

"Only if it's in my glass of rye." He grinned, leaning over to take a drink from the plastic cup beside him.

"Don't worry about him," my ex commented. "He's too smart anyway. He's an accountant. He's the oddball who never fit in the family because of his professional status."

His cousin laughed. "I have no idea what professional status a drummer holds."

"We beat to our own drum, my friend."

I pointed at Bernadette. "She needs a batting lesson. She's up next."

My ex ran over.

"Here—grip the end of the bat right here," he explained, placing her hands near the end of the bat. "Set your legs in this stance, bring the bat back, and watch the ball. It's all about timing. You don't need to swing hard."

"Why is this thing so heavy?" whined Bernadette, trying to get the feel of the bat.

"It's aluminum. Bats don't get any lighter than this one."

"Fine. Let me be like a caveman and try to hit the ball."

To help out, Aleksander stepped off the base, moving closer to Bernadette. He gently tossed the ball.

She missed.

He arched another soft throw.

She missed.

"On three," he called out. "One, two, three."

The ball fell past her before she swung. She tossed the bat down. "Stupid game."

She walked off and sat down on the grass next to me.

"Good try," I said.

"Like everything in my life. A swing and a miss."

"You gave it a good try. It's not easy. Today was only the second time I've connected with the ball."

"I just want to call Mike right now and ask him how he's doing, what he's doing, if he's missing me."

"Not a good idea. Get those thoughts out of your head. It's over for now. You can't make someone love you, Bernadette."

She bit her lower lip.

"Hey, team!" Charlene called out. "We're going out to the bases!"

"Let's go catch some balls," I urged, pushing Bernadette up onto her feet.

Bernadette looked terrified. "The last thing I need is a horn growing on my forehead."

"Keep your hat on. It'll provide some cushioning."

My ex signaled for her to cover left field. I was going to try pitching.

The first batter, Charlene's sister, caught my first lob and slammed it away for a home run. Charlene booed her.

Next up was Aleksander. He was smiling, swinging the custom-made bat he had carved himself years ago. I'd picked it up one time, and the weight had nearly torn my arms off. No one used it except him, because it was insanely overweight.

Now that the sun was out, he had taken off his T-shirt and wore just his blue sweatpants and runners. Gray duct tape was wrapped around his waist dozens of times.

"Shouldn't you be on the disabled list?" I joked, pointing at his homemade abdominal support.

"Listen, chickee-poo, this old man can still run circles around you."

"Aleksander!" someone called out. "You have an unfair advantage—half man, half tape ball."

"Don't come unraveled," joked someone else.

In the distance, a person hummed a few bars of stripper music and shouted, "Take it off!"

"Smart-asses, huh?" he said, swinging his bat to warm up.

"You still look sexy, honey," called out his wife.

"I'm going to wrap you up tonight," he said.

A few gagging sounds came from the players.

"Come on, bionic man—show us what you've got."

He grinned, stepping up to bat. "Make me work," he said to me.

I spun my arm around in circles, loosening my shoulder joint.

"Hey, Aleksander," someone from my team said, "you're looking like a life-sized fly strip."

I took advantage of the distraction and tossed the ball. He reacted at the last second, swinging wildly with a loud grunt.

He missed. He walked around in a circle, bending side to side.

"Nice try," I called out.

"Again!" he shouted, grimacing.

He readied himself.

I threw out a speedy underhand pitch. Aleksander put his entire body behind the bat and completely missed the ball. His momentum spun him in a circle. He crouched and squeezed his sides, groaning.

"This is no time to cry like a baby," someone heckled.

"You okay?" I asked, concerned over how pinched his face was.

"Again," he breathed, his face ashen.

He stood up, arching his back and taking a long, deep breath. His eyes watered.

"You sure?" I asked doubtfully.

He raised the bat to his shoulder, breathing heavily.

I tossed him a ball as gently as I could; it should have been an easy hit.

He released a tremendous grunt and swung, torqueing his hips and snapping his body in a large arch. He missed. Aleksander fell to the ground, writhing on the base.

We rushed to his side.

"My guts. I heard ripping." He clutched at the tape around his waist.

"Is it your hernia?" cried out Charlene. "Where's it hurt, honey?"

"I'm on fire. Stupid tape didn't work."

"Do you need medical attention, Dad?" asked my ex.

He shook his head. "I need a drink of rye. Quickly."

Someone handed over a silver flask. Aleksander chugged, lines of rye running down the cracks on each side of his mouth.

He pushed himself up. "More tape. Wrap this tighter."

"Should we cut that off first?" I inquired. "Redo the tape bandage?"

"No way," he breathed. "It's the only thing holding my guts in place."

"Dad, are you going to be okay?" said my ex, concerned.

"This is nothing," he growled. "Remember when I impaled myself on the canoe paddle? That was pain, sonny boy."

"What's he talking about?" I asked my ex.

"Dad's talking about when we went white-water rafting. He refused to wear a wet suit because that was for sissies. The instructor kept trying to tell him the suit wasn't just for the cold but also for protection. Well, he got tossed off the canoe, and when he landed on the paddle handle, it slid up the side of his Adidas shorts into his you-know-what."

"Good grief!" I cringed.

"Your father is one tough dude," commented Bernadette, joining the fray around the batter's mound.

"Everyone," shouted my ex, "let's call it a day since my dad can't compete! We can move along to the open-pit barbecue. I'm going to move my drums outside to play a little dinner music while we feast."

I was relieved. Sports were stressful for me. I'd had no exposure to them growing up, so I'd never related to why people became so competitive just to say they won, when they received nothing.

"Ready to eat?" I asked Bernadette, who was taking her hat off, releasing her hair.

She grimaced and let out a long breath. "Would I be a terrible person if I said I'd like to head back to the city? This sun has kicked the crap out of me. I think I just need to go lie down."

My ex turned to look at us.

"Are you sure? The pig roast is amazing. The baked potatoes rock. And I'm playing solo."

"I'm beat," confessed Bernadette. "Sorry."

He brightened. "Cool. I get it. Next year, my dad will be healed, and we can do the entire game. You must come back for it."

She nodded unenthusiastically.

"Hey." He turned toward me, wiping sweat off his forehead with the back of his hand and grinning. "I was thinking you and I should hit that cottage campsite thingy we stayed at while we were married. Summer's almost done. What the hell? Let's send it out with a bang."

I stared at him, unsure what he meant by that.

"Are you talking just us," I said, pointing at him and me, "or *us?*" I circled my finger around Bernadette, him, and me.

"You and me, man. Straight up."

"Things are different now," I said, studying him.

"Ah shit, on paper only. I'm me. You're you."

"I'm not sure that would be a good idea," I managed to croak.

"If you get your driver's license by then, you can chauffer me to the site. Show off your road skills. Burn some rubber, baby."

I was incredulous. "If we do it, it's all aboveboard. No funny business."

"As real as Baba's homemade pierogi."

"Sounds enticing and totally foolish. And my dad would kill me."

"My mom and dad would love it."

I pointed my finger at him. "No bullshit. We go out there to relax. No expectations."

"Get out of Dodge for a couple of days. I'll make all the arrangements."

I was shocked. "Take-charge guy. Impressive. I no longer have to be your personal travel agent."

"Just do it, Lars," Bernadette said, tossing up her hands.

I poked him in the chest. "No funny business, buster. This is only an end-of-summer getaway."

"I guarantee that's the way it'll go down," he replied, laughing.

CHAPTER 26

I Never Promised You
a Rose Garden

I think raising a daughter—me—was tough on my dad. I never really felt he knew what to do with me. I think every dad always envisions having boys. I'm not sure why, but I think it may be that male-to-male bonding thing. Dads just seem to know how to entertain their boys while they grow up. They know what boys like to do from being boys themselves, and traditions are handed down from dad to son, from son to their son, and so on, generation to generation.

My sex tossed all that out the window. My dad was left with a box full o' boy toys and a daughter who simply overwhelmed, confounded, and terrorized him over what to do with me.

We tried that toss-the-ball thing, but I didn't really get it. He did try bringing out a baseball bat once. Now, that was even stupider. He tossed the ball to me twenty times, and twenty times, I missed. Twenty times, I had to put the bat down, run after the ball, and throw it back to my dad. Exhausting. No fun.

We tried flying a kite. I found that fun—at least until the kite got up in the air. Then what? Hold on and watch it float. I finally let go and watched it fly far, far away—gone for good. I told my dad it slipped from my hand.

We tried tobogganing one time. I was maybe six or seven years old. It was fun climbing the tall hill, holding my dad's hand. He carried the toboggan in the other hand. Somehow, he convinced me the ride down would be fun. It was not. It was fast. When I jumped off from fear, I tumbled down the hill. We never did that again.

We tried skating. It hurt to put the skates on. The fall on my ass hurt even more. I cried. We went home. We never went back there again.

*****

I steered the Reliant into the parking lot of the Driver's Examination Services building. My dad sat next to me, having instructed me every minute of the drive from our place, as if it were a last-minute cram session. My head was full of dos and don'ts. I was ready for anything the roadways tossed my way.

Dad hopped out of the car, checking to ensure that all of the lights were functioning and that no violation would occur.

"Remember, Larissa," he said, taking my arm lightly, "count to five at every stop sign. Drive five kilometers below the posted speed limit. Double-shoulder-check before changing lanes. Use your goddamn turn signal every time you change lanes or turn a corner."

"I got it," I said, trying to sound confident despite my urgent need to pee.

He rubbed me gently on the shoulder. "Just do what we practiced all these months. You don't need to be perfect. Just keep the infractions in check to stay below fail, and don't make a big screwup."

That comment pressed harder on my bladder. My hands shook with nerves, and my fingers were cold. I was in the spotlight with this test—my dad wanting me to succeed after working hard to teach me, Dalton expecting a pass, my ex wanting me to drive us to the resort. When had it all gotten out of control?

"I'll do my best, Dad," I responded weakly.

"Chin up."

"Okay."

He pointed toward the door, and I left the car and headed toward it, walking into cool air. I felt as if I were about to throw up. The front desk quickly had me registered, and in a few minutes, a woman sauntered toward me in flip-flops, a tired look on her face.

"Larissa?" she said in a voice that wasn't really asking.

I nodded. "Present."

"Let's go," she said, holding a notepad.

"Long day?" I said, hoping to make conversation and warm her up, to make me seem a real person. I'd read once that psychos had a harder time killing their victims if they got to know them.

"My day?" she asked, raising her eyebrows. "Brutal. You're my sixteenth test this afternoon. All failed."

I looked at her, alarmed. "Aren't you supposed to curve the results?"

"Driving is a privilege. Today sixteen people should stick with walking."

I gulped. I was testing with an assassin. "I guess the odds of passing are in my favor."

"I haven't passed a driver in three weeks."

My heart dropped. "I hope luck will be on my side then."

She glanced at me. "You'll need more than luck."

She looked at her watch as we walked up to my car. "Let's make this fast. I have five more after you, and I need to get home to feed my cat. I forgot to leave out his food this morning."

I unlocked the car. "Perhaps we should do the shorter route to help you get home faster."

She leaned down to get into the car. "It's rush hour. You'll screw up in the first five minutes for an automatic fail." She shut her door.

My dad stood off in the corner of the parking lot, smoking. He shot me a thumbs-up. Good thing he'd missed my instructor's comments. They would have provoked a major tuning.

"Okay," said the instructor in a monotone, "the test begins the moment you pull out of this driveway and terminates when the car crosses back into the driveway. You will follow my commands. At all times, obey the traffic laws. At no time will I inform you about your collected violation points unless one of two occasions arises. The first is if you have reached the maximum violation points, resulting in a fail. In the second, for any automatic fail, I will inform you and terminate further testing."

"Do I get any bonus points for demonstrating advanced driving techniques?"

"If you pull any driving stunts, I'll ban you from a retest for a year."

"Okay then, let's stick to basics."

"Let's."

I backed up, sweaty hands on the steering wheel at the ten-and-two position. My instructor turned off the radio. Silence shrouded the car; the only sound came from me swallowing.

I reached the end of the driveway and stopped completely. I waited in the silence. I wondered if she was attempting to lure me into making a turning decision on my own. I kept my foot pressed on the brake. She nodded.

"Turn left."

I flicked on the turning indicator, looked both ways, and gently steered the car in that direction. I heard her scribbling a note in her book. My heart jumped. *What the hell did I just do wrong?* Already, in the first seconds, I was inching toward failure.

I focused on the speedometer, keeping it five kilometers below the posted speed limit, just as my dad had instructed. A sign partially covered by a tree branch caught my eye. The speed was to drop by ten kilometers an hour. I quickly reduced.

I heard a huff from beside me, followed by more writing in the book. I wanted to ask her what the hell I was doing wrong.

We came to a stop sign. I counted to five during a complete stop. There was more writing.

My instructor pointed to a residential street, and I turned the car down it. There were several parked cars. I searched my mind for procedure. My dad's voice boomed in my mind: *Signal around. Stay completely in oncoming lane. Give right of way to oncoming cars. Don't run over a cat dashing across the street.*

I steered around the cars and merged back into my lane. We came to the end of the street and another stop sign. I was about to approach and stop at the sign, when I noticed the pedestrian crosswalk before it. I brought the car to a standstill in front of the crosswalk before proceeding ahead. I merged onto a main roadway and stayed in the right lane while cars sped past. I held my speed. The instructor directed me to a side street. There was more writing. Ahead were pylons against the curb. It was time to parallel park. I approached and parked behind the markers, awaiting instructions.

"Move forward, and park the car between the pylons. Touch any of the pylons, and you will fail. You have one opportunity to complete the test by parking the car. A second attempt will result in failure."

I shoulder-checked, put on my turn signal, crept up, and positioned the car, procedures that had all been drilled into my head by my dad. I backed up, swung the wheel, and stopped the car where I wanted it.

Don't forget to put the car in park, boomed my dad's voice, and I followed by shifting into park. I waited. The instructor looked both forward and back, made a note, glanced my way, and then opened her door and looked down at the space between the car and the curb.

"You need to be within twenty-four inches of the curb." She slammed her door. "Continue down the street and turn into the first parking lot on our right."

I steered the car out of the stall, cursing myself for missing the distance. I had practiced countless times so that I was always within the allotted distance. Dad would kick my ass.

We pulled back into the testing facility's parking lot. We crossed the threshold.

"Your test concludes now," she said flatly as she scribbled notes in her book.

I pulled up to the parking stall, stopped, let out a long breath, and released the brake. The car rolled into the steel pole and stopped with a lurch and a bang. My hand shot up, putting the car into park.

"For the love of God!" I shouted. I placed my head on the wheel. *One for the curse. Zero for Larissa.*

I heard the tearing of paper.

"Here," she said, handing me a large piece of paper I intended to cut my throat with. "You passed."

"Get the hell out!" I shouted, stunned. "How? All that writing?"

"Perfect score. I was doodling. Good luck with your driving career." She hopped out and walked toward the building.

Tears rolled down my cheeks. I was a licensed driver.

My dad came walking over; I rolled down my window.

"Dad! I passed," I said, waving the papers outside the window in front of him. "I think this means I've dodged the family black cloud!"

"You dented the bumper," he replied, walking past me to the front of the car.

He bent down, examining the damage.

"How bad?" I asked, grimacing.

"Scuffed the bumper pretty bad. Reverse the car back a few feet," he instructed, signaling with his hand. I started the car and reversed. He had me pop the trunk. He reached inside and walked back to the front of the car, carrying a spray can of paint. He shook it vigorously, a metallic sound coming from inside it.

"What are you going to do?" I asked, leaning my head out the window.

He bent over; I heard the sound of paint being released. A plume rose from the front of the car. He stood back, waving off the cloud around his head.

"There," he said, walking past me with flecks of gray over his hands and face. "The scuff is gone."

CHAPTER 27

Yesterday's News

I stopped the Reliant directly in front of the house and honked. There was something special about being a driver. There was a sense of power to it.

My ex shuffled out the front door of his parents' house, his mom waving from behind him. I waved back.

"Congratulations on your license," I heard her say from the doorway. I waved at her again and smiled.

My ex opened the door and flopped down beside me.

"Cool ride," he said, studying the gray cloth-and-plastic interior and nodding in approval. Three variations of air fresheners hung from the rearview mirror to stifle the underlying smell of old car.

"I guess," I replied. To me, a car was a car.

"We're riding in style today," he said, grinning and putting on his seat belt.

"If you mean as opposed to the transit bus, yes. But I can assure you we won't be turning any heads."

"My mom wanted you to come in for lunch."

"That's nice of her, but we need to get on the road. This is my first time driving on the highway. I want to take my time."

"I hear you," he said, loudly chewing his gum. He drummed on his lap.

"How's your dad's hernia?" I asked, having not spoken to him since the baseball game.

"Brutal. He had to go in for emergency surgery. When he unwrapped the duct tape later that night, his stomach bulged out like a basketball. It was straight to the hospital. He's recovering nicely." He smacked his gum.

"And the toilet?"

"Still leaning against the china cabinet," he said, laughing.

I steered away from the city and entered the highway that would lead us to our resort.

"How'd your dad take the news of us hitting our hump shack?" he asked, chewing.

"Still wants to kill you."

He nodded. "Figured that."

"And just to clarify, we are not going to be spending time away at a hump shack. It's a cabin—got it? Ex-spouses don't go to hump shacks together."

"Just a term," he replied, snapping his gum.

"Get it out of your head."

"Whatever." He stared out the passenger window.

"Hey," I said, looking his way, "we've never actually driven together when one of us was the driver."

"Feels weird."

"Yeah. How'd we get out last time?" I asked.

"My dad, remember?"

I nodded. "That's right. He was thinking about sleeping in his truck overnight to avoid having to drive back the next day to pick us up."

"Actually, he did."

"He did?" I thought for a moment. "No, I'm sure he said he drove home."

"Nope. Just didn't want you to get upset. He parked down the road."

"Get out of here," I said, looking over with a grin.

"That's why he wanted to stop at the A&W on the way home. He was starving."

My eyes widened. "But we didn't, because I told him I had to get home and cook for us."

"I know."

"You guys should have told me the truth! Now I feel terrible. I starved your dad."

"He lived."

I was annoyed.

We drove in silence for the next few minutes.

"Nice hair," he said out of the blue. I'd had streaks put in a few days earlier. His comment caught me off guard. My ex had no powers of observation. He had always been oblivious to most details or to changes around him that didn't involve drums. Six months into our marriage, I had begun tanning sessions three times a week. I had even used an enhancer tablet, giving me a great Cuban-gold tan over the course of three months. My ex hadn't noticed. Each night, I'd lain down next to him in bed, my skin darker and darker, until my arms had looked like burned wood next to a cadaver. My tan had outlasted our marriage.

"Thanks."

"Welcome."

He took a CD from his knapsack and held it up.

"Where do I put this to play it?" he asked, looking at the dashboard.

"Back in your bag. This car only has a cassette player."

"Get out of here!" he said, not believing me.

"This car predates the conception of car CD players by three years."

He shoved it back in his knapsack. "I wanted to play you the latest set of tracks my band is going to be covering."

"You have a CD of original songs. When are you guys going to record your own tunes? I thought you had something in the works."

"Still deciding which ones to record."

"Is this the road?" I asked as we approached a sign along the highway.

"I think so," he said, leaning forward, as if that extra couple of inches would provide him the clarity to confirm the turn.

As soon as I left the highway and turned onto the gravel road, it all came flooding back. The trees overhung the road, resembling a tunnel. We had joked at the time it was the road leading to hell.

When the cabins appeared, déjà vu struck me. Except this time, I arrived as a divorced woman.

"Looking good," stated my ex, smiling, still chewing his gum after the ninety-minute drive. "Let's get at it," he said, popping open his door when I came to a stop in front of our cabin.

I turned the car off. The voice of Auntie Tina echoed in my head from when my dad had told her about my trip out there with my ex. "Good for her. Keep trying—two, three, four rounds—to squeeze money out of the son of a bitch."

That was never my intention. I wondered if that was how it looked to outsiders.

I got out of the car and closed the door. A horrific thought occurred to me. What if this wasn't simply the getaway my ex had promised? What if the bastard was setting me up for a shot at romance? What if, when I opened the door to the cabin, it was prestaged? Shit, what a cluster fuck that would be.

"Come on!" he urged, walking to the door and waiting for me to open it.

My steps felt wooden, ghostlike, as if I were walking to the gallows. I reached the door, and he signaled for me to take the door handle. My arm weighed a million pounds. A pulse throbbed in my head. My heart thumped. What would I find? I pictured the worst behind the cheap wooden door: flowers, champagne, a spread of four cheeses, rose petals covering the floor, the bath drawn, Barry White on the stereo, scented candles flickering, and a bowl of heated body-massage oil. *Shit.* My heart raced. *Yes, no, maybe so?*

A moan escaped my lips as I turned the handle, allowing the door to slowly swing forward.

I stepped over the threshold. Darkness and the smell of cedar surrounded me.

My ex's hand reached across me and hit the lights.

The room appeared—vacuumed carpet, drawn blinds, made bed, silence.

Romance, my ass. For my ex, romance ended with the rotting corn husk.

He pushed past me. "Let's unpack and see what's on TV."

I followed him inside, looking around the sterile room.

"Whoa. Wait a minute," I said, stopping and pointing.

"What?" he asked, confused, flopping down on the bed.

"That," I said.

"You got me. What?" He rolled onto his stomach with the remote.

"The bed, dummy. There's only one."

"There was only one last time."

"Last time, we were married."

"So?"

"So I don't sleep around."

"No funny business. I told you. This is aboveboard."

"Hard to be aboveboard with one bed," I protested.

"Don't worry. I'll face the other way."

"You do that. I'll also be stacking every pillow in this place between us. If you make one attempt to climb over, I'm pepper-spraying you."

"That's pretty nasty."

"So is my naked body. Don't attempt anything."

"Whatever," he said, turning on the television.

I put my duffel bag on the table. "Are we not going for a hike?"

He shook his head. "I brought the Wii."

I stared at him. "Are you saying we're staying inside the cabin to play video games, when we have canoes, hiking trails, and tennis courts outside?" Although I had never been an outdoors type, even I could see how dumb his plan was, driving all the way out there to play games on the TV.

"I have Wii tennis, you know."

"You're an idiot," I replied, taking my bag to the washroom to unpack my bath products.

"This is a fifty-five-inch television, Larissa," he called out from the other room. "The game will feel real, yo."

"Christ," I mumbled to myself. I opened the night bag and started removing items, placing them on the bathroom counter. I organized my lipstick, deodorant, and toothpaste in a row and was extracting my hair dryer, when my ex walked into the bathroom and stood behind me. Before I could say anything, I heard fluid hitting the toilet bowl.

"Are you pissing?" I said, seeing his reflection in the mirror. He was slouched, one arm braced against the wall.

"Yippers."

"Dammit, man. I told you I didn't like it while we were married, and I certainly don't want to see it, hear it, or smell it while divorced."

"What's the big deal?"

"Ah, it's disgusting."

"Don't look."

"I can hear it foaming, you idiot."

The toilet flushed. "There. Done." He walked past me back to the room. I heard the television turn on.

Some things never changed. He had the same gross habits, and he didn't wash his hands. I began to understand my dad's rage the first Sunday after my ex had moved into my parents' house, when my ex had walked into the bathroom while my dad was brushing his teeth after breakfast and taken a piss. My dad had gone ballistic. My ex had tried to explain he was acting out his European roots. My dad had reminded him he wasn't European and said if he ever tried to do that again while he was in the bathroom, he would zip it midsquirt.

I took my time unpacking my sundries, still steaming over the one bed. I was also in no hurry to play video games on a resort getaway.

"You coming?" he called out. "Do you want your same player— Olga?" he asked.

"Don't tell me she's still set up on there." I stormed into the room. Olga was the female Wii character I had set up back when we'd first started dating.

"Of course. Why not?" He stared at me, my controller in his hand.

"Because when you get divorced, you get rid of all your shit from your spouse."

"You want me to get rid of Olga?" He was incensed. "All your high scores will be lost."

"I don't care. They don't matter. I was never supposed to play Olga ever again."

"All the memories. You can't kill off Olga."

"She's dead to me."

He looked at me, hurt. "You're mean. What's happened to you since we got divorced?"

"Times have changed. I have changed."

"What's supposed to happen to Olga's nemesis, Spencer, if she's gone?"

"Kill him off, too. You and your next girlfriend can develop your own characters. I'm sure she won't be impressed to see your ex-wife's Olga on there."

"Of course she won't mind. No one kills off their computer character."

"Well, I just did. So do her."

"This is supposed to be our weekend," he whined.

"Correction. This is a weekend that happens to have the two of us together. Don't expect to be holding hands and singing 'Kumbaya'— got it?"

"Then what are we here for?" He sat up on the bed, tossing the controllers onto the quilt.

"You tell me! You said we should come out here."

"Like old times."

"We don't do things for old times. Our times were over when we signed the paperwork, remember?"

"So"—he leaned back on his elbows—"what are we supposed to do for the rest of the day before we go back tomorrow?"

"It sure as hell won't be playing Wii. Why'd we drive out into the bush to do that? We could play in your parents' basement. I figured you wanted to come back out here to do nature stuff—like backpacking, swimming, playing horseshoes."

He looked at me strangely. "Last time we were here, we played Wii, and anyhow, you don't like doing nature stuff any more than me."

My shoulders slumped. "Fine. But I'm killing off Olga and making a temporary character."

"Sure." He perked up.

I sat down on the bed next to him, grabbing the controller. I waited while he ran through the menu to select a game. He glanced over at me.

"What?" I asked.

"Your legs are shaved."

"They need to be. I'm a woman." I pulled down my sweatpants, covering the calf that was exposed.

"Since when?" he mumbled.

"Since when what?"

"Your legs. They were always hairy for me."

I was shocked he'd even noticed. When we had gotten married, I'd shaved my legs every second day. After the first three months, the routine had become every Sunday. He'd never seemed to care. Silence was acceptance.

"My dates like soft, shaved legs."

"You're still dating?"

"That's what I should be on right now, a date, not with my ex-husband."

He pointed at the door. "Why not go walk the campsite? There's bound to be a tent of boys."

"Funny."

He refocused on the menu. "Do you have a game in mind?"

"Sorry, but I don't. I brought my hiking boots, thinking we'd be walking around outside, not Wii bowling. It's so cold in here that I need to wear my jacket anyway." I shivered.

"Crawl under the covers."

"Now, there is a good idea."

"Take off your boots. We don't want to dirty the bed." He indicated my footwear. The asshole actually thought I was going to get into bed with my boots on. I should have said something, but I kept my mouth shut and pushed them off, each with the other foot. They fell to the floor.

"Happy now? The cleaners owe you a medal for saving them work."

"If we ever want to come back here again, we shouldn't leave it a pigsty."

My face lit up. "You and I are never coming back here. It's creepy enough we have the exact same cabin as before."

"That must mean something."

"It means we got the same cabin. Nothing more. If anything, it shows how stagnant we are together—we can't even change the place we stay on a getaway."

I pushed back the quilt with my feet and screamed. I jumped up, threw down the Wii controller, and stood back from the bed, pointing. My ex screamed, jumped up, fell to the floor, and scrambled to the door.

"What the hell is it?" he breathed, keeping a hand on the doorknob. "Spider? Snake?"

I pointed. "Blood. My blood."

He looked at me, lost. His baseball cap on his head faced sideways.

"Did you cut yourself?" He walked over to me, realizing he wasn't going to be impaled by fangs.

"Yes. Last year." I was panting, staring at the bed.

"So why are you in hysterics? You scared the shit out of me. I think I sprained my back." He tried to stretch.

I pointed at the sheets. "Look at that," I growled.

"Is that dried blood?" He bent slightly.

"I just told you it is."

"Looks shaped like a small heart. And that's yours?"

I nodded. "You're damn right it's mine. Remember when I caught my leg on that stick while walking up to the cabin door?"

"Yeah."

"And it poked a hole in my pants."

"Sure."

"And I bled."

"Yeah, I remember all that. It was no big deal. A small scab."

"The deal," I said, staring angrily at him, "is I picked off that small scab when I lay down in the bed, and I bled on the sheet in the shape of a heart."

He looked confused. "And? What's your point?"

I flushed. "You meathead, the point is my blood is still on the sheet! They've never washed the sheet we were lying on a year ago." I shivered. "That's repulsive."

"Actually, that's pretty gross." He made a face.

"There's no way in hell I'm sleeping in that bed."

"We have to."

I shook my head. "I don't have to. In fact, I don't have to stay here a minute longer. What else haven't they done? How many asses have sat on that toilet since it's been cleaned? What kind of excrement is on the quilt? You know those never, ever get cleaned. I just sat on that with my shaved leg exposed!" I rubbed at my calf.

He backed up a step.

"So what now?" he asked.

"We're out of here. I'm demanding we get reimbursed for this contaminated cesspool. We're driving back home tonight."

"But we'll be driving in the dark. Can you see?"

"I'm a novice driver. I'm not blind."

"What about deer on the highway?"

"Stick your head out the window, and tell them to bugger off."

"So no Wii?" He looked crestfallen.

I glared at him. "How can you even think about gaming, knowing year-old blood has been festering in this room? God knows what kind of fluids we're standing on right now. And you made me take off my boots!" I scrambled to put them back on. I'd be tossing the socks when I got home.

*****

Right up until my ex left my car after I pulled up in front of his parents' home, the drive back was silent. I was fuming. My ex, being himself, had no idea what to say.

I drove down to the end of his street and stopped. I wasn't ready to face a barrage of questions from my parents as soon I opened their door. I felt mentally exhausted. It was dark. Most of the stores and restaurants were now closed. I had nowhere to go to hide my head and make sense of my tumbling emotions.

I reached for my phone.

It was late. But my mind was in a state of emergency.

Dalton answered on the third ring.

"Larissa!" Even at this time of night, his voice boomed as if he had just been injected full of adrenaline. "Are you stuck on our project and need some direction to move it forward?"

I took a deep breath. I was bending the client–boss rule.

"I'm stuck. But not on the project."

His voice grew concerned. "Okay. Shoot. I'm here for you."

I hesitated.

My world came pouring out—the guilt, the shame, the need to be with someone I could trust.

"Meet me at my house," he said without hesitation. He provided me with the address.

He told me he was on the road, driving back from his warehouse. He instructed me to use the key to his house he'd given me if I arrived first.

I did. I let myself inside. The bungalow had a warm presence that dropped the anxious turmoil in my guts. The silence was comforting. Nothing about the interior screamed that a man lived there as a bachelor. There were no neon beer signs, oversized televisions, or dartboards. Dalton kept his home orderly. The mastery in how he ran his business was also evident there. I giggled; it took balls to pull off wall-to-wall shag carpeting throughout the entire main floor. My dad would have appreciated the decor.

I grabbed a Coke from the fridge and flopped into a leather chair in the corner of the living room. I tossed my head back and closed my eyes. What did Dalton think of when he sat in this chair? One thing was certain: his thoughts wouldn't be laden with guilt about having gone out with an ex. Poor judgment and decision making weren't concerns for him.

I could feel Dalton's pride over owning this home.

I snuggled my nose against the leather. It smelled of him. The turbulence inside me seemed to flush out, comforted by his scent. I was somehow protected and assured my world would make sense again.

The door opened.

I jumped up, splashing cola across my chest.

"Larissa!" Concern crossed his face as the door crashed closed behind him. He rushed toward me.

I held out my free hand. "No, I'm okay. I may not look it right now with half a can of Coke foaming down my body."

His expression grew darker. He led me into the kitchen and handed me a towel. "What happened tonight?" He leaned against the counter as I dried myself.

Where do I even begin? I flashed my eyes at him. "Long story short, I'm a fuck-up. Plain and simple. Today just proved it, in case there was ever any doubt."

I watched his eyes grow dark.

"First of all," he said, staring right at me, "that's the most-unfair remark you've ever made about yourself. Second, let's head back into the living room. I can see we need to talk."

I followed him and took back my place in the chair I had been waiting in earlier. He sat in the chair next to me.

He released a long breath. "Look," Dalton said, "I know you hate being back at your folks'. No one wants to admit defeat and have to show up on the doorstep with a suitcase because they couldn't handle it out in the real world. I get that. And to a tiny degree, I even accept you've placed blame for your follies on a supposed family curse that seems to derail any goal you've had in your life. Hell, from what you say, all of your family members have been smacked around by this curse."

My face was frozen. "Let me tell you about a genie who confirmed all of this over a bowl of ice cream and a deck of cards."

Dalton cut me off. "I don't give two shits what someone has said to you. Life is not influenced by a deck of cards. But I do take great offense when you think of yourself as a fuck-up. You're not. Not in any sense of the phrase. Hear me out." He held up his hand as my mouth was about to open. "Life is not easy. We can plan all we want, dream as big as we can, and do all the right things, and none of those dreams might occur. That's life. But we can keep going, keep focused, and become motivated by these hurdles, because that's what they are: something we can jump over. They sure as hell aren't roadblocks."

I snapped, "Easy for you to say. You've got it all—a house, a business. Your shit's together, man. What do I have? I have an account on a dating site that sets me up with losers. All men are freaks. Sorry. Where's normal in this world anymore? Who the hell treats a girl to McDonald's on a first date? Huh? I expect that once I'm married, but I want a little romance, a little effort, when a guy is trying to get on my good side. You know what I mean? I've reached so many lows this year. I'm dating guys my mom set me up with. My baba! For Christ's sake, Dalton, today I went on a date with my ex. Yes, I'll say that out loud. So you see what I mean? What kind of loser dates her ex-husband? There was blood on the sheets!" I flung my face into my hands.

"Blood?"

"Long story," I replied, my voice muffled behind my hands. "But take my advice, and don't go back to cabins with your ex. Nothing good can come out of seeing your dried fluids on the same sheets."

Dalton grunted but pressed me no further to explain.

"Listen, kiddo," he said softly. "Do you see one thing that's missing in this house?"

I lowered my hands, looking at him and then around the room.

"A large neon beer sign? What kind of bachelor are you anyway?"

He chuckled. "You're half right. I'm a bachelor. That's not because I want to be, Larissa. It was a decision I chose only because growing my business didn't give me time to take dating seriously enough. But that doesn't suggest I haven't been lonely. I've sacrificed loving someone, being loved. And it's been lonely as hell."

I looked at him skeptically. "Don't give me that crapola. A guy like you—successful, handsome—would have fashion models fighting over you. You're the type of guy with a different woman hanging off his arm every Friday night."

He barked out a laugh. "For your information, girlie, I do my weekly business summary reports on Friday nights. The only girl hanging off my arm is the girl handing me the interact terminal at the drive-through window when I'm grabbing a late-night burger after my reports are finished."

"Get the hell out of here!" I said, breaking into a grin.

"That's better," he said, pointing at me and smiling. "And let me be clear. My last date? You think *you're* a fly magnet for losers? This gal, on our first—and last—date, got so shit-faced drunk on my dad's homemade wine during supper at their place that she went into their bathroom—and this is yet to be fully explained—slumped forward, fell against the toilet, and knocked the tank off the bowl. The entire porcelain tank shattered against the tile floor! Water went one way, down the hall, and my date went the other, into the bathtub, out cold, ripping off the shower curtain on her way in. I got that without a family curse. Go figure."

I grabbed my sides, laughing. It was good to know other people shared my dating pain.

"Okay," I said, "I give in. You've dated losers too. Give me a high five in brotherhood." We slapped hands.

"Good." His look softened. "None of this came easy." He looked around. "The marketplace, tight-ass banks, competitors, bad decisions—many times, I was on the cusp of complete financial ruin. All I could do was keep pushing over those hurdles and convince myself they weren't roadblocks. Some luck. Some tenacity. And somehow, here I am with you tonight. Maybe I owe your ex a wad of cash because your rekindling date led us to this moment now."

I giggled. "Don't do it. He'll just blow it on more cymbals and drumsticks."

Dalton's expression relaxed.

I released a sigh.

I glanced at him, locking eyes. "So the takeaway from this Dalton lecture on life is that nothing comes easy, don't assume other people don't struggle, and I'm only a loser if I give up."

He grinned. "Well done, young seedling. You are a quick study."

I laughed. "Something about this house promotes good learning. Perhaps it's the well-cared-for plants scattered over your tables. What's up with that, huh? That isn't a guy thing."

He beamed. "I've been told plants rejuvenate the air with positive vibes. Besides, that's how I de-stress—by watering my plants after work each day."

"Watch it, buster. You've already won the praise of my mother. But if she finds out you're a plant guy like she is, I might get pressured into an arranged marriage."

He flashed a smile. "And would that be so bad?"

I scoffed. "What priest would find me competent to get married twice within twelve months?"

"We'll use a justice of the peace then," he said, smiling.

"You're such a problem solver. As your wife, I wouldn't ever have to use my mind. You'd make all the decisions."

Dalton fell back into his chair with a laugh. "Hey, remember, I delegate at work. You'd be run off your toes."

"Or maybe I'll be chasing you around the house so you won't have the breath to delegate."

"Oh my," he said. "I'd say you've shaken free from the sky-is-falling blues you had when you called me tonight. I like seeing your smile again."

"Thank my dad for the thousands of dollars in braces. I think he's still making time payments."

"He's a good man. He's the type of father I'd like to be."

I snorted a mouthful of Coke.

"Stop it! I'm wearing more of this soft drink than drinking it! Yes, he's a good guy. Couldn't he stop creeping into my life's plans?"

Dalton leaned over, briefly rubbing my shoulder.

"Deal. As of right now, he's reassigned as my whiskey-drinking partner only."

CHAPTER 28

Working Overtime

I was energized. My legs pumped, keeping up with the sixth level on the treadmill. I grasped the bars, hardly leaning my weight against them. Bernadette stood on the treadmill next to me, taking each step on level two as if it were her final step on Earth.

I was chewing gum. Bernadette was eating a muffin and drinking a Slurpee.

"It was the most ridiculous weekend." I explained to Bernadette about my woodsy getaway with my ex. "I knew it was stupid when he asked me at the baseball game. I convinced myself to say yes simply because I couldn't see how bad it might be."

"And?"

"And it sucked. He sucked."

"What did you expect?" She took a bite from her muffin.

Good question. What was I expecting? "I don't know. Maybe a surprise. Maybe I was thinking we missed something in our marriage and the retreat would help us discover it."

"Are you saying you were hoping you'd get back together?"

"Something like that."

"Either you wanted him back or didn't."

"It's like that unwritten possibility that a couple might reunite in the first twelve months of the breakup."

"Really? I never heard of that one."

"Yeah, well, I sort of thought maybe this was our window to get back together. Obviously not. I can't blame being Ukrainian and the curse on this weekend. I take the hit directly for my own poor judgment."

She glanced over at me. "It's like buying back a car you sold the previous year."

I grimaced. "Worse—like putting unwashed socks back on."

"Yuck."

I nodded. "Going back there with my ex was like putting those old socks back on, and they were damp and stinky."

She held up her hand. "Enough. I'm going to gag on this muffin."

I laughed.

"So it's reasonable to say your ex is a loser."

I laughed again. "Big-time. No reason to mull over what-ifs. He's still immature, goalless, passionless, not driven. I need to truly focus on my future and move past what we had."

"You never really had much, when you think about it. You guys were only married nine months. There were no assets. No kids either."

"We had love."

She smirked. "Look where it got you. Look where it got me. Frankly, love sucks." Muffin crumbs tumbled from Bernadette's mouth.

"I'm so over it."

Bernadette slurped at her drink. "Yesterday I killed my client's hair. She requested platinum blonde, and I killed it. It turned green. She was crying. Actually, she was hysterical."

"What happened?" I gasped. Bernadette was a skilled hairstylist.

"I screwed up. I was thinking about Mike. Thinking about my life." She shook her head. "I wasn't focused on mixing my formula. My boss told me to take a few weeks off and get my shit together. I completely ruined her hair. I ruined her life."

"No, you ruined her hair, not her life. Now you're being dramatic. Her hair can be fixed."

"You're right. It's my life that can't be fixed."

"Don't be silly."

She huffed. "This is the longest I have ever been without a man in my life. Ever. So it's the longest I've gone without sex. My loins are killing me."

I looked at her, surprised. "Your loins are getting cranked into a pretzel because it's been a few months since you last got laid? Honey, I went twenty-nine years before I fully became a woman. I could go months without a sleepless night over it."

She moaned. "This is brutal, Larissa. Men never leave me. I was the one to make that decision, whether they wanted it or not. And I always had three or four waiting in the wings. I put all that aside for Mike. I'll never invest my heart in a younger man. From now on, it's a prerequisite that they are older than me by another decade."

"That's a pretty old chunk of meat, my dear."

"I heard meat ages well with time."

"Not the kind of beef you're thinking about. I doubt it tastes better or works better."

She sighed. "I want a man who's had his heart ripped out of his chest, so he knows what I've felt."

"Ouch. Do you really want someone undergoing lifelong counseling and self-medicating? Crying men just aren't sexy."

Bernadette swept her arm. "Look at all the dudes in here. Not one of them is flirting with me. Have I been tainted? Don't they realize any one of them could have me right now? Right here. They could take me on this machine."

"Please don't. Not with me next to you."

"No need to worry about that happening. These guys are blind or dumb. I might as well be bouncing on this stupid machine naked; no one would be interested."

"I'm sure Leo would have something to say."

"I'd even do him just to make sure I remember how."

I laughed. "Maybe this is your time to take a man break. Sniff the air for a while without it reeking of High Karate or Axe. The space might give you a chance to realize there is a world that exists without men in it. It's fascinating us girls can actually survive, have a life, and laugh without hanging off the arm of the mighty male."

She snorted. "As if."

I looked at her and laughed. "You're oversexed and misled by all the propaganda telling us that without a man, we're miserable alone, spending Friday nights reading a book."

"Reading a book? Now you're describing purgatory."

I snickered. "You're nuts."

"I have to say," replied Bernadette, reducing her speed to a crawl, "your mom's been really cool during my entire heartbreak. We've had some really good chats while potting her plants and pruning. She's a real astute woman when it comes to life and relationships."

I looked over at her. "My mom? Astute? Has she told you her views on marriage and love yet? If not, ask her. That'll rattle your image of her."

"Nah, she's all right. I'd still be crying in my room in your basement if it wasn't for her talks with me. She's trying hard to show me different perspectives."

"Well, if it works for you, good. But I'd recommend you take it all with a really large grain of salt."

Bernadette sipped at her Slurpee. "How's this big project you're working on going? Your mom tells me he's quite the guy. Makes a lot of money, too."

"I don't know how much he makes, but he's certainly running a large business. He's convinced I can turn his company around with a new website."

"Does he realize your ambition is getting twelve hours of sleep a day?"

I laughed. "True enough. The funny thing is, I'm getting kind of motivated with this project. At first, I was like, 'This is crap. Who cares about tape and bubble wrap?' His zealous passion is rubbing off on me. Now I'm thinking about how can I make tape and bubble wrap sexy on his website."

"You're sounding more whacked than me."

I looked over at her. "I have to be honest with you. After the day with my ex at the cabin went sideways, I ended up calling Dalton. I think I needed unbiased man support."

Her eyes flung open. "Don't tell me you screwed your boss!" She laughed loudly, spraying chunks of muffin from her mouth.

I smirked. "Christ no. He's my boss."

"Hey, that seems to be the in thing on those Internet fantasy videos."

I looked at her, confused. "What videos? What are you doing in my basement?"

She laughed some more, opting not to explain further.

"Anyway," I continued, "I needed support, and he was a gentleman. I ended up meeting him at his house. He made me feel comfortable. I felt I was able to open up. It was a real adult conversation that never touched on drums or video games."

Bernadette shook her head. "All that hot man meat, and all of it off-limits for you. You got screwed too—just not how we'd want to."

I shut off my machine, wiping at the sweat on my forehead. "Listen, I need to get back home to work on the project. Our official launch is coming up, and I'm far from that point."

Bernadette stepped from her machine. "Good. I'm so not motivated to be here today. I think I'll veg with your mom over tea and gardening."

I laughed. "You're the daughter she always wanted, talking like that."

We arrived back at my place. I parked the car on the street. My dad was right—the freedom of driving beat walking and the inconvenience of the bus. *Chalk up another score for my old man.* Either he was getting smarter in his senior years, or I was starting to listen.

"Hey, we're home," I called out as Bernadette and I entered the house and walked into the kitchen. It felt as if we were sisters.

There was silence.

"Maybe she's out," I said to Bernadette as we both grabbed Cokes from the fridge.

"Nothing beats a postgame can of sugar," she said, managing a laugh.

"Mom?" I called out again. "You home or not?"

"Shopping?" said Bernadette with a shrug, sipping at the soft drink in the can.

"She would have said that before I left."

"People can change their mind."

"There's no note anywhere."

"In here, girls." My mom's voice came from the living room.

We walked into the room and saw my mom kneeling in front of a plant with clippers.

I should have known. "I was just about to call the cops on you," I said, taking a seat across from her on a sofa. Bernadette sat on the floor next to her.

"You okay?" said Bernadette.

I scrunched up my face. "What do you mean?"

"Looks like your mom's upset."

"I'm okay, girls," she replied, snapping vigorously at a branch.

"Really?" I said. "The way you're working that clipper, you could chop a tree in half."

My mom tossed them onto the ground. "I had a nasty conversation today with Dru, Sebastian's mother. She came over right after you left, as if she was watching for you to leave."

"That's creepy," said Bernadette.

"The whole family's creepy," I said.

"I think she gave me a tuning," said my mom, looking at us both.

"Over what?" I asked, feeling my temperature rising after all that Dru's loser son had put me through.

"That's just it. None of it makes sense. She's ultrapissed that you went on that retreat with your ex."

"What?" Bernadette and I squealed in unison.

"Who cares?" I said, getting angry. "It's none of her business."

"My thoughts exactly," agreed my mom. "Except she's peeved because now she believes you've been leading her son on all this time."

I said, "Leading what on? He's been a hanger-on, like a piece of snot from my nose. He just shows up all the time. Does she know the word *stalker*?"

"I guess since we've never told him to go away, he's taken that as a signal you and he were an item."

"Get the hell out of here!" I burst out laughing.

Mom nodded. "So when they found out you were back with your ex, they felt betrayed."

"Are you back with your ex?" Bernadette asked me blankly. "I thought you said you were done for good?"

"I am!" My arms shot up. "He's history—bye-bye."

"Then why's he saying that?" inquired Bernadette.

"Because he's a loser too. He and my ex should date. They're a perfect match—boring and geeky."

"Anyway," my mother continued, "Dru came over to vent her anger over you abusing her son's emotions. She's had him admitted to the hospital for a few days to stabilize."

"Stabilize what?"

"I don't know. 'Stabilize' is what she said."

"He needs a few shots of electricity to his brain. It's his mom who's ruined him with the morning wake-up back rubs."

"Gross," said Bernadette, laughing and shaking her head.

"I've said this before," I said to her. I turned to my mom. "What I do on my time is mine. Who I see is private. This burns my ass. I wish she had done this while I was home."

"Believe me," said my mom, "I wasn't any easier on her. I told her as strange as her son is, we've always welcomed him into our house."

"You said that?" I asked, amazed.

"You bet. Told her she needed to treat him like an adult and stop holding his hand."

"What did she say?"

"Nothing. Sucked in her breath. Stormed out of the house. Nearly broke our front door, slamming it so hard. I came in here to cool off by trimming my plants." She shivered. "Nasty woman, trying to attack my daughter."

"You've done good, Mom. You saved my honor."

"Good work, Mrs. Androshchuk," said Bernadette, rubbing her shoulder.

My mom looked at me. "You never made Sebastian any promises, did you? Gave him hope there was something between you two?"

"Gross. No way."

Her face tightened and reddened. "And, ah, no, well, you know, a little something-something out of pity?"

Bernadette and I cried out with laughter.

"Absolutely not," I assured her, holding in my guts, laughing. "No mercy anything from me to him!"

CHAPTER 29

What...The...

I closed my door and turned off the light—it felt like the right thing to do. Then I leaned against my door and speed-dialed Amy. I clutched my phone, and when she answered, I whispered harshly, "What the goddamn hell?" She had no idea what I was talking about and said as much in return. I grunted.

"*He's* here!" I hissed into the mouthpiece, as if that would make the realization slam into her brain faster.

"Who's *he*?" she said. I could hear one of her kids having a fit in the background.

"Who?" I shot back as if she should automatically know. "He! My ex!"

She was nonplussed. "So? This isn't the first time." She barked out at her kid to shut up, and the background instantly became quiet.

I growled into the phone, clenching it in both hands against my face. "So what? The *so what* is, he's across the hallway from my room, in Bernadette's room, and the door is closed!"

"No way!"

Now I had her attention.

"Yes way!" I closed my eyes, trying to squeeze out the image of those two walking past me. I hyperventilated while describing it to Amy. "He knocked on our front door. My dad answered. I thought he was here to see me. I told him to get lost. Next goddamn thing I know, Bernadette's greeting him, and those two saunter over to her room!" My stomach rolled; I was certain I was about to barf.

"So knock on the door, and ask what's going on."

I caught my breath. "I can't do that!"

"Sure you can—it's your house."

"No, it's my parents'."

"Then go get your mom to knock. I know your mom. She's probably nearly pissing herself right now, wanting to know what the hell is going on too."

"Hang on," I whispered, putting the phone down on the carpet and quietly opening the door. I didn't have to go far. I ran into my mom, who was crouched at the end of the staircase in her housecoat. We both breathed out.

"Go knock?" I said, signaling with my thumb toward Bernadette's room.

"And say what?" she murmured.

"Anything." I jerked my thumb. "Just find out what my ex is doing in there.

"The door's closed," she commented.

"That's why we have to find out what's going on in there, Mom. It could be relations, and you know that's not allowed inside our house!"

She nodded but looked scared. I dashed back into my room, closed the door quietly, picked up my phone, and leaned my ear against the door.

"My mom's going to knock," I breathed into the phone.

"Hello, you two," I heard my mom say, trying to sound indifferent to the fact that my ex was inside her house with my best friend. "Can I get you both a cup of tea?"

My mom was brilliant.

I faintly heard Bernadette decline. The door remained closed.

"Didn't work," I hissed into the phone to Amy.

"That's not good," she replied.

"No shit." My heart was double-timing in my chest. Time was of the essence. I needed to find out what my ex's game was about. I poked my head out my door. My mom shrugged. I waved at her to scatter.

"I didn't think your ex and Bernadette cared for each other much," remarked Amy.

"Neither did I," I responded, chewing on a nail. I heard a clink over my phone.

"What was that?" I whispered.

"I'm pouring myself a glass of wine, honey. This is turning out to be first-class drama. Screw cable tonight."

"Sadist."

"Bored. Remember, I'm married with children. I have to live vicariously through the exploits of others."

"Dammit," I groaned. "I'm going to try peeking in through the window."

"You're crafty," said Amy with a laugh.

"Desperate." I held the phone to my ear as I slowly opened my door. Bernadette's door was still closed. I snuck around the corner and ran into my mom again at the end of the staircase.

"Go back upstairs," I said quickly.

"Where are you going?" she asked, quietly following me.

"Outside to look in her window."

"Be careful!"

I scowled. "I'm not going to press my face against the glass."

She nodded, her hands clenched in front of her.

I opened the front door. The air was chilly on my bare feet as I stepped on the cold concrete deck that ran the entire length of the house. I crouched and moved in a flurry of quick steps, stopping at the edge of her window. I prepared myself for the potential horrors I might witness as I peered in on my ex and Bernadette.

I swore. The blinds were closed. Bernadette had never closed the blinds since she had begun staying in the room. Now my imagination was narrowing to the sick possibilities of the debauchery that could be occurring right that moment.

I ran back inside and shook my head at my mom when she looked at me, expecting an update. I shot past her up the stairs, heading to her bedroom, which was above Bernadette's.

"Talk to me," Amy said.

"She's one step ahead of me. Blinds were drawn."

"Damn, she's good."

"But why?" I screeched.

"Maybe your ex is pumping her for details on how to win back your heart."

"I hope that's all he's pumping."

Amy shrieked. "Gross."

"Yeah, tell me about it." I was breathing heavily.

I flung myself down on the carpet next to the furnace vent. I pressed my head against the metal floor grate.

"What now?" Amy asked.

I croaked, "I'm trying to listen to the vent. I hear voices."

"Don't tell your shrink that," she quipped.

"Shhh," I hissed. "I can hear them." The voice of my ex was clear. A rush of warm air began hitting my face.

The furnace came on, drowning out the evidence.

"For the love of God," I said, nearly bellowing.

"This ain't your night," said Amy.

"Sorry," my mom said from behind me. "Your dad was cold. He turned on the furnace."

"Tell him to put on his parka," I said, running past my mom. I was almost out of ideas for how to break the sick shroud of secrecy occurring right under my nose in my house—my parents' house, actually, but close enough.

I made my way back downstairs. *Screw stealth.* I bent down in front of Bernadette's door. At least the light was on inside her room. I could see shadows moving past the door. I leaped up and dove into my room. I closed my door just as I heard her door open. The bathroom door closed. The sink faucet turned on.

"Someone is washing up in the bathroom," I whispered to Amy.

"Why would they need to wash up?" she said. I could hear her swallow a mouthful of wine.

"There's the million-dollar question."

The water stopped.

"Weird," I whispered to Amy. "No toilet flush. Just the sink."

"What could they be washing?" Amy said. "Hands? Feet? Another body part?"

"Don't make me throw up." I gagged.

The door to the bathroom opened, and I heard footsteps pass my room. The door to Bernadette's room closed again.

"Okay. Call her," I said.

"What?" asked Amy.

"Make the call," I hissed.

"To Bernadette?"

"You bet," I said. "Flush it out of her."

"What do I say?"

"Just be casual. 'Hey, what's up?'—that kind of thing."

"Okay. I'll do your dirty work."

"Just play stupid. Don't let on that you know my ex is with her."

"I'll do one better," said Amy, the clink of the wine bottle against her glass ringing as she refilled. "I'll call her on my phone and put her on speaker. And I'll have you on my husband's phone so that you can hear the conversation."

"Damn, girl, you are devious!"

"How do you think I landed a husband who actually works and provides? Us women can be wily, you know."

"You're a true friend in times of emergency." I sighed into the phone, relieved I was about to dig out the truth behind the closed door across the hall from me. Whatever bullshit my ex was up to was about to be exposed.

I called Amy back on her husband's phone. She put me on speaker and then dialed Bernadette. I heard the phone ringing across the hall from me and through my phone.

It was on.

I could have used a glass of Amy's wine to steady my hands; they both shook. I hated secrets—especially when I wasn't the one holding them.

Bernadette answered.

"Hey, what's up tonight?" Amy kept her voice steady.

"Nothing. Just hanging around."

There was silence, and Amy tried again. "You and Larissa going out tonight?"

"Nope. Too tired."

I wanted to scream "Liar!" at Bernadette through my door.

Despite half a bottle of red swirling inside her guts, Amy was fast. "I was thinking of hitting a show. You in?"

"Nah. I've just done my nails; they need to dry."

"How about the late-late show?"

"Pass. I was planning on reading a book I've been putting off and then hitting the sheets early."

I yanked at my hair. Bernadette let the bullshit slide out of her mouth as if it were gospel.

Amy redirected her attack. "So anything new lately?"

"Same old, same old."

"Sounds boring."

"It sure is. Boring Bernadette."

I wanted Amy to go for the kill. She read my mind. She became my late-night phone heroine.

"Any word from your ex?"

"Hell no. And I never want to speak to him again. I'm still unpacking my shit from the garbage bags because of him."

"I'll come over right now and help you finish."

"Thanks, but I'll pass. I'm not feeling up for guests tonight."

I suppressed the urge to slap the door with my hand.

"Are you sure, hon?"

"I am. But thanks anyway."

Amy took aim for the bulls-eye. "What's Larissa up to tonight?"

"Not sure. I've been in my room all night."

"Doing what?"

"Not much. Just talking to myself."

"Really? Nothing else going on there I should know about?"

"Nope. Pretty low-key. Just kicking back with my book." Bernadette wasn't budging. I wanted to shout through my door, "Bullshit!"

"Well," replied Amy, the frustration evident in her voice, "I hope you're doing okay."

"Top of the world," Bernadette replied with a giggle.

I clenched my teeth. Amy terminated the call.

Amy came on the line with me.

"Can you believe her?" She laughed into the phone. "She wouldn't give up Little Bo Peep. The ice queen of crapola."

I shook my head. "Maybe there's more to it. Maybe my loony-tunes ex has a knife to her throat, forcing her to lie."

"Why would he be doing that?"

"He's a musician. They're crazy."

"They make music, not hold people hostage."

"Listen to their lyrics—confessions of the criminal heart."

"Okay. Whatever. I've got to go get more ice for my wine and a bigger glass. You just made my night, girl."

"You're welcome. Enjoy my pain," I said as the phone went dead.

I sat with my back against my door for the next two hours, feeling powerless. I ran every scenario through my mind, right up to storming into Bernadette's room, pointing my finger, and yelling, "Busted!" Except I wasn't sure what I was busting them on except for their secrecy.

Finally, I heard the door to her room open and a flurry of whispering. I hoped my mom had vacated her position at the bottom of the stairs, or she was about to get called out.

I squeezed my eyes tightly together, trying to avoid thoughts of what I might find if I suddenly opened my door to catch them in the hallway.

Bernadette's shirt on inside out? Heavy sweat on my ex's brow? An embrace or a nuzzle? Her hand on his ass?

Those scenarios were too emotionally traumatic for me to witness.

Then I heard the front door close. Footsteps shuffled past my door. I scrambled to my feet, my legs numb from the fetal position I had been in for the last two hours.

I lurched into the hallway. Bernadette's door was closed again. This time, no light shone under it.

I leaned against her doorjamb. What was she doing now—lying on her bed, staring up in the dark, replaying in her mind the last few hours with my ex? I scoffed. I didn't think I'd had a total of three worthy hours during my entire marriage to reflect on.

I went back inside my room, closed the door, flopped down on top of my blankets, and stared at the same dark ceiling Bernadette was looking at.

What the hell was going on?

The answer scared me shitless.

CHAPTER 30

Explorer-ing

October 3, 8:08 p.m.

Not a good day for Cousin Garth—in fact, a bad, humiliating day. A day of shame. Cousin Garth's nine-to-four-thirty gig of a lifetime as a techie in the computer department at a major insurance firm—a job that paid well and included four weeks' vacation, no weekends, his own computer, and his own office with a second-floor window—had been struck by a fatal virus.

His job description was to assist those in need of assistance when their computers didn't boot up or jammed, froze, crashed, and, in one case, burned. It was a dream gig—total control, power, authority. Sometimes that power goes to the head. Sometimes the head isn't thinking clearly. Sometimes you're just a freaking idiot. Sadly, Cousin Garth was number three.

The insurance firm, in a spot check, found Internet porn on his work computer. Apparently, the firm had a second set of computer wizards—dream-job guys who checked up on the computer experts fixing the computers. Nothing is sacred, I guess.

Cousin Garth assumed he was last in line, hence no one checked up on him. Check up they did, and did they find stuff on his computer. Contrary to the firm's Internet-usage policy and computer-usage policy—computers were not to be used for anything but firm websites and inoffensive material—Cousin Garth had loaded up his cache, bookmarks, and browsing history with every known website starting with XXX: *DP POV CREAM PIE KITKAT BUKKAKE BDSM COHF SCAT NAUGHTY NEIGHBORS GLORY HOLE PUBLIC DISGRACE TUG EXPRESS CFNM MANOJOBBERS.*

Cousin Garth did what any normal guy would do (although I don't think normal guys look at porn, especially not at work, and they definitely don't save bookmarked pages of porn on their work computers). *He went into disgraced-sports-star mode by denying, denying, denying.* Now, it takes balls to sit with a straight—albeit red—face in front of your supervisor, manager, department head, audit head, and firm president, denying you have porn on your computer. It takes balls because they have their smoking gun (your computer with porn on it), they have their evidence (your computer with documented times, dates, and locations of porn visits), and they have their proof (your access code used to log in each time).

Needless to say, the firm wasn't buying it. His demise was rather demeaning. His firm's ID was cut from around his neck; his computer ID swipe card was cut in half; his job was cut loose; and his chair, keyboard, and mouse were discarded by a hazmat team (too much of a health hazard to sanitize). In twenty minutes, he went from valued, cherished insurance-firm techie to a fired, heinous, loathsome, vilified, escorted-out-the-door-and-off-the-grounds employee. The only thing he retained was a lifetime ban from ever stepping back on the company's property.

*****

"I don't get this at all," I said to my mom and dad, who stood with me inside our garage while Bernadette was downstairs, cozying up with my ex. "This is total bullshit." I was fuming. I was livid. I was dumbfounded by Bernadette's betrayal. It had been two weeks since the night my ex entered Bernadette's room for their mysterious, closed-door romp. Now the cat was out of the bag. My ex and Bernadette were officially dating.

"Calm down," said my mom, who was sitting in a patio chair next to my dad's car. He was busy gluing on the Chrysler emblem that had fallen off the trunk.

"How?" I said, pacing, unable to settle. "My best friend suddenly jumps the bones of my ex, and I'm to be calm?"

"Good riddance," stated my dad, bent down in front of the trunk with a bottle of glue in his hand.

"You're divorced," reminded my mom. "It's not like she is having an affair with your husband."

"Sure this is like an affair!" I shouted. "I was married to him. He was mine. Best friends don't take sloppy seconds."

"She does come from a sordid background," reminded my dad, pressing and holding the emblem in place. "Shitty glue," he muttered. "This stuff sticks to everything but what it should."

"Have you talked to her about your feelings?" asked my mom.

"I can't do that!" I screamed. "It'd look like I cared."

"I'd say you do care."

"I care because there's a million men she can have. She can even have Sebastian. Why go after the one man I've ever been with?"

"Simple," said my dad. "She has the same poor taste."

"Maybe there's comfort in having known him?" suggested my mom gently.

"Bull crap," I growled. "She can't be without a man. She's desperate. So she went after someone who was vulnerable." I clenched my fist. "A person still grieving the loss of his marriage."

My dad grunted. "That dummy can take his drum set and set it up in her place when she moves out of mine. He ain't bringing it back to my house. I'll shove every single drum up his keister." He struggled to wipe glue from his fingers with a paper towel.

"Roman," my mom said.

Dad scowled. "He can run up the tab on her family from now on."

"Bernadette might be happy with your ex," Mom suggested from her lawn chair.

"Are you nuts?" I turned on her. "No one can be happy with him. He's a loser."

"I'll second that," my dad said, now attaching an extension cord to the front of the car.

"What's that for?" said Mom, pointing to the cord.

"Storms a brewin'. If the snow blows, I'll be ready."

Mom shivered. "I hope the forecasters are wrong about this one. It's too early for snow. We barely experienced a fall. If we get a blizzard now, the winter is going to seem so long."

I groaned. Snow was not my enemy. "I don't know if I want to punch Bernadette for her betrayal or hug her out of pity for a miserable future."

"Just be her friend," Mom said.

"Easy to say that," I said. "First, she moves into my house. Then she takes my ex. What if she convinces you two to become her parents, huh? Then I'll be parentless." I looked at them hopelessly.

My dad stood up. "I need another daughter like I need another hole in the head."

*****

I stood outside the garage, seething after the chat with my parents. Both had gone back inside the house. I stayed outside to make a phone call.

I hit a programmed number in my phone, crossed my arms, and leaned against the garage wall.

"Pick it up, you bastard," I growled. The call went to voice mail. The sound of my ex's recorded voice turned my stomach.

"Working on my drum solo, groupies."

I sucked in my breath at the sound of the beep.

"You loser," I bellowed. "You're a total bottom-feeder, a parasite. Feeding off my friends when they're vulnerable is despicable. You know what that makes you, huh? That makes you a predator. You're as low as a sex offender. Get some class, jackass. Go find your own women. In fact, you can find the blow-up ones for half price if you Google, you cheap-wad." I jabbed my finger to terminate the call.

"Take that, you douche bag," I said out loud with cathartic release. I turned to go inside the house.

*****

I approached the dining-room table with trepidation. We were eating at the dining-room table instead of the kitchen not because it was a national holiday, someone's birthday, or a party but because my mom needed the space to serve Bernadette and my ex, who was dining with us.

It was our first meal all together. It was an act of faith on my mom's part, trusting I would not use one of the dinner knives set innocently around the table to carve up my ex.

I took my seat, avoiding eye contact with both Bernadette and my ex. I was breathing hard. I jerked my chair forward after I sat down.

Out of the corner of my right eye, I saw Bernadette and my ex. Though I wasn't looking directly at him, his silhouette betrayed his classic ignorance. He was wearing his baseball cap at the dinner table.

My dad's face was contorted. Simple table manners were a requirement, and I knew wearing a hat at his dinner table was as bad as spitting on a priest. I was dumbfounded over why he wasn't tuning my ex.

I tapped at my cell phone on my lap, texting Amy to update her on my ex and his attire at the table.

"Heathen," she wrote back.

"Amen," I replied.

My mom passed around a casserole of pierogi. My ex scooped some out onto his plate with his fingers. He pushed a few more onto Bernadette's plate. She giggled and rubbed her shoulder against his.

"I hope you washed your hands, bucko." Finally, my dad made his entrance.

"Yes, sir. Clean as a whistle," my ex replied.

"Do that again, and your fingers will be in the garbage disposal. Use the spoon."

Snickering, I took the bowl and tried to pick the pierogi I thought had been missed by the fingers of my ex.

Next came a bowl of cabbage rolls. My ex used the spoon to lift the rolls onto his plate and Bernadette's.

"One more?" he whispered to her.

"One more, passion pusher," she replied, giggling and squeezing his thigh.

I texted Amy about the passion-pusher reference.

"G-r-o-s-s," she replied.

A plate of headcheese came next. Bernadette made a face and waved it off when my ex offered her a scoop of the jiggling green mass. He loaded his fork with a healthy portion of the wavering headcheese and lifted it to her mouth.

"Just a little taste, poopsy. Savor the delicious pigs' feet."

My dad stared at them from his side of the table.

Bernadette opened her mouth, and he slid a forkful of headcheese inside. He slowly pulled the utensil from her clenched lips. She moaned, swooshing the food inside her mouth. With a wide grin of approval, my ex scooped a large amount of headcheese onto his fork and put it into his own mouth.

I heard my dad's teeth grinding. I wanted to gag. Bernadette was sharing spit with my ex.

I lowered my head, texting Amy.

"She's wearing his old Zildjian cymbals T-shirt." The shirt had shrunk from so many washings that I was certain Bernadette's girls were going to explode into the container of cottage cheese in front of her.

My mom went around the table, filling all of the glasses with red wine. White was never an option. My dad hated it.

Bernadette and my ex each lifted a wine glass, intertwined their arms, and drank from opposite glasses, ending with a kiss.

"For the love of God, you two!" shouted my dad, the embrace exceeding his tolerance. "Use your own glasses."

"Dad just exploded," I texted Amy. "It's on."

My ex and Bernadette glanced at each other, giggling, a wine mustache on each of their upper lips. My ex used his finger to wipe hers away and then used his tongue to lick it from his finger. Bernadette did the same for him.

"Dad," I grunted, stomping my foot, glaring at him and then at the debacle in front of us.

"Use the goddamn napkins," my dad muttered, shoving two cabbage rolls into his mouth.

"Can you pass the pickles, Mrs. Androshchuk?" asked Bernadette, giggling as my ex brushed his hand over hers.

My mom handed her the plate.

"These are to die for," breathed Bernadette. She turned to my ex. "These are homemade by Mrs. Androshchuk," she explained to him, though he had eaten more jars of pickles while residing with us than my dad had in his lifetime. My mom was never able to can them fast enough.

"Everything is homemade here," said my dad. "I refuse to eat anything my wife can make that's bought in a store."

"Try it," my ex told Bernadette, who acted as if she had never eaten one of my mom's pickles in her life, despite having eaten them since she was in grade two.

She took a bite of his half-chomped pickle, the crisp crackle snapping in the air around us.

"Make sure you've had your shots, Bernadette," I warned, losing control. "You don't know what he's got from all his groupies."

Her face was dreamy. "I can accept all his cooties," she said, biting on the pickle while giving him buffalo eyes.

"Cooties," I scoffed. "What's that term from—like grade five? Already, he's lowering your intelligence."

She stopped chewing my ex's pickle and stared at me.

"He's a loving, intelligent sweetheart." She stroked his cheek. "He makes me complete."

"You're both going to make me puke if you exchange any more food in your mouths," warned my dad.

"Did you run out of shirts?" I pointed to Bernadette. "Did you have to wear that old thing of his? I remember washing it."

"I want to be closer to him and asked if I could wear it. You know he's passionate about his craft."

I choked. "Craft? You mean playing drums?"

"He's a musician."

"That's because he sucks at everything else considered a real job."

"He's going to make a CD."

I barked. "Oh really? He's been making that CD for so many years now, it's going to be vintage the day it's released."

"I just need to lay down the tracks," my ex said. "It's all up here," he added, putting his finger to his forehead.

"I'm sure it's the same tracks that have been up there for years now," I spat.

"Beets, anyone?" asked my mother, walking around the table with a ceramic bowl of the red vegetables, apparently oblivious to the exchange of words. She scooped some onto my dad's plate, and he nodded at her.

"Hey," I said to my ex, grabbing his attention, "why don't you eat those beets and do for Bernadette what you'd do for me—show her your red pee afterward? That'll certainly prove what a sweetheart you are."

"Not for this sweet lady," he said, nuzzling his nose against hers.

"Lady?" I said, rearing back in my chair. "I wasn't lady enough to avoid having to look in the toilet after you went? You left it in there for me to see when I picked up the lid."

"Knock it off," growled my dad. "I'm trying to eat my meal here, and I don't want to be hearing about red pee and toilets."

"Do my beets give you red pee?" said my mom, horrified.

"Beets do that to pee. Yours aren't anything special," my dad replied, spooning too many into his mouth and leaving beet juice around his cheeks.

"So are you going to take that hat off or not?" I finally said to my ex on my dad's behalf. "You've eaten here enough to know that's rude."

He looked surprised. He took off the hat and placed it on the table next to the pierogi.

"Come on," I urged. "That's disgusting. Your head sweat is on it. Put it on the floor, will you?"

He knocked it to the ground.

"You don't need to be nasty to my man," Bernadette said, cutting up a cabbage roll.

"Your man? You don't even know this man, and if you did, you'd be running."

"Oh, I know him very well. He completes me and makes me a better person."

"Is that right?" I snickered. "I don't know what load of bullshit he's fed you, but he can't con you for long."

"Larissa," she said, taking his arm and stroking it, "I can't account for your experience, but I can tell you that you let a good one get away."

My dad's knife clanked against his plate.

"Obviously, the yollup didn't get far enough away, because he's here again. I can tell you something right now, sonny boy," he said, pointing his knife toward my ex. "The same rules go when you're here again. No funny business downstairs with your girl—understand me? I'd better not hear anything through the venting that isn't the furnace fan running—got it?"

"Yes, sir," my ex replied, looking shaken.

I was about to add that I didn't want to hear any funny business next to my room either, when the doorbell rang.

"Any of my other past boyfriends coming over to hook up with you?" I said, looking at Bernadette. She looked away.

"I'll get it," I said. If I had to see one more pierogi mangled between two mouths, I'd never eat one again.

It felt good to get out of the dining room, which felt like a dirty blanket wrapped around my face.

I pulled the door open.

"Dalton?" I said, not hiding my surprise. He was holding two Starbucks coffees.

"Listen," he said seriously. "Tomorrow's the launch. Knowing you, you're pulling an all-nighter to iron out last-minute wrinkles."

I nodded despite the fact that my actual plan entailed hitting the sheets for a long sleep in la-la land.

"Of course," I said, taking a coffee from him. "I'll be doing several dry runs throughout the night."

"Who's there, Larissa?" called out my mother.

"Dalton!" I shouted back.

"Have him come up, for God's sake," she replied.

"We're just having supper," I said, pointing backward with my thumb.

"Oh," he said, waving his hand, "I'm intruding. Sorry. I'm just nervous about tomorrow's launch. I just finished a business meeting."

"You're coming up for a rye," called out my dad.

"Another time, Mr. Androshchuk. I'm just dropping off a coffee for your daughter. She's going to be up all night fine-tuning the presentation for tomorrow."

"Bring her a shovel!" shouted my dad. "Forecast says a blizzard's coming in overnight. We might be getting an unseasonably early dump of snow, I hear."

"I heard that too," he said to me, concern etched on his face. "Normally, I'd be here with my truck to drive you. Unfortunately, I've got to be at a premeeting and then set up for the presentation. What happens if we get this snow they're predicting?"

I shrugged. "I have no idea. I've never driven in snow before."

"And you don't have snow tires," called out my dad. His hearing was eerie.

"With this," I said, lifting the Starbucks venti, "I'll be wired to run in snowshoes to your business if it comes to it."

"Are you coming up?" inquired my mom. "I'm fixing a plate for you."

I grinned at Dalton. "You entered hell, and there is no escape."

He chuckled. "The heat's good for my sore joints."

I pointed behind me with my thumb. "There's plenty of heat inside right now. My ex is dating my best friend, who's living in my basement, having just been punted out of her relationship by her boyfriend, and they're both at the table, eating supper, feeding one another chunks of headcheese with their own forks."

Dalton burst out laughing, a broad smile stretching across his face. "You might want to add some of your dad's whiskey to that coffee. How weird. Sorry to hear the drama you're going through."

"At least someone understands. Thank you," I said, nodding.

"You realize this has nothing to do with that family curse, right? Shake that from your head."

"I have, sir!"

"Good. Tomorrow you're about to transform a company and its employees into a force to be reckoned with by every competitor out there. In my opinion, you've given that curse a royal ass kicking."

I bowed. "No thanks to your understanding, mentoring, and, may I add, substantial financial influence." We laughed together. "Needless to say, you helped me keep my head on straight when I came crying to you about my ex. You were a perfect gentleman and a voice of reason." Our eyes connected for a moment. I realized how soft his gaze was and noticed the way the crinkles around his eyes made him appear vulnerable. He reddened and began to say something.

My mom came around the corner, carrying an oval of tinfoil that covered a mound of food.

"Take this," she said, handing it to him. "You're looking thin."

He laughed, winking at me. I smiled back. "I will. Thank you. I enjoyed your last take-home so much I'd be a fool to say no."

"Tomorrow's my daughter's big day," my mom remarked brightly. "I'm hoping after her presentation, she'll finally realize we have no family curse."

"It's all bullshit," bellowed my dad from the kitchen table.

Dalton laughed, grinning broadly. "After all these months, she's kept her silence about the website. I'm ready to be blown away tomorrow," he said.

"Oh my," Mom said, looking past Dalton to the window alongside the door. "Are those snowflakes?"

He nodded, his expression turning grim. "The news is calling for a major storm overnight."

"My gosh," she said, holding her hand to her mouth, "the roads will be awful."

"Don't freak me out more than I am," I pleaded, my mom's worry compounding my growing anxiety.

"Are you coming up for that drink?" shouted my dad. "It'd be nice to have a drink with another man who can appreciate it and not by myself at this damn table every night."

"He can't!" I yelled back. "He's got big business to attend to."

"Another night, Mr. Androshchuk," Dalton called out, "when we can celebrate your daughter's fine work on my company! I'll bring the bottle and do the pouring." Dalton looked at me steadily. "You'll do fine tomorrow, even if it snows. Enjoy your coffee. Get through this weird dinner. And make my website rollout rock tomorrow." He held out his fist, and we tapped our knuckles together.

CHAPTER 31

Easy Come and Hard to Go

October 4, 11:10 p.m.

The fallout came swiftly after the axing. Juanita packed her shit, kids, and life and left poor Cousin Garth and his parents' homestead. She tossed out words such as *pervert*, *deadbeat*, *no job*, *no money*, and *good-for-nothing little boy*. What had he been thinking, looking at that? She should have known only deviants stalked the Internet, not loving, compassionate, solid-state men.

Cousin Garth was heartbroken. This amazing, wonderful, larger-than-life woman was the heartbeat, sweetheart, and heartbreaker he adored, cherished, and worshipped. The reality of her leaving and exiting his life forever was beyond comprehension. Cousin Garth locked himself inside his bedroom with a bottle of rye and stayed there day after day, not eating or sleeping, his soul wasting away. He didn't shave, eat, shower, or leave his room. He didn't have anything left to leave the room for, except shame. He'd had everything, and everything he'd had was now gone. There was no one else to blame or whine about except himself. His job was gone, his pride was gone, and Juanita was gone. Gone also was his desire to keep breathing.

*****

I woke up not to my iPhone alarm, which I had set to rouse me, but to my dad's forceful hands shaking my back—far from the soothing rub Sebastian was accustomed to.

"Get your ass out of bed, Larissa. It's a shit show outside."

In the haze of my sleepy mind, my dad's reference to outside was unclear—did he mean outside my bed, my bedroom, or our front door? I wasn't interested in the answer, just in going back to sleep until my alarm went off. That day was my presentation of Dalton's website, and every minute of sleep was my ally. I needed to be on my game. The day would include a lot of firsts for me, including my first time presenting a completed website I'd designed and my first time presenting in front of a group of people. And for the first time in my life, my dad was inside my bedroom, waking me up.

"What are you doing?" I mumbled. "I have to go to work today."

"Not if you don't get your ass out of bed now," he said roughly, shaking me again.

"Do you have the right daughter?" I sighed, trying to roll away from the hand that was rattling my world.

"Look, your mom is brewing coffee for you."

"Go bug Bernadette," I huffed, burying my face back in my pillow.

"In ten seconds, I'll drag you and your mattress upstairs."

I shot up in bed.

"What is your problem?" I growled, staring at my dad, who stood in front of me wearing his winter parka and toque, covered in snow.

He stared at me. He took a step toward the window and yanked the blinds up. I couldn't see outside.

"Is that snow?" I asked, confused. When I had gone to bed, dying flowers had sagged sadly outside that same window.

"Damn straight it is. We got blown in overnight. Your phone alarm went off an hour ago. Your mother tells me your meeting is in ninety minutes, and you're still wearing Spice Girls pajamas."

I sat up in bed. My heart thumped.

"Did you pile snow against my window to give me a heart attack?" I felt dizzy.

"Do I look like someone who has time to be silly with you? Not only can't you see out your window, but you can't see your car, buried under the same shit. Those idiot weather guys said we'd get a blast of snow, and here we are, buried. How they get paid is beyond me."

"What'd you mean you can't find my car?" My brain was starting to process everything my dad was saying to me.

"It's under a snowdrift."

"What!" Again, my heart missed a beat.

"I've been digging a tunnel from our door for the last hour, trying to reach it."

"Dad, what's going on? I have to present today!"

He pointed, nodding. "No shit. Now you're getting at why I'm standing in your room in my winter boots."

I groaned, frozen, unsure what to do first.

"I was supposed to be up an hour ago? No one woke me!"

"Hey, we give you a room to live in. We're not your babysitters, too."

"I can't believe I slept through my alarm," I whined, fear starting to surge.

"And you'd have slept through the day if your mom hadn't sent me in here to get you up. So get moving. The roadways are blown in. You'll be lucky to get to your destination by next week at this rate." He turned and left the room.

I flung myself from the bed, my socked feet fighting to grip the carpet while I spun in a circle, unsure where to start. My alarm had been set to wake me an hour earlier so that I could get ahead of things. I'd slept through my golden hour and buffer, and a snowdrift covered my window. I shivered. These were all bad signs. The curse had struck again!

I stripped down to my bra and panties. The Spice Girls were tossed onto my closet floor. I stood in front of my wall mirror in my underwear and pink socks, horrified. I was a disaster: my hair was a rat's nest, the skin on my face was puffy and discolored, bags drooped under my eyes, and pillow imprints were embedded in my cheeks.

The aroma of brewed coffee wafted down the stairs and into my room. My vision the previous night had been to ease into the morning—sipping coffee, getting my caffeine buzz on, rehearsing, prepping, and walking confidently to my car in my leopard-print pumps. Somewhere in the last eight hours, all hell had broken loose around me.

"Coffee's ready, Larissa," my mom called from upstairs.

"I'm a disaster!" I shouted toward my door. "Why didn't you wake me?" I ran to the bathroom to grab my blow dryer. Then I thought I should revisit my wardrobe, so I ran to my closet with the blow dryer in my hand. I grabbed a blue dress, remembered I had to get started on my foundation, and dashed to the bathroom with the dress and hair dryer.

"Why didn't you wake up to your alarm?" my mom called back from the kitchen.

"I don't know!"

"Now you're going to be late."

"I know that!" I screamed, running back to the bedroom to find a fresh set of underwear. I clutched the hair dryer, dress, and foundation brush in my left hand while pulling out socks and mismatched bras and panties, trying to find a new set, with my right hand.

My frustration boiled over. "For the love of God, now does everyone believe me that there's a goddamn family curse?"

"Anything I can do to help?"

I stopped. Bernadette stood at my door. She was wearing her blue flowered pajamas.

I took a heavy breath.

Things had not been right between us since she'd bottom-fed off my ex. I was still sore. Dinners were awkward, passing in silence.

I broke down. "Yes."

She walked over and embraced me. Tears welled in my eyes. I needed my best friend more than I needed to be angry at her. It was her life to live, and if it included my ex, it was her life to mess up.

"I'm totally screwed," I moaned. "I've overslept. I look like shit. My dad says my car is under a snowbank. Right now, I want to crawl into my closet and cry."

She looked harshly at me. "You will do neither. We'll tackle one problem at a time. That's what us girls do."

My shoulders slumped.

"Breathe," she said, grabbing each arm and looking me in the eye. "You did yoga with Amy. You learned how to breathe, relax the inner core."

"I learned that the hair on old-man balls turns gray."

She grinned at me. "You are wise beyond your years."

"Do you have any idea how difficult it's going to be for me today if there are any old men watching my presentation, now that I know what's down there? Talk about distraction."

Bernadette giggled. "Oh, honey, keep a tack in your hand. Every time your mind starts to wander to hairy gray balls, give your finger a stab."

"I might bleed out before my presentation is finished."

"Then let's get you looking your best for the handsome paramedics who will get to caress your body while applying the tourniquet."

I looked at her softly. "You always know what to say to calm me the hell down." I let out a long sigh. "I'm sorry for the way I've been acting toward you. I let my own crap cloud the fact that you've been screwed and are trying to heal too."

Her eyes crinkled. "Blame it on that ice-cream-cone bonehead Genie. He cursed my Belgian Waffle Delight, and we both paid a heavy price for it."

"Amen." I laughed as we embraced. It felt good to be back in the fold.

"We've got work to do before you rock out your presentation, girl. When I'm done with you, the bed head will be a memory—at least until tomorrow morning. With properly applied makeup, you will transform into a powerful businesswoman—a man-killer, take-charge, no-bullshit entrepreneur who's going to rock out with your Apple laptop and bedazzle your customers."

I bowed in front of her in my bra and panties. "Ladies and gentlemen, yours truly."

"With those granite-hard glutes, maybe presenting like this would be a home run."

"My glutes only harden during a seizure."

"Well, they're looking mighty fine to me right now," she said, taking a slap at them.

"Easy," I said. "If my dad walks in to see us fondling each other, we'll never hear the end of it."

She grabbed my hand and led me to the bathroom. "Makeover time," she said confidently, plopping me down on the toilet seat.

"Larissa," called out my mom, "are you coming up for coffee? I have toast ready for you."

"Bernadette is trying to make me look like I haven't just climbed out of my coffin," I hollered, my voice echoing in the small room.

"That's so sweet of her," said my mom.

"She'll be happy I won't still be looking for a moment to cut your throat," I said, laughing while Bernadette began combing through my hair.

"I put a chair against my bedroom door every night."

"I was planning to wait out in the hallway until you had to make a pee run."

"I have a milk container next to my bed. One step ahead of you, my dear."

"You always were the smart one."

"Survival. I've had my fair share of scorned ex-girlfriends wanting to draw my blood."

"The thrill of avoiding harm's way." I laughed. "My nerves would be shot, expecting an ex ready to disembowel me with every doorbell ring."

"Never answer on the first ring, and always have an escape plan," she replied, joining my laugh.

"Look at you two girls," said my mother, beaming. "You both made nice again? So lovely." She handed us each a steaming coffee mug.

Bernadette grinned. "I'm just covering up the bruises I left on her face."

"And she tore off my clothes," I said, commenting on my half-naked attire.

"Friends being friends," said my mom with a smile.

"How's Dad doing out there?" I said, feeling guilty about sitting inside, warm and dry, and drinking coffee while he was battling windchill and snow.

Mom grimaced. "He's making progress. I think he's shoveled nearly to your car. I worry he'll give himself a heart attack."

"There's no way Dad would ever die from shoveling snow or doing anything physical. He's an iron horse. If anything, when it's his time, he'll die from choking on a mouthful of pierogi."

My mother laughed and then looked serious. "I'd better start cutting his up into little bite-sized pieces."

"Just don't get him excited so that he starts yelling with his mouth full."

Bernadette nodded, grinning. "I've noticed that during supper, he tends to spray a little."

We all laughed.

"You kind of get used to it over time," I remarked, "or try to keep your plate out of reach."

"You're looking beautiful," commented my mother, leaning against the bathroom door. "This reminds me so much of when you were getting ready for your wedding day."

"This time, I have far more at stake."

"You also had a lot at stake last time with your vows."

"I'm talking a big payout here. For my wedding, I was as broke going in as going out. All that really cost me was a day of my life."

"Larissa!" My mom's face went white.

"Money can buy a helluva lotta men around a pool in Mexico," agreed Bernadette.

"You two girls are trouble together."

"Now we're a couple of vampires feasting on men, sucking out all their blood."

"And emptying a few pockets while we're at it!" screeched Bernadette.

My mom turned to go. "Enough. I'm fixing a platter for your presentation, Larissa. I have a few more pickles to cut up, some headcheese, and cheese and meatballs."

"Thanks. The two of you are the secret to my success."

"Your mom rocks!" exclaimed Bernadette, applying my makeup.

"Yeah, she can be pretty cool when she needs to be."

"Okay, Ms. Businesswoman. Lay it on me," said Bernadette, standing back while I stood up in my bra and panties in front of the mirror. I looked stunning.

"Ladies and gentlemen," I said, thrusting back my shoulders, "today you will be stunned by the brilliance of my mind and the website about to be unveiled before your very eyes. I ask that you withhold all your oohs and aahs and screams of ecstasy until the very end of the presentation. I will be taking autographs afterward in the back of the room, and cash gratuities are welcome." I bowed.

"Lovely! Let's hope you remember how to boot up your MacBook Air."

I sighed. "Dalton has millions of dollars at stake if this website bombs."

"It won't. You won't," Bernadette assured me. I tried to feel convinced, staring back at myself in mismatched underwear.

I turned and faced Bernadette. "You're a lifesaver. Thank you."

"And just as sweet, with zero calories. Now go kick ass, woman!"

We each let out a cheer. I ran to my room for my blouse. Once I had it on, I raced up the stairs to the kitchen.

My mom had wrapped a massive platter in tinfoil.

"You must have used an entire box to cover that monster," I said, staring at it while chomping at my toast.

"Almost. I wanted to make sure it was sealed. No one will go hungry today."

"Don't forget I've got to carry all this from my car in heels."

"Just be careful out there, for Christ's sakes, in this weather. I couldn't sleep a wink last night, worrying."

"Funny. I slept fine."

"One day, when you have kids, you'll see what I've gone through. You'll never sleep soundly ever again."

"Not a great endorsement for me to bear children, Mom."

"Just a reality. We all go through it. You will too." She dusted off her hands on her apron.

I stuffed the final piece of toast in my mouth. "How do I look?" I asked, crumbs falling from my lips.

"Stunning. Dalton will be very impressed by how professional you look. He's such a nice man. It certainly wouldn't hurt to work on more projects for him," she said.

"Cut the sales pitch. If I blow this, he'll blacklist me from every business in this city, and I'll never leave your house."

Mom smiled. "Go. Do well."

I put on my winter parka, slipped on my dress shoes, and grabbed the platter of food, which was twice as wide as I was. Mom stacked my laptop and purse on top.

"Is there anything else I can pile on here to really make it a circus act sure to fail?" I said.

"Just watch your step once you step out the door. It's icy." She pushed open the screen door. The blast of winter wind made me gasp and catch my breath.

"What the hell happened overnight?" I shouted, turning down the narrow path made by my dad.

"Watch the roads. Maybe your dad should drive?" Mom waited for my response.

"Not cool. Having Dad pull up would make me look like this was grade five."

I took cautious steps, balancing my packages and trying not to slip on the snow. Months ago, walking in my heels in this would have been impossible. Today I was pulling it off.

I reached my car. My dad was still brushing snow off of it. He yanked open the passenger door, and I placed my tray of goodies inside.

"The goddamn snow was as high as my chest," he said, icicles hanging from his nose and eyebrows. "This effort means a double shot of whiskey when I get inside."

"Thanks, Dad." I hugged him. Our winter jackets acted as large buffers.

"So you think you can manage the roads?" He looked at me. "Remember to brake twice as early. The black ice will get you every time. If you slide trying to stop, put the car into neutral and turn your wheels into the curb."

"Can you write all that down?"

He jabbed at his toque-covered head. "Use this. Be smart."

"I will." I kissed him and waddled to the driver's door. The snow on the driveway was higher than my ankles.

"Where's your boots, fer Christ's sake? And no gloves!"

"Can't wear them. I need to be fashionable."

"Stupid, more like it." He closed my door. "I put a shovel in your trunk."

"Why?" I asked through the window.

"To shovel yourself out when you get stuck."

I waved, having no intention of becoming stuck. I put the car into gear and moved it forward.

I went a few feet from the curb before my tires started spinning. I was making a lot of noise and going nowhere.

I rolled down my window as my dad walked up.

"What's happening?" I asked.

"You're stuck."

"Already? I haven't gone anywhere."

"Welcome to winter driving." He wiped the snowbank growing under his nose from his breath. "This is why the rule of thumb is that you leave an hour earlier to make up for slow driving."

"I'm already an hour late," I said in a panic.

"I'm going to push. Rock the car."

I rolled up my window. When I saw Dad behind me, I put the car into drive and hit the accelerator. Instantly, I was spinning.

"Reverse," I heard him call out. I shifted into reverse, back into drive, and back into reverse several times. The car pushed ahead another two feet and then wouldn't budge. I could see my dad's face in the mirror; he was going to give himself a hernia pushing so hard.

I yelled, "I can't believe my shit luck! I need to get going!"

I saw a figure shuffling toward us. The person was disguised in a full-body one-piece snowsuit. He wore a balaclava. I locked my door. I was about to be carjacked.

Instead, he got behind the car and joined my dad in pushing. The car's rocking caught momentum, and the summer tires gripped the snow, moving me into the middle of the roadway, where a snowplow had cleared the pavement.

I stopped.

The hero walked up to the window with my dad. I rolled it down. I smiled. "Thanks, man. You saved my ass."

The balaclava came off.

"Sebastian!" I wailed.

"I saw you struggling. Thought you could use help. I was heading home from a walk. It's time for my morning nap."

I felt sheepish after my treatment of him. I hadn't spoken to him since his mom had blasted mine.

"Thanks. A lot. I mean it." My mind was trying to process what he had just said. Why would anyone go for a walk on this day, of all days? His mom must have been freaking out. Maybe he was trying to lose the nerd image.

"Come over and play sudoku with me one day." Before I could respond, he took off his mitts. "You'll need these today." He handed them to me and walked away.

"Nice boy," my dad said. "A bit of a yollup but a nice boy." He turned and started back toward the house.

I was off.

The roads were brutal. Every intersection meant a hold-my-breath moment, trying to get the car to stop on the ice. I finally arrived at Dalton's business to discover the parking lot was still packed with snow. I'd have to walk across it from the street to the door. I was minutes away from having to set up, and I had one shot at carrying everything inside.

I got out of the car; opened the passenger door; lifted the platter, laptop, and purse; and kicked the car door closed with my knee. My months of gym time were paying off. I managed not to drop everything as I started walking through knee-deep snow. It was above my knees, to the bottom of my dress. Each step became a giant, slow-motion forward plod. Suddenly, when I lifted my foot for the next step, I realized my shoe was missing. I had no idea where it had fallen in the snow.

"Come on!" I shouted in frustration. I decided to continue forward. I took two more steps before my other shoe went missing. Now I was barefoot in subzero temperatures.

"Holy Christ, I'm freezing!" I yelled, jumping the remaining five feet to the door like a deer. Somehow, I grabbed the handle and pulled the door open. I stepped onto the tile inside. My feet were red. There was no way I could attempt to walk back in the snow with bare feet.

I walked to the second set of doors, whose glass had long ago been cleaned of my lipstick, and gingerly raised my arms until a finger found the button to press. The door opened.

Dana ran over to assist me.

"Larissa! You're going to hurt yourself." She grabbed the laptop and purse. I placed the tray of food on a table.

"Your shoes?" she asked, noticing my bare red feet.

"Somewhere in the snow. When you see them in the spring melt, can you call me, please? They cost me forty-nine dollars."

She held her hand to her mouth. "Can I offer you my boots? They aren't fashionable, but at least you won't be in bare feet."

"Any chance you're a size ten?"

She shook her head. "Sorry. Six."

"No worries. I wore a friend's father's slippers, which proves how big my feet are."

"Larissa!" Dalton boomed. He was wearing a blue pin-striped suit with a red tie. He looked damn good. "I've paced long enough to wear out a strip of carpet. But I held back from calling you because I knew you'd show up."

"So sorry, Dalton," I said, giving him a handshake. "Last-minute scrambling after my alarm failed me." I studied his attire. "I hope you didn't get dressed all fancy just for me." I winked.

"Absolutely!" He straightened and stood even taller. He looked awkward but refined, in contrast to his usual casual appearance.

"Well," I breathed, "it's a good thing I spent at least a few hours putting this website together. It's not often—actually, never—that a man puts on a suit for my sake. I'm sure this will be worthwhile after all the trouble you took to knot your tie so perfectly."

He beamed. "Atta girl. That's why I'm paying you the big bucks." He grinned. "Besides, I had the sales clerk cinch it for me before I left the store." He put an arm around me, leading me to the conference room. "Is this a new style? Shoeless? I don't mind the red toenails— let me say that much."

I grinned. "I do my best work barefoot. Makes me feel at home."

"Hey, whatever works. One guy wore hot-pink tights while he presented his company's products. Who's to judge, right?" We tapped fists.

I set up my laptop and linked it with the smart screen in the conference room. The employees began piling in, until nearly a hundred people surrounded me.

I was now in the spotlight.

My mouth felt dry. Dalton stood off in a far corner, smiling, hands in the pockets of his pants. He nodded and motioned for me to take a deep breath.

Standing barefoot in a boardroom full of strangers, I glanced down, thankful all of my toenails had freshly applied polish.

The audience was waiting, all eyes expectantly on me.

I straightened up and threw my shoulders back. *Screw you, curse.*

"Ladies and gentlemen," I began loudly, looking around the room as if I owned it. I felt okay. I was going to pull this off. "My name is Larissa Androshchuk. Yes, my last name is short on vowels, but I'm far from short on imaginative ideas. I was hired by Dalton to create and present a website that would kick your competitors' asses and dazzle your customers. Today I bring you that and more."

I was actually enjoying myself. I started the laptop and moved through a simulated demo of the website operations.

"From now on, customers will have real-time stock numbers, voice-directed by the customer to sweet Beth, their computer liaison, who responds. Interactive videos demonstrate equipment features during use in real situations. Anything and everything can be viewed from multiple angles and with zoom features—the next upgrade will implement taste and smell." I looked up into the sea of faces and smiled. I felt good. "Past client orders are on file so that with one command, they can reorder. That results in instant inventory adjustments for accounting. Shipper bills are generated, and parcels are tracked to their destinations. Beth scans all competitor websites for pricing, and every day, she automatically adjusts pricing to within ten percent for aggressive bidding." I cleared my throat. "Employee profiles interact with the customer, putting a face and voice to the department and making it real. Customers not only buy into the product but also buy into the people—you. Every one of you. Every Christmas, Beth issues a thank-you parcel to every company that has bought from you, personalized according to their profile for what they enjoy most. Beth speaks nine languages, never has PMS, and always shows up for work, seven days a week. This is Dalton's dream employee."

I turned and smiled at him while his staff laughed.

He took a bow.

"Welcome to the age of big business!" I tossed my hands up to cheers and applause from the employees and Dalton's wide smile.

I heard his laugh across the room, and it sounded comforting.

I grinned, feeling my heart pound from the adrenaline jolt of my presentation. I basked in the rush, thinking, *This must be the feeling that drives Dalton every day in his business.*

I'd pulled it off.

Dalton began popping several bottles of Mumm champagne, and he handed glasses around to his staff.

Dana walked up to me with a large smile across her face.

"The presentation blew me away, girl. If your system does what you're saying, I'll be able to retire with this company." She leaned forward, and we hugged.

"Thanks," I said. "I can sleep now, knowing I'm not the person solely responsible for sending the entire staff to the soup kitchens."

Dana pointed to Dalton. "I've never seen him put a suit on for anyone, not even his banker when he was begging for a credit-line increase." We laughed, watching him pour glasses of champagne that spilled over the edges. "And look at that grin on his face. You'd think this was his wedding day."

He approached us with a fresh bottle and three glasses.

"Maybe this is the next-best thing to my wedding day," he said, popping the cork and sending it all the way up to hit the ceiling. He then filled our glasses, bubbles fizzing to the top. "I'll consider this a dress rehearsal."

I laughed, and he leaned over and hugged me. "You're my heaven-sent angel," he said into my ear, and he pulled away.

I flushed. "That's why I came here barefoot. Aren't angels supposed to be barefoot?"

Dana laughed. "I'll leave you two lovebirds—I mean, business associates—alone to plan your next venture. But could I please be your bridesmaid?" She laughed harder and moved into the crowd of employees.

Dalton became serious. "Should I practice carrying you across the threshold?" He nodded toward the conference-room doors. "Those would have to do for today."

I smirked. "If you think you could lift this caboose," I said, slapping my own ass with my free hand, "thanks to endless homemade pierogi and headcheese, go for it."

His face relaxed. "You're an amazing girl—do you know that?"

"You're a pretty amazing guy, too—did you know that?"

"I think we could be pretty amazing together." He waved his arm between us. "Beyond the business part of it."

"I would have to agree with you. But you should know I'm way cheaper as an employee than a girlfriend. You'll need to put in a helluva lot more overtime to fuel my expensive habits. I wear makeup now, and that shit's exorbitant."

He stood a step closer. "You're priceless in my eyes."

I pointed at him. "Don't let my dad hear that, okay? You'll give him heart palpitations if he thinks I'm moving out."

He cocked his head to the side. "It's time you made him an empty nester forever."

"You mean make his life easier? I'm Ukrainian. I'm genetically programmed to remain with my parents until I'm sixty years old."

"You're breaking that myth. You have your driver's license. You have a career. And now you have a man."

I giggled. "Are you saying Beausejour's most-eligible bachelorette is turning off her red light?"

He nodded. "For good. The only light on will be the one in our home."

I grinned. "If you guarantee me you'll never, at any time, turn on the bathroom fan while I'm taking a shower, I'd say we have a deal, buster."

He barked out a laugh. "That I can promise you. As well as this," he said, signaling for Dana to return. She was carrying a white object that caused me to laugh crazily.

"Is that a pierogi?" I pointed, tears streaming down my face. The fake pierogi was the size of desktop computer.

"This," replied Dalton, grinning, tapping the pierogi with his fingers, "is your family-curse piñata."

"Say again?" I laughed harder.

"Yup." He nodded. "I had Dana go out and find a company to specially make this pierogi-on-steroids piñata."

I wiped a tear from my cheek. "And do what with this thing?"

"Smash it."

"You're nuts."

"Your belief in the family curse is nuts. If it takes this horror-movie-sized pierogi to forever shake that dogma, then today you're smashing the shit out of it."

"This is crazy," I said, laughing uncontrollably.

"Dana," he instructed, "hang this pierogi from that door." All of the employees were catching on to what was about to occur and began forming a large circle around us as we headed toward the door.

"Kill it, Larissa, just like you did your presentation!" someone shouted from the crowd.

"Girl power!" another bellowed.

I grinned. Dalton certainly had demonstrated creativity.

I raised my fist in defiance of the pierogi. A cheer went up in response.

Dana stood on a chair and suspended the piñata. She stepped aside. The mass of employees closed in around us. Someone began playing the theme from *Rocky* on his or her phone.

"Now what?" I said, feeling a little awkward. Dalton looked surprised.

"Of course! You need a stick!" He looked around desperately. There was a stir in the crowd as a female employee came forward. She carried a push broom.

"Go for it!" she said, handing me the broom.

I took it in my hands, testing the weight.

"Don't hold back," Dalton said. "Eliminate the curse that's dogged your family."

I gritted my teeth. "Generations of Androshchuks have been plagued by the curse. Today you're going down, baby!"

The roar in the room increased. It was time to strike.

I released a war cry and drove the stick, putting my hips behind it. I connected dead center, shattering the piñata. A shower of packets spilled to the floor.

"What in the hell are these?" I asked, bending down and picking one up.

Dalton walked over next to me.

"Garden seeds. You can join me at my house. Let's see what kind of green thumb you have. You talked about finding balance in your life. This is where it starts."

I stared at him, smiling wryly. "I guess I can use those pink work gloves you gave me for my birthday. Now that I have manicured nails, I don't do bullwork without gloves."

"Just wait until you show your mother your creations!"

"She's already shit a brick that I can make pierogi."

Dalton reached over and gave me a hug. He stepped back and handed me an envelope.

"One last piece of business for a job well done," he said, smiling, folding his hands behind his back.

I opened it gingerly, expecting a completed prenuptial agreement.

My eyes grew wide.

My heart raced. I trembled at how sharp Dalton's listening skills were; he'd remembered our conversation from months ago. This amazing man had earned more points.

I locked eyes with his glittering ones, and then I looked at the items inside the envelope: tickets for two to Bali.

CHAPTER 32

Wiser's, Number Sevens, the System

November 10, 1:12 a.m.

Why does my father harbor such hatred, anger, and venom toward Groundhog? My dad has no use for "the piss head," as he regularly lets us all know, including the Groundhog herself.

She applied for assisted housing—nice apartment—to earn pride, self-determination, autonomy, and self-sufficiency. She was a suppressed female—burdened, stifled, and crushed by society, men, and the system. She got it. It was downtown; quaint; and surrounded by hundreds of suppressed, underprivileged women just like her. And that would have been true had she lived there, surrounded by those women, those kindred spirits.

But why live alone—with no Wiser's, meals, cleaning, or dark basements—when she had it all with her parents? As far as I know, she never knew what color carpet was inside her feminist-empowered, government-paid apartment. Further, she was approved by the system to receive monthly stipend checks—moola sent via mail to her parents' home.

Being on assistance meant not owning any assets, so the car her parents gave her was unregistered and undisclosed to the system. Her driver's license had expired five years earlier, so she wasn't a registered license owner.

Groundhog had a good thing going. During her weekly Friday evenings at the Legion—with bingo, Wiser's, smokes, and slot machines—she celebrated her good fortune.

There were times in my father's life—most were fleeting, but nonetheless, they did occur—when comeuppance happened for him.

Groundhog left the Legion late one evening, three sheets to the wind with a gut full o' Wiser's, lungs expelling expensive packs of Number Sevens. She got in her unregistered, nonasset car to drive back to the comfort of her parents' basement. High on prescription Percocet from her mother's doctor, because of the dark rain, bad driving, bad luck, and fate, chance, or destiny, she mistook a row of fifteen cars along a street as her buffer zone.

Realizing something was amiss from the sparks and the noise, which was louder than her AM top-forty radio station, she decided leaving the area was best, because her parents' house was at the next corner. After wheeling the car around, she pounded the same fifteen cars.

For the first time, Groundhog set foot in her system-provided apartment, taking refuge on the canola-colored carpet. The apartment was sparsely furnished—actually, it had no furnishings. No cups, drapes, tables, or anything else.

She lay down on the living-room floor, tapping her ashes back into the cigarette pack.

Perhaps her last conscious thought was of the roughness of the rug beneath her ass, but for sure, her next conscious thought was being doused with foam and then carried across the back of a fireman. During her slumber pass-out, her cigarette had lit up the canola carpet and her clothing. They say she smoldered for a while before the smoke set off the system-mandated-and-provided alarm.

They say—whoever "they" are—that bad things come in threes, and Groundhog got her hat trick: drunk driving, leaving the scene of thirty accidents, and defrauding the system for assisted housing. She lost the license she'd never really had, the apartment she'd never really used, and the system-assisted stipend she didn't really need.

Did Groundhog learn a lesson? Not according to my father, who ranted that the piss head deserved to be taken out back and, well … He didn't really mean that. I think. But you should ask him yourself.

CHAPTER 33

Gimme My Couch

Love is fleeting, my friends. It is fleeting. Love in free fall. Auntie Tina was having a cold case of it—a total, complete, through-and-through breakdown of it. What's that Neil Diamond song— "Love on the Rocks"? She went right over the rocks and straight into the abyss.

I'm a believer. Love is love, and you love for love—not for the love of glory, of fame, or of money. You love for love—period. Auntie Tina's love was backfiring. She'd married for the love of money. And now her marriage was coming apart faster than a hand-knitted sweater. She was leaving her newlywed retired-city-worker husband, who was now farm-bound. She was leaving him and moving back in with her mother.

She wanted a piece of the farm, his pension, his checking account, and his household assets. She wanted, wanted, wanted. After all, she deserved all of this, she felt—she was his wife, his spouse, his legally bound-with-rights woman. She couldn't handle another minute on the farm. She couldn't take the farm smells, the mud, the shit, the isolation, the split ends, the corner store down the mud road, and the rough hands.

She had sacrificed everything to become his wife. She had standards he couldn't maintain. For her suffering, he now had to pay, pay, pay. It didn't matter whether the marriage was for five months, five years, or five decades. She demanded her comeuppance. After all, she had received absolutely nothing from her last drunkard husband, whom she had given the best years of her life. Not this time.

Her demands fell on the deaf ears of her soon-to-be ex-husband. He had worked, earned, and scrimped for a lifetime to get what he had, and he wasn't about to hand it all over to fair-weather wives. He had married for love, till death do us part. No one was dead.

She packed her suitcase full of salon products and relocated back to an ecstatic Baba and her one-room senior's apartment.

CHAPTER 34

Can I Borrow ... Your Ex?

December 11, 10:10 p.m.

Well, my father would consider today a happy day. Bernadette is finally moving out of our house. My mother's generous offer for her to spend the night became a series of nights—endless nights, in my dad's eyes. He is trying to shed children. He looks forward to being an empty nester. He's had more people living at his house during the last two years than ever before.

Bernadette is moving with my ex to his parents' house. They are shacking up. Bernadette is bottom-feeding on my relationship remnants, and my ex is bottom-feeding on the shattered relationship and pain of rejection Bernadette suffered. Two lovebirds—or two lost birds. I am still in shock.

Bernadette finally explained her feelings for my ex to me. According to her, he's funny (I don't think so); charming (childish, I'd say); sophisticated (he dropped out of high school—does she know that?); honest (he is too slow upstairs to be dishonest, I'd say); and dependable (then why am I divorced from him, huh?).

They really hit it off. They already have a master plan: live with his parents for a few years to save up a down payment to build a new home. Bernadette is thinking she can share an amortization with him!

I felt a stab of jealously. I made him the man he is today, and now Bernadette is getting this finely honed product! What about Mike and reconciliation? He is shacked up with a first-year university student in nursing. She moved into his place. What is going on around me? How is everyone shacking up so fast? Don't people go through Kleenex boxes, mourning the loss of the loves of their lives anymore? How about the word *rebound*? Where did it go? Does it not matter anymore?

Am I the freak? Is it now the in thing to bounce from one relationship to the next without a moment to change underwear? The cavalier attitude toward relationships seems flippant and, well, barbaric. Are we back to swinging wooden clubs to get our meat? Call me old school, but this girl still desires traditional romance and courtship—hey, what's your last name? I like the cat-and-mouse game, flowers, poems, holding hands, meeting the family, and, hell, having the car door opened for me. I stand by this attitude. I stand by the code of "no seconds" with friends' old spouses.

My ex at least showed respect by waiting outside my parents' house while Bernadette packed. She carried her stuff to the front door, and he loaded it into his dad's truck, his dad waiting in the driver's seat. It seemed so creepy having his dad there, reminding me of when he helped move his son in here prior to our marriage. I nearly succumbed to the urge to ask my dad for a shot of Five Star from his private stock to numb my nerves.

Dalton and I did fly to Bali together, and it was a sizzling time of drinks, sun, and carefree banter. I was able to be myself and forget about all of the drama back at home. The hedonistic vacation hit all of the targets to provide a lifetime of new memories. We talked dreamily of plans together—moving into a shared home and maybe even getting married and having children. Dalton continues to prove he is a chivalrous man, one I would risk exposing my heart to.

If this is love again, I am playing by my own rules. And it won't be scraps—leftovers. It won't be seconds, thirds, fourths—remnants of someone else's love. I want this relationship to be fresh-baked bread. It has to be a new adventure of surprises, self-discovery, and unexpected thrills. My philosophy is that I don't order the same meal each time at a restaurant, and I certainly don't scrape the food from the dish of the person sitting next to me, so why would I allow a similar style in a relationship? Wouldn't I be robbing myself of something special?

I won't allow that anymore.

Printed in the United States
By Bookmasters